SHELTER

After the Flare Book 1

SARAH JAUNE

Copyright © 2015 Sarah Jaune

All rights reserved.

We Are the Apex

DEDICATION

Dedicated to irony. You're an oft misused word, but your presence in this story, while veiled, is crucial. Also to the Internet, without which I would have never have been able to research this story. Together you two have been such an inspiring, and symbiotic team.

CONTENTS

Part 1: Mia		Part 2: Andrew	
1	Pg 1	14	Page 164
2	Page 15	15	Page 175
3	Page 28	16	Page 186
4	Page 42	17	Page 197
5	Page 55	18	Page 208
6	Page 68	19	Page 219
7	Page 81	20	Page 229
8	Page 93	21	Page 241
9	Page 107	22	Page 253
10	Page 119	23	Page 266
11	Page 131	24	Page 277
12	Page 141	25	Page 288
13	Page 153	26	Page 299

ACKNOWLEDGMENTS

I have a lot of people thank. First off, my amazing husband. I could not have written this without his support, and love. Next, my kids... you rascals are such an inspiration.

James, thanks for coming up with the idea of Apex, and asking me to be part of it!

My parents, thank you Mom for editing for me, and being a cheerleader. My dad for all of the times I picked your brain on the science for this book. By the way, readers, if the science is wrong, blame my dad! Although, admittedly, some of this is theory based.

A.M. for the countless hours editing! You are always awesome to work with. I appreciate you more than I can say.

My CDN gals for your cheerleading and for the help!

My fanfiction readers who braved this new world and followed me over to a new adventure. Thank you everyone for your support!

J. and A. for posing for my cover shot. You two were great sports about the whole nutty thing. To my youngest, also, for letting me stick you in a pink hoodie. Gender specific colors might be a social construct, but I doubt you'll thank me for that when you're fifteen.

Last, but not least, I need to acknowledge Tula Baby Carriers. www.tulababycarriers.com There have been so many "end of the world" stories where I've yelled at the page or screen "GET A BABY CARRIER!" Well, this was my chance to make it right. On the cover is a Tula, and when the world ends, I strongly suggest a good baby carrier, because dragging the baby and running from the zombies will get very old, very fast.

Part 1: Mia

1

Sunday September 6th

Seventeen year old Mia Harper ran her hand along the bridge of her nose, wiping away the sweat that kept collecting under her sun-glasses. She glanced up at the afternoon sun and wished that fall would come to Maryland. Up in Maine the trees were already turning, and the September heat was oppressive down through the Mid-Atlantic. She grabbed her water bottle and drank before attacking the weeds around her herb garden again. Most people would be relaxing that day. The Sunday of Labor Day weekend was always a reprieve with no work the next day, and barbeques all weekend long, but Mia was extremely thankful that she didn't have anywhere to be except her garden.

Her phone beeped in her pocket. It was her dad's ring tone, so she nearly ignored it. Sighing, she pulled it from her pocket, swiped and pulled up the text.

Please tell me you are home.

"Okay," Mia murmured softly. "Where else would I be, weirdo?" she asked the phone, like it was going to answer her. Even for her dad, though, that was an odd question.

I'm home.

She sent the message back to him.

Almost immediately her phone beeped again.

> *Stay put. Don't go out.*

She stared at the screen, confused. *What kind of bug had crawled up his butt?* Mia rolled her eyes, and typed back, *'You are a freak'* but on reflection, decided not to send that since she was hoping to get off of babysitting duty some time that century.

After deleting it, she went for a monosyllabic response.

> *Fine.*

"Keeee!"

Mia looked over to see her baby sister methodically chucking all the sand from the sandbox a few feet away with her red, plastic shovel. Jillian had been a surprise that had arrived shortly after Mia's sixteenth birthday. Now, at fifteen months old, she was starting to get into everything which usually resulted in things ending up in the trashcan. She grinned at the fair skinned baby wearing a purple sun hat that hid her riotously red curls. She'd been a surprise in more ways than one. Mia had expected to always be an only child, and when she did finally get a sister, it was one with red hair. No one else in the family had hair like Jilly's. Mia's hair was brown, just like her dad. Her mom was blonde, but that was mostly because of regular hair salon visits. They all shared blue eyes, though.

Sitting back on her heels, Mia stretched her arms up, trying to work out the kinks in her back. She grabbed the weeds she'd pulled and hauled them over to the compost bin that sat at the back of their property close to the fence. It wasn't a big yard, but except for Jilly's toys and sandbox, Mia had turned the whole yard into a garden several years before. She had corn that was almost taller than her that was nearly ready to pick. She also had pumpkins and squash taking over pretty much everything. They were going to have some excellent pies this year.

She heard a car door slam next door and nearly went to see if her neighbors were home, but that meant dragging Jilly from the sandbox, and her sister would pitch an almighty fit if she tried. Plus her parents would be pissed if she tried to pass the baby off to Mrs. Greene. Joyce Greene was always happy to take Jilly, but her parents were not so happy with Mia for pawning her off since they were paying Mia to watch her sister.

Mia glanced at her watch and saw it was almost four in the afternoon. She'd been out here a lot longer than she'd intended, and now it was too late for the baby to nap or she'd never sleep that night. She grabbed her water bottle and hoisted Jilly up into her arms and went in the back door. Jilly squealed and tried to throw herself out of Mia's arms to get back to her sandbox.

"Stop," Mia said, plopping the baby next to her toy box in the house and plucking the sun hat from her head. "If I keep you out any longer you're going to look like a lobster."

Mia dumped her gardening gloves in the bin she kept by the door and threw her sun-glasses on the counter. She grabbed the remote, flicked on the TV and saw that it was on CNN with a blond news caster pointing to something on a screen that she recognized absently as the Northern Lights dancing through a night sky. The TV flickered, the image distorted for a moment before it went blank. Frowning, she changed the channel and got the same result. She stuck her tongue out at it, and switched it off again. Stupid satellite TV. She didn't really want to watch it anyway. For a moment she considered putting on music, but decided against it.

She ran the cold water in the sink and started to dig the dirt out from under her fingernails. She looked around her spacious home absently. It was sparsely decorated and looked like a hodgepodge buying spree that had no coordination. The couch didn't match the love seat, and none of the wooden furniture matched. Neither of her parents cared much about how it looked as long as it was comfortable. The only pictures on the walls were of the family, including a recent photo shoot with Mia and Jilly out in a field of wildflowers. Mia's round face was framed by her shoulder length hair and it directly mirrored in her sister's face. They even shared the same slightly upturned nose. Both were liberally freckled from long hours in the sun, although Jilly's definitely stood out more. Mia could tan, but Jilly, with her fair complexion, only burned.

It was really their eyes, though, that drew a person's gaze. They were deep blue. Her best friend said they reminded him of a lake, which she'd found too fanciful, but oddly flattering. She and Jilly looked so alike, except for the hair. She loved that picture of the two of them most. She was lying on her side with her head propped on one arm and Jilly was standing behind her laughing, her red hair flaming in the late afternoon sun. It had been a birthday gift for her Mom, Diane, who had cried when she opened it.

The garage door, which led directly off the meticulously clean and well-appointed kitchen, opened. "Hey, I didn't expect you back so soon," Mia called to whichever parent it was that was coming in.

"I don't think you were expecting me at all," a familiar low voice said.

Mia spun and a wide grin split her face as she saw her best friend from since they were babies. "What are you doing here?"

Andrew Greene shut the door and came over for a hug, and she was squished against his tall, lanky frame. "I needed a break."

She pulled back and grinned up into his blue eyes. His chestnut hair was standing on end like he'd been running his hands through it all day. His face was tanned, mostly, she knew, because she'd had him out helping in her garden whenever he had been free that summer. His angular features ended in a strong jaw that needed to have been shaved a few days before. It did lend him a handsome, careless air, but she knew he didn't shave because he found the chore annoying. Andrew was a year and a half older than she was. Even though he was now eighteen, it never seemed to matter. They had been close as long as she could remember. "After only a week back? Johns Hopkins isn't exactly an easy party school, but that's a little bit excessive."

"It wasn't that," Andrew said, letting go and leaning back against the counter and running his hands through his short hair so that it stood up even more. She frowned a bit at that. Something was on his mind. He was starting his senior year, and he'd told her that this was going to be the hardest, which was part of the reason he'd moved onto campus rather than continuing to commute the thirty minutes from home. "My roommate got a girlfriend, and she hasn't left our dorm room in days. It's getting old."

Mia bit her lip and tried not to grin as she turned back to the sink to finish rinsing off the soap. "Sucks to be you."

"Thanks a lot," Andrew said dryly. "Where are your parents?"

"Work," Mia told him, drying her hands and turning to face him. She boosted herself onto the counter to give her aching legs a break. As much as she loved gardening it was a killer on the knees.

"On a Sunday?"

"Oh yeah," Mia assured him, crossing her ankles and swinging her legs a bit. "It looks like all those Saturdays over the last few weeks are turning into Sundays, too. My weekends are going to be shot. But at least they're paying me to watch her."

He nodded and looked down when Jilly toddled over and held up her hands to him. "Dew!" she cried happily as Andrew boosted her up and blew a raspberry into her cheek. Giggling she settled happily on his hip.

"You get smiles," Mia sighed. "All I get are complaints for not letting her stay outside to turn crispy."

"She loves me more," Andrew said, hugging Jilly to him. Jilly started to lean back to get down and he set her back on her feet. "So no plans tonight then?"

"Nope. Megan was going to come over, but her boyfriend didn't need to work, so they're going to the movies." Mia leaned her head back against the oak cabinets and sighed. "I am so tired of babysitting."

Andrew walked over and relaxed his hip against the counter next to her legs. "I know what you can do."

Mia raised an eyebrow, staring into his ridiculously handsome face. "Oh yeah, what's that?"

"Make dinner," he said.

"Uhg," Mia pushed at his shoulder playfully. "I should have known! You came home just so I'd cook for you?"

Andrew tried to look innocent. "No… I've missed you and… my laundry needed to get done and…"

Shaking her head, she hopped down and went for the fridge. "All right, what do you want?"

"Chicken and broccoli Alfredo," he told her instantly. "I'll be your slave."

Shaking her head she groaned as she pulled the heavy cream from the fridge. "Damn right you will be. That takes hours."

"I have been dreaming about it," Andrew promised, walking over to one of the cabinets and digging out her favorite skillet. "I'm going to starve when you go off to that Cordon Bleu school."

"I don't know that I'm going there," Mia huffed, trying not to get her hopes up. "I haven't gotten in yet."

"You're getting in," he assured her and got the garlic bulb. "Want me to peel?"

"Yeah," Mia said handing him a small, sharp knife before getting out her sauce pan to start mixing up the Alfredo. "Otherwise we won't eat until tomorrow. What did your mom say when you walked in?"

Andrew chuckled as he got to work peeling the outer layer off the garlic. "I threw my laundry in the washer and told her I was coming over to beg for dinner. She said to save her some. Hopefully she'll put everything in the dryer for me."

They worked companionably. Andrew followed her instructions for the prep work until she was all set to mix up the sauce. "Can I do anything else?"

"Nope," Mia said, squeezing lemon onto the chicken. "Oh shoot, yes. Can you put the diapers in the dryer?"

"Yup," Andrew called as he walked out towards the laundry room.

What her parents had been thinking when they wanted to cloth diaper Jilly, she'd never been able to figure out. Yes, it did help the environment, but it was so gross.

After he came back, Andrew sat on the floor with the baby and started to build towers out of soft blocks for her to knock over. Jilly laughed hysterically for ten minutes every single time she did it.

"She's got to be hungry," Mia called over to him. "Can you give her some of that baby food? I think there are a few jars left to finish up.

For the most part, Jilly would eat anything put in front of her, but the odds were good that the baby would be asleep for the night before dinner was ready.

Andrew plopped her in the high chair, put on the bib, and started spooning food in. More than once over the summer the two of them had babysat her sister. They had had a good routine down before Andrew had started back to school. She'd turned the burner down and left the chicken simmering in the olive oil and minced garlic.

She looked over and saw the baby's orange haired head leaning to the side, staring up at Mia in a way that meant any moment now she was going to pass out. "Okay, let's get you changed and in bed."

"Isn't it early?" Andrew asked looking at his watch. "Crap, how did it get to be six already?"

"Time flies," Mia sang as she hauled the toddler over to the changing table to get her ready for bed. It always did for her when she was cooking. It wasn't work when you loved what you were doing. She stripped Jilly out of her sandy clothes, and changed the wet diaper, throwing it into the dirty diaper bag. "Okay kid," she said, zipping up the cotton footed pj's, "bed time." She carried her up the stairs and dug her pacifier out from under the crib where Jilly had thrown it that morning. She stuck it in Jilly's mouth and put her in the crib. Jilly reached for her stuffed monkey as Mia covered her with a light blanket. "Night," Mia told her sister, and after flipping the light switch, she made her way downstairs. The only real saving grace about having to babysit was that her sister was easy to put to sleep as long as she was tired.

Andrew was standing in the kitchen, hands in pockets, staring down at the chicken in the covered pan. He didn't touch it. He'd been yelled at more than once when he'd lifted lids or opened oven doors to peek. "I'm starving."

"Me too," Mia agreed equably. "Why did you pick the dish that takes so long? I could have made bread faster than this sauce takes to thicken."

Andrew threw an arm around her waist and hugged her. "Because I had really bad Alfredo last week and I need to get the awful taste out of my memory."

Mia snorted. "Go set the table. We should be ready soon. I just need to steam the broccoli."

Fifteen minutes later, Andrew was groaning as he dug into the dinner. "I love you, Mia," he said with something akin to ecstasy. "I will be happy to sit here and get fat off your cooking."

Shaking her head, Mia ate. It was good. It could have been better if the broccoli had come from her garden, but the late heat that kept hanging on meant that the next round wasn't going to be ready to be harvested for a while yet. "I'm absolutely not feeding you until you get fat. Food should make you healthy."

"I can dream, though, and it's a good thing you won't feed me that much because I'm pretty sure I would never stop eating. This is amazing," he said between mouthfuls. "I hate campus food."

She'd met up with him for lunch a few times after she got her driver's license and had sampled it. She had to agree that it was pretty bad. She was a food snob. It was a small part of what had led her to stop regular schooling when she was fifteen and start homeschooling. She'd wanted to focus on her passion. Andrew had always been homeschooled, and he'd finished high school when he was thirteen. That had allowed him to enroll in college that next fall. He'd been at Johns Hopkins since. He wasn't the youngest student, by any means, but it was weird that his mom had been driving him to class for over two years.

After seeing Andrew's success, Mia had been able to convince her parents to let her leave her private high school which gave her more time to focus on cooking and gardening; her two real passions. She still did math, science and reading, but she could get that work done faster at home and focus on what she wanted.

Andrew leaned back in his seat, patting his flat stomach. "I'm good now."

"You can do the dishes then," Mia told him as her phone let out a chirp from the counter. She ignored it.

"Aren't you going to get that?" he asked, rising to take the dishes to the dishwasher.

Something in his tone piqued her interest, but she wasn't sure what. She watched him, but he didn't meet her gaze. Odd. Mia shrugged and took a drink of her water and decided it was her imagination. Besides, she knew the ring tone and Andrew probably did as well. "That's a text from my dad. He's probably telling me that they're heading home."

"It's a late night for them," Andrew said as he stuck some of the leftovers in a container to take to his parents.

His answer was just a bit too casual. She narrowed her eyes. "I guess. They didn't get home till nearly midnight last night," Mia stretched and stood up. Her parents worked in the Pentagon doing something. She didn't know what, and they weren't allowed to tell her.

Her phone chirped again. "Unbelievable," she grumbled and grabbed her iPhone. She swiped and entered her passcode and pulled up her texts.

The first one said:

> *Bug out!*

Mia blinked, her heart sinking. "No... no no!"

"What?" Andrew asked, coming to peer over her shoulder. He laughed. "You have the weirdest parents ever."

"Noooo," Mia groaned. "I do not want to go up there now! Damn it, why couldn't I have had sane parents?!" She clicked on the second message.

> *Now Mia! Tell me you got this.*

Mia typed in a message back.

> *I'm not going. Jilly's asleep.*

"That's not going to work," Andrew reminded her. "When he gets it into his head that you need to practice this survival stuff, he doesn't let up."

"I'm not going," Mia said mutinously. "The last time he sent me up to that stupid shelter I was there for three days with no word, and he was pissed at me for leaving Jilly with your mom." She poked him in the chest, annoyed by his amused grin. "It's boring and quiet, and it takes forever to get up there."

Her phone chirped again.

> *Go now or no Cordon Bleu. Take Jill.*

"You suck!" Mia said wishing her dad could actually hear her. She swung around, completely annoyed and ready to chuck her phone out the window.

Andrew caught her arm, saving her phone from smashing into the wall. "Just calm down."

"No, you have no idea how much crap I have to pack up to go! It will take me an hour to pack, and then by the time I get up to the shelter it will be close to ten." Her parents had nagged her, tried to bribe her, threatened her, but she'd never made up her bug out bag so that she could just pick up and go. She stared down at the message, hating her dad right at that moment. "Why is he doing this?" Mia heard the whine in her voice, but didn't care.

"How about if I go, too?" Andrew asked her. "We'd just have to come back by Tuesday morning. I have class in the afternoon."

Mia frowned at him. "You want to go hang out in the shelter, eating crappy food with a toddler? For the weekend? That's the kind of break you wanted?"

"It will be like camping," Andrew said, his mouth twitching into a grin. "Except the fact that we'll be sleeping underground."

Mia bit her lip, rocked with indecision. "Why did my parents have to be preppers?"

"I dunno," he replied and picked up the Tupperware with the leftovers. "I'll run this over to my parents, let them know where I'm going and grab some clothes. I'll be back in ten minutes."

Mia shook her head and texted her dad back.

Fine, I'm going.

She didn't mention that Andrew was going with her. She wasn't sure that her parents would be mad about it, but she also wasn't sure that they wouldn't be, and what they didn't know couldn't hurt them.

Mia pulled the check list of what to pack from a folder that sat behind the house phone and got to work gathering up what she needed to take. The list was exhaustive. She started with clothing for her and Jilly.

She grabbed a bag and got all of the baby's diapers out of the dryer, thankful that they were ready to go. She snatched the Tundra's keys and went to unlock the camper shell on the truck so she could start throwing everything in.

When she turned it was to find Andrew there with a duffle bag, which he chucked into the very back. "What needs to go?"

Mia handed him the list and Andrew groaned.

"Come on Drew," Mia said, using her childhood nick name for him. "Let's get hauling."

With his help it only took them forty-five minutes to get the truck loaded, most of which involved packing her clothes. He was loading in the last bit when she went up to get the sleeping baby from her bed. Her sister was completely out. Mia carried her warm, limp body down to her car seat and buckled her in, putting the blanket and her monkey in the car seat with her. She grabbed her purse, sun-glasses, and phone then locked the door behind her.

"All set?" Andrew asked as she walked over. "You want to drive?"

Mia shook her head and tossed him the keys which he caught easily. "You love driving this thing and you are doing me a favor. You can drive."

"Excellent," he said in his best impressions of Mr. Burns from The Simpsons.

A minute later they were on the road, heading for the Baltimore Beltway to drive north into Pennsylvania. They didn't talk much as they drove north on I-83 and crossed the border. The truck started to bounce in the ruts and potholes and Mia blinked, focusing on her surroundings. "We're in Pennsylvania?"

"Yeah, just crossed the state line," Andrew confirmed.

Mia sometimes wondered if the Maryland road crews intentionally made the roads smooth right up to the state line. Pennsylvania was notorious for potholes.

Andrew had the music on low, and a woman's voice was floating out of the radio, singing something about heartbreak and romance. "Are you tired?"

"No," Mia said, stretching out her feet. She'd kicked off her flip flops and ran her bare feet along the mat on the truck's floor.

"That's good, cause I don't remember how to get there," Andrew said reaching over and turning the radio down a bit more. "I don't think I've been up there since before your grandparents died."

Mia tried to think back, but couldn't recall another time. "I guess not. It was shortly after that that my parents lost their freaking minds and decided to start planning for the end of the world."

"They didn't lose their minds," he said amused. "They just watched one too many zombie movies."

"Or they lost their minds," Mia retorted annoyed. "Who on earth has a bunker built and buried in the middle of nowhere just in case the world ends?"

"All right, that is a little bit nuts," Andrew agreed affably. "Still, if you've got to ride out the zombie apocalypse somewhere, being that close to the Appalachian Trail is definitely not a bad place to be."

"I guess," Mia agreed and they fell silent again. It was beautiful up there. The forests were old and pristine, and the air always smelled clean. Down in the cities it tended to stink like car exhaust.

An hour later, just as they were merging on to I-81, her phone chirped again. She checked her texts and saw a new message from her dad.

Are you there yet?

No, getting on to 81.

Stop texting and driving.

Ooh... Mia sighed and tapped in her reply.

I'm not driving. Andrew is.

She waited, waiting for her ass to get reamed for bringing him to the shelter. It was supposed to be kept absolutely secret, but Mia didn't hide it from him, and her parents knew it. She'd needed someone to vent to when her parents had started stock-piling supplies and weapons to hide on the land her grandparents had left them. Mia missed her grandparents. Both sets had died in the last few years, and she wished that they were still around. They would have talked her parents out of all of this insanity. No amount of money left to her parents as an inheritance could make up for their loss.

The next text finally came through and gave her pause.

Good. I'm glad he's with you. Be safe and don't leave until I tell you.

"That was weird," Mia mumbled. "I just told my dad that you're going with me, and he said 'Good'."

She glanced over to see a wry grin on Andrew's face as he continued to drive. "By George, I think he likes me!"

She couldn't remember where that quote was from, but laughed anyway. "He loves you. They're just unreasonable about this prepping crap."

"Which way after this?"

"You'll get on I-78, and it's up a few miles after that."

2

The driveway into her grandparent's old property was a nightmare to find, even when you knew what you were looking for. The trees were so thick around there that it was easy to miss everything. There were thickets of trees in Maryland, but nothing like what they found up here. Here you could walk for hours and never find a road or a house. The only access to her grandparents' old property was off a state park road that was paved for about a hundred feet. After that it was gravel roads for about a mile. The state park had, at one point, belonged to a great-great something grandfather who had donated all but a hundred acres to the state with the stipulation that they get road access. The property had passed down from them.

Mia hung on to the aptly dubbed 'oh shit handle' as the truck bounced through the rutted lane. Miracle of miracles, Jilly slept through all the bouncing. "It's up here on the right. There," she said pointing out the hard-to-see entrance. It was just a narrow cut out from the trees.

Andrew turned and slowly drove up the steep incline for about 500 yards to a small clearing and parked near where her grandparent's old trailer had stood. They hadn't lived up here, just used it when they came to hunt. Mia looked at the clock before he turned off the truck and saw it was 9:34pm.

"Okay, let's get unloaded," she sighed, slipping her flip flops back on and hopping down from the truck. She retrieved the flash-light that was under the seat and made her way over to where the hatch of the underground shelter was concealed under a fake boulder. A rock stabbed her in the side of the foot. "I wore the wrong shoes for this."

"Did you bring other shoes?" Andrew asked as he opened the camper shell's top and dropped the tailgate.

"Yeah, they're in my bag somewhere," she called as she used the handle to swing up the molded plastic rock that hid the entrance. Mia dug the key out of her pocket and unlocked the padlock. She pulled the lock off and tried to stick it in her pocket, but her shorts were too tight so she locked it on her belt loop and pocketed the key again. The entrance looked a lot like a submarine's hatch, but about four feet in diameter so it was really heavy. She grasped the handle and pulled. It didn't budge. She pulled again. Didn't move an inch. "Hellllp," Mia cried, trying to sound like a southern belle. "I need a big, strong maahhhhn."

Andrew walked over and yanked on it. It swung free. "You loosened it for me," he told her brightly.

Mia rolled her eyes. "You didn't even grunt! You're supposed to grunt so I don't feel like a weenie."

"I forgot," he gave her a playful grin and grabbed three bags to descend down the dark stairs. "How far down does this go?"

"Stop when you hit the wall," she called out helpfully, grabbing a box.

"Such a funny girl," his voice said floating out of the dark space. "Where's a light?"

Shifting the box onto a hip she stuck the flashlight in her mouth so she'd have both hands for the heavy box and carefully made her way down the steps. She dropped the box and went over to a switch that would turn on the thing that would turn on the lights. She hadn't exactly paid attention to her dad's explanation of the whole setup. She flipped the switch and a soft hum filled the space. Next she went over to a light switch and flipped it. Dull, florescent bulbs blinked on; showing the bare entranceway and a sticky note stuck to the box that said, 'batteries last 2 weeks, then hook up solar panels'. Mia barely glanced at it.

"That's cool," Andrew said looking around. "How about you get Jilly settled, and I'll bring in the rest of the stuff?"

"I'm not arguing with that," Mia said and she ran up the stairs and over to the truck to unbuckle her sister. Jilly stretched a bit as she pulled her from the seat, but Mia popped the pacifier back in, and the baby relaxed. She grabbed her favorite things and carried her back down into the shelter. When she reached the bottom of the stairs she went to the door on the right and opened it, walking into what could have been the living room of any apartment in America. It had plush carpets and was beautifully furnished with a large, squishy couch that was a chocolate brown color. The walls, however, were completely bare and stark white. No art left its mark on the shelter.

She walked through the small but serviceable kitchen, past the wooden table that sat four, and to the smaller bedroom where the portable crib was kept constantly ready. Mia set the baby down and covered her up again. The ambient temperature around her made it feel cooler than the air conditioning at her house in Maryland, but it wasn't uncomfortably so. Her dad had mentioned something about geothermal cooling. What she'd heard when he explained it was 'water keeps the shelter cool' which was a good enough explanation as far as she was concerned.

She closed the door and walked out to finish unloading, but arrived to find Andrew bringing down the last tote. "I'm going to go lock the truck and text my dad," Mia said as he handed over the keys. She went back up and grabbed her purse before locking the doors.

She pulled out her phone and sent a message.

We're here.

She waited a beat, wondering if he was going to get back to her tonight. She knew they had cell reception because there was a tower not too far away, and she'd used her phone here before. When nothing came, she went back in and pulled the cord on the fake rock so it closed over her head and she was left standing in the hollow cavity it created. Carefully she made her way down into the shelter until she could close the door.

Mia turned the wheel which would completely lock out anyone trying to get in and let out a tired sigh. She hadn't hidden the truck under the camouflage netting like she was supposed to, but she was too worn-out to care, and her dad wasn't there to yell at her.

"Holy crap," Andrew whistled as he caught sight of the living room for the first time. "You said it was furnished, but this is better than my dorm."

"They didn't spare any expense," Mia agreed. "Jilly even has a whole other set of toys here. I'll let you stay in my parents' bed and I'll sleep in with Jilly. This way," she said, taking him to a bedroom with a queen sized bed. "I'm in that one," she pointed to the other door off the kitchen. "There's a bathroom over there."

"Okay, I can manage," Andrew said agreeably. "Night."

"Night... and thanks," Mia said taking his hand. "Thanks for coming with me."

"Sure," he gave it a squeeze and walked in to the other bedroom. Mia flipped off the lights and used the flashlight to make her way through the bunker.

She quietly made her way to the twin bunk bed in the room she shared with her sister and dug out the sheets to make the bed. She unlocked the padlock from her pants and stuck it on a shelf before she fell into the bed and straight to sleep.

~*~ ~*~ ~*~

Jilly woke her the next morning. It was pitch black in the room, and Mia was sure she'd only slept for ten minutes. "Mkay," she yawned. "Hang on Jilly." She was achy from moving all the stuff up to the shelter, and too tired, but she'd learned long ago that getting pissed at a baby was useless. They didn't really care if you were cranky or tired. They just wanted to eat, and sometimes a clean diaper. It depended on the baby's mood.

"Eeeaaaa," Jilly called out with a whine. It was as close to 'Mia' as she was going to get for now.

Mia stumbled for the light switch and the dim bulb above her head flickered to life. Her sister was standing on her chubby legs, chewing on the side of the pack and play. "Okay kid," she rubbed her eyes and took her out to the small kitchen. She put Jilly down and went in search of the bag with the clean diapers.

By the time Andrew stumbled out of his room she had Jilly changed, dressed, and was starting to fix breakfast from the freeze-dried food that was kept ready in the shelter.

"How are you awake?" Andrew groaned, sitting down and dropping his head onto his folded arms.

Mia quirked an eyebrow as she glanced towards him. "It's almost 8:30."

"It can't be."

"It's the dark down here," Mia said mixing water in with the powdered milk. "The first time I stayed it was a huge adjustment."

Andrew merely grunted.

Mia put the milk and a box of cereal on the table. "Here."

"Thanks," he yawned hugely, stretching up. "Sorry, I'm trying to wake up."

"This isn't my first rodeo, cowboy," Mia said dismissively. "I know how you are first thing in the morning."

Andrew poured the cereal into a bowl and nodded in acknowledgement. "I'm working on that. It isn't going so well, especially since I refuse to take up drinking coffee."

She put some of the dry cereal in a bowl and gave it to Jilly who was in a portable high chair. "Num-num!" Jilly cried happily before daintily picking a single piece of cereal from the bowl.

"I'm going to go up and call my parents," Mia told Andrew. "Don't let her dump that on the floor."

"Got it," Andrew nodded.

Mia made her way out and up the stairs. She turned the lock for the door counter clockwise a full turn and pushed open the hatch. She put her shoulder against the plastic rock façade and it swung up, allowing the fresh morning air to brush her face. She loved this time of day.

Birds were singing in the trees, everything was still damp from the cool night air, and the world was at peace. She took a moment to simply soak in the forest around her. The birch, oak, and pine trees all blended together to make a multicolored mosaic of greens and browns. Come fall the forests would be alive with the fire colors of the dying leaves. Mia grinned despite herself. Being out in nature and in the fresh air always made her happy, even in the spring when the pollen made her eyes water and itch. She pulled out her phone from her pocket. She had two new texts from her parents.

Good.

That must be in response to her text about them getting there safely.

The next was from her mom and came at 11pm.

Take care of Jilly. We love you both. We're sorry.

"What?" Mia said out loud to the morning. Why are they sorry? She tapped her mom's name and began to type.

When can we come home?

Then she saw it... her phone said 'no service'. "No..." she groaned. She went back over to the hatch and climbed down. She closed the hatch behind her but didn't lock it. It was more to keep mice out than anything. "I have no cell reception," she called as she kicked off her sandals and wended her way through the boxes and back into the kitchen.

"Great," was the response she heard. "I'll go up and check my phone in a bit."

"Mine normally works up here," Mia reminded him. "I called you the last time I was here."

Andrew shrugged. "Who knows? We're in the middle of no-where."

"Yeah," she agreed, but there was a nagging in her gut. "Yeah, I guess."

"So what do you want to do today?"

"I brought the baby carrier so we could go on a hike up on the A.T.," Mia said referring to the Appalachian Trail. It was about half a mile from the shelter. "Or we could play board games. There are a ton around here somewhere."

Andrew considered her. He did that a lot. He was looking at her, but he wasn't really seeing her as he was lost in a trail of thoughts that went along the path of his decision making process. Mia was used to this. Andrew wasn't the only one to get lost in thought in her life. Her mom could have a brain wave and stop midsentence to go write something down. It was as amusing as it was annoying, but her mom was brilliant with computers, and sometimes the ideas just needed to land on paper. "You're thinking too much," Mia reminded him.

He shook his head, like he was clearing it. "I think maybe we should stick around here today."

There was something there, but she didn't let herself dwell on why he'd want to stick around the shelter when he was such an avid hiker. They'd both hiked parts of the Appalachian Trail in Maryland and West Virginia. They'd talked about hiking through Pennsylvania as well. Mia scrunched up her nose in resignation. She wasn't likely to get out of him whatever it was that was causing those thought lines to form on his brow. Instead, she decided to switch topics and throw him off kilter. "I need to show you the text I got," Mia said handing over her phone.

He blinked in surprise for a moment before he swiped and entered her passcode, which he knew as well as his own, and pulled up her texts. He read through them quickly. "That's... weird."

"What did she mean?" Mia asked, reading it again over his shoulder. "Last night dad said not to come home until they told us, but of course I was planning on ignoring that. Do you think they're just trying to get me to take this drill seriously?"

"I don't know," Andrew said in what could only be a measured tone. "Let me look at my phone." He went back into the master bedroom and came back with his phone a moment later, already scrolling through it. "I have a text from my mom that says..." his voice faded off as he stared at the screen.

"What?" Mia demanded.

"She said that she loves me, to keep you two safe and stay where we are." Andrew's startled blue eyes met hers, this time he looked alarmed. "What does that mean?"

Mia shook her head. Panic was tickling at the pit in her stomach. "This has to be some sick joke, Drew. The zombies couldn't have actually invaded. All of that stuff is crap!" Jilly let out a shriek and Mia went to spring her from her high chair. She grabbed a dish towel and wiped her sister's face, looking into her baby blue eyes and her happy smile. Her heart clenched. Her breathing sped up as she turned to him. "We have to go home in a few hours. You have class tomorrow!"

Andrew came over and put her arms around her, the baby between them, as he rested his chin on the top of her head. "Take a deep breath." Jilly flailed with her toddler jabber that meant she was annoyed. Mia put her sister down so that she could toddle over to the blocks that were sitting by the couch. He pulled her in closer, holding her tight. "Come on, Mia. You can do this."

She closed her eyes and held on, soaking in the feel of his arms around her, her cheek against his warm chest, his heart thumping in a regular beat against her ear. She refused to give in to the panic attack. The panic attacks were the main reason she'd left her school, but she was pretty sure Andrew was the only one who knew just how bad they could get. "Okay… okay I'm calm."

"I don't know what's going on, but you should be able to use your phone," Andrew said. He kept his voice level and calm, and she could tell that he actually meant it. He wasn't really worried. He let go and pulled her into a seat next to him at the table. "Your parents might want you to practice for the real deal, but they couldn't have downed the cell tower."

"But does that mean-"

"It doesn't mean anything," Andrew cut her off. "It could just mean the tower is down for repairs right now and will be up again in a few hours."

She watched his jaw clench momentarily and Mia's fledgling hope sunk. "You think something is wrong." It wasn't a question. It was odd that he would think that but still not be worried.

"I don't know that anything is wrong," he hedged, his eyes meeting hers. "But I think we need to be careful and act like something is wrong."

Mia's bottom lip started to tremble, and she felt the prickling behind her eyes. "What about our parents?"

"I don't know," Andrew said with a hitch. "They might be fine."

"Eeeaaaa," Jilly called, coming over to her. "Mmmmm!" She grunted, hitting her stomach.

Mia nodded and picked her up to change her diaper. Jilly had mastered that trick only a few days before. "So… should we cover the truck?"

"Yeah," Andrew said standing. "Where is everything? I'll do it while you change her."

Mia gave him the instructions and changed her sister's diaper. She held her little body against her, smelling her sweet scent and wishing like crazy that she had parents there to pass the kid off to. She didn't want the responsibility for Jilly to be on her shoulders. Worse still she'd dragged her best friend into this mess with her.

But if something was wrong... if something was wrong she'd been part of saving his life. And what if she'd told him not to come with her?

"Da ah du goya go," Jilly told her seriously, patting her face with one hand.

"If you say so kid," Mia replied, standing up with her sister on her hip. She walked over to the storage area in the bunker and found Andrew looking through some of the boxes.

"I got the truck covered and put the rock back down over the entrance," he told her as he pulled out a couple of blankets.

"What are you looking for?" she knelt down at the box.

"I don't know," he admitted. "Just anything."

"There's a whole storage room back there," Mia pointed. "Dad packed it with all kinds of survival stuff. There's another one with food too, enough to last four adults for three years."

Andrew turned to look at her a little dumbfounded. "He really took this stuff seriously."

"Yeah," Mia agreed as she set her sister down and walked over to the door at the end of the small room. She pulled it open and showed him the rows upon rows of packed and labeled boxes.

Jilly toddled over and poked her head in. "Wuzat?"

"Proof that your daddy is insane," Mia grumbled.

"But maybe not that insane," Andrew said from behind her.

She glanced over her shoulder at him. "Drew..."

"We need to make a plan to find out what's going on," he said firmly as he flipped the switch and lit up the storage area. "Well... damn, how many guns are there?"

"A lot, so we need to keep this door locked," Mia said picking Jilly up.

"Definitely," he said. "It's a good thing your dad taught us to shoot."

Mia wrinkled her nose. "Just because I can shoot them doesn't mean I want to shoot them."

"Fair enough," he said backing out and shutting the door. There was a bolt at the top and he slid it up so it was locked. "I think maybe I should hike along the A.T. to the next town and scope things out."

"No!" Mia said instantly. "No, you can't."

He raised an eyebrow, crossing his arms. "Why not?"

"Because..." Mia faltered. "Because... we should all go." Even as she said it, she knew that it was a stupid idea. "Maybe I should go."

"No," Andrew said firmly, walking back over into the living room area and flopping on the couch.

Mia followed behind him reluctantly and put Jilly down. She went straight for the kitchen cabinets, opening and slamming them while Mia sat down next to him. "You can't go."

"You can't either," he retorted, rubbing his eyes with the heels of his hands.

"So neither of us is going anywhere, then," she said firmly.

He put his arm around her shoulder and pulled her close into his side just as Jilly threw a colander over her head giggling madly. Mia wrapped her arms around his waist and held on. "We need to know what's going on."

"I agree," she said as she studied the white letter on his shirt. She didn't even know what it was and it didn't matter.

"Mia..." Andrew said in exasperation. "You can't leave Jilly."

Mia didn't answer. She watched her baby sister's bright red curls bobbing around the kitchen and knew she couldn't leave her. She couldn't drag her into an unknown and possibly dangerous situation. For better or worse, she was in charge of her right now, and Jilly was still a baby. What could possibly be going on, though? Could there really be something so catastrophic that she needed to stay locked in a bunker underground? "Maybe we should just drive home."

"Both our parents said to stay here," he said, sounding exhausted. "I mean, look at where your parents work. Maybe they knew something was going to happen, and that's why they told you to get going."

"I guess," Mia evaded as doubt filled her again. Her parents did work at the Pentagon, but they were always saying that their jobs were boring. "Nothing could have really happened! We'd have heard a bomb or..." then she remembered the radio. "Oh God, I am an idiot!"

She sprung up from the couch and over to a cabinet. It was above her head, but she jumped and snagged the blue radio from the shelf. It was one that you were supposed to crank in order to make it work. She started turning the handle to generate the power needed to turn it on even as she slipped on her shoes and went for the hatch.

"What?" Andrew asked, following behind her.

"Grab Jilly," Mia said as she made her way up the stairs and opened the hatch. She kept cranking as Andrew came up with the baby. He'd also snagged Jilly's shoes, and he put them on her before setting her down. Instantly the toddler went off to pick up sticks.

Andrew had to stop her from chucking them down the hatch entrance. "That's going to be a problem."

"See hole; must fill it," Mia agreed as she stopped turning it and flipped the 'on' switch and began to tune the radio.

"Are you on AM or FM?"

"FM," Mia said as she looked at the switch. She flipped it to AM and kept tuning.

Static filled the small clearing as they stared at the machine, willing someone to come over the line and give them a clue as to what was going on. No sound came through other than the static. Mia kept tuning slowly, hoping for news of some kind. Something to fill the silence and ease the dread that was mounting.

Then she heard it, a single voice, but she'd gone past it by the time it registered. She carefully went back, tuning in to the monotone almost computerized male voice.

"-Broadcast System. Please shelter in place and do not leave your homes. Marshal Law has been declared. Anyone caught out on the streets after dark will be detained. Please stay tuned for further information. This is a message from the Emergency Broadcast System. Please shelter in pl-"

Mia cut it off and felt her arms drop as the enormity of what she had heard fell in to place. Her parents had known something was going to happen and had gotten her and her sister out of the way. They must not have been able to go with them.

They'd prepared years before for something to happen. What had they known that they hadn't told her?

"Ouch!" She hollered as Jilly stuck her in the leg with a stick. She looked down at her baby sister who held out her treasure. Mia took it without really thinking about what she was doing. She looked up and met Andrew's stricken eyes. "What happened to our parents?"

"What happened to the world?"

3

Mia strode away from them off towards the edge of the trees, her heart racing. "I can't do this," she wheezed out, feeling her chest tightening painfully as a movie of awful images played in her head. Her parents might be dead, the world might be ending, and she was stuck not knowing anything except that she had her baby sister to take care of. The whole thing was so surreal that she couldn't quite make it fit in to her mind. She spun back to Andrew, her heart trying to burst out through her throat. "What are we going to do?"

Andrew looked at her helplessly and swung Jilly up into his arms. "I don't know."

Jilly stuck her head on his shoulder and patted his chest. "Dew Dew."

Absently he kissed the top of the baby's red hair and strode over to her. "Mia, we can survive here, right?"

"Yes," Mia said automatically, trying to calm her racing heart. "We can live underground for up to three years as long as the ground water doesn't get contaminated too badly." She wrung her hands, and looked up into the air, fighting desperately not to cry. The sky was blue with fluffy clouds. The world didn't end when there were fluffy clouds in the sky! "There's a well and something that cleans the air, and there is some sort of plumbing. Why didn't I pay attention when Dad was explaining it?!" she cried out, stamping her foot. "Damn it, I never took him seriously!"

"Calm down," Andrew said patiently. He had a knack for staying calm when she was freaking out. Sometimes it was the best thing in the world to know that he'd be a rock when she felt like quicksand. Right now, however, it was a little irritating. "We can survive here," he reminded her. "Nothing else matters here and now but that we're safe."

Mia glared up at him. "Our parents might be dead!"

"But they might not be, and we can't do anything about it," Andrew told her, his expression unnaturally calm. She wanted to shout more. He didn't seem to get just how bad this would end up being.

"I now have a child to raise," Mia said pointing at her sister feeling the hysteria swamping her. "I'm not even allowed to buy cigarettes Drew! I'm not old enough to be in charge of her forever!"

"Maybe it won't be forever," he countered, his face finally starting to show some emotion. "Mia, you have got to pull it together. You aren't doing this alone!"

She closed her eyes and shook her head. "What the hell did I drag you in to?"

"I volunteered," Andrew retorted, "and it may have saved my life. And I can buy the damn cigarettes for you if you really want!"

Mia opened her eyes and stared at him as the giggle burst from her since she was never going to smoke. "Oh God... what the hell are we going to do?" She walked over and stuck her arms around his waist as he held her and Jilly.

Drew rested his cheek against her temple. "We're not going to panic. Between us we can take care of Jilly. We can stay here, stay safe and wait for news."

Jilly delicately pulled at a strand of her hair. "Eeeeaaa."

Mia held out her arms and her sister came to her, cuddling in. She closed her eyes and Andrew pulled them in against him again. Neither of them seemed to want to let go. "Why aren't you freaking out?" Mia asked, breathing in his comforting smell.

"Because you're freaking out," Andrew told her gruffly. "We can't both panic."

"I'm sorry," Mia murmured. "I just... how did our world change so much since yesterday? What would I do if you hadn't come along?"

"You'd have managed," Andrew said confidently. "You'd have had a couple of major panic attacks first, but you'd have been okay."

Mia pinched his side teasingly. "I am really glad you're here."

"All things considered, me too," Andrew told her honestly. "If I have to ride out the zombie apocalypse I'm glad I get to do it with you and not my roommate's girlfriend."

"There are no such things as zombies," she said rolling her eyes. "Zombies don't kill cell towers."

Andrew started laughing. "Maybe it's their new 'brains' and they've started eating them."

"You are terrible," Mia groaned, and set Jilly back down on the ground. "Okay... so the plan is to stay here. We'll keep checking the radio."

"I wish we had a Geiger counter," Andrew said, taking the leaf that Jilly handed him.

Mia gave him a blank look. "A what?"

"It checks for radiation in the air," he explained. "I had a class last year that used them to measure ambient radiation."

Mia eyed him suspiciously. "What kind of classes are you taking?"

"The fun kind," he said squatting down to Jilly's level so she could fill his hands with dirt. "Or I was taking classes," his blue eyes met her and some of his worry slipped out. "I suppose I might not have a college to go back to now. We can do this together. You and me, we make a good team."

Mia sat down on the ground and watched them, her knees drawn up to her chest. "What kind of life is this, though?"

"People did this all the time," Andrew shot back. "Way back when this would have been a luxury."

"I just..." she struggled to form the words. "I just want to know what happened."

"Is there a CB radio?" he asked, staring at the truck. "Down in the shelter? Maybe the truckers are talking."

She tried to think, to calm her racing brain. "One with the hand held microphone? Yeah, it's downstairs, but I don't know how to use it."

"I do," Andrew said standing up. "Is it up where the other radio was stored?"

"Yeah, should be up there somewhere," Mia said and watched him go back into the shelter. She turned to her sister who was experimentally sticking a rock in her mouth. "Don't," she groaned, swiping it from her hand. "We can't take you to the ER!" Jilly frowned at her and scrunched up her mouth in disapproval like a prissy old librarian when you yelled 'FIRE!' in the library.

Mia laughed at Jilly's expression and picked her up, kissing her soundly on the cheek. "You're so cute!" She watched Andrew come back with the radio. Jilly smiled at her while Andrew flipped on the radio, setting it down near them on the ground.

A voice instantly filled the clearing.

'news saying that the coast is gone. Everything is burning.'

'Anything confirmed?'

'No, just rumors around the hunting lodge. Everyone is getting restless.'

'Is anyone planning to hike down?'

'Not right now, maybe in a day or so.'

'Are you staying at the Ranger's Station?'

'We've been ordered to stay put.'

'If you hear something pass it on.'

'Will do.'

Andrew flipped the switch and turned to look at her. "It sounds like no one knows what's going on."

"How could the coast be gone?" Mia frowned, letting Jilly play with the ring on her thumb. "What fires?"

"I don't know," he said slowly. "But they didn't know either."

"So..." Mia thought through all the scenarios. "We could try to make it to a town, but we may not find anything out."

"Or we could be discovered and have all the supplies taken," Andrew warned. "Don't forget that to anyone who wants to survive whatever is going on, this place is a gold mine. Right now it's completely hidden from everyone."

She took a deep breath and blew it out slowly. "We can't use the guns. We'll have to use the crossbows. Sound travels through the valleys."

"We have crossbows?" His eyes lit up like it was Christmas as a grin stole over his face. "I have always wanted to fire one!"

"Good," she sighed. "You fire it and make sure we've got meat to eat. I'm going to have to figure out how to create a garden that no one will see."

Andrew held his arms out for Jilly. "Let's take a week and lie low. Then we'll start to plan everything out so we can get through the winter." He looked around at the clearing. "I imagine it gets really cold here."

"Yeah," she agreed. "I think there's cold weather gear. My dad's stuff should fit you okay." Mia glanced around dejectedly. This couldn't really be happening. She couldn't really be stuck up here and contemplating staying for the winter. "Maybe they'll come get us before that happens."

"Maybe," he said. "I want to scout around a little bit."

Mia raised an eyebrow. "I thought you said we were lying low."

"No, I mean just right around here," he said pointing around. "I want to see what kind of animal tracks I can find."

"Ohhh, your Eagle Scout thing," she said. She'd teased him up, down and sideways about going all the way through Boy Scouts, especially since he was in college for most of it. That hadn't stopped her from being there with his family to cheer him on when he'd gotten his award, but she'd still made a ton of jokes about him always 'being prepared'. Now it looked like she was going to have to eat her words. "Do you still have the truck keys?"

Andrew nodded, "Yeah but the key fob isn't working; you need to use the key to unlock the door."

"Weird," she said and caught the key he flicked to her. Mia went to the truck to unlock the doors and came out with the baby carrier which had been under the seat. She closed the door and he locked the truck, pulling the cover back down. "Do you want to take Jilly or should I?" she asked holding up the red carrier with the old fashioned bicycles on the fabric.

"What are you going to do?" Andrew said, switching Jilly to his other hip.

Mia wrinkled her nose. "I'm going to start digging through all the junk in the storage rooms and make an inventory list."

"Me then," Andrew said and turned around so she could fasten the baby carrier around his waist.

She had to let it out some to get it around him. "You're getting chunky," she commented dryly as she took Jilly and put her on his back, handing him the shoulder straps so he could shrug them on and clip the chest-clip in the front. She didn't need to mention that she'd worn it last, so it was adjusted for her smaller frame. It was implied between them. This wasn't their first go around with the carrier.

"It's your cooking making me fat," he said, amused, as he patted his flat belly and adjusted the buckles. "She'll scare off the bears for me, won't you Jillibean?"

Jilly settled in with her cheek on his back and looked at Mia, so content to just be where she was. She obviously felt safe as she nestled in and didn't think twice about where she was going. Jilly trusted Andrew to get her there safely, whatever 'there' ended up being. "She's got no idea," Mia breathed out, a little jealous.

Andrew turned back to look at her, and she gazed up into his face, one she'd known so well for her whole life. His gaze was so intense that Mia had to fight not to look away. "I'm not going to let anything happen to either of you."

"You can't make that promise," Mia said wishing that he could. "You don't know what's going to happen."

He shook his head and took her face in his hands, running his thumb along her cheek. "I can't control what anyone else does to us, but I can make sure we survive out here. I know how to do that."

"Okay," Mia bit her lip in trepidation. "I'm going to find the crossbow for you."

"It's like discovering I'm in Willy Wonka's factory," Andrew said grinning, "Only with weapons instead of candy." He took a step back and turned.

Jilly looked at her for a moment and then waved with a giggly, "Da ga oot goya!"

Mia watched them go for a second longer before she headed back down into the shelter to get to work. She found a notebook and pen in one of the kitchen drawers. She also found the log that her mom had stashed there, and set it on the table to start taking notes.

She opened the tall cabinet off to the side of the main kitchen cabinets and pressed in what looked like a knot in the grain of wood. She heard the click and stepped back, tugging on the cabinet which gave way to reveal the secret entrance to the food pantry. She went in and did a quick study of everything, but it was just as she'd left it when she'd set it up. Her dad had given her free reign on the food selections, and she'd made sure that they had it all plus heirloom organic seeds for starting a garden.

Mia had always found the whole thing nuts, but when given nearly an unlimited amount of money to buy food and seeds she hadn't really argued.

She closed the door and went back to the larger storage room where all of the guns were kept. Mia pulled the door, flipped the switch and blew her hair from her face. This was going to take a while. Most of the boxes weren't labeled. She'd griped at her dad about doing it, but he'd been adamant about just getting the stuff up here. She'd wanted to take just a few hours to label everything just like everything was labeled in her own closet. But it had taken them two trips to haul all the stuff. Mia could still remember the back ache from it, and had complained loudly until he'd let her go to the chiropractor.

It was the stupid things like going to the chiropractor, Mia realized, suddenly staring unseeingly at the bin of ammo in front of her. She wasn't going to get to go to Chipotle next week for lunch, and she wouldn't get to go see the new Woody Harrelson movie with her friend

Megan in October. She didn't know if Megan was okay, and she had to stop herself from reaching for her phone to text her just to check in. Everything was different now.

Mia didn't get to pass her sister off to her parents when she was being annoying.

Jilly couldn't send random texts to Mia's friends or suddenly, and maddeningly, delete all the apps on her phone when she was supposed to be playing Sesame Street.

Shaking her head, she got back to work and started lugging some of the bins out into the bigger room. It took her nearly twenty minutes to haul out just the first row of bins. She left the weapons in their racks. She'd started to count them, but gave up when she realized there were over thirty shotguns and several things she would have expected to see in a Mission Impossible movie. There was a gun that was taller than she was. It had a tripod. Mia stared at it dumbfounded. She couldn't even fathom what her dad expected to do with it!

She found blankets, all-weather clothing, canning provisions, fabric and sewing supplies, hand tools, books by the hundreds on survival, supplies for keeping the shelter running, replacement solar panels, and amazingly a Geiger counter. She stared at the label on the hand held instrument and shook her head. It was only the tip of the iceberg. It was going to take her days to fully go through the shelter's stock pile.

Mia located the crossbow and bolts, which were specific arrows for the crossbow. She set them off to the side for Andrew before searching out tape so that she could tack inventory lists to each Rubbermaid tub. She also kept the books out of the storage room and started to move everything else back in. She wasn't sure how, but they needed to make some kind of shelves for the books so that they could find them easier.

She was halfway done shoving a bin back in when Andrew came down the steps, closing the hatch behind him. "I found a lot of tracks."

"No bears I hope," Mia grunted trying to move a box full of tools by sliding it along the floor.

Andrew walked over and picked it up like it weighed nothing, and he didn't have a baby strapped to his back. "Where to?"

Sighing and stretching she pointed to the spot where she wanted it. "If you weren't useful, I'd be annoyed by that."

Andrew set it in place and grinned at her. "You know you love me."

"Yeah, I know I do," Mia agreed easily. "Where do you hide all these muscles anyway? You're skinny as a twig!"

He shrugged and turned so she could help him get a sleepy Jilly off his back. "I thought for sure she was going to pass out back there."

Mia took her sister and carried her back into their bedroom, putting her down for a nap. She came out and started digging food out for something that could pass for lunch. "What kind of tracks did you find?"

"Bear," Andrew drawled.

"You're hilarious," Mia quipped passing him a water bottle. "Seriously hilarious."

"I did see bear tracks," he said, twisting off the cap and drinking it down. "I also saw deer, rabbit, foxes, and something else that I think might have been coyote."

She turned slowly from the cabinets. "You really saw bear tracks?"

Andrew tilted his head to side, completely bemused. "How did you not know that there are bears up here?"

"Oh God," Mia groaned sinking into a chair at the table. "I'm going to be eaten alive."

"Nah," he shook his head and patted her knee consolingly. "They're black bears and they won't eat you. They might eat Jilly, though, so we do have to watch her."

"You are not helping me!" she spit out at him. "I can't deal with bears!"

"You can deal with bears," he corrected.

Mia shook her head numbly. "I'm going to have to carry a gun or something on my hip like one of those redneck freaks in Texas!"

"You could do that," Andrew said considering. "But if you shot a bear with anything that could be carried on your puny hip all you'd do is piss it off."

Mia dropped her head onto the table. "I'm going to get voted off the island."

Andrew tugged gently at her hair, something he'd done to her for years. "I'm never voting you off the island."

"Why not?" She looked up pathetically. "I'm useless."

He gave her a 'be serious' look. "Who's going to feed me?"

Mia rolled her eyes. "It's add water and crack open the heating agent! How hard is that?"

"Fine, you're out then," Andrew said earnestly. "I will raise Jilly all by myself."

A smirk flitted across her mouth. "You're going to have to hand wash her diapers."

"Oh damn," he moaned looking disgusted. "I completely forgot about that! How are we going to wash them?"

"I can do it," Mia sighed, resting her head on her arms. "I found a hand crank washer in the back. At least I know why they cloth diapered her."

"That's good... I think," Andrew said, digging in to the now rehydrated spaghetti. "I am going to miss your cooking," he said regretfully looking down at the limp noodles.

"I thought I wasn't getting voted off!" she griped, grabbing a fork and digging in. It was... "This is nasty."

"That's what I mean," he commented, making a face. "You can't really make good food from this stuff."

Sighing heavily, Mia took another bite, choking down the cardboard textured food. "If we're still here in the spring I'll have fresh vegetables. I've got olive oil and other spices so I can make some good dishes then."

Andrew gazed at her wistfully. "I am almost looking forward to that. But then that means we're still stuck here next spring and I'd rather find out that this whole thing was some elaborate plot to get you to take this prepping thing seriously."

"But why though?" Mia asked, all the while wishing it were true. "Why would they stick us up here like this? Why do that to Jilly?"

He took another bite and a large drink of water. "No idea. You know," he said contemplating the meal in front of them. "I've thought about marrying you just so you'd be there to cook for me every night."

"That sounds sexist," she said mildly.

Andrew arched an eyebrow. "If we were married would you ever let me fix dinner?"

"Nope," Mia said forking in another bite. "You're a crappy cook."

"I'm an adorable dish washer though," he said confidently.

She snorted and shook her head. "I found a Geiger counter."

Andrew's fork clattered to the table. "Seriously?"

"Yep," she confirmed, drinking from his water bottle. "What are you going to do with it?"

"Check to see if the trees are radioactive," he informed her with a straight face.

"Oh, of course," Mia clapped a hand to her forehead. "Why didn't I think of that?"

He kissed her cheek and stood, heading for the storage room. "You didn't take my science classes or you would have."

She finished eating as much as she could and stored the rest in a plastic container for when Jilly woke up. They had a refrigerator, but she didn't want to turn it on before they had to. It took a lot of the battery power generated from the solar panels. She'd have to can things this spring to help avoid having to refrigerate everything.

"Do you have a notebook?" Andrew called out from the other room.

"Yeah, hang on," she said grabbing the journal and bringing it over to him. "Here."

"I'm going to record the radiation levels outside for a bit," he said taking it and the pen from her. "That way we'll know if a bomb did go off." He was halfway up the stairs before he bent and looked back at her. "This seems like a really stupid question, but we do have potassium-iodide tablets for radiation poisoning?"

Mia stared at him blankly for a moment, trying to remember if she'd seen anything like that. "I... there was a whole box full of first aid supplies."

"Can you get to it easily?"

"Yeah," she said pointing. "I left it out in the main room just in case we needed it."

"Okay, go and check to see if we have them," Andrew instructed. "If we do, make sure they're near the top of the box and easy to get to."

"Okay," Mia agreed, and he was nearly out of the hatch when she called up to him, "what are they called again?"

Before she could even get to the box he was back again, slamming the hatch shut. His face was white. "The radiation levels are off the chart. We have to stay inside.

4

The days crawled slowly by, like a one-legged sloth, into the middle of September with a healthy mixture of boredom, tedium, fear, annoyance, exhaustion and complete disgust. The first time Mia had washed Jilly's diapers by hand, she'd nearly puked. It had taken everything she had to keep cranking the washer, and it had required Andrew hauling buckets of excrement filled water away from the shelter. They only went outside for short spurts of time when they absolutely had to, but oddly enough, the radiation levels had dropped down to normal again after only a week. Andrew was at a loss to explain it, but Mia didn't really care why it had happened. She needed to get out into the sun or she was going to go off the deep end in a hurry. She'd even taken to washing Jilly's diapers outside just to get out there.

"Potty train!" Mia griped at her sister who wasn't listening. There were sticks on the ground to be played with. It was no good, of course. They didn't have a hope of potty training Jilly before she was two and that was eons away. She wasn't willing to do the math or she just might cry.

"But imagine if we didn't have the cloth diapers," Andrew said as he hauled yet another foul bucket away for her. "We'd be using our t-shirts at this point."

Shuddering from the thought, Mia kept washing. It was starting to get cold in the evenings as they passed the midway point through September. They hadn't strayed far from the shelter and hadn't heard anything worth hearing. The chatter on the CB had fallen silent. There was still no cell reception, and the one radio station they could get to was still broadcasting the same message. They still checked daily, hoping against hope that they'd hear something different.

Nothing came.

Mia oscillated between being thankful for the shelter, to being pissed at her parents for ditching her; from being convinced that because they were in the government they had to survive, to being sure they were dead. Andrew never said much about his parents, and she knew he was keeping it together for her. She was swamped in guilt for not being able to hold it together long enough so that he could fall apart.

The nights were the worst. She'd lie in bed, and if she wasn't exhausted, the thoughts and images of what could be going wrong would swarm over her, hovering and stinging until she stumbled from bed the next day at Jilly's call. Mia kept busy as much as she could. She'd gone through almost the entire shelter from top to bottom, making detailed lists of all their supplies. She'd then organized those lists in a way so that they could easily locate whatever they needed.

She'd badgered Andrew into making bookshelves for her, and for four days now, he'd worked with a hand saw fashioning the planks into something that could be used. He seemed to enjoy the task the more he got into it, even though it was taking forever. Jilly certainly loved the saw dust that fell on the floor. Mia hadn't had the heart to sweep it up yet when the baby enjoyed it so much.

They still hadn't taken a hike to scout out the land. They hadn't ventured anywhere near the Appalachian Trail. There was still the chance that hikers might still be out, possibly unaware of what had happened. Or people might be using it as a kind of thoroughfare to pass safely from Maine down to Georgia without being on the roads. They hadn't discussed it much. They'd simply decided that they couldn't take the risk, at least not right now.

The joking comradery that had always been a staple of their relationship was taking a beating. Every day Mia struggled more and more to find even a smattering of hope in their situation, and Andrew couldn't carry both their parts. They ate, sometimes in total silence except for the toddlerese that Jilly babbled out into the empty air around her. He'd halfheartedly suggested that she start working on the garden, but every time she looked around the land, her mind rebelled at the thought that they'd need a garden in the spring. Mia felt too paralyzed to even start it.

As the last week of September began around them, Mia went to bed shortly after Jilly. She was so drained and needed desperately to sleep, if for nothing more than it was a way to avoid the awful silence of the room out front. Andrew had taken to reading all the survival books that her dad had bought and she just couldn't bring herself to sit and stare at the walls, too tired to work and too depressed to care. She stared up at the ceiling as her eyes slowly adjusted to the dark, aided only by the dim light that filtered through the crack from the kitchen. Her body felt heavy, her limbs aching from washing diapers again that day. It wasn't enough to quiet her mind.

Mia heard Andrew's footsteps and watched the lights flick off as he retreated to his room. She continued to stare, to count sheep, to try to tell herself stories of a happy time where she didn't know about how to build compostable toilets. She thought about Andrew, her childhood friend and a man she admired and knew that without him here, she would be sunk. Mia wouldn't be able to do this without him. She turned her head and looked to the wall. He slept two rooms away, and tears pricked in her eyes, the first real tears she'd been able to shed. He was hurting, too, and she didn't know how to help him. She couldn't help herself.

The tears continued to rain silently down onto her pillow, and she rose quietly, reaching out a hand blindly for the wall. Mia couldn't sob in her room. Jilly would wake up, and that would be the end of their peaceful night. She found the small dresser and felt around in the top drawer for the soft cloth hankies that she'd located a few days before. Mia silently opened the bedroom door and stepped into the kitchen, and her feet moved without her conscious thought until she'd opened Andrew's door and stepped through.

"Mia?" his groggy voice called from the shadows.

She knew the layout of the room, and she shuffled towards him, hitting the bed with her shins. She reached out a hand, and found his arm which was extended out to her. Mia crawled under the covers and into his arms just as the sobs broke her.

Andrew's hand fisted in her hair, holding her in close as she curled her arms protectively into her shoulders, trying to hold the pieces of her heart together. Moments later his tears joined hers. She wound her arm around his waist and held on to him as he held on to her. They grieved together; holding on to each other until they were both spent and fell quiet.

Mia felt him shift and a water bottle knocked gently in to her hand. She unscrewed it and drank deeply, trying to replenish some of what had been poured from her. She wasn't certain there would ever be enough, though. She gave it back to Andrew who finished it off.

They clung to each other, as the new life before them fell more and more into place.

"I was going to take Jilly trick-or-treating this year," Mia croaked out. Her voice was so raw that it felt like she was speaking through sandpaper. "Mom and I picked out a jelly bean costume for her."

"I would have come," Andrew said quietly. "I would have wanted to come along for that."

"I'm sorry," Mia sighed as she nuzzled her face into his shoulder, finding peace in the soft cotton and the warmth she felt beneath it. "I'm sorry I've been such a mopey jerk."

His chest rose and fell under her. "We had to get to this."

"To crying like babies?" She wondered aloud.

"We had to grieve and let go of what we've lost," Andrew told her. "We have to accept that this is what life is going to be like and move on from here."

"But where does that leave us?" Mia asked, pushing her messy hair away from her face. "We're still kids."

He shrugged. "I'm not; not really. You're only legally a kid for another few months."

She fought down another sob, looking up and biting hard on her lip until it passed. "We're here. We're making a life here."

"Yeah," Andrew agreed. "We stay, we raise Jilly, and we survive."

"You don't get to be an engineer," Mia whispered. "I don't get to be a chef with my own restaurant."

"Well," he half laughed. "You do get to do that, but you're only catering for three, and the menu is limited."

She grinned before another thought crept in. "I never got to go to the Homecoming Dance."

"I didn't either," he mused. "But I don't think I'd have missed it as much as you would have. Who were you going with?"

"Sean," Mia told him. "The guy from church, remember?" She felt him nod. "We were sitting in the back after the service right after school started again. He said something about starting to ask girls to go with him now since he thought he'd be turned down a lot. I said I'd go with him if he wanted."

"I bet that made his day," Andrew chuckled and kissed her forehead. "A beautiful girl throws herself at him? What a crappy way to get a date."

"Shut up," she grumbled and poked him. "You know he doesn't see me like that."

She could almost hear Andrew rolling his eyes. "Yeah, okay then."

She remembered her conversation with Sean as they sat on the solid wooden benches while their parents chatted and Jilly played with the pens that were in the back of the pews. His glasses had kept slipping down his nose and he'd looked adorably excited when she'd said she wanted to go. He was so nice, though, and she had felt good about it. Boyfriends were the one thing she'd really missed out on by leaving school for homeschooling. She'd been around boys, of course, but when she'd been in school it was all anyone talked about. It was part of what made her hate school so much. All the high drama and angst made her crazy and left her feeling out of control and wounded, even if she wasn't the one stuck in the mire of a break up. "It would have been my first date," she mused. "And I had to ask myself out, too."

Andrew started to laugh, "Poor Sean."

She nudged him. "I would have been a great date!"

"I'm sure," Andrew agreed equably. He ran his hand along her back and rested it on her shoulder. "I guess this means I don't get to see the new Bond movie."

"I was going to talk Mom and Dad into going down to Florida next year so we could go to the Harry Potter Theme Park," Mia said suddenly remember the plan. "They refused to take Jilly until she was two. I wanted to try Butterbeer."

"I was starting job fairs." He sighed heavily and shifted on the bed. "But I was really thinking about applying to MIT and going for my masters."

She turned her head up to look at him even though she could only see a dim outline of his chin. "You'd have loved that."

"Yeah, I would have," he agreed evenly. "I had a good shot, too. I'm near the top of my class."

Massachusetts. "We might have still been together," Mia mused. "If I'd made it into Cordon Bleu I'd have wanted to go up to the Cambridge campus."

"That was part of the appeal," Andrew admitted ruefully. "I started looking at where I wanted to go and there are a lot of great schools, but it just felt weird thinking about being so far from you."

Mia nodded. She understood that completely. They'd been best friends for so long that it would feel weird not to get to see him at least once a week. "Now you're stuck with me in a bunker in the middle of nowhere." They fell silent each thinking their own thoughts. "I may never get married," Mia breathed out. "I didn't even really think about it. If we're trapped here for the rest of our lives…"

"I didn't have to get you to marry me so you'd be stuck having to cook for me," Andrew said soberly.

Mia closed her eyes as a giggle bubbled up out of her. Pretty soon Andrew was laughing right along with her. They laughed until the tears meant humor, and the grief faded to a dull ache. "I'm going to do better," she hiccupped a few minutes later. "I'm going to make the best of this, Drew. I promise I'm going to stop being so…" she struggled to find the word, but it didn't really matter.

"Me, too," he promised. "We can't change where we are, so we'll make the best of it."

"No more living in the past," Mia said, mostly to herself. "What's done is done."

"This isn't really how I expected to ride out the end of the world," Andrew informed her. "I sort of pictured just having a beer and letting it overtake me."

Mia scrunched up her nose. "When did you start drinking beer?"

"Well, I haven't," he chuckled. "But, I didn't expect the end to come this soon."

She shook her head, bemused. "Do you want me to go back to my room?"

He pulled her in closer. "No, I like having you here."

"Kay," she said and kissed his cheek as the waves of exhaustion finally began to pull her under. "Night."

~*~ ~*~ ~*~

"My arm is numb," Andrew's voice said from somewhere near her ear. "I think Jilly's up."

"Okay," Mia yawned and rolled off his arm. She had a massive crick in her neck from sleeping on his shoulder. She twisted her head to the side and pushed with her hand until she felt the pop. "Uhg, why do people sleep together?"

"I think they usually sleep next to each other," he groaned as he shook out his hand.

"EEEEEEAAAA!" came the shout from the other room.

"Coming, Jilly," Mia called out to her sister as she hobbled towards the door. Her hip ached from laying on it all night. She flicked the light and heard Andrew's gasp from behind her as the brightness chased out the black.

She plucked her sister from the crib, changed her diaper, and came back out to find Andrew looking at her oddly. "Are you still okay?"

Mia took a deep breath, assessing just how she felt. "Yeah... yeah, I'm okay. I'm done freaking out, at least right now."

They ate breakfast, but it wasn't the tense affair that it had been in the past few weeks. They talked about plans for the day and Andrew mentioned making a play kitchen for Jilly once the book shelves were done.

"She'll like that," Mia said, staring at the undecorated wall of the kitchen. "Maybe it was Luke."

"What?" Andrew asked blankly.

"My cousin's son, Luke," she told him giggling. "Last summer he told his mom that he wanted to make antimatter. She posted about it on Facebook. Maybe he ended the world."

Andrew's eyebrow rose. "Is he the little orange-haired kid who was inside testing all the electronics with the multi-meter during the Fourth of July party?"

"That's the one," she agreed.

"Isn't he like five?"

"Six, I think," Mia said, standing to clear the table. "And you're one to talk! Didn't you take your mom's cell phone apart when you were five?"

His cheeks flushed slightly and he shrugged it off. "I put it back together again and it still worked!"

"Uh huh," she said shaking her head. "But anyway, if anyone could do it, I'd lay money on Luke."

Andrew brought his own dishes over to the gravity fed sink. "It couldn't be antimatter."

"Why not?"

"Because it would have valorized the planet," Andrew explained.

She frowned up at him. "Really?"

"Yep," he told her and got out the soap.

"Meh," Mia blew out a breath and tucked her hair behind her ear. "No wonder his mom was so freaked by it."

After she'd cleaned up from breakfast she went to the storage closet and got out the gardening tools. It was going to take forever to get a bed dug out of the forest soil, and she'd need it prepared for the spring. Besides, she'd missed digging in the dirt.

"Where are you going?" Andrew called out as she headed for the stairs.

"Gardening," Mia answered and waved as she made her way into the early morning sun. The problem with planting a garden in a forest was sunlight. Not only that, but she had to contend with the thick roots and tons of rocks that littered the forest floor. It could take her months just to dig up the rocks. She'd seen a spot earlier that she thought might make a good plot. It was relatively flat, and there was only one tree in the middle that could be cut down and would allow a decent amount of sunlight in. It dappled down now that the leaves that were already starting to change into their autumn hues.

She hiked up to the place and started walking around, picturing in her mind what she wanted to happen. She couldn't go very large scale, at least not at first. There was still the risk of it being spotted, but the risk of running out of food was greater. If they were truly stuck here for years, they needed fresh food to be canned in order to continue to survive. They only had three years of provisions, and they were going to use up several months' worth until she had a sizable garden started and could can it. They were also going to have to try to smoke meat if at all possible.

Mia grabbed her first big rock and went to the place she'd decided would be her northeastern corner and dropped the stone. She did the same for each corner until she had a clear line of where she was going to place her rock wall. Then she got to work clearing the stones. Eventually, Andrew came out with Jilly on his back in the carrier, and together they worked, clearing the field of stones. "What about this tree?" He asked eventually, slightly out of breath.

"We can cut it down," Mia said eyeing it critically. "But the roots are still going to be a problem. Unfortunately, we don't really have a way to clear the stump."

"We might be able to drag it out with the truck," Andrew supposed. "There's chain. We can hook it up."

She looked up at it. "That's an idea. We definitely need to fell it before we build the south wall, so we don't crush it."

"What's the wall for anyway?"

"Rabbits mostly," Mia said. "It won't really do much, but if we make it tall enough, it might also keep the deer out. I'm not willing to place a bet on that, though."

"Won't a wall be really obvious if someone spots it?" He grunted, picking up a large rock.

"A garden will be really obvious if someone spots it," Mia retorted. "We either grow food, or we struggle to continue out here past three years."

He let out an oof as he dropped it where she pointed. "Fair enough," he agreed. "We're so remote anyway that it's difficult to imagine anyone coming out here to find shelter. In all the zombie movies, people move into the Walmarts."

"No zombies," Mia huffed, grabbing another rock. "I refuse to admit to zombies."

"Well it isn't nuclear," Andrew commented, kicking a rock out with his foot before stooping to pick it up. "The radiation fluctuations dropped way too fast to signify a bomb had been dropped. I'm starting to wonder if that wasn't just an anomaly."

"Hang on, Jilly's asleep," she told him and pulled up the sleeping hood on the carrier that would keep her head from flopping around. "That's at least something. I didn't really want to die from radiation sickness."

"It's the living with it that would be worse," he said and stopped to stare up at the trees. "Do you hear that?"

Mia glanced around nervously. "No? What are you hearing?"

"I'm not sure, but it sounds like-"

He didn't get to finish. Something brown and hairy smacked straight into Mia's face with a resounding thud. It stung so badly where she'd been hit that she'd barely recovered enough to swat at it before it took off again. Then she heard it, although it was hard to tell from the ringing in her ears. It was an intense, high pitched squealing or squeaking. She couldn't tell with her face on fire.

"Bats!" Andrew hollered and ducked down. Mia didn't move, which ended up being a big mistake because three more of the buggers flew straight into her before she dived down and hit the dirt hard.

She peeked up into the sky and saw a huge cloud of bats swarming around. It was only then that she saw the dancing lights in the sky. "What are those?" she hollered to Andrew.

He couldn't hear her. Jilly had woken up and was screaming at the top of her lungs. Andrew had pulled Jilly off his back and was shielding her with his body. The bats were dive bombing them, and some were getting close. Jilly was pissed. She'd not only been woken up, but now she was pinned down.

Toddlers don't particularly like being confined.

Just as fast as they'd come, they dispersed. Mia got gingerly to her feet, brushing off her jeans. She squinted through an eye that was already starting to swell shut. "Well," she said, trying to sound cool and unconcerned. "That was fun."

Andrew snorted as he kept his arms around a squirming Jilly. "You can say that again."

"Northern Lights," Mia told him as she pointed up. She'd never seen the Northern Lights and had never heard of them being this far south.

Andrew's mouth fell open. "Well... that's..."

He stopped, and stared up at them. She watched him think it over. She gave him a full minute, before she poked him back to this reality. "What?"

"I don't know," he told her honestly. He hooked Jilly back onto his back. She fought him at first, but as soon as she was in the carrier, she calmed down. Andrew cupped Mia's cheek tenderly, frowning as he studied her cheek. "You're going to have a black eye."

"Lovely," she grumbled, and turned back to the tree that stood in the middle of her new garden. "We need to get this thing out of here."

He studied her for another moment, before focusing on the pine. "Without a chainsaw it's going to take me hours to get the tree down."

Mia crossed her arms and grinned at him impishly. "Are you sure you're up for it?"

"I'm willing to give it a shot," he said agreeably. "Let's finish clearing the rocks and make sure you really want the garden right here before I do anything, though."

They worked till lunch and had a good number of the rocks cleared. The soil was excellent. All of the years of composted leaves left it dark and nutrient rich. She was going to have to get the roots out, but there was still at least a month to work on clearing it before they would get snow.

They went in and Jilly, who had fallen asleep again after their visit from Dracula's minions, woke up just in time to eat lunch.

"I'm looking forward to fresh vegetables," Mia said.

Andrew handed her a glass. "I'm looking forward to venison."

"You're killing it," Mia said, wrinkling up her nose. "I really don't think I could do that."

"Some chef you'd have been," Andrew quipped with a wink. "You wouldn't have skinned the meat?"

"I'll skin it," Mia qualified. "I'll help you smoke it, and preserve it, but I am not killing it."

He sighed and dropped a kiss on the top of her head as he handed Jilly a cracker. "Wimp."

"Damn straight I am," she laughed.

"Geee Dew dadabada," Jilly said seriously.

Mia raised an eyebrow. "You don't say?"

5

It took them three days of clearing the stones in the garden before they were ready to try to fell the tree. Mia and Andrew stared up at the tree considering. By that point the bruise on Mia's face had turned a marvelous mauve that gave her the appearance of a losing prize fighter. Andrew was being very overprotective, which annoyed her, but she'd let it go. For the most part.

"I need to do this by myself," Andrew said finally as he pointed an accusatory finger at the tree, like it was the tree's fault that bats had gone crazy and attacked her. "If it falls the wrong way you could get hurt."

"If it falls the wrong way, you could get hurt," Mia said stubbornly, crossing her arms. "I should stay out here to make sure that doesn't happen."

He did not look amused. "Are you going to hold the tree up?"

"Andrew!" She griped, and shook her head. "Maybe we should just forget this and try to find a different spot."

He threw a companionable arm around her shoulder as his face softened. "Relax, it will be fine. This isn't the first tree I've cut down."

She raised her eyebrow skeptically. "Really, when did you turn into Paul Bunion, hmm?"

"At my uncle's house in Michigan," Andrew reminded her. "He had that dead tree that got struck by lightning. I helped him cut it down. Of course we had a chainsaw."

Jilly swatted at Mia from the backpack from Andrew's back, and she turned to her sister. "Yes, little miss?"

"Uhh!" Jilly said, reaching out her arms to be sprung from the carrier. "Da!"

Andrew unhooked the chest clip. "Go on, take her inside and I'll get started. If you don't hear from me in an hour, worry."

"You aren't funny," Mia grumbled. "Really, your career as a comedian is going to flop."

"I'm very funny," Andrew said equably as he unclipped the carrier and handed it to her. "You've just lost your sense of humor."

"Yeah, yeah," she sighed and started back with Jilly to the shelter while he picked up the saw. She opened up the hatch, climbed in and awkwardly pulled it shut while juggling her squirming sister. On the whole Jilly was a really good baby, which was lucky, or taking care of her sister would drive her off the deep end.

Mia dropped her sister down near her toys and went to investigate what they were going to have for lunch. Breakfasts of cold cereal with dehydrated milk was getting old, but there wasn't much they could do besides that oatmeal. She'd thought briefly of trying to find some live chickens, but gave it up. They required a home outside and feeding. It was too much to hope that chickens would make it in the woods with bears running around.

She shivered as she thought of the bears. Thankfully they hadn't seen any, but she was always looking over her shoulder whenever she was outside. It had to be her imagination, but it just felt like they were being watched, even though she knew they couldn't be. If they were being watched, someone would have tried to take this place from them. Mia pulled out a package of dehydrated organic peas and contemplated them. It was more likely that absolutely no one knew this place existed, and if they did, they were dead or unable to get here.

Mia cut the bag open and added them to a pot with rice and black beans. It wasn't the hardiest meal ever, but it also wouldn't be loaded with processed chemicals or heaps of salt. She was getting so tired of everything being over-salted.

She began to stir just as her lower abdomen cramped and dread washed over her. Mia glanced over at the inventory that she had taped to the fridge and the glaring absence of something she should have noticed before stuck out to her. Her dad hadn't thought to stock tampons. She groaned as another cramp hit. She spun around desperately, trying to think of what she could use, but nothing except Jilly's diapers came to mind and she'd be damned if she'd use those.

Her eyes stopped at the door to Andrew's room, and she remembered the large dresser in there. She knew her mother had stashed some things in there, but...

Mia hobbled over to the door as another cramp hit her, making her gasp. Her periods were always horrible and heavy, especially when she hadn't been to the chiropractor. With one hand she pushed open the door, stepped over a discarded pair of Andrew's jeans and went to the tall chest of drawers. She pulled open the top drawer and found, to her relief and dismay, the cloth pads that her mom had tried to talk her into using a few years ago. There were also a couple of boxes that she didn't recognize. She pulled one out, read 'Diva Cup' and frowning turned to the back. "Wow," Mia whistled and stuck it back in the drawer. She'd have to be desperate for that one. Grabbing the whole stack of pads, she slammed it shut and went to get one of the smaller bags that could be used for Jilly's dirty diapers. It had a water proof lining inside, which made it good for holding in messes.

She was damned if she was washing these pads with Jilly's poo, and she needed a place to stash the dirty pads.

Mia stepped over her sister and closed herself in the bathroom and cringed inwardly at how gross this whole thing was. It was this sort of garbage that no one thought about when the world ended. She'd never once thought, 'What am I going to bleed on every month?'

By the time Andrew came back in, she was in the fetal position on the couch, hoping death would just take her. She could take Tylenol, she knew they had that, but it wasn't going to do much good against the cramps.

"What's up?" Andrew asked as he walked in and went to wash his hands. He was covered in wood shavings and smelled strongly of tree sap. The odor of it wafted over to her as she turned her head to look at him. He glanced back and concern flooded his face. "You look awful Mia, what happened?"

"I want to die," she told him as her stomach rolled and pitched with the clenching in her gut. "And it's really crappy of you to say I look awful!" She was sure she did look awful. Her face was covered in a large bruise, and healing cuts, plus she was reasonably certain she looked as bad as she felt. He didn't need to reminder her, though.

Jilly chose that moment to try to hand her a wooden block and when Mia wouldn't move her hands from around her knees, her sister placed it carefully on the side of her head and toddled off. She turned her head so the block slid down to the floor.

He dried his hands and came over to crouch down next to her. "Did you eat something that was bad?"

"No," Mia said through clenched teeth. She was reminded forcibly of the first time she'd gotten her period. Andrew had wanted her to go swimming and when she'd refused, he'd kept badgering her until she'd shouted at him that she was bleeding like a stuck pig, and he could go away. She was never sure who was more embarrassed at that moment, her or him, and she almost smiled now at the memory. She'd been twelve and him nearly fourteen.

Andrew ran a hand over her brow, leaving his palm on her cheek. "You don't have a fever."

"I have my period," she said pitifully as her lower lip trembled ominously. "And I have to use cloth pads!"

Surprise flickered over his face, but was quickly followed by understanding. "How bad is it?"

"Very bad," she whispered as his hand traveled from her face down to her shoulder. She closed her eyes and fought off the tears.

"Do you want me to get that hot water bottle from the first aid kit?" Andrew asked gently.

Mia nodded. "Thanks. Also, can you turn off the stove? The rice and beans should be done."

He smoothed back the hair from her face. "Sure."

Mia must have fallen asleep because when she woke later, she was covered in a blanket and a now cool hot water bottle was resting by her side. She turned to look and saw that she was alone in the shelter. There was no sound of Jilly's happy chatter or the sound of movement. There was a bowl of beans and rice sitting on the floor near her and she reached for it, touched that he'd left it for her.

She ate slowly, letting the food settle in her tempestuous stomach. The cramps were still there, but after the first wave they seemed to have calmed from excruciating down to painful. Painful she could take. When she'd finished her lunch, she stumbled to the bathroom and then made her way slowly back to her bedroom so she could stretch out more fully in her bed. Sleep claimed her moments after her head hit the pillow.

Mia woke hours later with her stomach rumbling with hunger, and thankful that her cramps had passed. She stood carefully, feeling a little light headed as she felt her way through the dark room. She heard Jilly rustle and froze, not wanting to wake her sister. Slowly, carefully she inched towards the door and saw that a light still burned under the crack at the door.

As quietly as she could she opened the door and slipped through, closing it behind her. She looked over and saw Andrew watching her from the couch. He smiled and went over to the fridge, which they'd finally started to use. He pulled out a wrapped up sandwich. "I saved you the last bit of the bread that you made last week." He set it at the table and pulled a chair out for her to sit.

"Thanks," Mia croaked out. She cleared her throat and began to eat as he went back to flop on the couch.

"Are you feeling any better?"

"Yeah," she said between bites. "Still a little achy, but otherwise I'm okay. What time is it?"

"Almost nine," Andrew said as he flipped a page. "I was wondering if you were going to wake up."

"Thank you," Mia said as she popped the last bite in her mouth.

He looked up at her confused. "For what?"

"For taking care of me and Jilly," she said as she walked slowly over to sit next to him. He put his arm around her and she cuddled into his shoulder.

"I promised you that I would," Andrew said as he went back to reading his book.

Mia tried to focus on it, but it made her head ache to try to read, so she closed her eyes and tried to relax. "What's the book?"

"It's about smoking meat," he told her absently. "I got the tree down."

"Oh, thank you," she yawned. She'd completely forgotten about the tree. "Was it difficult?"

"Not too much," he explained. "It was on a bit of a slope, so it fell pretty quickly. I didn't get much done after lunch. I put Jilly on my back and we went out to start sectioning it up, but that's going to take a while with just the hand saw."

She nodded and sighed, thinking back over the day. "We're better than we were five years ago."

"It would be embarrassing if we were worse," he commented dryly. "In what way?"

"I remembered the first time I got my period," Mia giggled, thinking back to the look on his face. "I wanted to die! I was so humiliated."

"Oh, yeah," he drawled slowly as he ran his hand up and down her arm. "I wanted someone to come along and bash me in the head with a shovel. You didn't have bad cramps back then, though."

She shook her head. "That started when I was fourteen."

"Right. I'm never going to forget that first time the cramps hit," Andrew groaned as he let his head thump back against the couch cushions. "We were out in your garden putting up the stakes for the pole beans, and you sort of went white." He shuddered. "If you hadn't fallen on to me when you passed out you'd have cracked your head on the pile of stakes."

Mia remembered waking up in the ambulance as she was rushed to the ER. "That was a great day," she said sarcastically. "Five million tests and nothing wrong with me but cramps. I was mortified."

"Eh, you've done dumber things," Andrew teased.

"Thanks a bunch," she said without heat. She stared off across the room as he went back to reading his book. It had been a really horrible day spent in the emergency room, but nothing was wrong with her. One of the doctors even told her she had a low tolerance for pain. Jerk.

Her eyes flicked over to Andrew's door. "Did you look through the dresser in your room?"

"I opened the first drawer, saw that cup thing, and decided I was never looking through it again."

Mia giggled. "What on earth was my mom thinking?"

"I don't even want to imagine," he promised as he flipped the page.

She saw the drawing of where to make the first cut on a deer and grimaced. "That's going to be gross."

"Yes, it is," he agreed evenly.

"Do you have a girlfriend?" Mia wondered aloud.

She felt him shift and look down at her, but she kept staring across the room. "No."

"A boyfriend?"

"Mia!" Andrew growled in annoyance.

"I'm just asking!" Mia retorted defensively. "Have you dated anyone?"

He was silent for a moment before he answered. "I dated a few times last school year."

"You didn't tell me?" She was oddly hurt. "I'd have told you."

"That's because you're you," he said nonchalantly, and she frowned at him. "None of them were serious enough to mention."

"What if I'd wanted to meet them?" She asked, poking him in the belly. "I have to approve of who you date."

He snorted loudly. "I can't bring just anyone to meet you. They'd have no idea what to do with our relationship."

That was true. "It would probably take someone who was really secure." The more Mia thought on it, the more she was sure that it would be just weird for someone else to be in the equation. "I've never kissed anyone."

Andrew flipped the page. "I know."

She huffed out a breath. "How do you know?"

"Because you'd have told me," he reminded her reasonably.

"I can't die without kissing anyone," she said suddenly. The thought, once it implanted itself, started to grow. It would be weird to never be kissed. "Do you remember that line from the Little Women movie?"

"I refused to watch that one."

Mia scrunched up her nose, trying to think back to when she'd read the books and had obsessively watched the movie twenty times. She'd been about thirteen or so. He had said no, point blank, to watching it with her. "Well, in it the one girl tells the boy that she's never kissed anyone, and he had to kiss her before she died. Or something like that."

"You want me to kiss you before you die?" Andrew chuckled. "Mia, I kiss you all the time. Kissing you on the lips isn't going to change anything."

She looked up at him. "Have you kissed anyone?"

"Besides you, you mean?" Andrew said not looking at her. "Yes, a couple of girls. It's sort of expected if you're dating in college."

"Have you had sex?"

Andrew rolled his eyes towards the ceiling. "Why do you want to know?"

"I'm curious," she grinned, knowing she was annoying him and not really caring. "I'd tell you."

"This isn't a conversation I'd ever have with a guy friend, you know."

"Well," Mia reasoned fairly, "I doubt any of your guy friends were going to try to talk you in to watching Little Women."

Andrew looked into her eyes, and shaking his head, laughed. "No, I haven't had sex."

"We'll both die virgins," she mused and then remembered her first point. "You do have to kiss me before I die, though."

"Why do you care?" He asked as he put the book to the side and stretched his legs out. "It isn't like anyone but you and I will know."

She wiggled her feet under his thigh to warm them up and curled more firmly into his side. "Because I don't want to miss out on that."

"It isn't going to mean the same if I kiss you," Andrew told her gently. "When you kiss someone you like and you're attracted to it feels different."

Mia looked back up at him into his blue eyes and tried to read his expression. "How is it different?"

Andrew's lips twitched, and he bent and laid his lips on hers. It felt… it felt like Andrew kissing her, like it always did. Just this time on the lips. He pulled back and his eyes twinkled in mirth. "Did that change anything?"

"No," she said, finally getting what he meant. "Maybe I'm gay."

"I think your obsession with that Liam guy would point to otherwise."

"Liam Hemsworth?" Mia mused as she scratched absently at her arm. She thought about just how adorable he was, and then grimaced. "Obsessed is a strong word."

"You mean not strong enough, right?" Andrew quipped as he pulled her in closer.

She rolled her eyes but chose to not to argue further. "Why can't I be attracted to you? You're very handsome, and it would save me a lot of hassle since you already love me."

"Believe me, I've wondered the same thing. I'd know how to be married to you without needing years of therapy to deal with the fighting. You I understand, girls in general… not so much."

He sounded so… Mia couldn't think of the right word for it. Sad was the closest she could come up with. She could almost feel how unhappy it made him, and she wanted desperately to make it go away. She wrapped her free arm his waist. "Oh, you'd still need therapy. I'd do my best to drive you nuts."

She felt his laughter rumble through his chest. "Well, maybe. But I'd get to die fat and happy."

"I'm still not going to feed you that much," she said shaking her head. One of the biggest parts of her food obsession was proper nutrition and making good food for people, not food that would only make them sick. "Poor Jilly. If we're stuck out here forever, she's never going to get to see a movie or eat good Mexican food or… too many things." It was too depressing to think about.

"She won't know what she's missing," Andrew reminded her as he ran a hand through her hair. "If we don't make a big deal about it, she'll be okay."

"I really want a cheeseburger," Mia said longingly. When she made burgers she minced all kinds of vegetables and blended them in with the raw meat, rather than sticking liquid smoke in. Just thinking about it made her mouth water. "I never thought I'd miss them this much."

"Maybe you're low on iron," Andrew said absently as he picked up the book again. "Since you're bleeding like a stuck pig and all."

She blew out a breath and wrinkled her nose. "It's a good thing I love you or you'd really annoy me."

He grinned and it transformed his whole countenance with how happy he looked. "Right back at you."

"Are you going to work on the tree some more tomorrow?"

"If you're up for it tomorrow, I'm going to hike up to the trail and watch for a bit. I want to see if anyone passes. I'm also going to start hunting for deer trails."

Mia started to protest but bit it back. "Are you going to stay hidden?"

"Yes," he promised. "I'm going to set out early and make a stand near the trail where no one can see me."

"But," she tried to say reasonably. "I thought you said it wasn't going to matter what is going on out there."

"Well..." he hesitated. "I got a slightly elevated reading on the ambient radiation, and with the Northern Lights being seen, I'm getting curious. After the first spike went down there hasn't been anything, so this seems a bit weird."

"Ugh," Mia groaned, squirming around to sit on her knees and stare at him. "When did that happen Drew?"

Andrew shrugged, not quite meeting her eyes, "A few days ago. I've been checking just to make sure it wasn't an anomaly."

She studied his face and saw the small tension around his eyes. "What do you think this means?"

"If the power is out, then it could mean that the nuclear power plants have melted down. Do you remember after the earthquake in Japan?"

She nodded. She wasn't ever going to forget seeing the images of the tsunami wave rushing over Japan or the fallout from the reactors melting down. "But what about a nuclear bomb this time?"

Andrew shook his head helplessly. "I don't know. I don't think it could be a bomb, but..."

"Okay," Mia said biting her lip. "Are we in trouble? Like are we going to get sick from it?"

"Not at these levels," he assured her. "If it gets a lot worse then we'll have to stay in the shelter for a few months."

She tried not to worry and to think about how crazy she'd gone during their first week stuck in the shelter. She tried to remember that so far her dad's eccentric plan was keeping them safe, tried not to think about what it would mean to have to spend months underground but... the tears formed before she could stop them. Andrew tugged her into his lap and put his arms around her. "I miss my parents. I wish someone was here to tell us what to do."

"That's the thing about being an adult," he mused. "We're the ones responsible now."

They sat like that for a long time. Mia listened to his heart and wished that she could give her mom a hug right then. She shifted her cheek and frowned as she poked at his shoulder. "Do you have muscles?"

"Yep. Someone made me cut down a tree for them." He sounded just the littlest bit smug.

"Too bad none of the girls are going to see your new buff body," Mia said slyly, glancing up at him.

"If I am the last guy on the planet will you marry me?"

She twitched her nose back and forth as if considering. "I would definitely think about it."

He chuckled, his deep blue eyes flashing in amusement. Andrew smiled at her in that way he'd done since they were small, and it was security and steadfastness that brought her back to all of the good times from her childhood. Most of her happiest memories included Andrew. She didn't have her parents, safety or even a promise of a long life, but she had her best friend here with her. If she was stuck here with anyone, she was more thankful than she could express that it was with him.

"You can go up to the trail," she said finally. "But you have to stay safe and come back to us."

Andrew cupped her face in his hands which were now covered in thick callouses from all the woodwork. He gave her an Eskimo kiss by rubbing their noses together. It made her laugh. "I'm not going to do anything that puts you two in danger. I promise," he said solemnly.

Mia nodded slowly, hoping that this wasn't a bad decision.

6

Mia paced the small living room, trying not to wring her hands like a fussy old woman. Andrew had been gone for hours. He'd missed lunch, and it had started to rain gently, the kind of good, steady soaking rain that all gardeners longed for. Unfortunately, that meant that she couldn't be outside working in the garden.

She'd put Jilly down for her afternoon nap right after lunch. She'd cleaned the kitchen, twice, cleaned the bathroom, then swept the entrance room down, and still he wasn't back. She didn't have anywhere else to focus her nervous energy and it was driving her mad. Mia stopped outside Andrew's door and sighed. She pushed it open and went back to the dresser with all of her mom's stuff in it. She needed to inventory it, even though she really didn't want to know what she was going to find. It was a new dresser made from pressed board about five feet tall and three feet wide. If she'd had to guess, she'd have said it came from Ikea or some other cheaper furniture maker. It had five drawers and stealing her resolve, she opened the top drawer and started pulling everything out.

Most of it was stuff that Mia had never heard of. There was a book about natural birth control and five purple thermometers which were labeled 'basal body thermometer'. There were also several boxes of condoms, which was fitting since she was pretty sure that Jilly had been conceived here in the shelter. She smirked at that and shook her head, putting it off to the side.

The next drawer down held a book on potty training. Mia flipped through it quickly before sticking it up on the bed to read more thoroughly. If she could get out of washing diapers this winter, she was going to give that a go. Also in that drawer were books about natural remedies and a bunch of bottles of essential oils.

"Oh, sweet," Mia grinned as she found a box of acupuncture needles. She looked them over and then found a book with a how-to guide. After sifting through the rest she went down to the next drawer and found, to her shock, an old cigar box with hundreds of gold wedding bands. "What on earth?" She mused, pushing through the various bands. Then it hit her that these were easy for trading with someone. It was cash on the run. She tried on several until she found one that fit and left it on her left ring finger. She didn't expect to need it, but if she did, it was easy to hand it over. Mia put the box to the side so Andrew could pick one out as well.

"What are you doing?" came a deep voice from the doorway.

Mia jumped and relief flooded her. She grinned up Andrew and saw that his hair was plastered to his head and shirt was soaked through. "You're safe!"

"Yeah," he sighed and went to grab a dry shirt from a basket on the floor. He stripped off the wet one and hung it over a chair. "I had to be careful coming back. I didn't want to leave tracks and with the ground muddy it took forever."

She nodded as she looked back to the drawer and pulled out a packet. "I was going crazy so I decided to sort through this thing."

"That's a lot of condoms," Andrew laughed as he pushed them to the side to sit next to her while pulling on the dry shirt.

Mia scrunched up her nose. "Jilly was born nine months after we first spent the night up here."

Andrew eyed the bed and groaned. "That's just gross."

She grinned at him. "Pick a ring," she told him, holding out the cigar box.

"Ah, trading for goods," he said as he picked through them. "I guess we are getting married."

"That's a seriously lame proposal," Mia said reprovingly as she opened up the manila envelope. Her eyes went wide. "Holy crap!"

"What?" Andrew asked, looking over her shoulder as he put a ring on. He stared with her.

There were at least thirty different passports stuck in the envelope. Mia pulled one out and found that her picture, along with the name Vanessa Baxter, and she was apparently now twenty one. She pulled out another, and found her mom's photo with the name Violet Sumner. Jilly's photo was there, too with the name Kelly Rolands.

Mia kept pulling and Andrew started sorting them. She froze when she found one with his picture. Her hand trembled slightly as she showed him.

"Donavan Baxter," he read slowly. His blue eyes met hers and held. "What on earth were they thinking? Why did they make one for me?"

"I don't know," she whispered and kept pulling. Mia had been wrong about the number of faked IDs. She'd missed a whole separate envelope that contained more. In total there were twenty full sets of fake IDs for herself, Jilly and her parents. There were four sets that had Andrew, Mia and Jilly as a family.

He stared down at them, and Mia could see his mind racing. "We should probably keep a set out to grab easily, and hide our driver's licenses," Andrew added after a drawn out moment of silence.

"Okay," she agreed slowly. A glint of moisture from his hair caught her eye, and she remembered. "What did you discover?"

"Not much," he said as he stuck three of the passports on the bed and helped her shove the rest back in the envelopes. "I did manage to spy on a couple of hikers, but they didn't talk about what was going on."

She nodded and put the passports off to the side along with the wedding bands. "They didn't see you, right?"

"No, definitely not," he promised as he reached past her to pull out another cigar box which rattled just like the wedding bands had. "These dudes were armed to the teeth and were built. Both of them looked like they could have snapped me in half without trying. If they'd seen me, they'd have confronted me."

Mia swallowed involuntarily. "That doesn't make me feel better."

"It wasn't meant to," he replied honestly as he opened the box and stared. "Well... uhm... pick an engagement ring out too."

She blinked stupidly, too stunned to do more than splutter, "Did they rob a freaking jewelry store? What the heck?"

"I have never seen this many precious stones in one place," Andrew murmured and held the box out to her. There were diamonds, rubies, emeralds and many other colored stones.

Mia took it and picked through, trying them on. It was funny, too, because these were now essentially worthless except for the gold. You couldn't eat a ruby. "I can't wear this when I garden."

"Careful," Andrew warned with a smile. "You're going to lose your girl card."

"Hopefully, I won't ever have to use this." She slid on a diamond solitaire that wasn't huge and seemed to match the band she'd already picked out. "What did the hikers say?"

He shrugged and closed up the box. "They were talking about getting to the next town up and trying to see if there were any supplies left. Apparently, there is a large outdoor store not too far from here. They both had assault rifles and were dressed in well-worn fatigues."

"Were they heading north or south?" Mia questioned as she shut the drawer and started to pull the bottom drawer open.

"South," he told her as he pulled out a book and stared down at it. "Unassisted Childbirth?"

Mia nodded back to his bed. "You know, in case they ended up with another Jilly on their hands."

Andrew stared at her, obviously not amused. "I'm never going to be able to sleep in that bed again. I do not want to think about your parents doing that."

Mia ignored him and pulled out a small box. She squealed happily. "A neti pot!"

"You get excited about the strangest things," Andrew said mildly as he took it from her. "I'm not washing my nose out with this thing."

"You might come spring when the pollen gets bad," she told him as she got out the salts that went with it. "Only problem is that we have to distil water to use with it. We can't trust the well water."

"If you say so," he agreed and pulled out a small plastic tub that was taped shut. He turned it over to read the label. "Sterile birthing supplies. Oh God..." he thrust it at her.

She rolled her eyes. "Relax. We're not going to be helping anyone give birth." She stuck it over with the condoms and pulled out a small envelope. She flipped it over and saw 'Mia' written on it in her mom's handwriting.

Andrew looked at it, then at her. He looked as nervous as she suddenly felt. "Do you want to read it alone?"

"No," she whispered. She pulled out the handwritten sheets and stared at them, unseeing for a moment before she started to read out loud.

> *"My Dearest Mia-*
> *"If you're reading this then something went wrong and Dad and I couldn't join you in the shelter. I hope you and Jillian are safe, and that you have everything you need. I hope you've found all the supplies, and I'm begging you to stay in the shelter. Stay safe and keep your sister safe. If you end up staying there for a few years, I know that you have gardening supplies, but please*

be careful. You should be well hidden, but it could be fatal if you are caught. When society breaks down, it won't break nicely.

"Mia, I'm so sorry that I'm not with you. I'm sorry that Dad isn't there. We planned for us to be there, hoped we'd be there, but also made arrangements for you to have everything you'd need just in case we couldn't make it. Our jobs have made it nearly impossible for us to guarantee that we could leave to be with you. We've known that something was going to happen for years. We weren't sure what exactly, and we did try to prepare for everything. I want to be there with you two. I want you to know that I love you and that I'm missing you. If we can, your dad and I will get to you just as soon as possible.

"I'm sure you've found the wedding rings. Keep one on and pretend that Jilly is your child. Start teaching her to call you mommy right now. Mia, this is so important! If someone questions you, she needs to be your child and not your sister. You have more of a claim to her if she's your daughter. It will also help if someone questions your age. I don't know how old you are when you're reading this, but I'm writing it shortly after your seventeenth birthday. Make up a story about what happened to your husband, and rehearse it. If you are discovered, having your story straight might help you to keep Jilly with you if there is still some form of government functioning. Under martial law things might get tricky. No one can know who you really are. Your dad and I are a liability if we aren't with you. Don't ever, ever tell anyone our names if you get asked.

"But mostly, I hope you aren't found and that you don't need any of the IDs or the wedding ring. I hope that you are safe and that you aren't too scared. When we let you drop out of school to start homeschooling we knew that we were giving you the chance to gain a lot of skills that might be needed and I'm so

> proud of you Mia. You've got more than a green thumb. I've never seen plants respond like yours do. You can do this. You can feed yourself, keep yourselves alive and thriving. You know how to take care of Jilly. I've left patterns for making clothes and fabric with the sewing machine. I've also stocked up on a lot of clothes in all different sizes for you two, plus a lot of hiking boots. It's all in the very back of the main storage closet in the large purple bins. I also included work books and other items so you can school Jilly up through fifth grade. Hopefully you've found them, but if not, keep going back. There's a false wall in the back. I had to put it all back there because your dad insisted that the guns go up front for easy access.
>
> "I'm sorry. I know I keep saying that, but I am. A couple of the times we asked you to babysit, your dad and I made runs up here with even more supplies. I didn't want you to worry by seeing how much we were preparing. I didn't want you to get upset over it. I also didn't want you to roll your eyes and dismiss us as crazy. You haven't been hearing what we hear at work, Mia. Something was always going to come. I'm just sorry we aren't-"

Mia had to stop, her voice cracked. Andrew pulled her into his arms so she was leaning against him. He kissed her cheek and held on. "Do you want to stop?"

She shook her head and took a deep breath, flipped the page over and continued to read.

> "I'm just sorry we aren't with you. I wanted to talk to you about boys, and be there when you went to the prom. I wanted to help you pick out a wedding dress and cry when you had your first child. I wanted to cheer when you graduated college and be the first customer of your amazing restaurant and I wanted to be pointing to your picture in a magazine and telling all my friends that that's my daughter! That's my girl, and I'm so

> proud of her. You are so talented. Sometimes I wonder just how I got so lucky to have such an amazing girl.
>
> "Mia, please save this letter for Jilly. Please help her to know just how loved she is and how blessed we felt to have her. We never thought we'd be able to have another child, and Jilly has given us such joy. I can promise that I'm missing her baby grins right now, and I'm wishing that I could bury my face in her sweet smelling red hair."

Mia had to squint a bit at the slightly blurred words. Her mom had clearly been crying at this point.

> "Jilly, I love you and I want so badly to see you grow up. Your sister adores you and she will do her very best to take care of you. Be good to each other. You're the only family you each have and you need each other. Mia is going to teach you how to be a strong, smart and capable woman just like herself.
>
> "I have one last thing to say to you, Mia. Your dad and I talked about Andrew and what would happen if he's up here with you."

She blinked and looked back at him, but his expression was blank. She turned back to the letter and read on.

> "If Andrew has come along, please know that we are glad. We talked about it some last month, but we can't really come to an agreement about if we should plan to have him come with you or not. I'm hoping he did. You have been two peas in a pod since you were both in diapers, and I know just how much you love each other. I trust Andrew completely. I trust him to take care of you and Jilly. I also know that having him around will make the work load a lot easier on you, Mia. I think you can do this on your own, but if he's there, know we aren't mad about it. I know we pressured you to keep the shelter a secret, but your dad and I knew you'd never keep it from him. If Andrew isn't

there, don't feel guilty. Much of the time we can't control what happens in life, which is why your dad and I aren't there right now. If we can get to Andrew and his parents, we will try to bring them with us up to get you. I promise you that we will do all we can to get him back to you safely. I know you'll miss him like you'd miss your arm.

"Mia and Jilly... you are my angels, my brightest lights. I'm praying you are safe and well!

"I love you with all my heart-
Mom"

Mia stared for a long time at her mom's last words. Finally with a sigh she turned to the second page and saw it was from her dad. His messy scrawl was always a challenge to read, but he seemed to have made an effort to make his writing legible.

"Mia and Jill-
"When I started to prepare for the end of the world you told me that the zombies weren't actually going to come. Well, you're probably right, but something happened.

"Mia, you're in charge. You need to raise Jilly and keep her safe. You need to get over your fear of guns and learn to use them if you need to. Don't if you don't have to, the sound will travel and draw attention to you. I stockpiled a couple of cross bows and there are several handguns with silencers."

"Oh, geeze," Mia groaned as she stared at that. "Is that the weird thing on the end of the barrel?"

"Yeah," Andrew said as he squeezed her shoulders.

"You can do this, Mia. We've been training you to handle this on your own just in case we couldn't be there. I'm proud of you, and I love you and your sister very much.

"Be safe-
"Dad"

"Mom writes two pages and Dad fills less than half a page," Mia sighed as she carefully folded the pages.

"Wait, there was a PS," Andrew said taking it from her. He read it out loud.

"PS the code to the safe is grandma's birthday."

They looked at each other blankly. "What safe?"

"I haven't seen a safe," Mia said, looking around. "I've looked through pretty much everything."

"I haven't seen anything either," Andrew agreed. He grabbed the stack of passports that he'd kept out. "It looks like my fake name is now Donavan." He grimaced. "I'm not sure how I feel about that."

"Can I call you Donnie?"

"Absolutely not," he assured her and opened hers. "You're Vanessa, and Jilly is now… wow. Millicent."

Mia snatched it from him. "What? There's no way I'd name a kid Millicent!"

"We have a little-" then Andrew paused as they looked at each other, and it hit them at the same time. "Milly."

"One of the names for her was Kelly," she said slowly. "I didn't look at the other ones."

Andrew pulled open the drawer and took the passports back out. "We need to work on memorizing the different identities. We don't need the ones that had your parents, just ours. Where are they..." he quickly sorted through and pulled them all out.

Mia flipped through them and read off. "Ryan, Sonya and Ellie Trent. James, Claire and Nelly Beaumont. Conner, Emily and Lily Baker."

"I really don't want to be Donavan," Andrew said handing back the stack. "Pick a different one, any of the others is fine."

Mia giggled and pinched his cheek. "You're such a sweetie pie my little Donnie-poo."

"You're a brat," Andrew laughed. "Do you want to be Sonya?"

"No," Mia said studying them. "All of Jilly's names rhyme so we can easily switch her to something else."

"Yeah," he nodded. "It makes sense. It's hard to adopt a new name when you're a kid."

"Why did they go to this much trouble?" Mia looked back at him as her heart began to ache. "Why would they want to give us so many ways to hide? When did they plan for you to be here? Even back in June, when she wrote this letter, Mom didn't think you'd be here."

Andrew's jaw clench and his eyes clouded as he shrugged. "I don't know, Mia."

She looked back down at the names. "Which one, Claire or Emily?"

He studied her a moment. "I guess I think you're more of a Claire."

"Okay," she said pulling that stack out. "So we're Claire, James and Nelly Beaumont."

"I suppose we are," Andrew said slowly as he stuck them in his pocket. "We're going to have to find that safe."

"Yeah," she agreed as she started to put stuff back into the drawers. She kept out the books, though, intending to read up on everything her mom had thought worth setting aside. She looked back down at the letter one last time before sticking it back in the drawer and shutting it firmly. "I hope they're okay. I hope they can find your parents and make it up here."

Andrew stood and held out a hand for her. He pulled her into his arms and rested his chin on top of her head. "Me too. I really hope they made it out. They'd be able to hike out to the trail and walk up here without really being seen, except by other hikers."

"That could be a problem, though," she sniffed, trying to hold back the tears. "If there are armed people on the trail, maybe they'll be stopped."

Andrew snorted. "No one is going to stop your dad, Mia."

"What do you mean?"

"I mean, your dad was a Navy Seal!" He said exasperatedly. "No one stops those dudes."

"He wasn't a Navy Seal!" She argued, pushing away from him. "He was in the navy, sure, but he's a scientist."

He looked at her, frowning. "You didn't know?"

"What are you talking about?" She whispered, shaking her head.

"He was a Navy Seal," Andrew said slowly, holding his hands out, looking completely floored that she was arguing with him. "Your dad knows all about guns because he was a trained sniper."

Mia threw up her hands, exasperated. "Where did you hear that?"

"I asked him!" Andrew blurted out, sitting down hard on the bed. "I asked him when he took me shooting this summer. He told me. Why didn't he tell you?"

She bit down on her lip and shook her head slowly back and forth. "No... no that's not possible. They're like... they're like trained killers. He is a scientist!"

"He was that too," he said frowning. "Do you even know what kind of scientist?"

She didn't. Mia's mind went blank, and she tried to remember what the diploma on the wall said. "He went to the Naval Academy and had a degree in physics." Andrew stared at her, totally dumbfounded. He was silent for so long that Mia ended up stamping her foot. "I stopped asking! When I asked, he told me that he couldn't tell me."

"He had a Master's in Astronomy from Yale."

"Why did he tell you and not me?" She stormed as she looked up at the ceiling. She couldn't stop the tears this time.

"I don't know," he said softly. "But he was a Navy Seal. He has this picture in his office of him and another guy holding a flag. I asked him about it."

Mia froze. She knew the one he was referring to, but she'd never asked her dad about it.

Andrew continued hesitantly. "I Googled it because I didn't recognize the symbol on the flag. I asked Scott and he told me a little about it and how it was right before he got out of the Navy. I thought you knew. I mean, for being in his forties your dad is seriously ripped."

She shook her head and turned when she heard Jilly's call. "Oh..." Mia walked out and towards her sister, but it felt like walking through wet cement. She opened the door and forced a smile as she picked her sister up, knowing what she was doing was wrong on so many levels. "Hi, baby girl! Come to Mommy."

7

Mia carried Jilly back into the kitchen and set her down. "Look, there's Daddy!" she said as brightly as she could.

Andrew only stumbled a little before he plastered a smile on his face and crouched for Jilly to run to him. "This is only a little weird," he commented as he swung Jilly into his arms. "She doesn't even seem to notice."

"She's young," Mia sighed, hating that she was doing this. It felt wrong on every level. "She forgets fast. She already calls you 'Dada' half the time anyway."

"If we don't see anyone, though," Andrew said as he put her down near her toys, "it won't matter. What happens when your parents get here?"

Mia watched her sister toddle over to her blocks, babbling happily. Her bright hair stuck out from sleep, but she was already pulling the blocks out to play with. "Then we'll adjust. Right now this is what they wanted me to do. I've been saying for weeks that I wanted them to tell me what to do."

"I know but…" Andrew's voice trailed off as he looked between them. "We just need to not be seen."

"But Mom was right about the garden," Mia mused as she sat down at one of the kitchen chairs. "She was right that it was easy to spot. We need to have a cover story."

Andrew grabbed the pad of paper and pen that sat on the counter and handed them to her before sitting across from her. "Okay, let's make up a cover story."

She blew out a breath and stared at the blank lines on the page, wondering what could fill it that would be enough to capture a fake life. Questions still lingered, though. "Why are my parents a liability?"

"I don't know," he said honestly, drumming his fingers slightly. "It could be because of their jobs, but if the government has broken down, then I don't see why. It isn't like they're the president of the country or anything."

Mia worried at her bottom lip, wishing they had better answers. "I guess."

"We should stick to the truth as much as we can," Andrew pointed towards the page. "We were neighbors and childhood sweethearts."

She nodded and started making notes in her neat, precise handwriting. "When did we get married?"

"Let's make it something easy like New Year's Eve?" Andrew suggested. "We can easily remember that."

"So we make that a year and a half before Jilly was born?" She quickly did the math in her head. "That would make it December 31st, 2012."

"I guess," Andrew blinked. "I'd just turned sixteen."

Mia shook her head and held out her hand for the passports. "According to these you're twenty-one right now, not eighteen. So we'd..." she paused as she looked at the date on her own fake passport. "No wait, I'd have been seventeen. That won't work."

"Okay, so then we'll say it was the next year. We got married because you were pregnant and due in June."

She grinned feebly. "I guess that works. You'll have just turned twenty and I'll be eighteen. At least these list our actual birthdays. We don't have to memorize new ones, just different years."

"How does it feel to be an old lady?" He asked chuckling. "You're, what? All of twenty now?"

"Twenty-one I think." Mia flipped back to the passport and did the math again. "This is getting confusing. Jilly was born in 2014, and this lists me as having been born June 9th, 1995. So I'd turned nineteen just before she was born on June 25th..." she trailed off. "Okay, you're right. Twenty."

Andrew dropped his head to the table. "We're going to be eaten by zombies."

Mia rolled her eyes and chose to ignore him. "So we were childhood sweethearts. I got pregnant, and we got married New Year's Eve."

"We hate each other," Andrew said, not raising his head from the table. "Definitely fight constantly."

She laughed, gently pulling one of his dark locks. "You need a haircut."

"We don't trust each other enough to give each other haircuts." He told her, finally meeting her eyes with a grin. "Write that down."

"I can't write that down," Mia argued. Suddenly she just felt calm. "I trust you with my life."

His blue eyes softened and he reached out, taking her hand in his. "Right back at you." Then he grinned wickedly. "So does that mean I can cut your hair?"

"Not on your life," she told him firmly. "Touch my hair and die."

He shook his head. "Okay, so we dated for a while before we had Jilly?"

"Yeah, let's say a year before I got pregnant. You know," she paused and frowned down at the paper. "It's very weird saying I was pregnant."

"Uh, yeah," Andrew agreed. "It's even weirder to think that I'm the one who knocked you up."

Mia couldn't help it, she burst out in giggles as her cheeks flushed. Jilly wandered over and held her arms up. She pulled her sister into her lap and nuzzled her nose into her neck, making Jilly laugh. "I love you little girl."

"Gah!" Jilly cried happily. She reached out for the pen which Mia deftly pushed out of the toddler's reach.

She looked up to find Andrew studying them. "What?" she asked, bemused by his confounded expression.

"It's just..." he hesitated and his eyes flashed. "You really are her mom now. As far as anyone is concerned you're her mom."

Nerves jittered through her, shooting down her limbs. It was a daunting thought. "You're her dad."

"I know," Andrew agreed. His voice shook a little. "I get that. Back in our old life that would have been the end of everything, you know? It would have limited all of our choices and made getting a college degree really difficult."

"But here it doesn't change much," Mia said, following along his line of reasoning.

"Except it does," Andrew told her. "Here our lives are in danger. We may not starve right now, but we run the risk of someone trying to kill us for our food." He looked so careworn that Mia nearly stood up to hug him. His next words froze her. "It's on me to keep you two safe."

He'd said that more than once. Never had it sunk in so deeply into her soul. "It's on me too," she began, but she cut off when he shook his head.

"This isn't about being the caveman," he told her. "It's about the fact that you hate guns, and I'm a better shot."

"I never really tried," Mia agreed knowing that he was supremely better. Her dad had tried everything he could to get her to take shooting seriously, but she'd never wanted to learn. Most of the time she flinched and shut her eyes when she pulled the trigger and he'd eventually given up on her. "I'm glad he taught you."

"Me, too," he whispered hoarsely. "You need to get better, though."

"Yeah," she acknowledged, hugging Jilly tighter to her. "I need to stop being afraid of them. But," she said, taking a deep breath, "if it comes to it, I'll run with Jilly, and you hold them off."

Andrew gave her a tight grin. "That's a plan."

Mia set Jilly back down and her sister crawled under the table. "Why are we up here during the end of the world? Who owns this land?"

"It was your grandparents," Andrew said as she wrote that down. "We stick to the truth. It was your dad's parents."

"How did we know to come up here?" She looked up and could see them both struggling for something to that seemed plausible without giving away what her parents had told her. "How about we were up here to check on things and spend the night? It was coincidence? When we heard the radio and our cell phones wouldn't work we stayed?"

"I like that," he agreed. "We have to say we're from Maryland since the truck has Maryland tags. We're going to need to hide the registration paper."

She wrote, making notes on a separate page of things to take care of later. Mia stared at the page and then looked back at Andrew. "I don't want to do this right now."

"Okay…" he replied slowly. "What do you want to do right now?"

Mia looked over to Jilly, who was playing again. "I want to play for a bit and pretend we're not hiding for our lives."

Andrew reached over and covered her hand in his, but she didn't look back to him. "It won't change anything."

She watched her sister as her mind whirled. "No," she agreed slowly. "But since I can't change anything anyway, I can pretend that the world around us isn't actually falling apart.

~*~ ~*~ ~*~

The rain from the previous day had left the ground soggy, and the forest around them perfumed with the heady fragrance that always followed a storm. Mia inhaled deeply as she hauled out the gallon water jugs to the garden to start digging up the tree stump. Despite the damp she knew she was going to work up a sweat.

She set Jilly down in the partially walled garden and set to hacking up tree roots with a shovel while Andrew continued sectioning off the trunk of the tree. She'd been only a little shocked when he'd come out of the store room with a hip holster and some kind of handgun strapped to his waist.

"This is going to take days," Mia grumbled as she dove into the back breaking work.

"Ga!" Jilly shouted from near the wall as she picked up handfuls of mud. Her sister was going to be filthy in minutes, but it was better than wearing her constantly on their backs.

Andrew grunted, using the hand saw to start on another chunk of the fallen tree. "It's going to take weeks," he corrected as he got to sawing. Mia could see that he'd left off halfway through his first cut.

Sighing, she stuck the shovel in hard and stomped on it with her booted foot, trying to drive it further into the ground. It got stuck about half a foot down. She tried to jump on the shovel head, but it wouldn't budge further. Mia pulled back and shivered a bit as the metal head scraped on a submerged rock sending shivers up her spine, much like nails on a chalk board. "I hate that sound."

Andrew didn't respond and when she looked up it was to see him staring hard into the trees. Mia followed his line of vision but couldn't see anything. "What-" But she froze as she heard a twig snap. Her heart tripped and blood rushed to her ears as panic swamped over her in a tsunami wave. She couldn't move.

"Get the baby," Andrew ordered softly. She didn't move. Mia heard, but couldn't move as another twig snapped as something moved closer to them. Only when she saw him step forward, the gun raised steadily in his hands did she feel her limbs unfreeze. "Now!" He hissed at her, his eyes not leaving the trees.

Mia scrambled forward and grabbed her sister. Jilly wailed instantly at being removed from the dirt she was throwing. "Shh!" Mia whispered, moving back behind Andrew.

They didn't have long to wait and to Mia's horror, the red of a sweatshirt appeared through the trees.

"Freeze!" Andrew called out calmly, but forcefully.

The person froze, just close enough to see that she was short and female. A low, trembling alto voice called back. "Please, don't shoot! We're just trying to get through."

Andrew was silent for a full ten seconds before replying. "How many are with you?"

"Me and my sister," she called back. When Mia looked around she could see a light blue shirt off behind. Fear, greater than her own, coursed through her. The look on the woman's face was enough to solidify Mia's blood into ice. "We don't want any trouble! We just can't walk on the trail. We've had too many close calls."

Mia looked over to Andrew and saw his jaw clench, but his posture never wavered. She wanted desperately to run back to the shelter, but knew that was a dead giveaway as to the location. Finally he broke his silence. "Come forward slowly. I don't want to shoot you, but I will if I feel like you're a threat."

Mia saw her nod and very slowly the two women came into the clearing. They looked grubby and hungry. Both once had had blonde hair, but it was now liberally streaked with grime and dirt. Their faces were only slightly cleaner and everything down to their worn out hiking boots was coated and soaking wet. Both looked terrified, and it was impossible to tell their age under the grime.

"Who are you?" Andrew asked and Mia marveled at just how calm he sounded. She wanted to sink to her knees and maybe not ever get up again as a kaleidoscope of feelings assaulted her. These two didn't seem like criminals, but on the other hand, they were the first people they'd seen in weeks.

The one in the blue shrunk back, even as her sister answered. "My name is Donna. My sister is Gabby. We were hiking the trail… a through hike from Georgia, and we're heading back home to New York…" her voice cracked. "A few weeks back something happened. All the power was gone and suddenly there were men with guns everywhere."

Jilly peeked around to look at them and the sight of the baby seemed to spur the one in blue to speech. "We really don't want to hurt you. We both have kids… they're in high school and college now, but we just want to get through."

"We've had to stay off the trail, but try to follow it to stay on course," Donna agreed. "We were nearly raped a few times, and our packs were stolen."

Andrew nodded slowly and inclined his head to the right. "That's the way north. You aren't far from the trail."

"You can take that water jug," Mia piped in, shocked to realize that she'd spoken as she pointed to the jug that was sitting on the make shift wall halfway between them. It was almost as if the voice that had come from her wasn't her own, but someone with a lot more guts.

Gabby shook her head nervously, obvious reluctant to move forward. "We don't need anything, honestly. We're managing."

Donna frowned at her, but moved towards it slowly, keeping her eyes fixed on Andrew. She picked it up. "Thanks. This will help." She backed up again. "You two look really young to have a kid." Mia couldn't tell if it was meant as a criticism or to try to bridge the icy crevasse between them.

Neither replied, but Jilly yelled helpfully, "Da!" and tried to lunge for Andrew, even as Mia tightened her grip on her sister.

"We manage," Andrew replied. "Go on. If I see you again, we will have trouble. Keep moving. There is a town along the trail about twenty-five miles up, and a ranger station somewhere between here and there. You might find help from them."

"Thanks," Donna said quietly and Gabby inclined her head. The two turned and continued on through the woods along a line that Mia knew would keep them going along the general direction of the trail.

"Not a word," Andrew whispered. "Don't say anything."

She could only stare after the retreating figures, unable to form coherent sentences anyway. When they were out of sight Andrew flicked the safety on the gun, and holstered it again. Quickly he grabbed up the tools and the three of them made their way back to the shelter. Only when she was back inside, down in the kitchen that had become a sort of hub for them, did the shaking take over.

"I've secured the hatch," Andrew told her coming back in. He took off the gun and stuck it up in one of the top cabinets of the kitchen.

Mia nodded as she set her filthy sister down and sank into a chair. She noticed belatedly that her hands were shaking.

"Nuh uh," Andrew said coming over to her. He scooped her into his arms and took her over to the couch. "Lay down, feet up. You're in shock." He put her down and stuck some pillows under her feet. He disappeared for a second and came back with a heavy blanket to cover her.

Her teeth chattered as he sat on the floor next to her, and pushed her hair out of her face. She tried to focus on him, but everything around her was hazy. "You're okay now," Andrew said gently, stroking her cheek. "You made it through, and when I needed you to keep it together, you did."

Mia tried to speak, but even when Jilly came over to poke her nose she couldn't make her voice work. Slowly the warmth started to seep back into her limbs, and she closed her eyes. Almost immediately disgust began to fight with the panic. It was that, more than anything, which brought her voice back. "I can't believe I fell apart!"

"You didn't," Andrew's tone was gentle and she didn't need to open her eyes to know that his expression would be conciliatory. "You were great during-"

"I can't keep doing this," she said, cutting him off and finally looking at him. "I can't be like this, not with the world the way it is."

Andrew shook his head, and pulled Jilly into his lap before she could scale the couch to get to Mia. "You were fine. You gave them the water."

"I didn't get Jilly until you told me to," she whispered, and felt the guilt at knowing she'd left her sister vulnerable. "I was frozen! You moved, you acted, and I just stood there!"

His blue eyes radiated compassion. "That isn't a bad thing, you know. My dad would have done the same thing."

"Your dad wouldn't have frozen," Mia retorted and held out her arms for her sister. Jilly cuddled in to her embrace, for once laying still with her head on Mia's shoulder. "And anyway, he's a pastor. Of course he'd have given them the water."

"He might have frozen when he was seventeen," he argued reasonably. "But he's a peaceful man. He never goes looking for a fight."

Mia kissed Jilly's brow and ran a hand over her soft curls, finding just the tiniest bit of mud stuck there. "I'm a wimp."

"No!" Andrew said vehemently. "You're a peacemaker. You don't look for conflict. There isn't anything wrong with that."

Mia studied his sincere face. "I can't just rely on you to protect us. I can't just be the girl."

"I hate when people say that," he griped and stood up to walk across the room. His shoulders were tense and anger seemed to pulse from his rigid posture. "Why does everyone say that like being a girl means you're automatically a weakling?"

"I…" she faltered, thrown off kilter. "I didn't mean it like that."

Sighing heavily, he turned back. "Yeah, you did," Andrew told her flatly. "You meant it just like that. So does everyone else. You throw like a girl, or fight like a girl… it's all crap." His eyes were hard. "Girls are just as tough as boys, Mia. Sometimes, like you, they're tough because they don't fight. And sometimes they're tough because they can kick my butt like your friend Amanda with her black belt in karate."

Mia felt a small smile form on her lips as the memory came back to her of Amanda flipping him onto his butt. "She did, didn't she?"

"Yes!" Andrew said, coming back over and sitting on the edge of the couch near her legs. "Do you think that I see my dad as a wimp?"

"No," she assured him. "No, he does all kinds of things that take courage, like volunteering downtown with the homeless."

He watched her, so intently that she felt herself want to squirm. "It's the peacemakers who are going to rebuild this world, not the ones who shoot."

Mia reflexively tightened her arms around her sister's tiny body, "If they live long enough."

"They will," Andrew said confidently. "Real courage will always win out, Mia. It takes more courage not to shoot."

She frowned, trying to work that out, "Because they have to face things?"

"When you shoot someone, you're claiming all the power. There's a lot of cowardice in not being willing to confront what the other person might do," Andrew explained, leaning a bit to run a hand up Jilly's back. The baby only stirred slightly, and Mia realized she must have fallen asleep. "If I give up the power to kill someone, then I have to accept that I'm not totally in control. That's really scary."

Mia worried at her lower lip for a moment. "Would you have shot them?"

"No," he said without hesitation. "They weren't a threat. I probably wouldn't have offered them the water, though. That took courage. That was seeing them as people, just like you, and offering what compassion you could without jeopardizing our safety."

"I'm not brave." Mia didn't know much, but she knew she couldn't have done what he'd done.

He sighed heavily, exasperated. "You don't get it, Mia! Being able to shoot someone is not bravery. Looking at someone, and seeing their humanity— that takes guts. There are different ways of showing that you're tough."

She looked away towards the unadorned wall as her mind raced. "We should have swapped dads."

"Your dad loves you." Andrew's voice was low. "He told me once that you weren't the child he thought he'd get, but that you were the one he needed."

Tears sprang to her eyes but she didn't let them fall. She missed her parents so much.

8

They stayed underground for nearly a week after their encounter with the hikers. By the end of the seventh day Mia was ready to pull her hair out. "If we do end up having to live down here for months because of radiation, I'm going to go postal."

"That's not nice," Andrew said casually flipping through a book on solar panels. "Postal workers have a really hard job."

"Ugh," Mia huffed, stomping her foot. "I want to go outside again."

He raised an eyebrow. "You want to get outside? I think you've listened to those Katy Perry songs at least five hundred times. My ears are bleeding."

She grinned impishly. She'd finally remembered that she could play the music off of her cell phone, and she'd been blasting it as she searched, yet again, to try to find the safe that her dad had mentioned in his letter. She still couldn't find it. Mia looked over to the stairs that led up to the outside world. "Let's do it, then."

"Let me get the truck keys; I need to run it or it will be useless. Hopefully the battery isn't dead yet because figuring out how to jump it would be a nightmare," Andrew said as he fished the keys out of a drawer in the kitchen.

Mia huffed out a breath, grabbed Jilly's shoes and made for the stairs. "Come on, Jilly. Let's put your shoes on."

"Bababa, mmm," Jilly toddled over and sat for Mia to put on her shoes. "Mama!"

Mia grinned at her, but felt her heart clench. Jilly had taken to the switch immediately. It hadn't been hard to get her sister to start calling her that. She finished tying the shoes and swept her up just as Andrew came back with the gun strapped to his waist. "Let's go," he said as he also grabbed the garden tools.

She followed Andrew up the stairs and let out a slow breath as he opened up the hatch. Weak morning sunlight filtered down through the trees and there was a definite bite of fall in the air. Mia didn't care, though. She was just pathetically happy to see the sun and breathe fresh air.

They emerged into the open carefully, looking around. Everything was just as they'd left it, and only the sounds of nature flitted around them.

"I'm going to check on the truck," Andrew told her as he moved over it. The cover was still in place, although slightly askew. "Wait for me, and then we'll go up to the garden together."

Mia nodded and watched him pull the camouflage tarp off the truck, letting it fall on the back. Andrew froze, staring into the back window of the camper shell.

"What?" Mia asked, feeling her heart rate triple.

"There's someone in the back," Andrew answered simply. "There's a lot of blood."

"Oh God," Mia breathed out coming over to look. She saw a bloody handprint on the glass. It was a perfect imprint, brown and caked with a bit of dirt. A Hollywood horror studio couldn't have created anything better, and it sent chills down her spine.

Andrew dropped the tools and pulled out his gun. Slowly he opened the back hatch. They looked in to see a slight boy, about fourteen, with dark skin and short black hair. His white t-shirt was covered in blood. For a horrible minute Mia thought he was dead, but as she watched she could see his chest rise and fall in shallow gasps.

Andrew looked at her. "What do you want to do?"

She didn't even need to think about it. Calm unexpectedly took control of her mind, and her instincts kicked in to high gear. This was a kid, an injured child. "Get him inside."

"Okay," Andrew said. He holstered the gun and reached in for the boy. Even though Andrew wasn't very big, he had no trouble pulling the kid into his arms. "He's really thin."

Mia walked ahead of him back to the hatch with Jilly and went back down. She set her sister down and went for the first aid kit. "Put him on the couch."

"Okay," Andrew grunted and walked into the other room.

She ran in with the first aid kit and some clean towels. "We need to clean him up and see where he's injured. Is he unconscious?"

"Looks like it," Andrew said as he went for the towels. He dropped them next to her. "I'm going to go grab the tools and close the hatch. I'll be back in a minute."

"Okay." Mia was only half listening, and she dug out medical gloves and went to get water. Carefully she pulled his shirt up and found it was stuck at his right side. There was a black mark in the shirt, and dried blood crusted all around it. Jilly came over to inspect just as Andrew walked back down. "Give her one of our phones to play with. I need her distracted."

Andrew went and fished out his phone to give the toddler. Jilly toddled off happily, already swiping through the Elmo app. "How can I help?"

"I need to get his shirt off," Mia said softly. Together they slowly worked the shirt off of the boy and she couldn't help but gasp. There was a nasty, puss-filled wound in his side. "Let's stick some towels under him and start pouring the peroxide on it. I think he's going to need some of the antibiotics, though."

Andrew rolled him carefully so Mia could shove the towels under him. When she poured the liquid on, it started to bubble and the boy let out a small cry, his eyes fluttering open as he groaned and tried to roll away. Andrew held him still, putting steady pressure on his shoulders. "You're okay, you're safe. We're taking care of the wound."

"Shhh," Mia crooned as she ran a damp cloth over his face, trying to see if there were any other injuries underneath the dirt. There were a few bruises that looked like they were nearly gone and a deep cut that was mostly scabbed over on his temple. "What's your name?"

The kid's eyes flicked to hers once before closing again.

"I don't know what else to do for this," Mia said, indicating the injury on his side. "The antibiotics are all pills, so he's got to be awake to swallow them."

"Let's put on some bandages," Andrew told her as he dug some out along with the antibiotic ointment. It seemed useless in the face of such a large wound, but without anything else it was going to have to do. She liberally spread the cream on the cotton bandage and carefully placed it over the wound before they taped it to him. She pulled a blanket over him and went to wash her hands.

Andrew stood, staring down at him. His face was awash in concern. He looked back at her. "This is stupid. Your dad would kill us for bringing him down here."

"I don't care," Mia retorted as she dried her hands. "He's just a kid! We couldn't leave him up there to die."

"What about when he wakes up, Claire?" Andrew asked her, his eyebrow raised and she suddenly understood with blinding clarity what had him completely on edge. This boy wasn't going to be able to hurt them. That wasn't the biggest hurdle before them. They had another directive that would now be put to the test.

She wasn't Mia anymore. She was Claire, he was James, and they were married. Slowly she nodded and went to her room to very quickly, and quietly, grab all of her stuff. She needed to move into Andrew's room.

As efficiently as she could she got herself set up in Andrew's room and made it look like she'd been there all along. "Maybe we should move Ji-" Mia cut off, and shook her head. "Nelly into our room for now, just so we can keep an eye on her."

Andrew looked back and forth between them. "Yes. I need to go lock the storage room, too."

"Okay," Mia agreed gently as she went to take her sister's portable crib apart to move it. She didn't want to mistrust the kid, but at the same time she also knew it would be stupid to blindly trust him. Trust was earned. With her sister moved into the master bedroom, she stripped the bed she'd been sleeping in and put on fresh sheets. When Andrew came in behind her, she turned and was stunned when he leaned in and kissed her. "What-"

He shook his head, his blue eyes intense. "You can't react like that, Claire," he said quietly. "We've been married for nearly two years, and we have a daughter. I kiss you; you kiss me back, okay? We need to keep up this pretense."

"This is stupid," Mia grumbled, but this time when he kissed her, she leaned in and didn't recoil. "Okay, I got it, James. Now let's move him in here so he can sleep without Ji- grrr!" She cut herself off. "Without Nelly poking him in the eye."

He nodded and went to move the kid.

Mia checked on the boy every thirty minutes. She tried a few times to get him to drink some water using a straw, and after a couple of hours managed to get him to wake up enough to drink. Later that night, she even coaxed his eyes open enough that she was reasonably certain he could talk to her. She had planned out what she wanted to say to him, because it hadn't been completely natural. "I'm going to bed after I change your dressings again. My husband and I are just in the other room. If you need us, call out, okay?" Her voice had cracked slightly on the word 'husband,' but hopefully he was too sick to notice.

The deep brown eyes met hers briefly and she thought he'd understood. He closed them again and fell back into sleep.

Mia crawled into bed with Andrew twenty minutes later, and stared up into the pitch black above her. She was still not used to a life without the ambient lights of the city filtering in through windows at night. It was so dark underground.

Andrew rolled over and put an arm around her waist, burying his face in her neck. "He's too sick to hurt us."

"I know he is," she breathed out softly. "I'm not worried about him hurting us. I'm worried that he's going to die and that we won't be able to save him."

Andrew kissed her cheek. "All we can do is try."

She nodded. It would have to be enough.

The next morning came with the call from Jilly. "Mama! Dada! Mama!"

Andrew was up before her, pulling Jilly from the crib and bringing her back over to the bed. Mia rolled and found her wiggly sister between them. "Hi, Nelly." At least this time she'd remembered.

"Mama!" the baby said happily as she half crawled onto Mia's face.

"None of that short stuff," Andrew said as he pulled her off Mia, who was laughing.

"Num-num!" Jilly whined. "Pwee! Num-num!"

Mia yawned and stretched. There wasn't any light in the room, but her eyes had adjusted to the dark enough that she could make out the shapes around her. It was almost like the furniture was in grayscale. Except darker, everything was much darker. "I guess that's my cue. Can you get her diaper? I'm going to check on the kid."

"Okay," Andrew agreed with his own answering yawn. He was still not a morning person, but he was getting better. Suddenly he took her hand in his. "Are you sure you don't want me to check on him?"

She felt her gut drop, and she knew why he was asking. "No. I can deal with it." As she rose, Mia heard a voice start chanting in the back of her brain... please don't be dead, please don't be dead...

The walk through the kitchen to the smaller bedroom took seconds, but might have taken hours. She dawdled only long enough to pour out a bowl of oatmeal to stick in the microwave for Andrew to feed Jilly. Mia carefully cracked the door and peered in to find brown eyes watching her from the bed. She grinned in relief. "Do you want me to turn on the light?"

"Sure," came the tenor reply. He flinched a little when she hit the switch, but didn't otherwise react as he watched her warily. "Where am I?"

"That's an excellent question," Mia hedged as she walked to him and crouched down next to the bed and knelt on the carpet that barely padded the hard floor below her knees. "You're underground in a shelter."

He stared at her, unblinking. "You're crazy."

Mia couldn't help but laugh. "I'm glad you're feeling better. What's your name?"

He paused for just a moment before answering. "Jamal. Jamal West."

She held out a hand and he carefully reached over to shake. His hand was slightly bigger than hers and sweating a bit. She wasn't sure if it was nerves or a fever, but decided not to comment on it. "I'm Claire Beaumont. You really are underground in a bunker."

"How—" he broke off when his voice cracked a bit, and Mia knew that her estimation of his age was probably pretty close to fourteen. Jamal cleared his throat and tried again. "How did I get here?"

"Well," Mia said slowly. "I'm not entirely sure how you got into my truck, but you got down here when we found you. My husband carried you down. How's your side?"

"S'okay," he mumbled and shifted a bit, wincing a little. "You look too young to be married."

Mia smiled grimly. "I did get married really young. How old are you?"

"Seventeen," Jamal answered, looking away.

"Try again," Mia countered, waiting.

His eyes flicked back to hers. "Sixteen."

Mia stared at him expectantly, waiting.

"Fifteen."

This time she snorted.

Jamal sighed and let his head fall back. "Fine, I'm thirteen. I'll be fourteen in February."

"Okay," Mia said. This time she believed him. "Are you hungry?"

"A bit," he admitted. "My stomach's not feeling so good."

"I can imagine," she said and turned when she heard Andrew's call. "My husband is James and our daughter is Nelly. She may wander in here, but if she bothers you, just let me know."

His eyes widened in surprise. "You have a kid, too?"

"Yeah," she answered and stood. "I'll get you something light to eat, and then I wanted to give you some antibiotics for that wound. You aren't allergic to anything, are you?"

"Nah, well," he hesitated as she looked at him expectantly. "I'm allergic to strawberries."

"We don't have any of those, so you're safe. I'll be back shortly." She left, leaving the door cracked in case he called out.

Andrew was eyeing her, not speaking as he sat at the table with Jilly in the high chair.

"MM GAH!" Jilly shriek at Andrew. "DADA! Num!"

He turned back to Jilly and spooned up some more oatmeal for her. "I'm sorry, sweetie."

Mia grabbed the container with the oatmeal and poured some into a bowl before adding a bit of water. She stuck it in the microwave and heated it. "He seems okay. I'm going to grab the antibiotics and I'll change the dressing after he's eaten."

"Okay," Andrew said. "Do you need any help?"

"No, I have it," Mia promised and went for the medicine, which was in the other room in a tote. Once alone she paused and closed her eyes, drawing in a deep breath. She was supposed to be twenty, a mother and wife. She needed to keep her poise and remain calm. Feeling slightly more centered, she dug through and found the right bottle.

After he'd eaten and taken the pill, she changed his dressing and found that the wound looked slightly better than the day before. He hissed out a breath as she put the bandage on, but didn't other make any noise. "What happened?"

"Shot," he told her through gritted teeth, his eyes were white slits as he fought with the pain.

Mia gasped, but didn't otherwise comment. "Okay, you should be good for a bit. I'll check on you once in a while, but otherwise just stay here and rest. If you need me, call."

"Thanks," he mumbled.

She gently patted his shoulder and turned off the lights as she went out. Andrew and Jilly weren't anywhere around, and she also saw that the back pack was gone from the coat rack on the wall, so she presumed that he'd taken her up top. When she checked she realized that he'd taken the hand saw, which meant he'd intended to work on sectioning up the tree. With Jilly on his back. Mia could only shake her head. They had arrived at the point that the baby was almost like an extension of him, and where he went she was there with him. Both of them loved it, too. Jilly was always calm when Andrew wore her, and Mia had to admit that it did look appealing. To her, the world was safe because she was riding along on a big, strong back, on a person who never let her down and always protected her. If only life could stay like that.

Mia had sometimes, when she was younger, felt that way about God when she was in church, but as she'd grown into a teenager it had become more complicated. Believing in God didn't isolate anyone from pain or suffering. Sometimes, she just knew that God had her back... and sometimes, like right then, it didn't feel like it was enough.

Sighing, she went to get out the hand washer and the dirty diapers.

Jamal slept most of the day. He managed to make it to the bathroom once with Andrew's help, but slept through lunch and only wanted a bit of beans and rice for dinner.

Mia stood in the door staring at his sleeping form, worrying at her bottom lip. Jilly was asleep already for the evening and the laundry was finished, and drying on lines in the other room. Her back hurt from the work, but her heart hurt more staring at the kid before her.

She started slightly when Andrew came up behind her and wrapped his arms around her waist, resting his head on top of hers. "You ready for bed?"

"Yeah," she said, leaning back into him. She could feel his warmth on her sore back, and it was almost as good as a heating pad. A heating pad... something else she missed from her old life. "I want to complain that my back hurts from the laundry, but since you kept sawing at the tree with a baby strapped to your back, I'm not sure that you'd want to hear it."

"I'm okay," he promised, pulling her back out of the door. "Come on, let's get some sleep, and I'll try to work some of the kinks out."

She followed behind him and flicked the lights out in the kitchen. Mia pulled out the sweatpants and shirt she was sleeping in as Andrew did the same and they both turned their backs on each other to change. There was no need for words. They'd been camping together many times over the years and had a routine. "Done," Mia whispered, not wanting to wake Jilly.

"Me, too," Andrew replied and she got the light before carefully making her way back to the bed. "Roll onto your side," he instructed and she did, giving him her back. He stared to knead at her tight muscles.

Mia let out a sigh of relief as he worked out some of the knots. "This is so unfair to you."

"When I really need one, I'll ask," he assured her with a quiet chuckle.

Letting out a final sigh as the tension seeped from her, Mia closed her eyes. "I'm good now, thanks."

"Okay," he said and she felt him shift onto his back. "Night."

The next day went about the same as the day before. Andrew worked out in the garden on the tree with Jilly as much as he could. Jamal slept for most of the day again, but he did eat more and his wound was continuing to look better. By the third day he was awake and ready to come out of his room for a while. He joined them at the table for lunch, looking around the place with wide eyes. "It's unreal that we're underground. You only hear about these things on TV."

"It was my dad's idea," Mia said after she swallowed a bite of stew. It wasn't the worst she'd ever had though and she was heartened to see Jamal eating more like a normal teenage boy. "I thought he was nuts, but it ended up being a lifesaver."

"Seriously," Jamal agreed, taking a drink of water. "How did you get the truck up here?"

Mia and Andrew looked at each other. "What do you mean?"

"Well," Jamal looked between them, confused. "I mean... none of the other cars work."

Mia felt her jaw drop. Andrew gasped. She could almost hear the cogs turning in his mind, and she could tell that this new information meant something huge to him. "None of them?"

"No," Jamal told them. "I don't get it."

"We..." Mia hesitated. "We actually came up here to check on things that weekend. It was coincidence that we were here. We didn't know it was so widespread."

Intelligent brown eyes met hers, and then flicked back to Andrew. "But then why did you stay up here?"

This wasn't part of the story that they'd worked out. Andrew jumped into the silence. "When the truck didn't start, we thought it was a coincidence at first, but then the phones weren't working either. We don't really have a way of getting home with Nelly. We decided to stay and wait to see if anyone came, but then we saw some hikers along the Appalachian Trail just a few days after everything stopped working. They said the world was going crazy, but they didn't know much."

"Crazy is a good word for it," Jamal said as he relaxed back and took another bite. "All kinds of strange stories floating around, and I've been spying on people when I can to try to learn more, but no one knows anything. What I did see was that no one has any electronics that work anymore, well, except you guys."

"The shelter must be a Faraday cage," Andrew mused as he glanced around them at the blank walls, seeing something that Mia couldn't see. "That's why the solar panels weren't hooked up before we got here. I thought that was a little weird."

"A what?" they both asked.

Andrew shook his head and blocked Jilly from grabbing a bowl off the table. "It protects electronics from electrical surges or signals. Do you have a phone?"

"Nah," Jamal said quietly. "My mom did, though. It stopped making calls."

They waited a beat before Mia finally spoke. "What happened to you? Why are you out here by yourself?"

He sucked in his bottom lip for a moment before answering. "We were driving back from my mom's friend's house. We'd gone to see her for Labor Day since my mom didn't have to work. Suddenly the car lost power, and my mom lost control. We hit another car and spun out."

Mia reached out and squeezed his arm gently. "What happened to your mom?"

"She..." tears filled his eyes, and he roughly swiped at them. "She and my little brother didn't make it."

"Oh, Jamal," Mia wanted to cry with him. She could almost see the pain pouring off of him in waves. "I'm so sorry."

He nodded once, not looking at them. "I'm kinda tired. I think I'll go lay down again."

They silently watched him close the door to his room.

"Duh," Jilly said, and Andrew let her down from the high chair.

"So what does it mean that none of the cars work?" Mia asked him.

Andrew shrugged helplessly. "It could mean a couple of things. It could be an EMP or a solar storm called a Coronal Mass Ejection. It could be some sort of terrorist attack, although I'm not sure how they'd have gotten to everything."

She could guess what Coronal Mass Ejection meant. That clearly meant the sun had thrown up all over the place, and whatever it spewed out wasn't good. "What's an EMP?"

"Electromagnetic pulse," he explained as he gathered up the dishes. "It just means something knocked out the power. A nuclear bomb set off in the atmosphere is supposed to do that, but the damage wouldn't be like this. It's supposed to be powerful enough to kill people on the ground."

Mia put away the leftovers and turned to look at him. "So a solar storm?"

"I guess, but I think they would know that's coming days before it hit," he said as he dried the plates. Andrew walked over and pulled her into his arms, kissing her lightly on the lips. She tried not to freeze up, but it still felt weird. "What?" Andrew probed carefully, his eyes intent on her face.

She shrugged. "I just... it's still weird, and we're not being..." Mia flicked her eyes to the door and back up to his.

He knew what she was getting to. "We are what we are now. If we don't do certain things, then when we need to it's more like work and doesn't come naturally."

Mia closed her eyes and leaned into him. "You're right. I guess I'm still not used to it." Tears wanted to form as she thought of that poor kid having to see his dead mom and brother. "I feel so bad for him."

Andrew ran a comforting hand up into her hair, cradling her to him. "I think we're only starting to see the tip of the iceberg on just how bad it's going to get."

9

"What day is it?" Jamal asked the next morning. "I tried keeping track, but I lost it a few weeks back."

Mia reached over for her phone and swiped at it to check. "It's October 10th."

"Wow," he exclaimed as Andrew walked in with Jilly.

Andrew's arms were covered in mud, but he looked pleased as he set the baby down by her toys. "I got the trunk sectioned, up and I was able to move it out of the way so we can finish the garden wall." He ran a bit of water over his hands, washing away the dirt. "The stump will be a problem since we can't haul it out with the truck."

"I can help," Jamal offered immediately, looking between them.

"I appreciate that," Andrew said as he took off the gun and hip holster and left it out of Jilly's reach on the counter before coming to sit by Mia and casually draping an arm around her shoulder. "But until you can do a push up, you're not going to be much help."

"Yeah," he sighed grumpily.

Mia smiled sympathetically. "It won't be much longer. Do..." she hesitated a moment. "Do you want to tell me how you got shot?"

"No," Jamal answered instantly. "But I should 'cause you don't have a clue what it's like out there on the roads."

"We don't," Andrew agreed. "It would be helpful to have a better picture."

Jamal picked at a spot on the table, not looking up at them. He traced a knot in the wood grain slowly with one finger, over and over again. They waited him out, giving him time to put his thoughts together. "When we crashed, we hit another car. Everyone was killed except a little girl. She was in one of those car seats that's got a harness like a race car driver, you know?" they both nodded. Jilly was in one like that. "Everyone else was thrown from the car. When I came to, I checked on my family and then went to check on hers, but they were dead. She was crying and I helped her get down. She was sort of hanging down from it."

Since the little girl wasn't with him, Mia knew that this wasn't going to be a happy ending, but she didn't interrupt.

"We gathered up all we could and started to walk. It was daylight by then, and I just knew that no one was coming." Jamal sighed heavily and looked up at the celling. "Her name was Dana and she was seven. She was this tiny little thing. We finally found a house, and a lady let us stay for the night, giving us dinner and such. Dana and I were both from Philly, so we were both going back there. That's where her mom lived. She'd been with her dad and stepmom for the weekend."

"What happened after that night?" Mia questioned. Andrew squeezed her shoulder almost reflexively.

He met her gaze and looked back to Andrew. "We kept going. The woman who we stayed with didn't want us to stay longer. I thought she might keep Dana, ya know, 'cause she was this cute little blonde girl, but she wanted us out. So we kept walking. We passed a lot of crashed cars and a lot of dead bodies. It got to the point where I didn't even look anymore for survivors. We had to sleep outside the next night, but it wasn't cold, so it was okay. We ran out of food and water so we went up a driveway to find another house to see if we could... could get something..." his voice trailed off and his eyes were haunted. "I knocked on the door, and a minute later a large dude with a gun opened the door."

Mia's hands flew up to her mouth. "Oh no! That's how you were shot?"

"No," Jamal corrected her morosely. "I ducked, but Dana was behind me. I…" he licked at his dry lips as tears filled his eyes again. "If I hadn't ducked it would have been okay, but he shot her straight in the face."

"Oh God," Mia groaned, feeling her insides twist in horror as the images played in her mind.

Andrew swore softly under his breath and leaned forward on the table. "She didn't make it."

"No," Jamal agreed, and his stricken eyes met Andrew's, reaching out for reassurance. "James… I swear I wouldn't have–"

"It's okay," Andrew grasped his shoulder. "It was reflex to duck. You couldn't have done otherwise."

Jamal shrugged off the comforting words. "It doesn't help."

"No," Andrew agreed softly. "It doesn't help."

"The dude, he started screaming that I'd killed her, and I ran for it. There wasn't anything I could do for her." Tears filled the boy's eyes again but he didn't let them fall. "I didn't go to no one's house after that, though."

Mia and Andrew joined hands, entwining their fingers. She wished that she had something she could offer him. "Are you still trying to get to Philadelphia?"

"Yeah," Jamal agreed. "My grandma lives there. If she's still alive, she's going to need me. She doesn't have anyone else."

"So how did you get shot?"

Jamal groaned and rolled his eyes. "It was 'cause I was stupid. I was crossing that main road out there, and I didn't wait to make sure no one was watching. Once I got to the middle of the street someone opened fire, and I had to run for it. I hit the dirt road and kept going, and when I saw the cutoff that led up here I thought it might lead me to some place

I could hide. I stumbled upon the tarp and realized it was a truck, and that's when I climbed in. I didn't realize I was hit until I lay down to catch my breath."

"You don't have to go," Mia said softly. "You can stay here."

Jamal shook his head resolutely. "I have to go. My grandma isn't young, and I know she may not be okay, but I have to check."

"We understand," Andrew said evenly. "We have no idea what's happened to any of our family, but with Nelly, we just can't risk going to find out."

"Nah," Jamal agreed, grinning over at the baby who was toddling around talking to herself. "I wouldn't have moved from here if I'd had the choice, not with a baby anyway. So..." the boy paused, studying Andrew. "So, if this was a solar flare what does that mean? I've only seen the effects here in the boonies. What about in the city?"

"I don't know exactly, although it's not technically a solar flare because that wouldn't cause this sort of damage," Andrew answered honestly. "If it was a CME, or a Coronal Mass Ejection, then a lot of what people think might happen is speculation. There have been a few flares that have hit, but nothing that is widespread. A flare hit the very tip of South Africa a few years ago and everything blew. Another hit part of North America in the 1800's and it took down all the telegraph lines."

Mia stared at him, a little flummoxed. "The things you have studied just flabbergast me sometimes."

"I didn't really study this," he admitted tentatively. "Your dad told me about them a year ago. I needed help with a project for my physics class and we got off onto a tangent about electromagnetism."

"Right," Mia drawled out, not ever being able to imagine herself getting caught up in a discussion like that. Cross pollination, sure; genetically modified foods, yes; water rights over the Colorado River, definitely; electromagnetism, no.

"I know what that is," Jamal said suddenly, and then smiled sheepishly. "That's the thing that makes a roller coaster shoot off fast."

Andrew nodded, and he looked impressed. "Essentially, yeah. When a solar flare hits that's the power that floods the earth, and that's why it's so damaging. It fills the earth with a lot of radiation and energy. It overloads everything and basically blows it all up."

"Does it always blow things up?" Mia asked. "I thought the Northern Lights were solar flares."

"Technically they are," Andrew agreed. "But a CME is more powerful, rather than the typical output from the sun. Some flares aren't all that dangerous and bounce off the atmosphere, while others knock out satellites and can cause power surges. This must have been a huge surge of electromagnetism in order to knock out all the power around here."

A memory flooded back to Mia, and she blurted out, "But remember what they said on the radio about the coast being gone?"

Andrew shrugged helplessly. "I don't know what that meant. It might mean that the power is gone there, too, or something else."

Mia felt tears prick but refused to cry, especially not in front of Jamal. "I hate this."

Andrew drew her from her own chair and pulled her into his lap, tucking her head under his chin as his arms wound around her. "I do, too."

"Mama!" Jilly demanded, toddling over to them.

Mia reached down and pulled her sister into her lap. She kissed the soft red curls and breathed in the baby smell that Jilly always had. "I wish we had more answers."

Jamal cleared his throat and Mia jolted, feeling guilty at sitting in Andrew's lap but when she looked over at the boy he didn't seem bothered by it at all. "How long would it take to get the power back up around here?"

Andrew sighed heavily. "It took them months to get the small part of South Africa back up and running. But that's South Africa. They don't produce most of the world's electronics. We'd have to replace all the big transformers that send the power out, and that would take years, especially because the places that make them are probably in the dark like we are."

Jamal groaned and his eyes flashed. "We make most of them."

"Yep," Andrew confirmed. "But China probably produces some of the parts too. If this is really widespread and China was hit, we're screwed. It could be years or a decade until we could get everything up and running again."

"And if all the computers were fried, then we lost all the knowledge on how to make everything," Jamal said flatly.

Mia was, at once, completely depressed by the conversation and deeply impressed by Jamal's quick grasp of the situation. She ran a hand over her brow and slowly stood with her sister in her arms. "I'm going to change Nelly's diaper and then go and get another look at my garden. I really need to start clearing it before we get snow."

She headed for the bedroom door away from the conversation of doom and gloom. Once her sister was changed, she found a pink striped hoody for the baby that clashed wonderfully with her red hair, and her sneakers. Mia had noticed, as she held the baby on her lap that her hands were freezing. Her mom had, true to her word, put aside clothes for Jilly in a lot of sizes. Thankfully, that also meant shoes because Jilly's feet had already grown a size in the month since they'd arrived at the shelter. With fall settling in, the air in the shelter seemed cooler, even though the temperature was kept regulated by the heating system. Still, there was something in the air that made her shiver. Winter was just around the corner. Jilly was definitely going to need warmer clothes until spring, even in the shelter. Mia came out and found Andrew and Jamal still deep in conversation over the problem of blown transistors, whatever those were, as she went towards the kitchen counter.

She knew she should take a gun, so she set her sister down and grabbed the one that Andrew had just taken off and strapped it around her waist, cinching it until it wasn't going to fall off. She grabbed her sweatshirt and pulled it on. "I'm going to leave Nelly down here, okay?"

"Yep," Andrew said before falling back into the finer points of the gases that the sun emitted and how they messed with the gadgets here on earth.

She was halfway up the stairs when she heard the knock from above. Mia froze. It wasn't loud, but it was definitely there. She tried to open her mouth to speak, tried to call for help, but all she could was stare at the locked hatch in horror. It was definitely locked because the lock was in place, but how would someone know to look under the fake rock?

"Mia," a muffled voice called from beyond the hatch.

"Oh God," Mia groaned, astonished that not only could she hear the voice, but that she knew the voice. Her limbs awoke again as relief flooded her. She dashed up the rest of the stairs, quickly unhooking the lock and turning the hatch despite her shaking hands. The cold metal of the hatch turned so slowly that she was sure that once she finally got it open, the man who owned the voice would have disappeared.

The hatch flew open and her dirty father stared down at her.

"Dad!" Mia exclaimed, and then squeaked as he hopped down, pulled down the concealing rock and slammed the hatch shut, efficiently locking it again.

"Go down," her father barked and she realized that it was uncomfortably crowded with the both of them standing on the narrow stairs.

Mia climbed back down quickly and heard Andrew's voice as he spoke to Jamal. Reality crashed over her, even as she flung her arms around her father, bringing her mouth as close to his ear as she could. He grabbed her tight, holding him to her. He smelled of sweat, dirt and undeniably of gunpowder. He kissed her brow. "I missed you," Scott Harper said gruffly.

"Dad," Mia said hurriedly and softly, so only he could hear her. "I'm Claire Beaumont, married to James and mom to Nelly. Got it?"

With a speed that left her dizzy he nodded in understanding. "I've missed you, Claire." With another noisy kiss, he set her down and marched into the other room, Mia following behind him, nervous at what he was going to say to Jamal. "James, it's good to see you safe." To say that Andrew was stunned was an understatement. He rose halfway out of his chair, his mouth agape.

Mia watched her dad pull Andrew into a quick hug. Jamal hadn't moved from his chair. His eyes were wide as he stared at the dirty, wild man, but unbelievably her dad didn't take any notice as he crouched down and looked at Jilly, who stared back with curious eyes.

It had been weeks since she'd seen her father, and right now he looked nothing like the man that Jilly might have remembered.

"I bet you don't remember Grandpa, do you Nelly?" he said gently, and only Mia saw the regret in his eyes, because he quickly masked it. "Well, once I've had a shower you might remember me."

Mia finally looked over to Andrew, who was staring at her dad with an unreadable expression. "How did you get here?" Andrew finally asked.

"I walked," her dad said, standing again with a sigh and dropping his large pack next to the table. He finally grinned at Jamal. "Hey, I'm Claire's father, Levi Hudson." Mia could only blink in surprise at the name change as her father stuck out his hand for Jamal to shake.

"Jamal West," the boy hesitated before grasping his hand. "James and Claire saved my life."

Her dad nodded and grinned wryly. "I'd have expected nothing less. It's nice to meet you."

"Are you hungry?" Mia asked him, studying the hard plains of his face.

Her dad grinned. "I am always hungry for your cooking, but right now I think my clothes could stand up on their own."

"Go get a shower and James will dig out some clean clothes for you," Mia told him as she went to find something to prepare. She watched him walk through the bathroom door and turned to Andrew. "I think some of Dad's clothing is in the storage room in one of the tubs in the back on the right. I labeled them."

"Got it," Andrew said as he went out and was back shortly after with clothes. He knocked briefly before cracking the door and dropping the clothes down on the bathroom floor.

Mia turned from the stove and shot Andrew a nervous glance, but his face was still blank as he plucked Nelly up into his arms. "I'll change her diaper," he said. Mia was still so off kilter that she didn't even remember that she'd just changed her sister before Andrew was gone from the room.

Sighing, she decided just to let it go and focus on food, which was something she knew how to control. Her options were limited when it came to meals. She could either open up an MRE, a meal ready to eat which was what the military used when they couldn't cook, or she could make rice and beans with some dehydrated vegetables. She went with beans since she could add spices to it.

"Can I help with anything?" Jamal asked from behind her.

"No, I'm fine," Mia assured him as she went to the fridge and got out some beans that she'd precooked a few days before.

"Your dad looks..." Jamal's voice faded off, and she turned to see his consternation.

Mia tried to smile, but only managed half of one, and it wobbled ominously. "He's a very good man and we're safer with him here."

Jamal nodded slowly. "Yeah... yeah, I think I can see that. Dude looks like Indiana Jones."

"You aren't far off," she agreed as she went back to stirring the beans as she reheated them. Mia thought briefly about what Andrew had told her about her dad before pushing it to the back of her mind.

She heard the shower turn off just as Andrew came back out of the bedroom with Jilly who was smiling happily. "Duh!" her sister shrieked happily.

He walked over with the baby on his hip and put his free arm around her waist. Andrew kissed her cheek and whispered, "It will be okay."

"Yeah," Mia agreed just as quietly as she stared into the pot of brown rice that was finally starting to boil.

"That smells good," a gruff voice said and Mia jumped. She turned and saw her father, but this time completely clean. His short, dark hair was still damp from the shower, but he was clean shaven again and his face was clear of grime. His expression was just as neutral as Andrew's had been and fear skittered through her arms, tickling through her veins. She shivered, suddenly not wanting to hear anything her dad might say to her.

Mia half expected Andrew to move, but he didn't. He kept his arm around her waist, and watched her father silently.

"Food will be ready shortly, Dad," Mia told him. "Why don't you have a seat? Do you want some water?"

"That would be great, thanks, Claire," he said, accepting a glass of water.

Silently Mia went back to the rice and nervously began to stir as her thoughts raced. She wasn't sure exactly what was going on, but she knew she wasn't going to like it. She heard Andrew moving around and Jilly's excited chatter, but no one spoke while she kept her back to the room, staring down blankly at the gently bubbling water. She desperately wanted to ask about her mom, but the words wouldn't come. Methodically, and without really thinking about it, she drained off the excess water from the rice. She preferred this method of cooking rice, which was more along the lines of how one would steam broccoli with a metal colander in a larger pot. She poured the drained rice into a large mixing bowl and began blending in spices without really looking at their labels.

Still no one spoke. Mia spooned in the black beans and blended them together. She portioned some off onto a plate, grabbed a fork and put it in front of her dad, finally meeting his gaze. He didn't move to eat, just watched her levelly. "Sit down," her dad commanded mildly, and automatically, she sat. Her mouth felt glued shut, but his blue eyes never left hers. "Your mom is fine and she sends her love. She and James' parents are hiding in our other shelter out in western Maryland."

Mia's mouth dropped open. Conflicting emotions raged through her. She simultaneously felt joy that her mother was okay and stunned that her parents had had yet another shelter that they hadn't bothered to tell her about. She dimly registered Andrew's relieved sigh as he dropped into the chair next to her. "You…" her voice cracked as she tried assimilate these two facts. "Mom is… she's…"

"Yes," her dad agreed evenly. "She and I made it back to the house shortly before the first of the flares hit. James' parents already had the jeep packed up, and we grabbed our go bags and left. It was dicey driving after the initial flare hit. Most of the cars died immediately, and there were a lot of wrecks, but we managed to get most of the way before we had to abandon the roads and walk. We were able to hide the jeep well enough, and I've checked on it a few times. So far it's safe."

Andrew shook his head. "So it was a CME?" At her dad's nod he went on. "The jeep is new. It shouldn't have worked after the earth was hit. All of the electronics in it should have been fried."

"It would have been fried," Scott agreed in a measured tone, "if I hadn't pulled the whole engine and removed all the electronic parts. I put in an old Chevy pick-up's guts a few months back so that it would look like a new car, but function like the older ones. It was tricky, but I got it working. I'd intended to do the same with the Tundra, but I didn't have time. In any case, I knew that if you had the chance to get up here before your mom or I could get away, and if you were stuck with a broken truck, you'd have to stay put."

"But..." Jamal started, but then froze when they turned to him. "Never mind," he mumbled, blushing a bit.

"Ask," Scott said to the boy, studying him speculatively.

"Well," Jamal hesitated. "It's just, you said you walked up here. Why walk if you have a car that works?"

Her dad laughed, but it had a hard edge to it. He took a large drink and a bite of rice before answering. "The roads are choked with broken cars, and for those who have survived, a working vehicle would have made me an easy target. Everyone wants a car that still drives. It was safer to walk. There was less chance of getting shot."

Mia stared at him as he tucked in and closed his eyes.

"Claire, this is as good as anything you ever made at home," he assured her. "I love your mom, but she just can't cook like you do."

10

Mia stared at her dad, trying to take in all that he'd just told her. How could her parents have stocked a second shelter without ever having told her? Why would they have kept it from her? The air around them hummed with tension, even though the only ambient sound was the small whirl of the motor on the fridge. Nothing moved, not even Jilly who stood silently nearby, watching the adults with her curls wrapped in her fat fist, a sure sign that she was anxious. Mia wanted to respond, but her mind seemed to be stuck as she stared across the small kitchen table at the chiseled lines and hard edges of her dad's face.

"You..." Andrew paused and shook his head before trying to go on. "So wait, you have another shelter?"

Mia's voice suddenly came back, full force. "How could you!?" she shouted, standing quickly and nearly knocking her chair backwards.

"Mama!" Jilly hollered and raced over, tugging at Mia's pant leg.

Mia hoisted her into her arms and glared at her father. "How could you have kept this from me?"

Her father glanced up once, but didn't otherwise react as he continued to steadily eat his way through his dinner. "You thought we were crazy to have this place."

"You are crazy!" Mia retorted with a bite to her voice. Jilly laid her head on Mia's shoulder and buried her face in Mia's neck. Her father's raised eyebrow only increased her ire. "Just because you ended up being right, doesn't mean you're sane. Why on earth do you have two shelters?"

Her dad polished off the last bite before leaning back in his seat and crossing his arms. Neither Andrew nor Jamal seemed inclined to jump into the battle, both sat back, looking between them without comment. "We have two in case one was compromised, or in case we couldn't get to one of them. We didn't tell you about the second one for a lot of reasons. The main reason is that you thought it was a waste of time. You never took prepping seriously, and if you'd known we'd had two different plans, then you'd have been even less inclined to do what we asked of you. You ignored us half the time when we wanted to practice. If we'd told you about the other shelter, you'd have been convinced that you were right about us being paranoid and insane. We couldn't take that chance. We needed you willing to at least play along with what we were doing."

Jilly wrapped her arms more fully around Mia's neck and whimpered. "Alright, fine," she said as calmly as she could, hugging her sister and running her fingers gently through the toddler's hair. "We can't argue; Nelly is getting upset. Are there more lies?"

"Yes," Scott replied with a satirical grin. "There are always more secrets and lies."

"Great," Mia muttered, knowing she had to calm down or Jilly would have a meltdown. She started to bounce Jilly, holding onto the warm little body. Her sister was innocent in this. Her baby sister who liked to giggle at Mia when she made silly faces. Jilly loved to play with blocks. She loved dirt, and tried her best to throw everything in whatever basket or bucket happened to be handy. She kissed Jilly's cheek and closed her eyes against the tears that wanted to flow out. She turned her back on the men and walk across the room, still rocking her sister in her arms. She stared at the shelter walls. Except for the fact that there were no windows, it might have been the room in any place. The couch, now with slight stains to the chocolate brown color, stood out to her. It had been new. Her parents must have spent so much time and money to do this. Not only that, but they'd done it twice and kept the second shelter a secret from her.

Because she would have thought them completely nuts; she'd likely have told them that they were completely insane, straight to their faces.

Her dad was right that she'd probably have blown everything off. If she'd done that...

Mia heard Andrew clear his throat. "How did you get my dad to evacuate? I'd have thought he'd want to stay and help."

"Oh, he did," Scott assured him. Mia heard something clink but didn't turn back to see what it might be. "I had already told your dad about the plans we had made, about a week before the flares hit when we were reasonably sure that something big was coming. He'd said he was staying, but after I explained about the radiation, I was able to convince him to hide, at least for a bit. Paul wanted to stay and help those who were hurt, but he couldn't do anything if he got sick from skin cancer."

"Skin cancer?" Jamal asked and Mia distinctly heard the fear. It pulled at her heart, too.

Andrew sighed heavily. "The radiation levels! That's why they were so high those first few days after we got here."

"Yes," Scott said. "The radiation from the flare was bad enough that a lot of the people who were out and exposed are going to be at risk for developing skin cancers in the next several months."

Mia felt Jilly's head totally relax and her arms loosen their grip. She walked over to their room and went to lay her sister in her crib. When she came out it was to her dad reassuring Jamal that he might not get cancer.

"We don't know who will get sick," Scott told the frightened boy. "It's going to be hit or miss and we have no idea just how bad it will be. There is no instrumentation in place anymore to measure just how much damage was inflicted."

"How far did it go?" Andrew asked as she walked slowly over to sit down next to him at the table. Andrew took her hand and squeezed it, keeping it on his thigh. "I mean, how wide spread?"

Her dad shrugged. "We don't have firm answers on that. In general we're reasonably sure that most of North America has been affected.

We're speculating that parts of Central and South America are also damaged, but it all depended on how the flares hit the earth. Whether Europe or China or Russia have had issues, we don't know. If we're lucky, Australia survived, and we'll be able to start piecing everything back together again eventually. There is a good shot that they did since they're far from where most of the flares were set to hit."

"How bad is it?" Jamal's voice shook a bit when he asked. "My grandma is in Philadelphia."

Scott studied him silently for a long moment before answering. "It's worse than I can possibly describe. With no electricity, the food was gone in a matter of days, and the cities turned to mass chaos, at least the parts that didn't burn down. There isn't a working fire department any longer." He breathed out a long, exasperated sigh. "A lot of people died, but not enough to make the food supply stretch because cities typically only have a two day supply of food at any given time, and without the truckers able to bring in new supplies, the cities fell hard. Water is also a problem as well since there is no way to keep up with cleaning the water. We were out of the worst of the chaos because the second shelter is in a remote area, but I was able to keep in contact with someone who was hunkering down near Baltimore. He said it was bedlam. People were looting and killing each other. A lot of people fled the cities to try to find food, many died on the roads since no one knows how to survive anymore without electricity."

Mia's heart ached for all of those people and disgust filled her. She'd been so mad at her parents for stranding her here when thousands, maybe millions, of people had been dying around her.

"When I finally left to head up here," Scott said as he sat up and laced his hands together on the table, "I was hopeful that I would be able to stay with the Amish. I knew that they'd likely not be affected by the outside world. What we called the end of the world, they'd call Monday, you know? They didn't have electricity to lose, but every farm I came to I found overrun with people who had taken the farms by force."

"Oh God," Mia breathed out, tears filling her eyes. "Did they kill the families?"

Her father sighed in disgust as pain filled his eyes. "Some did. Others kept them alive to show them how to keep the farm running. There aren't a lot of women around, though. I've seen mostly men on the roads, and all of them are heavily armed."

"Am I going to be able to get to Philly?" Jamal asked quietly.

Scott shook his head. "Not by yourself, no. I can take you down there when I leave in a week. It will only add a few days to my trip, but I doubt you're going to find what you're looking for."

Jamal's jaw tightened as resolve filled his face. "I have to try."

Mia wanted to argue with him. Even if it would be a pain in the can to keep up the pretense of a fake name, she wanted this bright kid to be safe. She trusted her dad, and thought he could get him to his grandmother safely, but it was a lot of risk for a possibly small reward. "You're only staying a week?"

"Yes," Scott said simply. "I have to get back to your mom so she doesn't worry about you. We also have to start making a plan to get civilization back to some semblance of order. Most of the central government is gone, or in hiding. I won't be able to keep Paul in the other shelter for long. Your dad," Scott said wryly to Andrew, "is a force unto himself, and you wouldn't think it if you were just talking to him after church on Sunday."

"I know," Andrew agreed with a chuckle. "When it comes to helping people, he's a bit of a fanatic."

There were a lot of other questions Mia wanted to ask, but none she thought her father would want to answer in front of Jamal. Finally one came to her. "What about the government? What happened?"

"I can't tell you much," Scott said. He stood and took his plate to the sink. Mia watched him rinse it as he continued. "Most of them are safe, or at least the plan was for them to be safe, but with the flare as big as it was, a lot of the plans fell apart. We couldn't hope to maintain a government when the whole country was devastated and no aid was coming. Every other country around us was getting knocked out as well."

"I need help with the stump before you go," Andrew said suddenly, and Mia frowned as she turned to him. "I can't get it out on my own."

"I said I'd help," Jamal reminded him.

"No," Mia interjected firmly. "You were shot, and if you want to leave in week then you need to rest."

"You were shot?" Scott asked, frowning at him. "Is that how they saved you?"

Jamal nodded. "I got shot crossing the road and climbed into their truck. They found me a few days ago."

"Let me see," Scott said walking over and hesitantly Jamal stood and pulled up his shirt. Mia watched her dad pull back the bandages and examine him. "It's mostly just a flesh wound, and it's healing up nicely. You should be okay to leave in a few days."

"So you're going to rest," Andrew said with a smile. "With Levi's help, I can get the stump out and then we can finish prepping the garden for the spring."

Mia saw her dad glance over to Andrew. His mouth tightened briefly as he nodded. "Yes, let's go look at that stump and see what we might do about it." Andrew unbuckled the gun from Mia's waist and put it back around his, tucking it under his sweatshirt.

Then it finally clicked, and Mia got what Andrew was up to as she watched them head out of the room, grabbing the tools. The two of them were going to talk, and they didn't want to be overheard. It wasn't particularly subtle of them, but she merely rolled her eyes as she started to put the food away.

"I feel bad," Jamal said. "Isn't there anything I can help with?"

"Yes," Mia said, as she remembered a chore she'd been putting off for two days. "I need to do laundry. You can help unless it hurts your side."

Jamal groaned good-naturedly, but rose none-the-less and followed her to the hand cranked washer. When he saw it, he groaned again, but this time he meant it. "We have to use this?"

~*~ ~*~ ~*~

The two men came back covered in dirt but looking pleased several hours later. Mia had to shove down her jealousy that they had been outside working in the dirt while she'd been stuck inside doing laundry. It was her garden, and she wanted to have her hands in it, not constantly be the one inside tending to the house work.

Although, admittedly, Mia knew that without heavy equipment she wasn't going to be much help against the large stump. She wasn't a weakling, but realistically neither was she a match for hundreds of pounds of wood. "How did it go?" she asked them as she kneaded some dough before setting it back in a bowl to rise.

"It's out," Scott told her and for the first time she saw a real smile on his face. "It was a beast, but we kept hacking at the roots until we could wiggle it."

"We dug a hole under the stump as far as we could go, then stuck a thick tree branch in use as a lever," Andrew told her while he filled a water glass. He drained it in one go. "That way we could push the branch down and figure out where the roots were still attached, so we could cut them up. We broke a couple of branches doing it, but it worked in the end."

Mia snorted and handed Jilly off to him. She could just imagine the two of them out there working through the logic of getting the stump out. It would have ended up as a game or a science problem. It was how the two of them had always worked. "Well, I want to go up and see it, so you're on kid duty."

"Hang on," Andrew said quickly. "Let me get her back pack and I'll go with you."

"I can watch her," said a low voice and they both turned to see Scott eyeing them. "You know Grandpa can be trusted, right?"

Mia blushed as guilt and embarrassment rained over her. She'd been so used to just the two of them having charge of Jilly that she'd completely dismissed her dad keeping her. "Uhm, sure, Dad. Nelly, do you want to play with Grandpa?" She looked at her sister who eyed them all suspiciously. "Let's cheat and give her my phone," Mia said, and she grabbed her iPhone and handed it to Jilly who started to flip through to the preschool apps, babbling happily.

Andrew set her down and she plopped onto her butt with a joyful, "Mamagaba!"

Scott waved them off. "I've got this. Go on."

"We're going," Andrew assured him. He grabbed Mia's hand and headed for the hatch.

Mia heard her dad say to Jamal, "So tell me about yourself," as they climbed the stairs. Andrew reached up for the hatch and his sweatshirt lifted enough that Mia was able to see the gun strapped to his waist. She wasn't sure she was ever going to get used to it, although it would likely be part of her life for decades if what her dad said was true.

In the back of her mind Mia had known that something had to be very wrong, but even now that she'd heard from an eye witness, it was difficult to imagine just how chaotic it really was. She'd seen zombie TV shows that showed a world that had fallen apart, but in those it had seemed like the zombies were the biggest problem, not the people who were still in their right mind. Maybe that was just her warped way of looking at it, and the people had always been dangerous. She inhaled deeply as she climbed up into the fresh autumn air. Fall was truly on the way. The leaves were starting to turn and all around her leaves of crimsons, oranges and yellows as bright as fresh corn danced in a slight breeze. She stared up into the lovely foliage, and it was easy to forget, just for that moment, that around her people were starving to death and others were being killed because they had food or shelter.

Andrew stood next to her, his hands in his pockets. She knew he was watching her and not the trees, but she didn't want to break the silence with the conversation that was about to come. Mia wasn't sure what was coming, but she was certain that she wasn't going to like it.

"I knew why we were coming up here," Andrew said quietly.

Mia stiffened and closed her eyes against the pain that was as acute as a punch to the gut. "I knew I was going to hate this."

"Mia..." his voice faltered. "Early in August your dad and I went shooting, and we talked about a lot of things. Mostly we talked about what we were going to do if something happened. We arranged a code because Scott knew he was being watched. He and I had called each other every few weeks for the last year or two, especially as my engineering classes got harder. I'd call to ask him questions, or he'd call to check up on me. We'd worked out that if something bad was going to happen, that I was going to come with you up here to the shelter. He would call me, and it wouldn't be out of his ordinary pattern, so no one would know. He'd call and warn me by telling me to take you out to lunch."

She couldn't look at him. She didn't want to hear it.

"He wanted to make sure that you and Jilly were safe, and I promised to do it. I promised to make sure that I got you two away and up here. He knew that by the time he'd be able to send you a text telling you bug out that no one could stop us, but it also meant he wouldn't have enough time to make you go himself." He hesitated, and when he spoke again she could hear the remorse in his voice. "I hated lying to you, but he'd made me promise not to tell you until... until we saw him again."

That did it. Her temper flared as she turned on him, glaring up into his face, not caring about the pain she saw written all over his features. The last rays of the sun filtered down onto his dark hair, highlighting it almost like a halo, but all she could focus on was how betrayed she felt. "So, if we'd never seen him again, you'd never have told me?"

"I would have told you," Andrew said quickly, holding out his hands pleadingly but she backed away from him. "Mia, I didn't want to keep it from you, but your dad was sure that if he told you that the world was really in trouble that you either wouldn't believe it or you'd want to wait for them, and he wasn't sure they'd be allowed to leave D.C. He wanted you two safe."

Mia's mind raced as she thought back to a few months ago. She'd not wanted to come up the shelter. She wouldn't have come up if Andrew hadn't promised to go with her. Now she knew he'd come home to make sure that she did go.

What would she have done if her dad had made the arrangement with her; would she have believed that the world was about to be blasted to bits?

"No," Mia breathed out, answering herself, looking away from Andrew and off into the darkening forest. She'd thought her dad was crazy, and her mom was a fruitcake for going along with his nutty plan to stock a shelter. Mia turned and stalked off towards the garden. She didn't even wait to see if Andrew was following her. At the moment she didn't care. She stared at the ground as she picked her way over fallen leaves, half rotten logs and around small bushes. Nothing registered as she thought through everything that had happened so far. She only looked up when she reached the low stone wall that bordered the small garden.

Mia's eyes swept the plot. There was a large hole where just that morning the stump had been firmly entrenched in the ground, unwilling to give no matter how much pressure she'd put on it. A few hours against her dad and Andrew, and now there was only a crater that would need to be filled. She jumped when she felt hands rest gently on her shoulders. She hadn't even heard Andrew come up behind her.

"Why do we deserve to live?" Mia whispered into the void. Not even the call of the first crickets starting to sing in to the late afternoon air made a dent into her senses. "Why are we here safely when other people are dying? When babies are out there starving and assholes are killing off the Amish because they won't fight back?"

"We don't deserve it," Andrew answered simply as he gently tugged her back against his chest. He wrapped his arms around her shoulders and rested his chin on top of her head. "But we're here so we're going to make the best of it. Mia, I'm sorry. I'm sorry I lied, and I won't do it again."

She didn't want to forgive him. That small, petty part of her that relished holding grudges wanted to cling to this and never let go. Mia thought, just for a second, about wanting to hurt Andrew like he'd hurt her, but just as fast as it had flared, the urge was gone and was replaced by the guilt of knowing that she'd brought this on herself. Time and again her dad had tried to get her to take prepping seriously. Time and again she'd blown him off. Even Andrew's gentle nudges and her mom's quiet understanding hadn't cracked her stubborn pride.

Mia had been so sure that the world would go on as it was, at least for another few decades until climate change made that impossible, that she wouldn't consider any other possibilities.

The east coast didn't have major earthquakes.

The super volcano under Yellowstone was not showing any imminent signs of erupting.

There weren't any mega-asteroids that were heading straight for earth right then.

No one was stupid enough to nuke America because they'd just get nuked right back.

Terrorists could cause damage, but the damage was always on a small enough scale that it wouldn't stop the whole of civilization in its tracks.

Hurricanes could be run from, because there was a week of warnings.

Solar flares were constantly hitting the world, and never did they cause worldwide damage. How many times had she seen news stories on large solar storms? They never amounted to anything.

The twenty-four hour news cycle meant that everything had to be hyped to keep people glued to their screens or their phones. It was all touted that things were getting worse and going downhill, but really it was the media's fault. People were gullible, and Mia had believed her dad had bought into it.

When the reality was that it was she who'd misread the signs.

11

Mid-October

Mia turned slowly around to face Drew. His arms slackened a bit from her shoulders so they could look into each other's' faces, but he didn't let go, and she was pathetically grateful that despite her, he'd done what was right and moved them to safety; even if they didn't deserve it more than anyone else. "Are there any more secrets?" Mia asked tentatively.

Andrew hesitated for only a second, but it was enough to cause the fear to creep back in. "Nothing that I can think of or nothing I was asked not to tell you. I might have forgotten to tell you things, but nothing that I'd hide if you asked."

That was fair. "I'm tired of doing all the house work." She had no idea why that spilled out, but it had been eating at her. "Now that the stump is out I want to work in the garden, and you can take care of the shelter."

Andrew let out a deep sigh, but a grin tugged at his mouth nonetheless. "Does that mean I have to cook?"

"Worse," Mia said, smiling again. "Diapers."

He let his forehead drop to hers, and he pulled her against him fully, engulfing her in a hug. "Your dad asked what's up with us."

"What did you tell him?" Mia asked with trepidation. She'd known that would happen, but she hadn't wanted it to happen quite so soon.

"The truth," Drew admitted wearily. "I told him we were doing what they'd said and keeping up a false pretense and that nothing else was going on."

She turned her head and stared off into the fading light. One lone lighting bug flickered in the darkened trees, but was soon lost to sight. She didn't know what she'd expected him to say, but the answer felt hollow somehow, although for the life of her she couldn't have begun to explain why. "Did he tell you why we were supposed to keep ourselves secret?"

"Nope," he said shortly, exasperation filled his voice. "Of course not; we're just the good little soldiers, and we should follow orders."

Mia looked up at him in surprise. He wasn't normally so annoyed with her dad. "Why are you so pissed?"

Andrew let go of her and walked over to a tree. He leaned against it, his shoulders slumped. "It's my family that's stuck in this. It's my life, and he says he can't tell us or we're in more danger. I know I should trust him, but…" his voice faded off.

"He's going to keep your mom safe," Mia said certainly, her tone low and soothing as she walked over and took his hand, lacing their fingers. "Your dad isn't going to stay put, but–"

Andrew cut her off, his piercing blue eyes meeting hers. A dimple that she so rarely saw in his thin face stood out as he clenched his jaw. "It isn't that part of my family that I'm worried about."

Mia's breath hitched, and she let go of him, stumbling back a bit as his words hit home. "Are you in love with me?"

His eyes closed and when he opened them again, he looked older than she'd ever seen him look. "No, but it doesn't really matter. I do love you, Mia. I love Jilly and I'd die for you two. You're my family and he hasn't been here." Andrew straightened and snagged her hands, holding them firmly. "He's not been here to hold you when you cry, or take care of you when you're sick, or make Jilly's Christmas present. My parents haven't been here to make sure I eat well, or that I have clean clothes; and it hasn't been my parents that I've talked to when I've been scared or feeling unsure. It's been you. It's been us, and it's going to keep being us for a long time."

And just like that she understood. Mia walked back into his embrace and felt a burn behind her eyes. The crickets chirped around her, a squirrel rustled in a tree above them, and the stars began to wink on. They were brighter than any stars she'd ever seen in the city, and Mia knew that they were only so bright because there was no light on earth to drown them out. Those stars that for so long men had studied and wondered at what they could possibly be, although no one really dreamed they could be massive burning balls of gas. Now they knew, but they were a mocking reminder that civilization had taken a tumbling step backwards into a darker age where the stars and the moon were a source of light and navigation. No one had GPS anymore. No one had guidance of which way they should go. But now, too, no one knew how to read the stars for guidance any longer. It was knowledge that was lost to the arrogance that the lights would always stay on.

The smell of the woods and the faint, distinct odor that always came at dusk while she was in the forest filled her senses. It was of dew and grass and something metallic that she could never quite put a finger on, but the smell always made her feel a lift like the rush of smelling a newly opened rose. Mia didn't want to go back down into the shelter. She wanted to stay here in Andrew's arms and forget that the world was still turning.

They broke a moment later and Andrew leaned in and kissed her gently, resting his lips on hers. She wanted to say that it was weird, but it didn't feel that way this time. When they pulled apart, she studied him carefully. "Why did you do that?"

"It felt right," he said slowly, looking just as confused as she felt. "I don't know why, but it just did."

It had felt right. "I sometimes thought that no one was going to want to kiss me," Mia giggled nervously then felt instantly stupid. She moved swiftly over to the garden and started to pull her dark chestnut hair up in a ponytail, using the band that she had on her wrist. "Forget it, Drew. I don't know why I said that." She knelt down on the ground and in the fading light started working at the smaller roots that were left from where they'd uprooted the stump. When he didn't say anything, she kept working. Her face was flushed with embarrassment. He'd not wanted to kiss her because he was attracted to her, but she'd made it sound that way with what she'd said.

Movement came from her left and Andrew crouched down next to her. He rested a hand on hers, stopping the effort of pulling out a weed. "Are you in love with me, Mia?"

Mia shook her head. "That would be awesome, though, wouldn't it?" she bit out sarcastically. "If I was in love with you, and you weren't with me? But no."

"Why are you so upset?" he asked her gently, his voice low.

Mia picked up a dead leaf and shredded it, trying to come up with some kind of answer. "I don't know. I guess I'm embarrassed about what I said because I know you didn't kiss me out of passion, but I've never been in a relationship, and the whole thing is really confusing because we are and we aren't."

Andrew lowered himself to the ground next to her and mimicked her action with another leaf, shredding it like she had. He tied the limp and bared stem into a knot before tossing it to the ground. "My relationships have been crappy. It starts off with this huge crush and feelings that are really intense and then you go out and you kiss and fool around and... well, then the feelings start to fade and the little things they do drive you nuts. Then we fought and broke up. It was the same way all three times that I dated someone."

"That doesn't sound like any fun," Mia whispered. "I'm sorry."

"Me, too," Andrew grumbled. "I want to be in love with you, Mia." He turned to her, and she could see the sorrow in his eyes, even though his face was only highlighted by the scant moonlight that filtered down through the trees. "I want to be with you because I always thought that this is what marriage would look like, but..."

"But there isn't that insane crush and those big feelings," she said, finishing where he left off.

"No," he agreed sadly. "But I want to be. That's what I want and if not, well, it doesn't matter because for all the world knows, you're my wife and I do love you. That's good enough for me. If being in love means all that crazy emotional crap, then forget it."

She nodded, not sure of what to say because she agreed with him. If she never fell head over heels in love with anyone, she could still live a happy life with Drew. It wouldn't be horrible to be stuck with him for the rest of her life.

They were silent for several minutes, neither moving to weed the garden, nor taking heed of the dark that had fallen around them.

Andrew finally broke the silence. "You know you're beautiful, right?"

Mia was startled, but a grin flashed over her features. It was too dark for him to see it, but it came through in her tone. "Is there ever a girl that thinks she's beautiful?"

"Yes," he retorted dryly. "But not many."

"Really, who?"

"My grandma knew it," Andrew said laughing. "At her last birthday party before she died, she told me it was nice that she was still beautiful, and she meant it."

A moth flittered by, ticking her nose. She swatted at it absently. "I guess I can see that." Her grandpa had said he was fat, ugly and old, and he'd cackled over it; actually cackled. Old people didn't seem to have the same set of standards. Warmth spread through her arms as she thought of what he'd said. "Thank you for telling me, although I suppose it's subjective."

"I think a lot of guys would have wanted to kiss you," Andrew mused. "It's more that your dad scared the crap out of everyone."

Mia bit her lip, trying not to laugh. "There is that, of course. I wonder if he ever threatened someone."

"Me," he admitted, bumping her shoulder with his. "He told me I had to be good to you or no one would find my body, but he didn't really need to. I was never going to hurt you. I think he knew that, but felt like he had to say it anyway."

"Oh well, for form, sure," she replied evenly. "It was expected."

"We'll be okay," Andrew said after a moment. "You and me, we'll be fine. I don't really want to wash diapers, but you have taken the lion share of the cleaning, and it's my turn."

"Don't married couples fight more?" Mia ruminated. "We rarely fight."

Andrew laughed and stood, holding out a hand for her to hoist her to her feet. "I am even tempered and you like peace, even if you have a bit of a temper. It would be weird if we did fight a lot."

They held hands as they walked back to the shelter. "I hope everything can go easily like this."

It didn't go easily, although it could have been worse. Her dad informed them that the couch in the living room area of the shelter was actually a sleeper sofa and it had a fold out bed when the issue of sleeping arrangements had been broached. "That's why it was so heavy when we moved it in," he'd told her, his eyes twinkling in amusement. Mia remembered all too well complaining about moving it in.

So her dad had claimed the sofa bed, and Mia had walked into Andrew's room as if it weren't ridiculously awkward to be sleeping with a boy with her dad in the other room.

"I think I want to die," Mia whispered as she crawled into bed next to him. "I can't believe we're doing this, and he's going along with it."

The light was out so she couldn't see him, but she groped around until she found his hand and brought it to her cheek. "Can you feel that? I'm going to be red permanently."

He ran his thumb along her cheek before letting go and rolling onto his back. "I think he can tell there isn't really anything going on between us."

"I guess," she agreed with a yawn. "Still, after how closely I was supervised before, this just feels weird. I'm still seventeen."

"Yeah, but how many times did we camp out in the back yard together growing up?" Andrew reminded her. "Remember that trip to Yellowstone? We've shared tents for years."

"That's true," she conceded. "Okay, going to pass out now. Tomorrow I'm spending all day in the garden."

~*~ ~*~ ~*~

As soon as she'd eaten the next morning Mia was out working in the garden, her dad at her side even though he hated gardening. She'd inherited that love from her mom's mom, her Gran. Gran had spent hours working with Mia to teach her how to tend and love a garden, and her parents had happily turned their whole yard over to their seven-year-old child. Mia had proved to have a green thumb.

She and her dad worked in silence for a long time. When she couldn't stand it any longer, Mia asked, "Where is the safe?"

Her dad glanced at her, before going back to pulling up the roots that she'd told him to work on. "It's behind the wall in the master bedroom. It's closest to the secret food storage room."

"What's in it?"

"Not much," Scott hedged. "Nothing critical, but you can hide other things in there like your driver's license."

Mia tugged at a clump of grass. She'd had so many questions. "Why didn't you tell me you were a Navy Seal?"

He was silent so long that she thought he might not answer. "You aren't one for keeping secrets."

Her mouth dropped open in stunned disbelief. Mia stared at her father, but he just kept working at the soil, not meeting her gaze. "You're blaming this on me?"

"I'm not blaming you for anything, Mia," he said patiently. "I'm simply stating the fact that if there was a secret to be kept, generally you didn't keep it, especially when you were younger."

"I..." she faltered, feeling guilty. "I kept some secrets."

He nodded grimly, glancing briefly at her. "Are we clearing this bed or not?"

She sighed heavily and got back to work. "I want to know why we have to keep our identity a secret."

"If I told you that then there wouldn't be any point in my asking you to keep it a secret," Scott said. He chucked a root over into a large pile of discarded vegetation. "I have my reasons, and I think I've earned your trust."

Mia wanted to argue, but the truth was that he had. "Am I ever going to know?"

"Maybe," he said. "If we make it through this and put the world back together again, then you'll know."

She pulled up a weed and started shaking out the clump of dirt that clung to it. She pulled out an earth worm that was clinging to the dirt and stuck it back in the ground before throwing the weed to the pile. "You're going to take care of Jamal, right?"

"I will get him to his grandmother's house safely," her dad promised. "Beyond that I don't know. He's a bright kid, though. I'd hate to see him hurt."

"He went through a lot," Mia said. "I'm glad we found him."

After another minute of silence her dad finally spoke. "I don't want you to take anyone else in, especially not over the winter."

"I make no promises," she told him. "I might, especially if it's a kid."

"Mia..." Scott's voice was full of exasperation. "You can't take everyone in. It's dangerous. He could have hurt Jillian."

"You want me to trust you," Mia retorted. "You gotta trust me. You won't be here. I need the autonomy to make decisions."

"Mia," he said again with frustration but this time tinged with something else. "I understand that you want-"

"You don't know what I want," Mia cut him off quietly. "Right now I'm taking care of myself and my sister without you or mom. Andrew and I are doing fine. You want me to cut you some slack about all of your secrets? Fine, but you have to accept that because you're not here, we're in charge of what happens. Are you taking Jilly with you?"

"Of course not," he said, sitting back to give her a hard stare. Her father studied her face, and she kept quiet, letting him see just how serious she was. "You can't take in every stray."

Mia shook her head sadly. "Jamal isn't a stray. He's a human being, and he deserves to live just as much as I do."

"What about the ones that would kill you so that they could live?"

Mia studied his blue eyes, eyes that were so like hers. She looked so much like him except that his face was chiseled in a way that every single aspiring actor would have killed for. He even had a scar on his right cheek that only lent to his air of toughness and dashing good looks. Her face was smaller, rounder and she had her mom's nose. No one, however, could mistake him for anyone but her dad. "I don't want to take stupid risks, but a kid who was feverish and had been shot wasn't a stupid risk."

"No," he agreed. "That was a calculated risk that I would have probably taken myself. But this winter if people are still up here, they're going to get desperate. It's going to get cold and people will be hungry."

She knew that, of course. Mia also knew that it was torture seeing people starving to death. So many did all over the world, and there wasn't anything she could realistically do to stop it.

"I want you and Andrew to be careful," Scott said. "I want you to move back into the other room once I'm gone."

Mia rolled her eyes, then felt stupid and childish for having done it when he gave her that look that all parents given their kids when they're acting exactly how parents of teens expect them to act. "Dad, I'm not risking us having a baby, *but*," she put a heavy emphasis on it even as her cheeks flushed hot with embarrassment, "there isn't anything going on between us. We're just friends."

"You're more than just friends," Scott countered. "You two always have been. I used to think it was more like brother and sister, but now I'm not so sure."

She'd never really seen Andrew as her brother. He was her best friend; it was as simple and as complicated as that. "Whatever we are, we aren't dating."

Scott opened his mouth to comment, but then snapped it shut and shook his head. "It's strange seeing you wearing a wedding ring, even though I'm the one who bought all of them."

"Yeah," Mia grumbled. "Speaking of which, do I actually have a college fund or did it go to all those rocks you have in that dresser?"

Her dad chuckled. "Oh you had one, but since the banks are all gone it's worthless now."

"That's just peachy," Mia grumbled. She went back to the soil, back to doing what she knew how to do best. She didn't have any control over the rest of the world, but she did know how to grow food. Who needed to go to college now anyway?

12

3rd week Oct

Three days after her dad arrived he took Andrew and Jamal out to kill a buck. He'd offered to take Mia but she had, not so politely, declined and much to her amazement they came back only three hours later with a dead deer, a crossbow wound in its side and the three of them looking way too pleased with themselves as they hauled the carcass down to a tarp in the large room of the shelter.

Mia held Jilly in her arms and watched them from the door to the living room as they struggled to haul it down. "There is no way that's all fitting into the freezer," she commented dryly, trying to cover up her encroaching nausea at the sight of the lifeless animal. "We can't smoke it right now, that would be sending up a red flag saying 'hey come kill us'."

"You didn't look all the way in the back of the storage room did you?" her father asked her, grunting as they set the deer down. Andrew went up immediately and pulled the hatch shut, locking it.

"I…" Mia faltered, and then shook her head. "Uhm, no, I didn't. There were a lot of boxes that were ridiculously heavy and I didn't want to haul it all out."

"Go sharpen your best knives darling," her dad told her. "We're going to wash our hands and dig out the chest freezer."

Her mouth dropped open. "You have got to be kidding me!"

"Nope," he grinned at her. "We need that food vacuum sealer too. It should be in one of the cabinets."

Over the next several hours they worked together to skin, cut up and store the meat in the small, cubic freezer that Andrew and her dad had hauled out from storage and plugged in to what Mia was now calling the work room. It was disgusting. There was blood everywhere and even after only a few hours the smell started to get to her. Several times Mia had to take deep breaths to keep herself from vomiting as she worked on the kitchen table sealing up all of the cuts of meat.

"You have to cook it thoroughly," her dad warned her.

"I know," Mia grumbled as she swiped a sweaty lock off of her brow with her forearm, trying to keep her hands clean. "I know how to cook meat, Dad. I'm not going to take a chance on us getting sick off of it. I'll overcook it, I promise."

On it went with her dad explaining how after thirty days in the freezer she could take some of the cuts out and make jerky from it. "Lovely," she muttered.

"Did you say something?" Andrew called.

"Nope," she said.

Thankfully Jilly slept through most of it and only got up when they were ready to take the bones and skin out to bury them. Mia had a ready-made excuse to duck out on that as well.

"Maybe I'll be a vegetarian," she told Andrew later that night as they changed for bed.

His only reply was, "bacon," which settled the matter.

"Okay, so not vegetarian. If we never get a pig it won't matter, though." Mia's dreams that night were full of sizzling bacon, which didn't help make choking down oatmeal any easier. Then she remembered that there were a lot of people starving at that moment. The oatmeal suddenly sounded pretty amazing.

The days with her dad there passed by so quickly that Mia was startled when they reached the night before he and Jamal were going to leave. The weather was getting cooler day by day and she knew they couldn't put it off any longer. She stood awkwardly, shifting from one foot to the other, and watched her dad carefully folding stuff into his hiker's back pack.

"I wish you didn't have to go," Mia said quietly.

Scott glanced up at her quickly before going back to work. "I don't want to go either, but I'm not useful here."

"You could take James with you," Mia told him. "He would be helpful."

"I'm absolutely not taking him," her dad replied definitively. "I want him here with you."

Sighing, she looked away from him. "You don't think I can do this on my own."

"I wouldn't want to do it on my own," he countered. "I wouldn't want to be by myself, up in the woods, alone with a baby. It isn't fair to ask you to do that alone."

Jamal walked in just as he said that. "James has to stay here," he said looking at Mia, his young face set and determined. "You don't take a dad away from his kid unless you have to. It's his job to protect Nelly."

Mia's gut clenched at the words. She flicked a glance down at her father, but he refused to look her way as he zipped his bag shut. That was exactly what her dad was doing. He was signing over care of his child to another. He was walking away to fight a different battle and nothing he said could erase that. In effect, he was handing Mia and Jilly over to Andrew and saying, 'Here, they aren't my responsibility anymore. Have fun.'

"I'm not going anywhere," Andrew piped in, coming over to put his arms around her, and kissing the top of her head. Mia hadn't even known he was listening, but with a small living space it was hard to get privacy. "Pretty much nothing could get me to leave you two alone."

The three males exchanged glances, and Mia had to fight not to roll her eyes. Whatever it was that they were silently communicating, she wasn't going to get in the middle of it. She didn't really want to be on her own with only Jilly, but it was galling to know that her dad didn't think she could make it without someone else there to help her.

On the other hand, Mia definitely didn't want Andrew to go anywhere. She wanted him here with her, if for nothing else than that she had someone to talk to. It was too quiet as it was with just the two of them when Jilly was asleep.

They packed up a back pack for Jamal, but didn't stuff quite as much in it. He and her dad would start out for Jamal's grandmother's house early the next morning, and if all went well, they would be at his grandmother's in three or four days. It would then take her dad another four days to get to the second shelter. He'd make better time on his own without Jamal, but Mia hoped that he would take the kid with him if they found his grandmother wasn't at her house any longer.

"I'll come back in March," her dad promised as he kissed them goodbye on the morning of their departure. "But if not March, early April. It depends on the snow levels this winter. If it's bad, I'll put it off for a bit, but I want to come before more people start to migrate."

"Is anyone still going to be able to move?" Andrew asked him.

"Yes," Scott said, running a hand through his short, graying salt and pepper hair. "Those who make it through the winter will start heading south, if they haven't already. They'll need to be in a warmer climate, and it will become apparent to everyone as soon as they realize that the power isn't coming back on."

Scott hoisted Jilly into his arms and buried his face in her neck, holding her tight to him. Jilly squirmed a bit, but finally snuggled in. "I'm going to miss you," he said kissing her cheek.

Scott handed Jilly over to Andrew and Mia saw that in the exchange more was being said than was spoken out loud. Mia hugged her dad, holding on for longer than she'd normally have. She didn't know if this would be last time she'd see him. Realistically, if anyone had a shot of making it through, her dad did, but he wasn't Superman. The bristle on his chin scraped against her cheek as he gave her a kiss. "I love you."

"I love you, too, Dad," Mia choked out then she stepped back and gave Jamal a quick hug. "Take care of yourself."

"I will," Jamal said, embarrassed as he awkwardly hugged her back.

She watched them walk up the steps and out of her life, not knowing what they would find out on the road, but sure that it wasn't likely to be friendly. She walked slowly up the steps behind them. Her legs felt like lead as she forced them up yet another stair. Finally, with a last *thunk*, the hatch closed. Mia turned the lock, feeling dread and many more unnamed emotions fill her gut. She turned to look at Andrew, who was watching her from the bottom step. "So what now?"

~*~ ~*~ ~*~

The answer to what now ended up being a lot of uncertainty over their family, hard work and drudgery as October slipped away and November rolled in. They had two light snow covers in the beginning of the month, which made it difficult to continue to prepare the garden, but Mia had a solid handle on it and knew that as soon as the ground was thawed enough in the spring she'd be able to start planting.

What was worse was knowing that the planting would be essential to their continued survival as was hunting. Andrew had started setting out small snares and catching rabbits for them to cook rather than constantly using up the supply of venison that the men had caught. The first time she'd skinned a bunny Mia had cried, even as she kept working. Feeling the soft, matted fur had sent her over the edge. Andrew had been tactful enough not to comment.

Their relationship, which had always been easy, was strained in the first few days after her dad had left as they tried to get to what they had been before Jamal had come into their lives. Mia had moved back into the other room with Jilly, but hadn't made it through the first night without climbing back in with Andrew. She'd done better the second night, though, and managed to sleep through without crying. After that they were back on a more even keel. Andrew was helping more with the household chores, except the cooking, and Mia was able to spend a few hours every day up in the garden. The ground had frozen quickly this year. She'd not expected a hard frost until into December, but Mother Nature was having a grand time screwing everyone over this year.

First it was solar flares; then early snows. The only mediocre bright side to the whole situation was that the carbon footprint of the country was cut to almost nothing overnight. By the time America was back on its feet the environment might have had enough of a head start to truly begin to heal itself from all the damage humans had been inflicting upon the earth. They'd have another shot, as they rebuilt, to rebuild with renewable resources and not screw the planet all over again.

In her darker moments, it almost felt to Mia like the planet had flipped off the US Congress and said, 'Fine, since you can't stop fighting between the parties long enough to make any decisions, I'm going to force you to destroy the planet in your life time and see how you like it!'

It would be the ultimate revenge for those old dudes to get their just desserts, rather than punting the problem off onto their kids and grandkids. Unfortunately, a lot of her generation would have died before then, so it wouldn't really matter to them.

"I'm so maudlin," Mia told Andrew, who merely quirked an eyebrow at that and refused to comment.

Jilly was growing like a weed and had truly embraced the word, "No!" She said it with attitude and style. She said it often, just to make sure they got the message. Her hair was getting longer and Mia was able to start pulling it up into pigtails. Her sassy, chubby cheeks would break into a mischievous grin as she told Mia, "No, Mama!" to pretty much anything Mia wanted her to do, even if it was what Jilly herself wanted, like eating.

"You can't laugh," Mia groaned in exasperation as she and Andrew tried to give Jilly a shower. They were both getting misted from the spray, and she knew she was going to have to change her shirt after this.

"It's so cute, though," Andrew argued with a grin. He blew a raspberry into Jilly's cheek and handed the naked baby over. At Mia's steely glare, he shrugged in resignation. "I can promise to try."

Mia shook her head as she stuck Jilly under the shower spray. "You have to do more than try or we're going to have a terrorist on our hands by the time she's two."

Life went on as normally as it could be. It was too cold to take the baby out for long, but they tried to spend time outside. Up through what would have been Thanksgiving the only really exciting thing to happen was Andrew outgrowing all of his jeans.

The day of Thanksgiving, which was a sick joke now as pretty much everyone around the country was starving, including the Native Americans, he'd come out of his room complaining that they were tight.

"Did you actually make me fatter?" he asked Mia, pulling up his shirt to show that he couldn't button the top snap.

Mia glanced at him and then looked down to the ground. She started laughing. "That's not your only problem."

Andrew looked down and swore softly. They were a good inch too short on the bottom. "That's just great."

"We didn't shrink them because we don't have a dryer," she mused, drying her hands off and coming over to kneel at his feet, trying to tug the leg down. It didn't budge. He'd definitely grown at least an inch over the last day or two. "I think you're still a growing boy, Drew. That's adorable!"

"Shut up, brat," Andrew chuckled as he pulled her to her feet and lifted her easily in to the air.

When he set her down again, she looked up. And up. It was clear as a bell that he was taller. "How come you get to get taller while I'm still stuck at 5'4"?"

"Are you really that short?" he asked, and ducked when she swatted playfully his arm. "So the real question is, do we have any bigger jeans?"

Thankfully the answer was yes. In the bin of clothing she found a wide range of pants in varying sizes. "What size are you now?"

"32x32," he answered her, pulling a box out of her way so she could dig through the one behind it without having to climb over it.

"What the hell kind of sizing is that?"

"What the hell kind of sizing is zero?" Andrew countered. "Are they saying the girl doesn't exist if she's a zero? And what if she's smaller than a zero? Do the numbers go into the negative, and does she start to implode?"

Mia rolled her eyes. "I'm not a zero so it doesn't matter."

"But some girls are," he said stubbornly. "That's just stupid."

"How about 34x34?" Mia asked. She decided to ignore his rant.

He took them from her. "That might do, let me try them on."

Thankfully they fit, and even more thankfully, there were a bunch of them. "You need a belt," Mia scrunched up her nose, studying them. They were a little loose at the waist.

"I have a belt. I'll have to eat more so I can fill them out," he said.

Mia shook her head in amusement as they put the storage room back in order. "They're still a little long."

"Boys take longer to grow, but I'd kind of expected to be done by now," he told her. "I'm going to have to make this work, though. We've got years to live here and no way to get more jeans."

"If you need new jeans, you're sewing them yourself."

"Fair enough," he said agreeably.

Years... Mia knew that they were going to be stuck here for years. Stupid things like needing another pair of jeans. But compared to starving or freezing to death, it was a small price to pay. "I don't even want to imagine how much money my parents spent on the stuff in here," she said, pointing to all of the bins. "But I guess since money doesn't mean anything now it was a small price to pay."

"These aren't new," Andrew said, holding up one of the pairs. It had a yellow tag on it that read '$4'. "She must have raided Goodwill or something."

"I guess that makes sense," she agreed as she folded up his old jeans to stick in the storage bin. She didn't anticipate that they'd need them, but nothing was going to waste now.

"Especially if someone was watching what they were buying," he mused. "I wonder if they bought a lot of things with cash."

Mia didn't reply as she made her way back to the kitchen. "At least I'm not getting any bigger."

Andrew laughed. "Weren't you just complaining about being short a few minutes ago?"

"Are you trying to get yourself in trouble?" Mia asked him, her eyebrow rose as she peeked into the oven to check on the rabbit that she had in a baking pan. She still couldn't get over the fact that she was now regularly cooking rabbit. Andrew was getting good at snaring them in traps so they had a few extra in the freezer.

She jumped a bit when she felt his hands snake around her waist. He noisily kissed her cheek and let her go. "I'm always looking for trouble."

She snorted. "Right."

"Hi, Dada!"

They both turned to the closed door. "Jilly must be up from her nap and," Mia smiled sweetly up at him, "she's calling for you."

"Yeah..." he shrugged in amusement. "I guess I'm on deck."

He emerged a few minutes later with Jilly. Her cheeks were still flushed from her nap, and she rested her head against Andrew's shoulder. Mia froze and looked at the picture the two of them made; his arms around her and her heart seemed to flip in her chest.

"What?" Andrew asked, looking curious at her.

"You two..." Mia didn't know how to find the words. "You just look... right."

He flushed a little, but was clearly pleased. "I have a really good dad. I always hoped that, you know, that when I got the chance I'd do half as good as he did."

She knew exactly what he meant. Andrew's dad was so involved in everything. He was a pastor in a church and a volunteer in the community. Unless someone was dying and in need of prayers at the hospital, Paul Greene had always been at Andrew's soccer games or his Boy Scout events. Mia had wondered often about how such a quiet, thoughtful man could turn on a dime and stand firm against injustice like a police officer harassing a homeless man or melt into a puddle while holding Jilly when she was a newborn. Their two families were so close that Mia had looked at him as a second father for her entire childhood. Mia's dad had his own strengths, but if she needed advice on how to deal with a tough personal situation, Paul had been who she'd gone to.

Yet, despite their differences, Paul and Scott were close friends and often hung out just the two of them to go fishing or running. It was only in the last year or so that the two of them had let Andrew run with them. Andrew had tried to convince Mia to run, but she hated running. Cycling was more her speed. "What did you guys talk about when you went running?" she asked.

Andrew stared at her blankly, rubbing Jilly's back. "Come again?"

She laughed. "Sorry, I jumped topics in my head. When you and the dads went running, what did you talk about?"

"Oh," he said, sitting down at the kitchen table. Jilly sat in his lap for only a second before squirming down to run to her toys. Mia handed him two cans and the can opener and he got to work. "We talked about lots of things, but nothing too serious. Just, you know... guy stuff."

"Guy stuff," she drawled out slowly. She took the opened can of green beans and dumped it into a pot to heat. Mia hated canned vegetables. They tasted terrible, but it was better than no vegetables, and it was something different from the dehydrated vegetables. "What exactly does 'guy stuff' mean?"

Andrew's mouth moved for a second, and then he snapped it shut as if he'd thought better than to say what he was going to say. "What am I doing with the pineapple?" He held up the second opened can.

"It's our dessert," she answered and took it to dump in a bowl. "Since it's Thanksgiving I thought we'd splurge a little today." She glanced back to him. "Guy stuff."

"Right," he sighed. "Well, we talked about the normal stuff like soccer and guns and God. We also talked about... about girls, and what it means to be a man and..." he turned bright red and shook his head. "Come on, Mia," he pleaded, his blue eyes meeting hers imploringly. He ran a hand through his brown locks, making it stand a bit on end. "Some of it was private."

She turned, crossing her arms and studying him carefully. "You don't want to tell me, and you don't want to lie to me."

"Basically," he admitted.

"Well, I can accept that," she said, turning back to the stove. "I guess I wouldn't want to tell you all the things my mom and I talked about."

"Probably not."

Mia grinned into the pot of beans so he wouldn't see her impish look. She tried to keep the laughter from her tone as she added, "Especially not about how it feels to push a baby out of your—"

"STOP!"

She could only smirk.

13

Last Week of November

November was quickly coming to a close, but a warm snap had made it bearable to be up in the garden for a few hours. Mia still had about a million stones to dig out of the ground, and since she was doing it by hand with a hoe and rake, it was taking forever. Her hip itched under the gun holster and scratching it was nearly impossible without taking it off. If she took the gun off her dad might just yell at her all the way from Maryland. Hopefully, he was in Maryland. Hopefully, Jamal was either safe with his grandmother, or he'd continued on with her father. She worried about them constantly, but tried hard not to let it get to her. She couldn't do anything to help, so worrying wasn't going to achieve anything.

Mia blew out a long breath and watched the frozen vapors as they curled into the morning air. Even if it was above freezing, the air from her lungs still froze when it hit the outside world. She didn't have long to work in the garden. Andrew wanted to check on the solar panels before they were buried under more snow. There was a generator, but optimally they wouldn't have to use it since fuel was scarce, and once it was gone, it was gone. They needed to try to survive without it.

She'd half-heartedly suggested storing the frozen food outside since it was freezing out now, but Andrew had shot that down and reminded her of the bears. They hadn't seen any bears, nor had Andrew spotted any tracks, but it wasn't worth the risk. They were going to have to conserve fuel in case the winter was really harsh and the sun didn't shine enough to keep the shelter running. The only good thing was that even if the lights went out, they wouldn't freeze. The shelter's ventilation system could be turned into a fireplace. They had a small wood burning stove, and if they needed it, they could hook it up to the exhaust vent and use it to heat one room of the shelter.

Life was, on the whole, dull. In another time Mia would have whined to her mom that she was bored and wanted to go do something. Now she had a lot to do and not much of it was fun. She and Andrew played games at night or cuddled on the couch to read, but they both went to bed early now. Gone were the days when she spent hours distractedly playing on her phone, or reading on Twitter. She didn't have electronics to tease her out of boredom, and while she'd hated it, at first, she'd quickly adapted to the new change of pace. There wasn't much excitement, but neither was there drama, and Mia had to admit she didn't miss the drama that her friends had constantly dished out all over the internet for everyone to read.

Now she and Andrew were up early and much of the day was spent in keeping their daily lives going. She'd started to wish for a bit of excitement several times, but that would probably mean that something was going horribly wrong. It was better that everything remained completely boring.

Something rustled in the bushes to her left, but she didn't glance up. Deer had been through a lot over the last several days, and she'd stopped panicking every time she heard a noise. She'd been working really hard on her nerves so that she didn't fall apart any time something scary happened. It was a mantra that she kept repeating to herself, that she could handle things, and she could stay calm. She didn't know yet if it was working or not, but it was worth a try, and it did seem to help her not scream when a squirrel crossed her path. That had been embarrassing.

The noise came again. Mia turned her head, but didn't see anything coming towards her. She rose slowly, pulling the gun from the holster as her heart began to hammer. Her hands shook as she flipped off the safety on the pistol and stood waiting with the weapon pointed towards the ground in front of her. Her finger was not in the trigger guard because it would be just like her to jump and accidentally fire the stupid thing, maybe right at her foot. It was the same drill her dad had pounded in to her head over and over again. The drill that she'd never wanted to pay attention to, but somehow it stuck anyway.

The braches moved again, but this time Mia was watching. She saw that the branches all the way up the four foot tall bush moved, meaning that whatever was behind it was big. It could be a deer. Mia kept saying that to herself as her breath caught in fear.

Snuffling noises floated towards her then a sickening, grotesque *crunch*. She started to back quietly back towards the shelter. One step carefully back, her eyes never wavering from the spot, then another until she backed into the stone wall of the garden. Gingerly she lifted her leg and tried to step backwards over the wall. Her foot landed squarely on a small stick and it snapped with such volume that Mia was sure it must have had a microphone attached to it. She froze and watched the bushes.

For a second nothing moved, then the branches parted and she saw it. A bear, its beady black eyes stared at her curiously. Her entire body vibrated as it tilted its head a little to the right.

Mia felt her mouth open as she prepared to scream, but no sound came out. The thought of raising the gun never once crossed her mind.

The bear's nose rose, its nostrils flared for a moment, before it turned around and picked something up in its jaw. Distantly Mia realized belated that it was eating. She knew there was little danger. Andrew had told her more than once that the bears weren't going to attack an adult unless they were ill or starving. Oddly enough that wasn't really comforting at the moment, even though it stood to reason that if the animal already had a meal that it wouldn't want to chase her, but still she couldn't move. Still something kept her riveted to see what the bear was munching on. Call it morbid curiosity, or the same sick fascination that made people slow down to look at a car accident, but whatever it was, Mia didn't move.

At first she couldn't tell what it was, or maybe her brain wouldn't let her process exactly what she was seeing. It couldn't possibly be what Mia thought it was. Seconds ticked by lasting for hours, slowly, and with a loud clunk of every rapid heartbeat pounding through her ears. It couldn't be a foot because that couldn't be a hiking boot hanging limply from the blood stump that was being crunched in the bear's great mouth.

It couldn't be.

Her brain felt fuzzy as a tinny whine filled her ears and spots began to race across the edges of her vision. Mia felt dizzy, wounded as though the bear had taken a swipe at her. Bile rose quickly into her throat making her nearly gag. Violently, she swallowed it down and took another halting step back over the wall.

The large jaw cracked into the bone and the shoe dropped with a sickening *thump* onto the dry leaves, landing unbelievable upright. A jagged bone stuck out from the shoe into the air, a sick marker to denote that someone's life had ended there.

Rage flared in Mia, coming from a previously unknown reserve deep in her soul. She raised the gun, spread her legs and fired directly in front of the bear, spraying the animal with dirt and rocks, the silenced gun only letting out a small *bang* even though the jarring was enough to nearly knock her back a step if she hadn't been braced. The bear reared onto its hind legs, dropping its prize. It howled at her, and the noise was as bone chilling as it was horribly loud.

"Crap!" Mia exclaimed, trying not to panic as time sped up again. She'd forgotten that that stupid gun had a silencer on it, and it wouldn't make enough noise to scare off a rabbit. The bear's roar was a lot more effective at scaring her. Unbelievably, the bear was slightly shorter than she was. It was almost at her eye level twenty-five feet away.

She didn't want to kill it, but she'd already pissed it off by shooting at it. It lurched once towards her, and she hesitated only a fraction of a second longer before emptying the clip in rapid succession into the bear's chest, aiming for as many vital organs as she could manage. It was so close that she probably managed to sink the whole of the ten rounds into it.

Blood began to spurt from the open wounds as the bear thumped down onto all fours. It took a couple staggering, halting steps towards her, and still looking immeasurably pissed at being disturbed. Then the features slackened, and it slumped to the ground about ten feet from her.

The bear's tongue lolled out of the mouth and a fine trickle of blood dripped down to the earth as the bear panted.

This time she did vomit. She bent over and heaved up everything her stomach had to offer and then some more that it didn't. Her hands shook as she propped them on her knees, the .45 Smith and Wesson nearly falling from her limp fingers. When the spasms stopped, Mia stood shakily and wiped the puke from her mouth with the back of her sleeve. Slowly she walked closer to the dying creature as she fumbled to remove another clip from the gun holster.

She dropped the spent magazine and inserted the fresh one, pulling back the slider to load the first shot. Then she took careful aim for the bear's skull, right into the eye and fired. With a direct hit, the animal was out of its misery.

Mia's legs gave out and she sank to the ground as she stared into the small, clearly juvenile face. Tears slid silently down her cheeks as the enormity of what she'd done flooded her. If she'd backed off quietly, they'd have both lived. Whomever the bear was eating was already beyond help, and now it was dead because she'd acted without thinking through the consequences.

Involuntarily, she glanced over to where the leg still sat, propped up in the hiking boot. Her instinct was to run for Andrew and let him deal with the aftermath. Instead, Mia got unsteadily to her feet and forced herself, step by step towards the bush that hid the rest of the body. If she hadn't already emptied her guts, she would have again. Most of the skin was gone, as was the meat as well. All that was left were the bones with some small bits of flesh still stuck to it. Every step closer brought on a stronger assault of smells to the point where she was shocked that she hadn't noticed it before while working in the garden. There were shreds of bloody clothing around the body, but not much else. The other shoe, presumably with the other foot, was gone. She could only assume that it had been dragged off by some other creature.

Mia closed her eyes and felt herself sway slightly. She took several deep, cleansing breaths and turned to get the shovel that she'd left near the garden wall. She holstered the gun again and moved off down past the small dirt road that led to the shelter and down to a tiny clearing among a copse of trees. She stuck the point of the shovel in to the ground and began to dig.

She didn't let herself think or get tired. She didn't focus on making a huge hole because the body was mostly bones and didn't need anything too elaborate. She dug into the thankfully soft earth until her back ached and her head hurt. She hit rocks that jarred her when she jumped on the shovel, and found roots that were as wide as her hand. She went for nearly two hours straight before she'd managed to dig a hole five feet deep and about three foot square wide.

Her hands throbbed horribly as she pulled herself from the hole. She now had blisters that had ruptured and were oozing all over her palms, but she didn't care. She left the shovel at the hole and stumbled back up towards the garden. She paused at her water bottle and drank deeply. Flies were already converging on the dead bear, but she couldn't focus on that right then. Bracing herself, she grabbed her gardening gloves and walked over to the body. She had to scare off a couple of birds from the bones. The black ravens cawed angrily, but moved away when she kicked at them.

Gingerly Mia reached down and picked up the skull that still had dark clumps of hair attached to it. The heavy, smelly weight with its sightless eyes made her stomach roll. Bile shot up her throat, but she held her breath until it calmed and walked back down to the makeshift grave. It took her several trips to move all of the body parts down. Her feet moved of their own volition, a conveyer belt of carnage and death. Finally it was done, and she placed the booted foot, the one that had started the cascade of horrible events, in with the other bones. She stood and said a small prayer for the person, whomever they were, before picking up the shovel again to cover the body.

Mia dumped heaping scoops of wet earth and rocks into the grave, straining to pick up at much as she could and finish the task as fast as possible. She wanted it done and over with while she was still numb to the horror and running on adrenaline. Twenty minutes later it was all over. Her muscles screamed for a rest as she walked back to the bear. She tried several times to drag the animal by its hind legs but hers were shaking so badly that she couldn't make them function enough to even move it a foot. It would need to be dragged much further away or it was going to attract a lot of scavengers to the entrance of the shelter.

She took one last look at the pathetically still baby bear before heading back to the fake rock. She'd done all she could, and now she needed help. Mia dropped her gloves on the ground and pulled open the hatch, not seeing the mess she left on everything she touched. Almost in a trance she made her way down the steps.

"Mia?"

She heard Andrew's voice but it was all she could do to not fall over. Mia looked up to see him coming quickly towards her. She was in his arms a second later. He half carried, half dragged her over to the couch and she slumped back against the cushions, letting herself sink in as exhaustion took over.

"What happened? I was starting to worry and was about to come check on you," Andrew said. His gaze was intense and his eyes flashed an even deeper blue than normal. His hands were on her knees and he squeezed them comfortingly.

Mia didn't know what to say. So many things wanted to come out of her mouth, foremost was that someone had died, and that she'd just dug a grave. Instead all that came out were tears and a muffled, "I shot a baby bear."

"What?" he spluttered, looking stunned. "You shot a bear?"

"I-it was a b-baby," she stuttered. Her teeth started to chatter.

Andrew grabbed her hands and started to rub them vigorously between his. She barely noticed the fiery pain that shot through them when her callouses rubbed together. "Calm down and breathe, I need to know what happened."

Mia closed her eyes and took several breaths. She felt so dizzy and tired. "I need something to eat," she managed to whisper. She heard him get up and grab something. Seconds later she felt a piece of bread pressed to her lips. She opened and chewed, forcing it down past a lump that was lodged in her throat. The carbs fell hard into her stomach, soaking up some of the acid that was making her so nauseated. After she'd managed to swallow all of it, she blinked her eyes opened and forced herself to focus on him. "I shot a bear. I couldn't m-move it. It needs to get dragged away."

"Okay," Andrew said slowly, taking it in, his face contorted in concern. He reached down to her waist and unclipped the gun holster. He stood, his eyes never leaving her face. "Why are you covered in mud?"

She looked down at the blistered hands that lay uselessly by her sides. They were caked completely in dirt. Her jeans were filthy and a hole had opened up in the knee where she could see red mixed in with the brown. She hadn't even noticed it until now. "It's the grave."

"What?" He asked her sharply.

More tears poured from her eyes and she shook her head, unable to say more just then.

He cupped her cheek gently, swiping at the tears. "I'll be back in soon. Jilly is asleep. Don't move, okay?"

She may have nodded, but Mia couldn't have said for sure. After his footsteps receded, she closed her eyes again and let herself fall sideways onto the couch. Sleep claimed her almost instantly.

What felt like only seconds later a hand shook her awake and Mia jumped, sitting up with a gasp. "What happened?"

Andrew's face was smudged with dirt and his jaw set. "Come on, you need to get in the shower. The bear was covered in fleas and mange. You've got scrapes and wounds all over, so you need to get cleaned up."

She didn't move, just looked at him dispassionately. "Did you get it moved?"

"Yes," he assured her. He reached down and hoisted her to her feet. When her knees started to buckle, he grabbed her around the waist and hauled her over to the bathroom. "In you go," Andrew said as he deposited her onto the closed toilet lid. "Strip and get in the shower. I'll grab some of my clothes since Jilly is still asleep in your room, and I want to get everything cleaned up before she's moving around."

Mia sat right where she was. She looked down at her booted foot and nearly reached for the laces, but the horrible image of the rotting bone sticking out from another boot made her dizzy and she couldn't move; couldn't manage to do something as simple as taking off her shoes.

"Hey," Drew's gentle voice broke her reverie. She met his gaze with dead eyes, and he sighed. He knelt at her feet and began to undo the laces. Quickly and efficiently he got her shoes and socks off, and he helped her pull her arms from her jacket which was covered in guts and mud. She lifted her arms so he could pull off her t-shirt and sweatshirt. Here she sat in just a bra and jeans and Mia knew she should feel weird about it, but she just couldn't work up the energy to care. The eyeless skull stared back at her from her mind's eye and stupid crap wasn't even worth thinking about. "Put your arms around my neck," Andrew instructed her and she complied. He carefully pulled her to her feet and she rested her head on his chest, smelling his familiar smell in his shirt.

She heard him undo her jeans and moments later they puddled on the floor. He moved her over to the shower and turned it on. He helped her step in and the water hit her like a warm blanket. Mia let out a sharp breath and felt the spray on her face, soaking her hair and her undergarments. It felt heavenly and somehow it infused her with enough reserve to stand on her own.

Then she tried to touch her face. Hot knives stabbed through her hands as the pain from the open sores ripped up her arms, making her gasp.

"What is it?" Andrew asked, taking her hand. "Oh damn! You really tore the shit out of your hands and fingers!"

Now that the water was washing away the grime, Mia could see that she had not only blistered her palms, but also most of the pads of her fingers. "I can't wash..." the thought of picking up the soap was too horrible to contemplate.

"It's okay," Andrew assured her. He pulled off his shirt, which was already getting wet, and reached for a wash cloth and the bar of soap. He ran the cloth over her arms and her face, getting off the worst of the muck. "Keep your hands in the water," he told her and she did, even though it stung like crazy.

He tried to wash her hair, but she had so much of it that he only succeeded in turning it into a tangled mess. "How on earth do you do this?" He grumbled, trying to get his fingers through it.

"Conditioner," she said and pointed to the correct bottle. "Don't use too much."

Minutes later she was cleaned off enough and he handed her a towel. "I left a pair of boxers, a t-shirt, and some sweats on the toilet lid. Can you get dressed?"

"Yeah," Mia said. She felt refreshed enough from the shower that she was sure she could manage. After he'd left, she stripped off her sodden bra and panties and dropped them onto the pile with her other clothes. She pulled on Andrew's stuff and had to carefully roll the waist band on the sweat pants several times before they'd stay on. Her fingers protested every single contact, but she didn't stop until she had the sweatshirt on as well. It went down well past her fingers, but she didn't bother to roll them up. "Can you open the door? My hands..."

Andrew opened it and she briefly met his eyes. He wrapped a dry towel around her hair and guided her to his room. "Go rest in my bed. I need to clean up the couch and get all of our clothes into the wash bucket before I get a shower."

Mia climbed into his unmade bed and used her feet to pull the blankets up over her legs while she curled into a ball. She felt the towel scrape gently along her cheek as she turned to face the wall, and she wished she couldn't still smell the rot of decay. She heard Andrew moving around for a while, and heard the vacuum go. Belatedly she realized that she must have dropped a lot of mud onto the couch, and she felt bad that he had to clean it up. Then she heard the pipes click against the wall as the water in the shower was turned back on.

Sometime later, it could have been five minutes or an hour, Andrew came into the room and crawled in behind her. He stuck one arm under her neck and the other around her waist as he pulled her in close to his body, warming her up like the blankets hadn't been able to. His sweatshirt smelled just like him, and it was like breathing in liquid sunshine.

"Tell me about the grave, Mia."

Part 2: Andrew

14

Andrew walked over to the bed and saw her curled in a ball, facing away from him. Even in the dim light from the kitchen he could see her shaking, although he didn't know if it was from cold, shock or both. From what he'd seen of the bear, he wouldn't have been surprised if she had been in shock. He climbed in beside her and pulled her back against his chest. He could feel how cold she was through the sweatshirt as he wrapped his arms around her from behind, her slight frame practically folding into him. He had so many questions, but one that stood out most because he'd found where she'd dug a hole that she'd then covered up again. He'd also seen where she'd puked. "Tell me about the grave, Mia."

She was silent for a long time, but he knew how to read her and knew he needed to wait it out. Her voice came out like she had a bad cold when she finally spoke. "It's why I shot the bear, it was eating the foot."

"The foot?" He prodded.

"I saw the shoe, and I got so mad and..."

Andrew groaned inwardly. If there was a shoe then there was a dead person and all the pieces made sense, even though he only had a tiny fraction of the story, he knew her well enough to guess what happened next. Still he waited, knowing that she'd need to get it out or it would haunt her.

Slowly the story poured from her until she got to the place where she couldn't drag the bear. "It's okay," he whispered into her hair. "I took care of the bear, it's fine."

"I'm not weak!" she blurted out suddenly, looking back at him.

He blinked in surprise. "I know."

"Just... the bear, and I was so tired and..."

"I had trouble moving the bear, and I'm bigger and stronger than you are," he said, trying to reason with her. "Plus, I hadn't just spent hours digging a grave. That doesn't make you weak."

Mia sighed and turned away again. "I shouldn't have shot the bear."

"It probably wouldn't have made it through the winter anyway," Andrew told her. He'd seen the size of the bear and knew in his bones that it should have still been with its mother. "The mom was probably killed, and it was sick. You likely kept it from starving to death this winter because it should have already been in hibernation by now with its mom." Black bears didn't technically hibernate, but he knew she wouldn't thank him for an explanation at that moment.

She sniffed, and wiped her eyes with the back of her hand. "That doesn't really help."

After what she'd seen he wasn't sure anything would help. Andrew couldn't imagine having to face a dead body. "Why didn't you come for me? We could have worked together."

"It was my fault," she said. "I needed to do it on my own. I can't always run to you."

He shook his head, trying not to feel stung that she'd refused to turn to him. "This isn't about fault. Even if you make a mistake, which I'm not sure you did, you still don't have to do everything on your own."

"I'm not helpless."

"I never said you were," he retorted, trying to keep his temper in check. "I just meant that-"

"I needed to do it on my own," she said again, quietly interrupting him.

Then he got it. Andrew knew that burning need to do it by himself, even if just to prove to himself that he could. "Okay," he said reluctantly because there was nothing else to be said. Mia had needed to prove something to herself, for whatever reason. He could only hope she had.

He thought back to when he'd first started at Johns Hopkins. He'd been thirteen and scared out of his mind to walk into the classes with all the adults. His mom had offered to go in with him, but he'd said no, knowing that he'd look like a complete baby if she accompanied him. It had been his idea to start college early. He'd called the university when he was ten and asked them what he'd need. Then he'd worked for three years to make it happen, because he'd already known that he wanted to be an engineer. He'd filled out his own application and set up an interview when he was twelve. He'd even applied for the scholarships that would help make the expensive tuition feasible. Andrew had found a way to get most of his education paid for, and he'd been accepted without help from his parents.

Andrew's mom had had to drive him to class, and she'd pick him up at the end of the day. He'd forced himself to wave goodbye to her bright, if somewhat apprehensive, smile, and he'd walked purposefully onto the beautiful campus. He'd memorized the layout of the school, but he still had the map in his pocket just in case. He'd ignored the stares of other students who were clearly wondering what this kid was doing there. He'd gone to his first class, which had been a calculous class. By the end of it he was excited and his nerves were gone. Within a few months he'd met a few other young students, including an eleven-year-old girl who had a nanny that was hired to take her around. He'd stopped feeling alone, and had started to have fun, and he'd been glad he'd pushed himself. He'd done it to prove that he could.

Mia's shoulder's relaxed and her breathing began to even out. A wave of protectiveness filled him as he looked down at her sleeping face. She'd always been there for him, and it amazed him now that his best friend was this girl. He'd never connected with anyone like he had with her. He'd met lots of guys through Boy Scouts and soccer, but nothing had clicked quite as easily. At first he'd been set to watch and protect her when they'd played as small kids, but pretty soon she was standing on her own and insisting on doing everything he did. When she'd started experimenting with cooking, he'd been happy to taste anything she made. It wasn't always great, but when she got stuff right, it was magical.

Just over two years earlier she'd started to complain to him about school. She'd brushed most of it off, at first, saying that she didn't like the classes, but soon after she'd told him about how mean some of the kids were and how everything was about who was hooking up with whom. She didn't say much about it, but Mia always had a weird way of knowing how people felt. Big emotions seemed to affect her more than other people and he thought it was this, more than anything that made school so painful for her.

He'd told her to drop out and start homeschooling, and to his amazement she did. She'd been happier for it; now the angst filled teenage drama wasn't in her face day in and day out.

Mia had always been more of a tomboy, although not in the strictest sense of it. They'd gone hiking and camping together often, but never really out in the wild. Most of it was at state and national parks where the wildlife was a lot tamer. Typically, if one of their families was going on vacation, both kids went along, which was how they'd gone to Yellowstone together.

Mia had a 'girly' side, but mostly she was just her being her. She'd had a tougher time acclimating to high school than her other friends, and when she'd dropped out to homeschool only a few of her closer friends had stuck around. It had been hard to watch her lose those friends, but in a lot of ways it had brought them even closer.

Andrew had been teased a few times by his guy friends about dating her, but it hadn't ever been like that between them. Their relationship, however, wasn't typical, and he'd never talked a lot about Mia to any of his three girlfriends. He'd known, somehow, that it wouldn't go over well, and he'd always pick Mia over them if it came down to it. She was his best friend and he'd never cared about another friend like he did her. She had never made him feel weak or stupid when he'd told her things that scared him. She was his sounding board, his confidant, and his comic relief. That was the one thing that had been sorely missing since they'd come up to the shelter. They didn't laugh like they'd used to.

When he was sure she was asleep, Andrew carefully extracted himself from the bed and went to start the laundry. He didn't make it more than a few steps before he heard Jilly babbling. Sighing, because he knew doing the laundry with the toddler would be twice as difficult, he went to grab her from the crib.

Jilly grinned up at him, "Hiya, Dada!"

Andrew couldn't help but smile at her. She was so cute with her curly red hair and amazing blue eyes. When she smiled, she could make him forget that she'd just dumped an entire box of rice all over the floor. "Hey, Jillibean," he said as he plucked her from her bed. Then he caught a whiff of her foul diaper and groaned. "You just had to gift me with it, didn't you?"

Jilly ignore that, of course. "Mama?"

"Mama is sleeping," he told her as he set her down on the changing mat to change the nasty diaper. "Really lucky Mama," Andrew said, and then he remembered what she'd done that day, and he decided that, on the whole, a poopy diaper was better than a rotting corpse that had been half-eaten by a bear.

Mia slept for several hours, and he ended up heating up some leftovers for supper. Andrew put some of the stew into a bowl and brought some in to her. Jilly trailed behind him, babbling happily as she dumped all his dirty clothes from the basket. Mia turned to look at him, blinking slightly from the light of the kitchen.

"Dinner," he told her, setting the bowl on the end table. He reached over and helped her sit up against the headboard. "Can you hold the spoon?"

"I think so," she answered quietly, licking her dry lips.

He handed it to her and went for a glass of water for her. When he came back he flicked the lights on and sat down next to her, meeting her red rimmed eyes. He didn't comment when he saw her fumble with the spoon. Slowly she ate. "How long have I been asleep?" she asked him.

"A while," he said. Andrew held the glass to her lips and helped her drink. "Once you're done eating I'm going to bandage up your hands. They will probably feel better tomorrow."

"I'm sorry you got stuck with all the work," Mia mumbled, not looking up her from stew.

Andrew shrugged that off. "You'd do the same for me."

Mia went to bed when Jilly did about an hour later, and Andrew ducked under the drying clothes in the work room so he could get back to work on Jilly's Christmas present. It was a small wooden play kitchen that he kept tinkering with, trying to overcome the obstacle of no power tools or hardware. He pulled back the tarp that was hiding it and stared at the wooden blocks that he was attempting to turn into a hinge. The problem with the end of the world was that there wasn't a Home Depot. He couldn't go out and buy anything to make this go easier. He had an idea about taking two blocks and cutting out notches to lace them together, but with only a hand saw, it was going to be tricky. Still, there wasn't much else to do in the evenings, and he was tired of reading.

Sighing, he got to work. He knew Jilly would love the kitchen. She was forever trying to peek under the tarp. She tended to get mad and yell, "Nonono!" when she couldn't get at it. It was adorable, which was, admittedly, a problem. She'd stamp her feet and scrunch up her little nose as she said it, staring right up at him like she was the boss, and he should be listening to her. Andrew had had to bite his cheek more than once to stop himself from laughing.

There wasn't much that was normal in their lives right now except Jilly, and Andrew was determined that at the very least, Jilly was going to get a present for Christmas.

The next day Mia was nearly back to her old self. She had to be careful with her bandaged hands, but her spirits had improved greatly, and she even managed to tease him about his abysmal attempt at oatmeal.

Andrew could never pinpoint why, exactly, he couldn't manage stupidly simple tasks when preparing food in the microwave. It was like he had a block where common sense should have reigned. At first, when he was younger, he'd been annoyed and frustrated with himself, but Mia had pointed out to his fourteen-year-old self that he couldn't be good at everything, and he'd given up. He'd become better at some things under Mia's teasing tutelage, but every now and then, like this morning, he still managed to burn the oatmeal.

He sheepishly met her amused grin. "I tried."

"That's all anyone can do," she agreed amiably before directing him on how to fix the mistake. She smiled a little, but it didn't reach her eyes. Andrew wished that something could give her back her smile.

The next few days Andrew spent outside preparing for the worst of winter to come. Mia refused, point blank, to go out until her hands were healed, and unfortunately the blisters weren't healing quickly. She was able to function now, but she couldn't grip a gun.

The encounter with the bear changed the rules of the game for going outside. Although they shouldn't encounter any other bears this season, Andrew wasn't taking any chances. He'd exchanged the .45 Smith and Wesson for a Glock 20 which was a more powerful hand gun and would be better against a fully grown bear. He'd also found bear mace in one of the bins. He'd had to shake his head in wonder. Mia's dad, Scott, really had thought of pretty much everything. Andrew even found a KA-BAR which was a huge knife that could be used to defend himself if he lost the gun. He attached the Glock, the sheath for the knife, and the bear mace to his belt before heading out. He'd looked over Mia's inventory sheet over a month earlier but hadn't realized that when she'd written "ten knives" and "twenty canisters of mace" that this was what she'd meant. 'Knife' didn't do the KA-BAR justice. The thing was as long as his hand.

Mia giggled at all of the crap he had around his waist. "You look like Crocodile Dundee without the hat."

"And I'm wearing a winter coat," he mused, throwing it on. He needed to rotate the solar panels, chop more fire wood and make sure the vent was clear. There was a bite to the air that had settled in over the last twenty-four hours and Andrew was starting to think that meant snow. Possibly a lot of snow.

The frigid, still air that blasted his face as he exited the shelter told him he was right. If they had any sort of moisture over the next few days they were in for a lot of snow, which could mean he'd need to set up the wood burning stove. Scott had gone over the setup before he'd left, but Andrew decided to preemptively get it into place so that he could quickly turn it on and get a fire going if it was needed. Jilly wasn't going to be a happy camper if she was too cold, and they could only layer her so much before she wouldn't be able to walk. All three of them could sleep in the same bed, but Jilly kicked like crazy, and no one slept except her.

It was weird, Andrew mused, as he walked over to where the solar panels were hidden that he was now functioning as a parent when he was not yet nineteen. It was frustrating sometimes, but without the outside world interfering, their lives were boring and predictable. Except when they weren't, and then their lives were complicated. He still couldn't believe Mia had had to kill a bear.

His birthday was in two weeks. In years past he'd have had a small party with his family and close friends, but not now. Now Andrew had no idea if any of his college friends were still alive and if they were alive, where they were. It was depressing to think about.

He reached the trees that hid the solar panels. Scott had cleared out some trees in a thick patch of woods so that they were hidden, unless you knew what you were looking for, which also gave them a clearer shot to the sun. Andrew rotated them a bit to the left, giving them more access to the winter sun and cleared a few of the fallen branches, and scraped the crap out of his knuckles in the process. He contemplated the oozing blood. He should take a break, and go rinse it out with soap and water. If it was Mia, he'd insist on it. They couldn't risk infection. He shook his head, and fished his glove from his pocket. He'd deal with it later.

He double checked the cables, and made sure that they were fine. Next, he was on to the vent for the shelter, which was disguised as a tree. When Scott had showed it to him, Andrew had laughed. He'd never have been able to pick it out. It was as if someone had hollowed out a tree, but in reality, it was a metal tube that was decorated like a tree trunk with a small hut top. He knocked a few leaves off the top that had landed there after falling from a neighboring tree and moved on to the pile of logs from the tree he'd felled for the garden.

Andrew spent the next several hours chopping logs and the only wild life that he saw was a couple of squirrels. It just figured that Mia would be the one to spot the bear. He hauled all the wood into the work room in the shelter and put a tarp over it so Jilly wouldn't get any splinters and went to set up the wood stove. The wood wasn't completely dry, but he'd already piled up a bunch of dry wood, and if need be they could burn the wet wood, it would just smoke more.

The shelter's ventilation system kept the air fresh and breathable. It also expelled a lot of the humidity that would have otherwise accumulated. Scott had redone the venting so that the filter could be removed and a metal tube fitted onto the stack so that they could vent the smoke from the wood fire. It was a potbellied stove, not very big, but big enough to heat the living room. He could only leave it attached for about twelve hours before he'd need to run the fan for the air filter for two hours, but it would allow them to heat up. The stove would funnel out a lot of the humidity just by virtue of it heating the room, but they needed fresh oxygen. The filtration system was very efficient, though. It only ran a few hours a day so removing it was not a huge loss.

"You really think we're going to get snow?" Mia asked as she held Jilly on her hip. Jilly was way too interested in the stove and they both knew it would be a problem trying to keep her from burning herself. The ventilation was in the right corner of the living room behind the couch, and they were going to have to get creative in putting up a barrier.

Andrew grunted as he wedged the stove into place, wincing slightly when he jammed his foot with one of the legs. "It smelled like it."

"Ah," she said.

That was something he appreciated about Mia. As a gardener, she understood things like that without much explanation.

He twisted it a bit and stood back, surveying it. He'd pulled the carpet up around it so that it was sitting on the bare floor. Deciding it was good enough, he grabbed the pipe and stuck it on the stove, connecting the potbelly to the ventilation system and pushed hard on the clamp to keep them connected. Then he preloaded it with wood and kindling so that if he needed to light it, it would be ready to go, and he wouldn't have to fumble with it.

There was an alarm on the batteries that were connected to the solar panels. On the off chance that they couldn't generate energy the alarm was supposed to sound an hour before the batteries ran out, but Andrew wasn't willing to take any chances. He'd rather have the whole thing prepared. He thought fleetingly about doing a trial run just in case the smoke didn't vent out correctly, but after a look at Jilly's excited, curious face, decided to wait until she went to bed later that night.

"Okay, she can be let down," Andrew said wearily. His shoulders ached a bit from chopping wood, but it was a good feeling. Much of the time he didn't have anything really physical to do.

Mia stood watching him, her arms crossed, as he washed the dirt off his hands. "I have a rabbit stew simmering for dinner."

"Oh great," Andrew said, his mouth suddenly watering. "I'm starving."

"I bet." Mia crossed to the pot and lifted the lid to stir it. "It should be ready in about ten minutes."

He pulled out a chair and sat, grabbing his water glass and downing it in one before studying her. "How are you feeling?"

She opened her mouth and he knew it was to say, 'fine', but at his raised eyebrow, she paused. "I'm still a little shaken. I keep seeing the skull when I close my eyes. And the dead bear. I keep wondering if..." her voice hitched and she shook her head.

Her eyes looked so haunted that he snagged her hand carefully, so as not to hurt the healing wounds, and pulled her down into his lap so he could wrap his arms around her. "Get it out, Mia. You'll feel better."

Mia sniffed and after a moment, finally spoke. "I keep wondering if the bear killed that woman."

Andrew nearly asked how she'd figured out it was a woman, but decided that the shoes probably gave it away, so he didn't press that point. He did, however, know the answer to her question. "There is no way that little bear could have killed an adult, even a teenager. It wasn't even a year old yet." He'd had to study bears pretty thoroughly for a Boy Scout project. Black bears were born in early spring and lived with their mothers for at least a year. This bear hadn't even weighed sixty pounds. "I'm pretty sure that she'd died before, and then the bear got to her, along with other scavengers."

"It was so awful."

"I know," he said softly, running a hand up and down her back.

His stomach let out a loud growl and she chuckled weakly. "I better get some food in you," she said as she stood and went to the stove.

Andrew watched her for a moment, but was distracted by Jilly who had started to climb the stove.

15

December 2nd

The snow started to fall in earnest right after dinner. When Andrew checked before bed it was already up six inches and still coming down. It was that type of snow where the flakes were fat and fluffy, making it perfect for building up large quantities. If there were still forecasters giving the weather on the seven o'clock news, they'd be urging everyone to stock up on milk, bread and toilet paper. He'd never quite figured out how people would run out of toilet paper in the two days it took to get the roads cleared, but had to admit it wasn't something he'd readily want to do without. Thankfully when Mia had stocked this place, she'd bought a whole lot of toilet paper. The powdered milk he could do without, though. Sadly, they had tons of it.

He went quickly to check the vents and the solar panels, but both were fine. Solar panels are notoriously inefficient, which was good news in a snow storm. The light and heat that comes in from the sun, but doesn't get converted to energy, warms the panels and keeps the snow on them melting. Still, if it snowed for more than twenty-four hours, they were possibly going to face their first power outage.

By the time he arrived back into the shelter he was soaked through and shivering. He stripped out of his wet clothes and put on the sweats that he'd left in the work room before hanging up the snow caked pants and jacket. Andrew shivered as he walked over to the control panel and switched off the heat to the work room. Sighing, he went over to the small chest freezer and pulled the plug on that as well. It would work like a cooler for a while, and it was going to get so cold in the work room that it probably wouldn't need to be running anyway.

Opening the door to the living room was like sliding into a hot tub, even though the room was only set for about seventy degrees. It would have to go down, and regretfully he turned the thermostat down to sixty.

"You're trying to kill me, aren't you?" Mia mused as she watched him over his shoulder. "Is the snow bad?"

"Very bad," he said turning back to her. He resisted the urge to put his cold hands on her cheeks, even though he knew she'd have done it to him. He grinned at her.

"What?" she asked, her eyebrow raised in curiosity.

He shrugged and went past her to grab two of the kitchen chairs. "You make me smile," he told her as he tipped the chairs onto their sides near the stove. He moved the couch just enough so that he could wedge the chairs and form a pen around the stove that would keep Jilly from touching it. It boxed the area in nicely.

Jilly walked over to investigate the new make-shift gates and immediately she tried to climb them. "Nah!" she yelled, turning to him with righteous indignation written all over her tiny face.

Andrew hoisted her into the air, throwing her up a bit before catching her and blowing a loud raspberry on her chubby cheek. "Sorry, Jillibean, I'm about to test it out, and it's going to be hot."

"Owwee," Jilly said instantly, looking back at it and pointing.

They'd been working on 'hot' being painful, and he was relieved that it was sinking it. "Yes, indeed."

He set her down and immediately she went right back to the chairs, trying to climb them and singing out, "owwee," over and over again.

"We tried," Mia said, coming up next to him.

Andrew put his arm around her and kissed the top of her head. "Yeah, we did. Thankfully she doesn't seem to be able to get over the chairs."

"For now at least," she added helpfully.

"You are so cheerful, Mia," Andrew chuckled, hugging her to him. "I don't know how you manage it."

"It's a gift," she giggled.

Much to his surprise and relief the stove worked perfectly and all of the smoke vented out of the shelter with only a minor adjustment to the hose. Andrew wasn't worried about someone seeing this smoke. It was snowing really hard, and anyone out in it wouldn't be able to see the smoke well. Also, the smoke vented at six and a half feet up a fake tree. Anyone walking around wouldn't be looking up into a thicket of trees to find smoke. There was always the possibility that someone might smell it and come looking, but even before the world ended no one was stupid enough to go walking in the woods during a blizzard. Now, it would be suicide with no way to warm up and no shelter for nearly a mile in any direction.

Andrew let it burn through the first round of wood before banking the fire and heading to bed. He set an alarm so that he wouldn't sleep through switching out the vents, but he didn't end up needing it. Because it was so cold in the shelter, Jilly woke up crying at around four in the morning and wouldn't be comforted.

"Let's camp in here near the stove," Andrew yawned as he watched Mia simultaneously rock Jilly and make her a bottle out of powdered milk. They almost never gave her a bottle, but it was a surefire way to get her back to sleep if she was upset. Andrew built up the fire again before pulling out the sleeper sofa. He grabbed all the extra pillows and blankets he could find and piled them on, making a sort of nest.

Mia crawled in and propped herself up while she gave Jilly the bottle. "I'm so cold," she said, her teeth chattering.

Andrew heaped the blankets around her and the baby, trying to cover them the best he could. "The fire will heat us up in a bit." What he didn't say was that if it wasn't out in four hours, he'd need to dampen it with some sand so that he could reattach the air filter, and they'd have to spend at least two hours shivering. If this is how winters were going to be, it would definitely be interesting and not in a good way. He was cursing himself for ever thinking that life up here could be dull. Right now all he wanted was boring regularity, and heat that worked all the time.

He made sure he could hear his phone alarm before climbing in next to her. In her sister's warm embrace, Jilly was barely awake as she sucked at the bottle.

"It's a good thing you know how to do all of this stuff," Mia mused quietly.

He looked sideways at her and saw the glow of the stove's fire dancing across her rich, brown hair. It was loose around her shoulders, brushing her cheeks. "You could do it, too." Andrew was confident of that. Mia was very smart, especially when the subject interested her. She could be extremely driven to learn.

"I never wanted to know," she mused. "I just assumed it would be okay. How stupid and arrogant is that?"

"Pretty darn stupid," he told her, deadpan.

Mia rolled her eyes. "You weren't supposed to agree with me."

"I love you too much to lie to you," he assured her and was thankful that she had an arm full of Jilly or he'd have received a pillow to the side of the head. "Seriously, though, Mia you'll learn now and it will be fine. You've got the chance to learn everything."

She was silent for a moment before replying. "I think we were all like that, though. We were all caught off guard. I sort of thought that if the end really came, I wouldn't be able to survive it, and maybe I wouldn't want to."

"You should have watched The Walking Dead." Andrew told her, not for the first time. She'd always dodged watching it with him by telling him it was too gross.

"I did, a bit," she admitted with a small smile.

He blinked in surprise. "I thought you said you wouldn't!"

"Well, I didn't watch it the real way," she said, shifting a bit to put the empty bottle on the floor. "When the new seasons came out on Neflix I'd watch the parts that didn't have the zombies. I could make it through the whole season in a few hours."

Andrew mouthed wordlessly at her, totally flummoxed. "What was the point in even watching it, then?"

"I liked the romantic bits."

Romance in a zombie movie... okay, then. "You are the weirdest girl I have ever met."

"I'm going to take that as a compliment," she said, grinning widely for the first time in days. She shifted to her side and set Jilly on the bed between them before scooting down to get fully under the covers. The tiny redhead slept through the whole thing, now that she was warm and fed. Mia's bright blue eyes met his, he was relieved to see that she was really amused by all of this. "I also liked the parts about how people reacted to each other. I guess, in some respects, the zombies weren't the most dangerous part of their new world. It was all the crappy things that the living people did to each other that made the difference between life and death. I didn't used to think of it that way, but now with the world the way it is, I'm starting to reevaluate. I think mostly I didn't watch enough of the show to really get it, though."

He couldn't argue with that, although he'd personally liked all the bloody parts of the show. He and his mom would watch it together every week in the fall. They would heckle the characters or comment on the good makeup jobs. His dad, though, just rolled his eyes at them and said, "Joyce, you're as bad as a teenager." His mom had thought that was funny.

Andrew lay down on the other side of Jilly and covered his shoulders. It was already starting to warm up nicely in their corner of the shelter, but he still felt the chill from the air around them. He closed his eyes, hoping for another three hours of sleep.

They rotated the stove with the vent and back again and he quickly figured out how long one load of wood would last so that he could time it correctly and put it out before they needed to switch it. Andrew showed Mia how to do it, and by the second time she was able to manage on her own, although she struggled to get the clamps tight enough around the metal tube to make sure the smoke vented out properly. In a pinch, though, she could manage it. They kept all but one light off and tried not to use the power as much as possible. After lunch Andrew went back out again with a shovel to check the solar panels and found that enough snow had built up around them to partially cover them. It was still snowing, but it had tapered off, and there was a good foot of snow all around, making walking a challenge.

Andrew used the shovel to knock snow off of surrounding branches so that as soon as the clouds cleared the panels would start to work again. Then he cleared and shoveled the snow away from around them, leaving the area in front cleared out. He checked the vents on the way back in, but found that the smoke was keeping the vent melted and cleared perfectly.

Life here was routine. Routines that sometimes shifted depending on the circumstances, but basically everything fell neatly into a set schedule, and that he could deal with. Andrew knew how to be methodical and meticulous. If he hadn't before he'd started school, his engineering classes had certainly beat it into him. For a moment, as he walked back down the stairs into the shelter, he longed for his classes back in college. There he had a plan for his life. He was going to graduate, maybe get a masters, hopefully get a job, then get married and have kids.

Here he had no job, and he wasn't likely to get one, at least not for a long time. He wasn't going to get his degree, and even if he'd had it, it would be useless right now. There were no companies and it didn't matter if you had a hundred billion dollars in the bank or not because the bank had been electronic and paper money was worthless. No one would be hiring because they had no way to pay anyone. It was weird to think that he'd never get an income and he wouldn't support himself in the truest sense of the word. Andrew knew he'd been lucky. His dad had a good job, and before his mom had decided to stay home and homeschool him, she'd been a very successful bariatric surgeon.

There was more to the story, of course, but it was a painful memory since he'd nearly lost her before he'd have ever remembered her. When he was one, his mom had been in a horrific car accident on her way to work. She'd been hit by a driver who had been drinking. She'd come out of it a mess while the other driver hadn't lived. Her right arm was so badly broken that she'd needed surgery and pins. Even after months of physical therapy, she hadn't been functional enough to operate the delicate tools needed for a gastric bypass operation. Joyce was a good doctor, well-liked by her patients, but the accident had led her down another path and had shifted her priorities. She'd nearly died, and she wanted her time to be spent with her son.

She'd given up her job rather than move into some other form of medicine. It still sometimes floored and humbled him to know that she'd given up medicine for him, but Joyce had always said that he was better medicine than anything. Life was too precious. The cushion from the insurance money, plus a hefty check from the other driver's wealthy family, had allowed them to live comfortably, if frugally, even with only a pastor's salary.

He knew they'd wanted more kids, but there was only him. His mom and Mia's had had that in common until Jilly came along. Andrew knew his mom had loved Jilly utterly, and had enjoyed spoiling her rotten. As he opened the door to the living room, he grinned down at Jilly, who was putting blocks into a plastic tub. She made life way more complicated than it would have otherwise been, but she was worth it.

"How was it?" Mia asked, interrupting his thoughts.

"It was okay," he said as he shrugged off his coat and hung it over the back of one of the remaining kitchen chairs. "The snow has stopped, so that's something. We got about eighteen inches."

"Wow! I wish we could play in it," she said, ladling up some stew for him.

Andrew wasn't quite sure how she did it, especially with no cook books, but every single time she made stew it tasted differently. It was always delicious and she managed to keep the meal from getting to be boring. "You are a genius," he promised her through a mouthful of food. He hadn't even bothered to sit down, just stood wolfing it down. His pants were slightly crusty from snow and if he sat the cold would press into his legs.

"I know," Mia agreed cheerfully. "On what in particular, though?"

"This," he said, indicating the bowl with his spoon. "I have no idea how you do this."

"I'm going to keep it that way so you can't declare me the weakest link," she said before snatching the empty bowl from his hands. "Go change before you freeze to death, and I have to take over chopping wood myself."

Andrew laughed and went to his room.

Despite the auspicious beginnings of winter, the snow only stuck around for three days before a warm front moved in and melted everything, turning the ground to sludge. They were able to go back to full power on the solar panels, and Andrew was able to devote more time to Jilly's Christmas present. He managed to round the hinge blocks down by sanding them for hours. It was tedious, but by the time they were done, he could lock them together and keep them from shifting by sticking a long nail down a -hole that he'd drilled through the blocks with a hand-cranked drill.

When he'd discovered the existence of the drill, sometimes referred to as an egg beater drill, he'd breathed a sigh of relief. Mia held the blocks for him while he cranked the handle which spun the drill shaft and created the small hole. He didn't have many drill bits so he needed to work carefully so as not to snap them. At home he wouldn't have worried so much since they were easy to replace at a hardware store. That was not possible now. After he'd drilled them out and nailed in place, he put the drill bit away and watched Jilly turn the crank on the drill for a bit. It made an odd clicking noise that she seemed to like.

"I believe that was my grandfather's," Mia told him. "I think I remember that being in his workshop."

"It's a good thing your dad saved it," Andrew told her. "It looks like I'll be able to get this done by Christmas."

She sighed heavily. "I don't know what to give you for Christmas."

"Just forget it," he said honestly, carefully positioning the block on the kitchen's little cabinet door. "I don't need anything."

When she didn't respond he glanced over at her and saw her smiling. "What if I want a cashmere sweater?"

"What's cashmere?" Andrew asked curiously.

Mia burst out laughing. "Why did I think you're gay?"

"I dunno," he said, grinning despite himself. He remembered being stunned at the time when she'd asked him, but now it just seemed funny. "Why did you think that?"

She shrugged dismissively. "I guess I was just surprised you'd never told me about your girlfriends. Do you remember that line in Legally Blonde?"

"Uhm," he hedged, not able to place what she was talking about. "No."

"Well, she figured out someone was gay because he knew shoe brands."

Andrew stared at her blankly. "What?"

"Do you know what Prada is?" Mia huffed, grabbing a block from Jilly before she could throw it.

He tried to place it. The name seemed familiar but he couldn't put his finger on it. "Is it clothing?"

"They're really known for their shoes," she told him. "But, see, a gay man would know that."

"That's a bit of a stereotype," he mused, forgetting about the cabinet. His dad was forever going on about not judging others and to never try to stick someone into a category. No one fit neatly in any one spot. "It would be like saying all girls have to like pink or all boys must like Wolverine."

"I like Wolverine! He kicks butt."

"My point," Andrew said as he picked up the hammer and stuck a nail between his lips for safe keeping, "is that we shouldn't pigeonhole people."

Mia plucked the nail from his mouth. "If you swallow that we're screwed."

"I'm just so used to doing it that I don't think about it anymore," he said as he carefully tapped a nail in place. "I've taken our local E.R.'s for granted all these years."

"I'm going to make a small cake for your birthday."

He would have told her not to bother with it, but she sounded so excited that he kept quiet. It was something she could do for him and in her way, that was how Mia really showed that she loved someone. She didn't particularly like baking as much as cooking, but with no fresh ingredients her passion for creating meals was stymied. Andrew, at least, could continue to tinker around with the complicated system that was the shelter, and to try figure out ways of improving it with the limited resources that they had available to them. It was fun in its own way.

"I can't believe you're going to be nineteen soon," Mia ruminated. "That makes you seem so old."

"Thanks," Andrew snorted. "That's just what I need, to be old before I'm twenty."

"I've still got six months until I'm eighteen and legally an adult."

"No one is paying attention to what's legal anymore," he reminded her. "I can't even begin to imagine what it's like out there, but I doubt it's pretty, and just how old you are doesn't mean jack."

She handed over the nail that she'd been fiddling with so that he could attach it to the other side of the makeshift hinge. "Actually, I imagine that being older might be better. Girls my age are probably not fairing very well."

Andrew had been intentionally not thinking about that. He couldn't imagine what he'd do if he ever saw someone being attacked that way. He hated rape; hated how cowardly it was and all that it did to the victim. He'd been friends with a girl in school who'd been raped at a party. They'd taken a chemistry class together and had been lab partners. She'd dropped out halfway through the semester to try to get her head straight and cope with the aftermath. It had torn her up. When he looked into Mia's face he knew that she was right, and the thought of anyone hurting her like that filled him with a rage so blinding that it took him a full minute to get it under control. "I'm not letting anything like that happen to you."

"I know," she said quietly.

There was nothing but trust in her eyes, and he hoped like hell that he could keep it up. Jilly broke the mood between them by coming over with a book and sitting herself in his lap. It was a Sesame Street book that she particularly loved, and he'd read it at least five thousand times that day. "Again?"

"Pwees!" Jilly called out, delighted that he'd got the message.

"You may as well give in," Mia said, standing up and brushing the dirt off her jeans. "She's relentless."

"I wonder where she gets that from," he called after her as she went through to the living room.

"No idea."

16

December 14th

His birthday crept up on him quickly and before he knew it, it was the fourteenth. Mia, true to her word, made a small chocolate birthday cake and sang Happy Birthday to him while Jilly clapped with delight.

"We haven't had chocolate in months," Andrew said through a mouthful of delicious, moist cake.

"I know," Mia said longingly. "I should have stocked up more of it, but I didn't consider chocolate a necessity for life. How wrong I was."

Jilly didn't really eat the cake, but smashed it all over her face and the table. "Num num!"

"Then why don't you eat it?" Mia asked rhetorically. Jilly daintily picked up a crumb and dropped it on the floor. "I give up," she said to Andrew before letting Jilly down from her high chair. "So how does it feel to be nineteen?"

"No different than eighteen, although according to my fancy fake passport, I'm twenty-two."

She nodded, looking thoughtfully into the distance. "Age is a social construct anyway."

"Excuse me?" he asked laughing.

"I've been thinking about it a lot. Age is relative. The term teenager is a recent invention, and a few hundred years ago you were treated like an adult when you were fourteen or so." Mia sighed heavily, and rested her head on her crooked elbow. "I've been stuck in this mentality that I have to be a certain way because I'm not an adult, but it hit me last night that age has nothing to do with it."

He wanted to say that he'd told her as much, but decided to refrain. "How does that change anything?"

"Well," she said slowly, "if I accept that age is not a magic fixer, and that I'm as old as I act and feel, then I don't have to be stuck feeling helpless and like I don't have a direction."

He blinked in surprise, more than a little dumbfounded. "So just like that you're done being a kid?"

"I think I was probably done shortly after I started homeschooling," Mia admitted wryly. "I was responsible for my own education, and my own way in life. After Jilly was born I was responsible for her a lot, including getting her to day care some mornings if my parents had to be in to work early."

She looked so serious, so contemplative, that Andrew didn't want to interrupt her, but he wanted to know. "What's changed now?"

"I think it... it was the bear," she said, scratching self-consciously at her arm and not meeting his gaze "I think by accepting that I took the bear's life to save my own, and to save another person's body... it just shifted everything, and I knew I couldn't stay the same. I was different and I needed to accept that."

He studied her thoughtfully. "I think it would change anyone."

"Maybe," she said noncommittally. "I hope I never have to kill a person."

She glanced up at him, and he nodded. "I can't imagine having to kill anyone. I think it would kill a part of my soul."

It was something that had weighed on him more than once since they'd run for it Labor Day weekend. He'd thought, or maybe just hoped, that everything would blow over quickly and that life would go back to the way it was. But life had a way of screwing with your plans. He'd never planned to have to fight for his life. The military had never appealed to him, although he wasn't quite sure exactly why. He'd had a couple of friends who had joined up and were enjoying it. He respected Mia's dad immensely, and he'd been in the Navy.

Andrew assumed that it was his pastor father whispering into his subconscious telling him to talk things out, not fight them out. He could fight if he had to, but he really hoped he never had to. "I'm glad you've made the switch."

"Tired of me acting like a spoiled brat?" Mia asked straightening her shoulders. He could tell she was only half kidding.

"No, it isn't that," he told her honestly, thinking about how her laughter and sense of humor, while still present, had definitely taken a hit since they'd had to come to the shelter. "You weren't happy. I think this will make things easier. I agree that it's stupid to say that the day you turn eighteen is the day you're an adult. There's no magic wand that makes that change, and it's important to think for yourself."

"I think I know why it happened, though," she said, grinning impishly.

"Why what happened?"

"Why they extended childhood," Mia said, rolling her eyes like he should be keeping up with her.

It made him smile. "Was it the greeting card companies, cause I hear they're responsible for a lot of the ills of the world."

She laughed, sitting back in her seat and pulling her hair up in a tail. It was getting really long now. "No, I think it was to keep kids out of the labor force so there would be more jobs for adults."

"What?" This was a new one for him. "Where did you hear that?"

"I read it somewhere, and it seemed like a good theory," she said shrugging it off. "I have a question for you, though. It's something that's been bugging me." He nodded for her to continue. "Why did you ask for Alfredo for our last meal?"

It took him a moment to put together what she was talking about. "Well, you have to admit it was a good last meal."

"Yes, but it takes forever," she argued. "What if the text had come through sooner from my dad?"

"It wasn't going to," he told her simply, standing and taking his plate to the sink. "Your dad said he'd give me as much warning as he could, at least four or five hours if he could manage it, then he'd warn you as late as he could so we'd both still be able to get away, but he wouldn't get caught and have us possibly stopped. He knew his texts were being monitored."

Mia bit her lip, worrying it between her teeth. "I guess it's still hard to believe that anyone cared that much about what my dad was saying."

"Believe it," Andrew said, getting her plate and Jilly's before wiping down the table. "I have no idea what he did, but more than once he pointed out someone tailing us as we went shooting last summer. I thought he was being paranoid for a while, but the cars always followed at a distance, and pulled off right before we got to where we were going. It tended to be the same make and model car, too. They were always black."

"That's not subtle," Mia grumbled, standing up to do the dishes.

"He told me they weren't trying to be subtle." That had been what worried Andrew most. Scott hadn't ever been very concerned by it, but Andrew had thought it was just plain weird that he was being watched so closely. He still didn't know why.

"This whole situation is cracked," Mia said, swiping at her nose with the back of her hand and leaving a small trail of bubbles there.

Andrew used his thumb to wipe them off. "Oddly enough the solar flares didn't even come at the peak of the sun's cycle for storms. They were supposed to be really bad in 2013, but here we are in 2015, and that's when the sun decided to go nuclear."

"Science doesn't explain everything," she said, turning at a sound from the couch. "Jilly, get down."

Andrew walked over and plucked the toddler from the back of the couch where she was attempting to scale it to reach the stove. "You're dangerous, you know that?"

Jilly smiled happily and patted his cheeks with her fat fist. "Dada!"

"Yeah, yeah," he griped good-naturedly. "I love you, too."

~*~ ~*~ ~*~

The run up to Christmas was not too bad. Often times Christmas at home was stressful and filled with commitments. They often had parties to attend and a number of church services that were part of the church calendar. His dad would have appointments and people to visit. With Andrew's birthday mixed into that chaos, it was almost never peaceful. This time, though, he had no presents to buy, just one to finish. They wouldn't have a tree, so there weren't decorations. His mom wasn't baking endless rounds of cookies with Mia. All he had to do was the work of the day and nothing more. In a lot of ways, he missed the hustle and the stress. It didn't feel much like Christmas without all of the trimmings, but a larger part of him was thankful for the reprieve from the commercialization of the holiday. And the carols... he could cheerfully take a year off from the annoying songs twenty-four hours a day on the radio. He didn't dislike all of them, but some were definitely grating.

Andrew wondered how his parents were doing. This would be their first Christmas apart in his life and he still found it hard to believe that he wasn't going to see them again; maybe ever, or at least for several months until winter ended. This would be the first Christmas in a long time that his dad wouldn't be preaching on Christmas Eve, and he and his mom wouldn't be there sitting with Mia and her family. Last year Jilly had cried through half the service while Mia's mom, Diane, had rocked her in the Mother's Room.

Mia had started singing to Jilly over the last few days, much to Andrew's amusement and annoyance. He hadn't told her how much Rudolph annoyed him, and she didn't exactly have a wonderful voice, but it was clear and sweet and Jilly had laughed when Mia danced around with her.

Christmas Eve came and Andrew felt itchy inside, like something wasn't sitting right. Unfortunately, he thought he knew what it was. His dad had a tradition of reading the story of the birth of Jesus every year, and to him it felt wrong not to continue it.

Andrew had been born into the faith and had grown up solid in knowing that Jesus was there and that God loved him. Then he'd gotten into science and things had started to evolve in a way that didn't lend towards having a faith in a God that science couldn't prove. In his soul he was a born engineer, always tinkering with things and taking them apart to see how they worked. It was his passion and his gift. He wanted to figure out how things worked, but there was nothing to prove with God. Either he had faith or he didn't.

He'd been freaked to tell his dad. He didn't know why it had been such a huge deal, but as he'd stared at a book that explained evolution, he couldn't imagine telling his dad how interested he was in it.

Except his dad had known already, and when Andrew was fourteen, Paul came to his room and knocked at the door, asking to talk. He'd told Andrew that he knew he was having doubts.

Everything had poured out of him and it felt like poison leaching from his system to come clean to an open and loving ear. Paul hadn't been upset with him. He'd asked his dad how he could reconcile science with faith.

"Faith and science don't have to be at odds," Paul had told him, clapping him gently on the back. "They aren't really in the same realm in my mind. I believe in the dinosaurs and in evolution. I've seen evidence and scientific proof to support lots of things that aren't mentioned in the Bible. I'm okay with that because the sun doesn't revolve around the earth."

He'd looked so earnest that Andrew had started to laugh. "What does that have to do with anything?"

"The things we can explain now are simply amazing," his dad had said with awe in his voice. "I recently saw a video on YouTube about where our solar system fits into the galaxy, and it was just stunning. We make strides and advancements all the time, but we still don't have all of the answers. A couple hundred years ago everyone thought that the world was the center of the solar system, not the sun. A hundred years ago you couldn't talk on a telephone, and thirty years ago we hadn't yet cracked the human genome."

He'd understood what his dad was telling him. "Just because science can't explain God now doesn't mean it won't be able to in the future."

"It might not," he'd said gently. "We may never have answers, and science may work to prove that God doesn't exist. That's where faith comes in, and Andrew, I don't want you to have blind faith. It isn't real or authentic if you don't embrace it for yourself and find where it fits in your own world views. Only you can come to that in your own way, but know this; some of the brightest scientists on the planet are also religious men and women. You aren't alone in your struggles. Some turn away, others turn towards it, but you aren't the first, nor will you be the last to stare into a microscope and wonder where God fits into everything."

It left him, today, with many unanswered questions about where God was in this mess. There weren't any answers, and the Bible he'd packed, pretty much out of habit, was still sitting untouched in the bottom drawer of the dresser. Slowly, almost painfully, he went to retrieve it. He stared for a long time at the worn and fading cover. Inside were answers to some people's every question, but Andrew knew that all of the answers weren't there. He'd heard people ask his dad, over and over again, 'why am I suffering?' or 'why did they die?' or even better 'why do bad things happen?' There were no good answers to those questions except that God would use the suffering for good. At the moment that seemed hollower than it ever had before.

He turned the cover page and saw the inscription his dad had written for him before he'd given it to him.

Andrew, you are a child of God on loan to me for a few years, and you've been the best gift I've ever been given. No matter how much I love you, God will always love you more. –Dad

Slowly, feeling suddenly older, he walked back into the living room and sat on the couch, holding the Bible.

Jilly, who was always up for a story, came and crawled onto the couch and into his lap.

Carefully he turned to the book of Matthew and began to read the familiar story to her. Mia glanced over at them from the kitchen where she'd been preheating the oven and came to sit with them. She didn't comment as he finished reading, just kissed his cheek and went back to preparing dinner.

The itch was gone.

After Jilly went to bed Andrew moved the play kitchen into the living room and stood back to admire his handy work. It wasn't every day that he got to build something, and this time he'd outdone himself, especially with his limited tools and resources. It was one thing to build a bookshelf when you had a power drill and router. It was another thing when you had to sand everything by hand and invent a way to make a knob for the drawer.

"It looks amazing," Mia said as she put a few small bowls in the cabinet. "She's going to flip."

He beamed, feeling pride at what he'd done. She straightened and walked over, hugging herself to his side. They stood together, silently looking down at it. They'd both agreed not to make a huge fuss over Christmas, but he found that not having a tree was just a little weird. "Are you sure?"

He didn't need to elaborate; she knew what he was asking. "I'm sure. We'll pick out a tree next year and Jilly can help decorate it. It's pretty much for her anyway."

It was such a switch from who they had been even a few years ago. When stripped of everything that they thought really mattered, they were forced to confront life in its simplicity. They had time to think and talk. They discussed books, gutted animals, and stopped a toddler from scaling the furniture. They had to work hard all the time to keep up their existence. There was no one who had the latest model car to envy. No one was telling them now that they had to try this new product, and there were no ads on TV that made their mouths water for a cheeseburger. No one got distracted on Facebook or Twitter. They couldn't get lost in the latest blog post, or watch a hundred movie trailers on YouTube. This life had nothing to it that they'd have said mattered, but to be together and survive was oddly, and unexpectedly, freeing.

"I miss Jon Stewart," Mia sighed, tugging him over to the sofa. She flopped and pulled him down next to her so she could stick her cold feet under his thigh.

Andrew tried not to flinch. It was unbelievable how cold she became, even with socks on. "That's a non sequitur."

"Not really," she mused, taking his hand.

Her fingers were frozen. Sighing, he started rubbing them. "How can you be so cold?"

"It's a gift," she retorted, shrugging. "I want to watch The Daily Show again. I hope he survived all of this."

"He probably didn't if he was in New York," Andrew said heavily, his hands slowing as he felt hers thawing out. "The cities were probably the worst hit."

"You're depressing."

"I'm realistic," he said. He pulled her over to his side as he stared unseeing at one of the kitchen chairs. "The cities have the most concentration of people. We know violence has erupted in some places, so it stands to reason that it's fairly widespread, especially because there isn't likely to be any form of effective government or law enforcement in place."

Mia shook her head. "The cops in New York have police horses. They'd still be able to get around."

"That's a thought. But with no way to communicate, it makes everything a lot more dangerous. A mob could overpower the lone cop and take the horse, either to ride or to eat."

"Okay, that's just gross. This is why I want Jon Stewart. He'd have made the end of the world bearable by making us laugh about it."

"But in our here and now we don't need him," Andrew said thoughtfully, absently rubbing her arm. "A good bit of what he was poking fun at was the idiocy of the system and the people who ran it. They're either dead or out of power, and the system is so far broken that it won't be fixed for years."

"What if they try to put it back the same way?" she asked. "I wish we could stop it from ending up like that again."

"That's what your dad is going to try to do," he told her. "He didn't say as much, but I know that's his goal. He doesn't want it to go back the same way. As humans we want to live in cohesive units. We want to live peaceably, and to have order in our communities. Some outliers will always cause trouble, but for the most part we're a social animal that wants to live in a group. When the panic finally dies down people will start to form communities again, and they will establish their own order."

She tilted her head to the side and looked up at him. "Where on earth did you read that?"

"Honestly, I don't remember," he said grinning. "I've read so many books that they blend together and remembering names was never my strong suit. When I was about nine or ten... do you remember? Mom told me to pick what I wanted to learn next. The library turned into a playground and suddenly everything was open to me. What I couldn't find there, I found on the internet."

"I don't really remember, honestly," she told him, yawning. "It was so long ago and homeschooling just seemed so weird to what I was doing in school. I remember there was a lot of drama about who wasn't so-and-so's best friend anymore because she wore a purple shirt, too. I think we learned about Maryland when I was nine."

For Andrew, education had been a joy because he'd learned what he wanted and how he wanted to learn it. His mom had taken a lot of criticism for it. He'd heard people say that he was going to be a social reject, or that he was going to have holes in his education. There had been stunned silence for a few days after he'd been accepted into Johns Hopkins, then it had started again. This time it was whispers that he was too young for college, and he'd lost out on having a childhood.

It would have been laughable if it hadn't been frustrating. Andrew had had a great childhood. He'd played with friends, been on soccer teams, become an Eagle Scout and managed to get into trouble a few times. He'd debated politics with one of their local representatives when he'd visited the state capitol. He'd volunteered in a local soup kitchen once a week for over a year. He'd even managed to have a few girlfriends, plus a best friend who was one of the best people he'd ever known.

When it came to his life, Andrew was only sorry that he couldn't have done more to save more people even though he knew realistically that there wasn't anything he could have done. Selfishly, he was glad he was safe. He was glad Mia and Jilly were safe.

Andrew glanced down and saw that she'd fallen asleep. Grinning, he stood and pulled her up, leading her over to her room while she walked along like a zombie.

17

Jilly's reaction to the play kitchen was worth every hour, every splinter and every whack to the thumb with the hammer. First thing on waking, even before she ate breakfast, she toddled over and started pulling at the cabinets and drawers, discovering the little plastic bowls and spoons that Mia had stuck in it. She'd turned to him and pointed, beaming with delight.

Mia put her arms around him and kissed his cheek, and in her best southern drawl said, "You done good."

Andrew laughed, completely amused. "It's really cool that she likes it. Now we have to get her away to eat."

"Not yet," Mia said, tugging him back to the table. "She can have some fun, and we can eat in peace."

Their morning progressed like many other mornings except that Jilly spent well over an hour shoving every block that she had into the kitchen. They finally got her to eat, and then bundled up to go for a walk outside. Andrew put on his coat, and then put the back pack on. It was awkward with the bulk of the coats, but he was able to put Jilly on to his back with Mia's help.

Just to cap a beautiful Christmas day, there was a light dusting of snow on the ground. It was just enough to be pretty, and not so much that it soaked their shoes.

"It's beautiful," Mia sniffed. The tip of her nose was already turning red from the cold as they walked sedately into the forest along the familiar paths that Andrew took to set traps for rabbits. He didn't have any snares set at the moment, but he would set them again in a few days.

They weren't running low on meat, but having too much on hand was not a problem as long as there was freezer space.

Andrew reached out a gloved hand and snagged hers. If ever a day called for walking hand and hand it was this one. He felt lighter inside than he had in months. It seemed, although intellectually he knew it was an illusion, that nothing could touch them. Rationally he knew that they were only safe to walk around any distance from the shelter because it was cold and it was unlikely that anyone would be out. Also by the time the afternoon had arrived, the temperature would raise enough to melt what snow there was, thus erasing the evidence of their trek through the trees. He didn't voice any of this to Mia. She'd humor him and listen, then tell him he thought too much.

He did think a lot. Andrew had been given literature at a young age that most wouldn't have picked up before college. It had made him think. Mia's comment wouldn't be a criticism, though. It would be a gentle nudge to remember to enjoy the moment for what it was, and that not everything had to be thought through.

Yes, nerd that he was, Andrew sometimes overthought not thinking about things.

"Stop," Mia said, half exasperated. "I can hear you thinking over here."

He grinned down at her, and leaned in to kiss her. He still had no idea why he was doing that. He didn't like Mia that way, but it was something that he did, and for once in his life he didn't want to overthink it. He enjoyed it too much and overthinking would ruin it. "You know me so well."

"That I do," she agreed. She shivered a bit, and tugged on his hand. "Let's walk a little faster so I don't freeze."

"How's Jilly doing?" Andrew asked her, turning slightly so she could see her sister.

Mia laughed. "She's just staring around at everything. "I think she's warm enough. She's in that snow suit, and she's got your body heat keeping her toasty."

They moved along at a good clip for about twenty minutes before turning around and heading back. By the time they reached the shelter's hatch, Jilly's head was starting to nod.

Unbundling from the snow and cold was a chore in itself, but when adding in a baby the tasks seemed multiplied by ten. He'd never figured out how one little person could add so much work to every task, but she definitely did.

Mia fed Jilly some soup before she put her in bed for a nap. "What should we do this afternoon?" she asked him.

"Nothing," he told her as he reclined back into the sofa. "I want to do nothing."

He saw her glance at the pile of laundry that still needed to be washed before resolution stole over her, and she went to sit with him on the couch. "I guess nothing works."

"It's Christmas, and the laundry can wait till tomorrow. I'll help you wash it."

They settled in together in a comfortable silence. They were the type of old friends so used to each other that words weren't really needed, but Andrew had been giving it a lot of thought, and he knew what he wanted to give Mia for Christmas. His family had always been big on communicating and expressing their feelings. Things were never bottled up. Grievances were aired in family meetings, and almost every night they'd spent time together discussing what had happened that day. He'd heard all his life the words of love, praise, acceptance and guidance that his parents had for each other and for him. His mom had told them that they wanted to model that behavior for him so that he'd know how to do that when he was in a relationship. It hadn't worked quite like that. Andrew hadn't ever known what to say except, 'I like you' and girls never seemed to find that sufficient. But Mia wasn't just a girl. He'd skipped rocks with her for hours, braided her hair for her once- even though he was terrible at it- when she'd sprained her wrist, and laughed until they'd hurt over jokes that only the two of them shared. He could tell her anything.

"Do you know what I love about you?" Andrew asked her. He took her hand and threaded their fingers together.

"How I cook?" she teased, laughing a bit.

He grinned but shook his head. "Nope, what I love is that with you I get to be exactly me and there is no pressure. You accept me exactly as I am."

Her voice was soft as she spoke. "I'm glad you feel that way. I do love you as you are. We're opposites in a lot of ways, but we seem to mesh well."

"I also love the fact that you love to have fun and be silly," he said. "I have a hard time letting go and you help me do that, and help me laugh at myself."

This time she didn't comment, so he plowed on.

"I really love how smart you are and how much you love to learn. I love the fact that we each have different interests, and I get to learn from you, and you learn from me. We don't get bored talking to each other because there's always something new I didn't know." Still she didn't speak, and he had one more thing to tell her. "What I love most about you is just how big of a heart you have. That boy you asked to the dance..." he paused, struggling to find the right words to tell her just what that said about her. "Mia, there are so many girls, especially ones as pretty as you are, who would have just turned away from him and left him to be miserable. You see into people's hearts and see the goodness and the person behind the exterior and you have compassion for them along with genuine fondness. I admire that more than I can say."

Andrew relaxed fully. He hadn't realized he'd been tense as he said it, but he'd wanted to get it right. He'd spent a lot of the previous night planning it out... because he thought through things too much.

When she didn't say anything, he started to panic.

Mia tipped her face up and tears were running freely down her cheeks. He pulled her in close and hugged her. "Don't cry!"

"It's g-good tears," she hiccupped. "Thank you. That was really nice." Mia fished a handkerchief from her pocket and blew her nose. "I don't even know what to say to that."

"You don't have to say anything," he assured her, and he was thankful at least that he hadn't upset her. "That's my Christmas gift to you."

"Definitely better than cashmere," she murmured into his shoulder.

"You never did tell me what that was," Andrew pointed out.

Mia let out a watery giggle. "It's goat's hair."

He frowned while trying to picture it. "Why on earth would you want to wear goat's hair?"

"Well, when it's spun correctly, it can be very soft," she explained. "A lot of women like it."

"I wonder if it still smells like a goat," he murmured, scratching his chin in thought. "I can't imagine it would or no one would like it. But that sounds a lot like wearing mink, which is popular, and I've heard those can start to stink if they get wet."

Mia sighed dramatically. "You are such a boy."

"Thank you," he chuckled.

"Really..." she said hesitantly. "Thank you for what you said. It was really nice to hear."

"You're welcome, and it's the truth," he promised her. He squeezed her hand gently as the hushed noises of the shelter wafted around them. Andrew wished again that his parents were there, but at least he knew they were safe. Or they were probably safe. He prayed a silent prayer that they were to a God that he didn't know existed, and he hadn't yet made up his made if he wanted God to exist or not. On most days he did want God to be there, and with the world the way it was right now, he thought it might be a good idea because surely only God could pull them out of a mess this big.

Humans were bound to screw it up. Again. But if God did exist, then he'd let everything fall apart. That thought wasn't exactly comforting either. He was left with a lot of questions and almost no answers, and that was not typically how things went for Andrew. Usually he had the answers, or he could find them. This was the conundrum that he kept coming back to. He had no scientific proof that God existed, and no proof that God didn't exist.

Everything with his faith was as clear as mud. He doubted he'd ever know exactly where he stood with it and he was coming to accept it, albeit somewhat grudgingly. Some things were just going to stay unknown.

"Stop thinking so much," Mia said, poking him in the ribs. "It's making my head hurt."

Andrew rolled his eyes good-naturedly. She knew him too well.

~*~ ~*~ ~*~

"I'm fine!" Andrew grumbled as he hobbled over to the couch with his arm around her shoulder. He sank carefully onto it, grateful that he didn't have to move any further. Getting down the steps back into the shelter had been hell enough. New Year's Eve had arrived along with an ice storm that had knocked over the solar panels and clogged the ventilation hole with icicles. Thankfully he'd repositioned the panels and scraped off the vent before he'd slipped and banged his knee hard on a rock.

Blinding pain had shot through him, jarring every bone in his body until he'd been unable to breathe. It had taken him fifteen minutes to get back to the shelter and Mia's help to get him down the stairs. He'd nearly knocked her over twice before she'd told him to sit on his butt and scoot down the steps.

He watched Mia fill a bag with ice and wrap it in a towel. Briskly she walked over, stuck it on his knee, and then went into his room. He heard her rummaging for something, but as he leaned back against a cushion he wasn't sure he really cared what it was. His knee was on fire.

"Dada," Jilly said quietly somewhere to his left.

He looked down to see her anxious little face looking up at him. Andrew tried to smile, but it came out as a grimace. Tears filled her eyes as he reached down and pulled her onto his chest. Jilly cuddled her face into his neck, her breath tickling him. He tightened his arms around her and willed his mind away from his throbbing knee. If he'd broken it or torn something, he was screwed. Beyond screwed.

Mia emerged from his room with a book and a small box. She set them on the floor next to him and pulled the ice off. Gingerly she began to work his jeans up his leg. It was agony. Pain licked like fire radiating out from his knee.

"I'm trying to be gentle," she said soothingly.

"I know," he said through gritted teeth. Andrew tightened his grip on Jilly for a second before forcing himself to relax.

Jilly started to squirm, and using only his upper body, he lifted her over and down onto the floor. Immediately she went for the little box, but Mia deftly snatched it and handed it to him to keep out of her reach before going back to working on his pants.

Andrew looked down at the box in his hands and groaned. They were the acupuncture needles. "This isn't necessary."

"Thankfully you can't walk away, so you're in my clutches and I can do whatever I want," Mia said, trying for a bit of levity. "We're going to try this. It won't hurt."

He doubted that. "They're needles, Mia! Needles hurt. That's what they're for, to cause pain."

"Don't be a baby," she sighed as she pushed his pants up above his knee. It was already swollen and discolored. "It's a good thing you're skinny and I can get these up so far. Getting you out of these pants right now would be horrible." Mia blew out a slow breath. "You really did a number on it."

Andrew closed his eyes and let his head fall back. "I hate ice."

"You were always crap at ice skating," she mused.

He heard her start to flip through the book, but didn't bother to look up. He didn't want to watch her stick needles into him, and he knew that arguing with her would be pointless. "You don't know what you're doing."

"I kind of know what I'm doing, but frankly we've got no other options," she said grimly. "If we don't do something you could be laid up for weeks. Anyway, what would your mom say?"

"She'd laugh that I was letting you stick needles in me," he grumbled, but finally grinned reluctantly. "She does love acupuncture."

Mia laughed softly. "Joyce was the one who got me into acupuncture when my allergies started to get bad. It's just funny that a surgeon's kid is afraid of needles."

"I am not afraid of them," Andrew muttered. "I just have a healthy respect for them. Anyway, she's not a surgeon anymore."

"No, but she's probably going to be working as a doctor again," she said as she started to carefully poke at his skin. "I can't get to the exact spots because it's swollen, so I have to guess a bit."

"That's just great."

She took the box from his hands, and he assumed she's pulled a needle out, because she stuck the box back on his stomach. "Take a deep breath and blow it out slowly."

He did as she asked and winced slightly at the small sting as it went into his knee. It lasted only a second, before it faded. "That wasn't too bad."

"I told you so," she said, getting another needle. "Two more."

Less than a minute later she had the three needles in his knee. Andrew cracked an eye and looked down at them. The needles disturbed him less than the color his knee was turning. "I really hope it's just a bruise."

"Me too," she said anxiously. "I'm leaving them in for fifteen minutes, and then we'll take them out and ice it again for another ten. We'll try the needles again tomorrow, too."

The fifteen minutes crawled along, and the only excitement was Mia having to save the needles from a very curious Jilly and her amazing pincer-like fingers.

By the time she pulled the needles out, the pain had lessened enough so that he wasn't ready to scream anymore. Mia stuck the ice back on and went to soak the reusable needles in a bit of alcohol. "The battery warning lights are starting to flash. Should I kill most of the power and start a fire?"

Since he couldn't get up to do anything about it, and they had to wait for the batteries to recharge now that the solar panels were ice free, Andrew didn't see another option. "Yeah, that would be good. Do you remember where the kill switches are for the other room?"

"Yes," she said, walking out into the storage room.

Andrew watched her go, and he was really thankful that he'd shown her how to do all of this stuff weeks before. He was awake and could walk her through the steps, but if something happened to him, he wanted her to know how to do it on her own. It was just a stupid fall, one tiny misstep and he was unable to get up or care for himself. It would be really easy to make another stupid mistake, and she'd be here with just Jilly. He heard her flip switches, and when she came back in, she firmly closed the door behind her. Mia turned off all the lights but one before climbing over the chairs that still kept Jilly from getting to the stove.

He looked over the back of the couch and watched her unscrew and then remove the air filtration. She set it off to the side and hoisted up the metal tube that would vent out the smoke, fitting it in place. She clamped it to the stove before maneuvering the other end up to the vent shaft. "I hate this clamp," she told him, not for the first time, as she pushed on it. He watched her lean all her weight on the ratchet that would hold it tight before it finally snapped down in place. If it weren't so far above her head she'd likely have been able to do it easier, but it was up at about six feet from the floor, so she was working well above her eye level. Mia swiped at the sweat on her brow before kneeling to light the kindling.

Andrew had taken to keeping the stove stocked all the time with wood so that if they needed to light it, it could be done in a matter of minutes. Moments later, the flame from the lighter caught and warmth began to waft from the small potbellied stove.

"You're getting better at it," he told her.

Mia shrugged but looked pleased with herself. "I still feel like a wimp when I put that stupid vent on."

"It's hard to do," he said trying to reassure her. "You can do this, though."

She came around and pulled a chair over to sit next to him. Her eyes glimmered with an emotion that he couldn't name. The blue of her iris looked so dark, like the sea during a storm. "I don't want to do this without you."

"Believe me," he said quickly, "I don't want to do this without you either, but you can if you have to."

She scrunched up her nose, which looked pretty adorable, as she glanced away. Mia looked so much like Jilly when she did it, and he grinned despite himself and the pain he was in. "I guess it's important that I can do this myself," she said finally. Andrew heard the reluctance in her voice. "A few months ago I'd have thought that I couldn't, but you always knew you could do this alone."

He shook his head. "Just because I can do this alone doesn't mean I want to, and we'd starve after three years. Every time I try to grow anything it dies to spite me. The best I can do is dig holes for you and weed. Even then, half the time I pull up the wrong thing."

She bit her lip, as she glanced back at him. "I guess that's true. You need to pay more attention this spring as we do the planting."

"I will," he promised, even though it made his gut clench in a very painful way to think of having to do it without her. "I'll get it right this time. But I hope that I don't need to know."

She nodded and stood. "I'll get dinner going. I think we'll do MRE's so we don't have to use the oven. Hopefully we won't have to sleep out here."

Andrew glanced back to the stove which was pumping heat into the room. He couldn't imagine having to move so that they could pull out the sofa bed. Stupid ice.

18

Early January

Andrew wasn't able to walk without Mia's help, or using a make shift crutch, for almost a week after he hurt himself. Acupuncture did seem to be helping, but it wasn't a miracle cure. Between that and the bags of ice, the swelling was gone after a day, but the pain was still really bad. Mia wrapped it in an ace bandage to see if it would help, but the pressure only made it feel worse, so they'd decided just to let it rest. By day three, he was ready to tear his hair out. He hated being inactive and watching Mia do everything was excruciating. She'd had to go and clear ice again, but she'd attached ice cleats to her shoes before she went out on to the slippery ground. They were too big for her shoes, but she'd said they worked okay. It took Mia longer to get everything de-iced, but she'd managed well enough.

It wasn't that she wasn't coping, but between the cooking, cleaning, laundry, caring for Jilly, keeping the stove going, and the shelter running, by the end of the week Mia was worn out. There were bags under her eyes, and she seemed to drag through everything. Andrew hadn't realized just how much the work load was shared until it was just her doing it. The evenings free to talk, read or play games were no longer possible, and Mia often worked through until eleven before she passed out from exhaustion.

He tried to push himself to walk, but his leg shook badly, and the pain returned almost immediately when he tried. Mia found a fallen tree branch that was tall enough for him to stick under his armpit to hobble around. With this method, at least she didn't have to walk him to the bathroom anymore. All of this combined to make him broody and cranky. He was doing his best to keep it under wraps by letting his mind wander, and to think some things through that had been bothering him for months. At home if he was laid up, he'd have books to read or the internet to troll. There were things to learn and do, or distractions that could be found. Andrew had read almost every book that was stocked in the shelter, and there was no possible way of getting to a library or buying from Amazon or going to a local book store and losing himself for hours in the shelves of new books.

Andrew hadn't truly appreciated just what being cut off from the rest of the world would be like, especially if he couldn't walk. He couldn't help but think through all the twists and turns that had led him to this shelter in the middle of Pennsylvania when by rights he could be dead just then.

He'd been born to parents who lived next to a couple who worked at the Pentagon doing God only knew what. Joyce and Paul Greene had become good friends with Diane and Scott Harper. Diane had given birth to a daughter when Andrew was eighteen months old, and the two kids had grown up together, clicking in a way that people rarely do, especially so young. Scott had taken an interest in him and had shown him basic survival techniques, plus taught him how to use a gun. At some point, and for reasons that Scott hadn't shared, he'd decided that Mia needed Andrew with her up at the shelter. Andrew knew the reason why now. By herself, Mia probably would have been just fine running everything. Even now she was coping, but the added strain of a toddler meant that everything was twice as difficult as it otherwise would have been. Looking at it objectively, this was a two-person job.

Andrew had been encouraged to think critically from as early as he could remember, and when pissed or bored, he coped by looking for patterns. He always had. Part of being homeschooled was learning to educate oneself and to do that effectively, one had to look analytically at everything to decide if a source was worth studying. It was a goal that his mom had drilled into him from as early as he could remember. She taught him to read and to write. She'd helped him learn to count, and she'd held his hand for the first few years of schooling, but gradually she started to push him out to find the answers for himself, and to question where those answers had come from. He could still clearly hear his mom ask him, "Is there another side to that story? Is that fact or opinion? How can you tell? Can you prove it?" His mom, although brilliant and certainly capable of teaching him, didn't call herself a teacher. "I'm the facilitator, Andrew. I gave you the basics, now I'm the wallet and your cab driver."

After he'd figured out the basics and mastered how to find the real answers, or the best he could find, Andrew had started to follow his passions. Sometimes that got him in trouble. One of his first professors had not taken kindly to Andrew showing up in that second story classroom at Hopkins. He'd walked into class, a skinny kid with a backpack that nearly weighed more than he did, to find a large, graying man with miniscule wireless glasses. The professor, and Andrew couldn't now remember what his name had been, had taken one look at him and told him the elementary school was down the block. Andrew hadn't known what to say, so he'd taken a seat and waited for class to begin. The man had started lecturing on what they'd be covering that semester and handing out the syllabus. He'd then begun to write out Maxwell's equations on the board and had told the class to call out what they were.

Andrew had answered first, his voice cracking a bit because of nerves and because he was thirteen, so a cracking voice was par for the course. Every eye had swiveled towards him, making his cheeks burn. The professor had turned slowly on the balls of his feet to face him, his expression pinched. "Are you one of those obnoxious know-it-all geniuses?"

"No, I'm not a genius," Andrew had answered as politely as he could because he wasn't a genius, and he only understood the basics of the equation. "I'm just interested in light."

The professor stared for a moment before grunting and turning back to the board. He'd wiped out the equation with the back of his hand and went on to something else. That professor hadn't ever warmed up to him, but he'd at least stopped antagonizing him. Andrew came to class prepared. He always had his homework done, and he was always caught up on reading. He debated and argued when needed. He had his own ideas, and sometimes he was flat out wrong. He'd loved college.

With a pang, Andrew was snapped back to his present reality, one where Mia was cooking something that smelled good, and he was stuck on the couch unable to walk or help. He didn't get to finish college, and he regretted now that he hadn't pushed himself harder in his first two years. He, and his advisors, had advocated hard for him taking the minimum course load to be considered full time so that he could adjust. Andrew had agreed, mostly because his parents had been all for it. Now he couldn't go back and redo it, finishing in the normal four years rather than five. All of this was stupid, of course, because a degree was basically a worthless piece of paper in their current reality.

Pity party, table for one. He knew he was feeling sorry for himself, and he couldn't seem to stop.

He'd been planning on taking up an internship that he'd been accepted to at a local engineering firm. It was a dream that he had to let go, and most of the time he assumed that he had. However, sometimes it climbed back out of the swamp to torment him, a dead dream that looked exactly like it had wandered off the set of The Walking Dead. Season Five, not Season One. His zombie was gaunt from hunger, and his skin was falling away from its bones.

Andrew shook his head. He was going on a mental tangent trying to distract himself, and it wasn't working well.

Thoughts about Mia's dad, Scott, circled in his brain as he tried to fall asleep most nights. Scott had to have known, at least twelve hours out, that the CME was coming, but he wouldn't admit to it when he'd been there. Scott could have predicted, although maybe not this accurately, how widespread the damage was going to be. No announcements made the news. No airplanes had been diverted. No one, except the very high up in the government, had had any clue as to what was coming so no one had been able to prepare.

He could see several plausible scenarios for why it would be kept quiet. The government could have believed that the effects weren't going to be as severe as predicted and didn't want to cause a panic. They would prepare for the worst and hope for the best. Or they may have discovered too late to effectively implement any meaningful changes that would save people's lives. But the theory that was currently winning in his mind left a bitter taste in Andrew's mouth. The government knew it was coming. They intentionally silenced all of the scientists who would have been able to observe the flares coming. They'd hid it from the public because there was nothing that could be done to stop it, and prepared to save themselves and as much of the main government as possible. They'd let planes fall from the sky, cars crash, and people on life support in the hospitals die.

How they'd kept the scientific community from revealing what they must have seen through their telescopes, Andrew could only speculate. He didn't know exactly how many telescopes watched the sun, but he knew that it had to be a decent number. Somehow, they'd been kept quiet.

Then there were foreign governments and scientists all over the world who had to have seen what was coming. Andrew could well imagine that a couple of countries would be only too happy to see the United States wiped off the map, but others had to know. The scale of the cover up was colossal, and he was starting to think that part of the cover up was the reason that people might want to get to Scott and Diane. He didn't know precisely how Diane was involved. He didn't know exactly what she did, but when asked, she claimed to work with computers. Mia's mom was funny, much like Mia herself, but she was also brilliant in an absentminded professor sort of way. What, if any, role had she played in this?

How many people had died because they'd kept the secret?

Mia's voice jarred him from his musings, derailing his train of thought. "Are you ready to eat?"

"No," he snapped before he'd even had time to think it through.

Mia let out a low whistle through her teeth and crossed her arms, her eyebrow raised.

"I'm sorry," Andrew said letting his head thud back into the couch cushion. "I'm in a crappy mood."

"Okay," she said. She turned and went back to the stove and dished up a plate for herself and for Jilly. Mia snagged the toddler as she walked by chanting something in baby-eeze and stuck her in her high chair.

Annoyed with himself, Andrew grabbed his makeshift crutch and pushed himself up to his feet so he could walk over to the table. Mia watched him, standing rigidly by his chair, ready to help him sit down. He didn't sit, though. Instead, he awkwardly put his arms around her tense form and pulled her to him as close as he could. Slowly she relaxed, wrapped her arms around him as well. It was half a hug, and half holding him upright. "I'm sorry, Mia. I'm frustrated with myself, and that's got nothing to do with you. I shouldn't have taken it out on you."

"Okay," Mia whispered against his chest. She withdrew and helped him to sit before going to get him a plate.

Later that night, after he'd hobbled off to his bed, and the shelter was dark and silent, Andrew's thoughts turned back to all that had to go into fooling the world. In the age of the internet, that was nearly impossible to do. He'd not even heard that the sun was getting more active again, and he regularly checked the headlines of most major news sources online.

Andrew had, for the most part, accepted that there was part of the government that operated without the public's knowledge. He understood that certain things would need to be done in secret. He might not like it, but he understood. It wasn't a black or white situation where there was an absolute right or wrong. If the public knew where all of the troops were and what they were doing, then the enemy would know, too. If the opposition had spies, then they had to have spies. If the public knew everything that the police were investigating, then the criminals would also know. He found most of that to be common sense. Some things were blatant, and everyone knew they were wrong, even as everyone felt powerless to stop it.

The most obvious corruption was with money. Congressmen spent most of their time campaigning and raising money. Because millions needed to be raised and spent to get elected, it meant that either one must be independently wealthy to run, or they had to raise enough cash from the wealthy to get to Congress. This then ended up with a vicious cycle. If one followed the money, then one could find the power, and the wealthy pulled the strings. Bills would end up going through

Congress with ridiculous addendums that had nothing to do with the original bill, but it would be necessary to ensure that it was passed. The Supreme Court had even declared that corporations were people, as far as campaign contributions were concerned. Andrew had lost pretty much any respect he'd held for the Court after that, even though he'd read through the transcripts of the debates and understood their reasons for making the decision. Understanding did not mean acceptance, and their justifications had been weak. Just thinking about it was enough to make his blood boil. He'd spent way too much time wondering just whom had financed that ruling.

In the last few years, Congress hadn't accomplished much. What they had accomplished was pretty useless, but they did succeed in driving a wedge among the American people. It blew his mind that no one seemed to be able to change it. The president had run on a promise of change and nothing had come of it, although he knew that was as much Congress's fault as the president's. Blame was shared on all sides, and in order to change it, they would have to start working together. It was more likely that Mother Teresa was going to come back from the dead than that Congress would resolve their differences.

However, it wasn't just America that was struggling. Wars were being fought all over the world. People were starving everywhere. Countries were polluting faster than the earth could correct for. Those who screamed for change were either ignored or pushed off as the extreme fringe. He'd seen people freak out over Ebola the previous year, but then refuse to get a flu shot. People were more likely to die from the flu. For the record, he hadn't received a flu shot last year, but he also hadn't panicked about Ebola. Everyone's attention was fixated on the wrong issues, and the real ones were largely ignored. Andrew thought that maybe it was because everyone felt helpless to institute a change.

What they'd been left with was a planet that was quickly heating up and would soon be unable to sustain life. That might not have happened in Andrew's lifetime, but there was a good shot that it would. They were left with a government that, while functional, was also so weighed down in bureaucracy that it was unwieldy at best, and ineffective at worst. They were left with so much debt to China that if the loans were ever called, the United States would be screwed.

No one stood up and said, 'enough is enough' with any real authority or drive to actually make the change. He'd never said it either, although it had bothered him a lot. Andrew knew, because he'd read up on uprisings before, that in a true democracy the real power was in the people. America hadn't been a true democracy in a while, though. Too many things were set up to convince people that they didn't really have enough power to change anything, so they didn't even try. He'd talked to his peers and been told that they couldn't fight the government, and he felt like yelling that the entire government was started by a revolution.

He'd been called a Tea Partier, which had made him laugh. He'd not voted in any election. The world had been blown to bits before he could get to vote, but that wasn't the party he would have aligned himself with. Even they were started by a large corporation, though no one seemed to be aware of it.

Andrew didn't want to pick a party and stand hard on a party line. He didn't want to pick a dogma and refuse, point blank, to ever change in the future. He believed firmly that if he couldn't change his mind, maybe he didn't have a mind to change. Life was not static, and things always evolved and grew. He didn't want to have the mentality of a nineteen-year-old when he was thirty. He hoped like hell he'd have it more together by then. He'd even thought maybe he'd be married by then.

Mia's face popped into his mind, her smile and her laugh, and he grinned into the dark room. He'd talked all of these things out with her once. She'd thought about it for a bit and told him that if he wanted to start a revolution that she'd be his right hand man, but she didn't know how to go about it. Honestly, he hadn't known how to either. He could probably get his homeschooled friends on board because they'd have the time to go protest with him. Most of them had been down to the capitol in Annapolis, Maryland more than once to see how the state government worked. They'd even visited Congress in Washington D.C. a few years ago. He could get them to take a stand with him, but when he'd asked one of his soccer team mates what he'd thought about it, he'd said it so poignantly that Andrew could still hear his raspy voice.

"Man, they aren't ever going to change. We can't fight the system, so why try?"

When had it become about sitting back and accepting the status quo? When had worrying about illegal immigration or job growth been enough to stop any meaningful action to save the very planet they lived on? Why did it matter if someone lived in a red state or a blue state? How could people be so blind to the fact that they might have a job today with a big oil company, but it wasn't going to matter in a few years because the planet would be so warm that life would be unsustainable? It blew his mind that oil company CEO's were so cavalier about destroying the planet for their own children. As long as they made millions, who cared if their grandchildren starved to death?

Droughts were going to kill off all the crops in California. It was coming down the pipeline as surely as anything. Rising temperatures warmed climates up further and created deserts where there used to be forests. All of the people in southern California were going to have to migrate out because there wouldn't be enough water to keep everyone going. Food prices would sky rocket because of a large demand and low supply as California produced most of the produce in the country. People would starve at higher rates. Government programs would have to step in to feed the hungry, which would raise taxes on the middle class, who would also start to go hungry. No one would have any disposable income to buy anything but food, which meant that the economy would tank, and no one, except the super wealthy, would have any money to fix it. Even the super wealthy would lose out. Life, as they had known it, would be over, and that would have just been in the United States. That didn't take into account that whole entire island nations that would be swallowed by the rising sea levels.

But it hadn't happened that way. No one had tried to pull the power grids offline before the flares hit. It might not have saved the whole power structure, but there was a small chance that if they'd been offline, it wouldn't have blown out and fried the entire system. By doing that, they'd effectively hit the reset button on America. They'd wiped the slate clean. Things weren't perfect. Anarchy reigned in the streets and people were probably dying by the thousands because they no longer had the skills to survive, nor any way to feed themselves long term.

Someone had made the call to end the modern world this way. If he weren't so horrified by the results, Andrew would have been amazed that they'd pulled it off in complete secrecy. But they had killed what would probably add up to millions of people, and if China and India were still functioning, they'd only delayed the carbon emissions needed for extinction of most life on the planet by a few decades at most. Contrary to what most people believed, the world didn't have to warm up much for the coral reefs to die off, and for the oceans to become uninhabitable. Shortly thereafter, a lot of the animals would start to die. Humans would eventually follow.

"Andrew."

The whisper was low as the door swung open and then closed. He heard Mia's sweatshirt rustling as she moved over to the bed and climbed in with him.

"What's up?" he asked gently as he pulled her to his side.

She was careful to avoid his leg, and she curled up next to him. "Jilly's snoring and I could hear you muttering. Why aren't you sleeping?"

He debated on how to answer, but he'd promised her the truth. "I think your dad let the world end on purpose so that they could redo all of it."

"Oh," she squeaked. "Uhm... well... nothing too depressing."

"You don't sound surprised," he commented, running a hand up into her soft hair as he felt her body heat melding with his.

"I'm not," she said with a sigh. "I wish I was, but I'm not. Nothing surprises me anymore. It would explain why people might want to kill us, but that's only if they knew it was him, and he was not well known."

A yawn snuck out of Andrew's mouth before he could stop it. "Sorry. I can't believe you're still awake. You have to be exhausted."

"I am," Mia agreed. "I just couldn't get my mind to settle."

"Roll over and I'll rub your back," Andrew told her, nudging her side.

It was a mark of just how sore and tired she was that Mia didn't argue, and within a few minutes she'd fallen fast asleep.

19

Mid-January

"Push," Mia instructed as she held his injured leg up a bit, putting counter pressure on the knee.

Andrew tried to move her, but his knee was still weak from several weeks of lack of use. It was already the middle of January, and he was unable to walk without his crutch. He watched her from his prone position on the couch, trying to focus on her face and not the discomfort. His knee was improving, there was no doubt about it, but it was slow, painful work. Mia was, essentially, trying to give him physical therapy on top of everything else she had to do, and it was maddening to still not be able to do more than the most basic tasks around the shelter.

What was worse was that it had started to snow the day before, and it hadn't stopped yet. The last time Mia had gone out to clear the solar panels and the ventilation there had been nearly a foot of snow. With her short stature it had taken her almost two hours to get through the drifts and accomplish what needed to be done.

Unfortunately, Jilly's snoring had turned into a full blown cold. Except that it couldn't be a cold since they weren't exposed to other people. It hadn't taken long to figure out that it was allergies that were filling the baby's sinuses with mucus, and they'd realized that the ventilation system had needed a filter change. When they'd opened it up, it was to find mold growing in it. It was no wonder Jilly was struggling to breathe. After changing it, and chucking the old filter out into a snow bank to be dealt with in the spring, the shelter had started to dry out more efficiently. It was a combination of dehumidifier and air purifier, and it was a minor miracle it had lasted as long as it had.

"Okay, pull," Mia said, bringing him back to the present. She held gently onto his foot and created resistance so that he had to work harder than he cared to admit to retract his leg.

"I need to be done with this," Andrew grumbled, trying valiantly not to flinch from the combination of pain and weak muscles.

She changed her hand position to the flat of his foot and without speaking, he began to push against her again.

"Mama pweas," Jilly chirped happily, coming over to them with a book.

"Daddy can read it to you," Mia said and Jilly brought it to him.

She was nearly nineteen months old now, and the amount of words that she understood still managed to surprise Andrew. He wasn't sure what he'd expected, but it wasn't a child that could understand what they were saying when she was given simple commands.

Whether she followed those commands or not was a completely different story. Andrew took the book and flipped to the first page to read. He kept working with Mia, following the unspoken instructions of where she placed her hand on his foot as he glanced over the page. "Sally the caterpillar was sad. She wanted to be a-" Jilly flipped the page prematurely.

Andrew was used to this. She loved books, but she didn't always want to hear every word on every page. Without missing a beat he went on, even has he pushed against Mia's firm hand. "Sally's friend Bill told Sally-"

A warning beep sounded.

"Oh no," Mia groaned, putting his leg down on the couch. Instantly she went in to action, shutting down all the non-essential lights and anything else that drew power. Within minutes, she had the fire lit in the pot-bellied stove and was back at his foot, ready to continue with his therapy.

SHELTER

Andrew watched her move through everything, now so efficient that it hardly seemed like effort. She still looked exhausted, but there was a new toughness to her that he'd never really seen before. Mia had hit a challenge that was higher than any wall she'd ever had to climb. She'd been forced to work long, hard hours for weeks on end. She's been physically taxed to a point that she'd never been before, and she'd found herself capable of the task. It gave Mia's whole countenance an assurance and poise that she'd never had before, and to Andrew's surprise, it made her somehow more attractive to the point that sometimes he found himself just staring at her.

"Push," she told him, squeezing his foot gently, and Andrew realized he'd been doing it again, just staring at her lost in thought.

"Sorry," he said, grinning sheepishly. "I keep losing my train of thought."

This time she resisted more, and he felt the effort it took to repel her. "What can you possibly be thinking about that's so enthralling? Nothing around here is that interesting."

"You're that interesting," he assured her and chuckled when she blushed. "I'm so proud of you, Mia. You're doing a great job around here."

Her smile was transcendent in her obvious pleasure. "If only my mom could see me now."

"Your mom couldn't boil water and do laundry at the same time to save her life," Andrew laughed, remembering how distracted Diane would get if she was working at the computer. "I think that's how you got so good at cooking. You didn't want to starve."

Mia's mouth quirked a bit. "Mostly it was The Food Network that was responsible for me learning to cook, but it didn't hurt that Mom was all too happy to pawn the task off on me. Your dad always preferred cooking, right?"

"Yeah," he agreed. Jilly had lost interest in Sally the caterpillar and had wandered off to her play kitchen, so he set the book down on the floor.

He pulled his leg back slowly. "Mom would cook, though. Dad just liked the fancier meals when he had time to fix something."

"I miss Mom," Mia said, not looking up from his foot. "I miss her trailing off in the middle of a sentence as she wrote something down, even though it always drove me nuts."

"Your mom is way too smart," Andrew agreed. "She constantly had her head in her work."

Mia's expression was thoughtful, as they continued to work. "I keep wondering what her part was in all of this. I can't help but think that she couldn't have really had much to do with deciding the world was going to end. She stopped hackers."

Andrew had been thinking about that a lot, too. Her job, as best as they could work out from the limited amount that Diane would tell them, was to help maintain cyber security. It was never fully explained to them exactly what that entailed, but Andrew was starting to form an idea of how that could have been beneficial, although it was still only guesswork. "If they'd wanted to stop information leaking out on the CME, they'd had to have someone monitoring the internet and trying to stop the leaks. It didn't have to be for very long. They would have only had twenty four hours warning before the flares were going to hit, but it might have been enough to keep people from talking."

Mia's hand jumped a bit as she pushed. "I guess so. I don't really have any reason to think that she wouldn't have done it. I think... I think part of me hopes that they didn't want the world to end this way."

"It was going to end this way, though," he said quietly.

"You don't know that," she argued, sitting down at the edge of the couch and staring at him. "If we hadn't had all those guns then people wouldn't be able to kill each other."

"They'd have still killed each other," he said quietly. "They'd have done it with bats or knives. The system is not set up to function without a central authority. It used to be. The country was founded that way, but it wasn't sustainable long term. Now for the short term, people will fight it out to survive, and once the population has dropped to a level that is sustainable either because enough food can be produced, or because only the self-sufficient are left, then a new form of government and control will begin to emerge."

"You are so cynical," Mia grumbled, her lip trembling. "You don't know that."

It was what happened before. Sometimes, after a major crisis, if aid was provided quickly, then civilization was able to be maintained. When the resources were limited, it didn't turn out that way most of the time. People were greedy by nature and often only interested in how to keep their own families safe. He couldn't even blame them. Andrew was, right at that very moment, only safe because he was part of a family that had made the provisions. He was going to do his best to make sure that no one else took that away from them. He looked between Mia and Jilly and knew that he was exactly like everyone else; he wanted his family safe.

A week later, as the over two feet of snow finally began to melt, Andrew managed to walk alone without the crutch for the first time. He still took it easy, still didn't push himself too quickly, but he walked slowly around the shelter in a large circle over and over again in order to build up his strength. They were running out of wood for the stove, and they were nearly out of meat in the freezer. He needed to be back up and moving again shortly.

Mia had managed to cut a bit of wood by herself, but she couldn't keep up with their demand. As strong as she'd become, she still couldn't swing the axe for more than two hours before she was too stiff to move. Her dad hadn't planned on Mia being the one chopping wood and had supplied the shelter with a large, heavy duty axe. It was sturdy and likely wouldn't break for many years, which was something that Andrew appreciated. Unfortunately, it weighed about five pounds. That didn't sound like much until you had to swing it several hundred times. Then it became very heavy, very quickly.

Three days after regaining his ability to walk, Andrew was walking up and down the stairs dozens of times all through the day. He next moved on to squats and then to jogging lightly in place. Jilly thought the whole thing was funny. She'd taken to toddling along after him as he walked, trying to follow him up and down the stairs, but only making it up two steps before he was already on his way down again. When he started doing squats she'd climb onto his back and held on like a little monkey. This actually worked out nicely because she added weight and resistance. When he started to jog she would stand next to him and attempt to jump. She couldn't, though her attempts were really cute.

Jilly's absolute focus on Andrew meant that Mia was able to catch a break for the first time in weeks. He found her napping on his bed next to some unfolded clean laundry. He'd shut off the light and left her too it, and he and Jilly had used that time to wash the dirty diapers. It was a lot more complicated to dump the dirty water because of the snow, but Andrew pushed through it and hauled the water up the stairs after he'd put Jilly down for a nap.

The walk through the slushy snow was difficult and pressed his healing knee to its limits. He took several breaks as he walked the thirty feet to dump it down the embankment. On the way back, Andrew looked around at the barren trees. Only a few evergreens still had any color, and the world was a melding of browns and whites as the snow melted to mud at the base of all the tree trunks. The air smelled crisp and new, just as it had back home in Maryland when the world was covered in a blanket of white. He'd missed going out in to the fresh air. The shelter was equal parts haven and prison. Sometime the line was so blurred that it was difficult to decide what it was at that moment. How a place could be so convoluted in his mind, he didn't really know and didn't try to separate them. Down that path was nothing productive.

Andrew walked slowly back to the shelter, moving gingerly down into the depths and closing the latch behind him. He didn't need to slip.

He took it easy that night after Mia scolded him for overdoing it, but by the next morning most of his pain was gone. He awoke early, something he'd never really managed before without being cranky, and stretched his leg. Andrew didn't even wince as he rolled to the edge of the bed. Tentatively he stood, and his leg held without shaking. He dressed, managed to tie both of his shoes without any assistance and went to dig up breakfast.

Remarkably, Mia and Jilly were still asleep, so he ate quickly, threw on his coat and grabbed the axe. There was a pile of wood with his name on it, and he wanted to escape before Mia could stop him.

By lunchtime that day, Andrew had cut enough wood to get them through another few weeks of cold weather if the solar panels weren't able to charge the shelter's batteries. By the time he'd hauled the last load of wood down into the shelter Mia was glaring at him.

"I can't believe you just did that," she growled, her arms crossed. "You couldn't walk a week ago."

Technically he could, but he wasn't going to argue the minutiae. He shrugged off his coat and hung it on the hook. "I'm fine."

"But what if you hadn't been, hm?" She asked, tapping her foot.

Andrew walked over to her, his knee aching only slightly from the long workout. He hooked his arms around her waist and hauled her up until she was at eye level. It wasn't as easy as it would have been a few weeks ago, but he kept her still as she squeaked in protest and amusement. His eyes felt caught in hers and he couldn't look away as he leaned in and kissed her gently.

Mia tentatively wrapped her arms around his neck and kissed him back. They broke apart a moment later. They watched each other and neither knew what to say. Slowly he let her slide back to the floor and he took a step back. "I'm fine, Mia, and it's time I start pulling my own weight again."

She didn't contradict him, or say anything about it as they ate lunch. They were back to eating mostly vegan meals in order to ration what meat they had left.

"I'm going hunting," Andrew told her as he rinsed off his plate.

"Okay," she said lightly, not meeting his gaze.

He turned to her, and he wanted to say something about the kiss. Something had felt a little different. It wasn't like anything he'd ever experienced before, although that wasn't a bad thing. It was just... he didn't have the words to explain it. He stuck his hands in his pocket, feeling uneasy. "Are you okay?"

"Yep," she said in a clipped voice.

"Mia..." he faltered. "Was that kiss weird for you?"

She glanced once at him before looking quickly away, "Nope."

Andrew reached out a hand, but let it drop. He didn't know what to say or do just then, and she clearly didn't want to discuss it. "I'm taking the crossbow to practice."

"Take the rifle, too," she told him, still not meeting his eyes.

"I will, along with the pepper spray," he promised. Turning, he went to grab all of his gear along with the crossbow and made his way out of the shelter. He had the rifle strap slung over his back and the crossbow in his hand along with a few extra arrows in a small quiver. It was a lot of things to carry, but if he was able to get proficient at the bow, they wouldn't waste bullets, and the meat would be a little easier to clean.

Andrew had a few trails that he knew the deer often frequented, and he'd managed to make a few hiding places in the vegetation for himself. He made his way carefully up to the first one he'd created only to find that it had collapsed sometime in the last few weeks, probably from the weight of the snow. He set down his gear and began the tedious task of reconstructing the blind. Most of the pieces were still there, and he was able to reuse them and set it back up. Standing back, he took a look around and saw that almost nothing was moving out in the semi-frozen land.

He continued on to his next blind and found it in a similar state of disrepair. By the time the sun was falling into the western sky, he'd fixed his blinds and he'd strung up four snares to try to trap more rabbits. He didn't know if they would be moving about, but having the snares meant that he was prepared if they did.

By the time he made his way back to the shelter he was ready for Mia to stick food in front of him, and maybe sit with an ice pack on his knee. It wasn't until he'd dumped his muddy boots in the storage room and walked into the kitchen that he remembered that their parting had been awkward and a bit tense.

Andrew heard his soccer coach's voice boom in his brain as a memory flashed in his mind. The best offence was a good defense. He strode confidently over to her and kissed her cheek nosily, making her grin despite herself. "What's cookin' good lookin'?"

Mia's stern gaze was ruined when she started giggling. "Any luck hunting?"

"Not really," he told her as he went to wash his hands. The pressure between them had dissipated and although he couldn't really pinpoint it, it felt like things were back to normal, which was just how he wanted it. "I ended up doing repairs on the blinds, and setting up a few snares. We may have some rabbit again shortly, but I'll probably spend a lot of time out looking for a deer. We really need that much meat to get through the next few months."

Mia nodded and passed him plates to set the table. "I couldn't believe we ran out so quickly. I didn't even cook meat every night, but it still went so fast."

"It's been a few months already," Andrew reminded her as he set out forks. "We've been here for about five months now."

She shook her head. "I still can't believe it's been that long. Time doesn't seem to be flying like it did at home, but it still seems like we were just driving up here yesterday."

"We've managed this long with only seeing a few people," Andrew mused as he took the pot she handed him and set it on the table. He sat across from her, watching her contemplatively. "I don't think your parents could have picked a better spot for us to hide. This is remote enough that we haven't really been found, but not so remote that it was impossible to get here in a short time."

She chewed thoughtfully on her rice and beans. "We're going to have to start planting soon. It depends on when the snow stops, but I'm thinking towards the end of February."

Andrew nodded, and then glanced at the closed bedroom door. "Is Jilly still asleep?"

"Yeah, I just checked on her," she said. "I decided to let us eat in peace before waking her up. She might be going through a growth spurt or something. Her pants are getting a little short."

He took another bite and chewed thoughtfully. "It won't be long before she's two and you'll be eighteen."

"Is it weird that I don't feel seventeen anymore?" Mia asked, pushing the pot over to him. He took the hint and dished more onto his plate. It was difficult to get full on rice and beans, and he'd burned a lot of calories that day.

"I don't think it's all that weird," he said with a snort. "You're functioning like an adult here."

"I guess," she said absently, pushing the food around on her plate. "What I had to do at home was stuff for myself. I didn't really have to think about anything but me, and it was easy to lose sight of the big picture. I didn't have to pay any bills, and I only had to babysit sometimes, but I always got paid for that. I think..." she paused, flicking her gaze up to his. "I think I like the new me better. I respect myself more now."

Andrew reached across the table and took her hand. "I loved you before, but I love the new you, too. You are turning into an amazing woman."

Mia's cheeks went bright red. "I'm not going to call you a man until you can remember to shave every day."

He raised his hand to his chin and felt the stubble that was liberally coating his cheeks. "Touché."

20

Mid-February

By the middle of February they were getting desperate for a deer. Andrew had managed to trap a couple of rabbits, and they had made that stretch, but they were completely out of venison. He was now spending most of his days out in the woods trying to track deer. He'd seen a few tracks, but had only seen one small doe that wouldn't have even fed them for a few weeks. It wasn't worth killing her when they had other ways of feeding themselves.

In desperation, Andrew decided to move up to the Appalachian Trail. It was a long haul back to the shelter, and he risked being seen, but if he got a deer, it would be worth the backbreaking work to get it back to the shelter. It would also allow him to watch for traffic and to see if anyone was already moving along the trail now that the weather was starting to warm again. He took up his position in his blind near the trail at just before dawn. It was still bitingly cold, and he had to breathe into his scarf to hide the plumes of steam that issued from his mouth at every breath. He settled in, the crossbow in his gloved hands, and prepared to wait.

He waited in the cramped space for several hours without seeing anything. He'd nearly decided to emerge and go back for lunch when a faint voice floated over to him. Andrew tilted his head a bit to the side, trying to hear where it was coming from.

"Shut up," a man's deep voice growled.

It was distinct now, and coming from the south along the trail to his left. Andrew couldn't see anything, even though he was only a few feet from the trail. He'd intentionally hid himself so that he could hear but not be seen. He could only watch for deer that were walking down from his position near the trail.

"Okay fearless leader, am shutting up so you can think of another brilliant plan." This time it was a woman's voice, harsh but brittle. Andrew could hear the anger, hear her condemnation.

Louder, the man's voice barked out, so close to him now that he had to force himself not to move. "The fuck have I told you about the back talk?"

Instantly, the woman snapped back dripping with sarcasm. "Oh, that's right! I should be making you a sandwich. Too bad you're such a pussy I don't have anything to make a sandwich with."

The sound of the blow was so visceral that Andrew almost felt it, rather than just hearing it. The woman screamed, "Just like a coward!"

But it was cut short by another loud blow. Then another, and another. Her screams, which had pierced the cold, still air rapidly faded to pitiful moans in just seconds as the hits fell rapidly. Andrew felt sick just listening to it.

He couldn't stay hidden, yet he couldn't risk Mia and Jilly. As silently as he could, his heart pounding in his throat he rose to his feet and saw the large man wailing on a small, dark haired woman. She was curled in the fetal position on the snow-covered ground as he kicked viciously at her.

He didn't stop to think it through. He raised the crossbow and fired straight at the man's back. The hulking guy staggered away as Andrew moved rapidly to intercept him. He was afraid he was going to have to fire again, but the close range shot was enough to send the arrow all the way through, and he could see the point of it sticking out of the front, right where his heart and lungs were located. The man's scruffy face was blank with shock, as he stumbled back once before falling to the ground near the edge of the trail. As he fell back, he landed awkwardly on the arrow and it forced it even further out the front of his chest.

Andrew felt the bile try to spew from his gut. He'd just killed a man.

He'd just killed a man. Numbness paralyzed him as he stared down at the man's face, his brown eyes full of hate before they slid seamlessly to nothingness.

He'd killed him.

A moan crawled over the frozen earth to knock him back to his senses. Andrew glanced quickly back and saw the woman rolling onto her knees, coughing and holding her stomach. He turned back to the dead man and grabbed his feet. He needed the guy off the trail. He couldn't have any evidence that they were living nearby, and that someone had been killed here. He hauled him twenty feet down the embankment on the northern side of the trail, away from the shelter to a drop-off that fell sharply down to a small creek. Saying a prayer that had no meaningful words, he rolled the man off the cliff and watched in sick horror as his body tumbled down the steep incline before coming to a stop. He stared for another moment before turning back to the small woman.

He didn't know what he was feeling at that moment, and it didn't matter.

She had lank, filthy, brown hair. Her face was already swelling, and blood was dripping from her nose. She could barely stand, and she favored one side. It was probably the side the man had been kicking. Her green eyes were defiant, but also haunted or dead, he couldn't tell which. She might have been pretty at one point, but now she was so wraithlike that she looked ill.

She waited for him to speak, waited maybe to flee from him.

"If you want to keep going, I won't stop you," Andrew managed to say and thanked God that his voice sounded steady.

She didn't speak for a long moment, clearly assessing him. When she did speak, it sounded labored and painful. "Thank you for saving me."

"You're welcome," he said, although he knew that at some point what he'd done would make him hate himself passionately. Not yet, though. Now he was still numb.

She nodded and turned to walk. Her legs gave out, and she stumbled to the ground swearing.

Several things flashed through Andrew's mind simultaneously. The first was how she'd talked to the man. He'd likely deserved it, but it also spoke of her not having enough sense to keep her mouth shut when traveling with someone dangerous enough to beat her to death. Also, she'd been with someone dangerous enough to beat her to death, which likely meant that she'd chosen to be with him. Something in her had decided that it was worth it. She was clearly starving, and probably desperate. The man, however, hadn't looked like he'd skipped many meals.

But she'd been beaten pretty severely and whatever else she was, she wasn't faking that she couldn't walk. His decision, no matter how much his instincts screamed at him not to do it, was already made for him.

Andrew walked past their dropped packs and crouched down next to her, not touching her and not close enough for her to strike out. She turned her head, and calculating eyes filled with pain met his.

"Do you want to come with me?"

She sniffed in, and he saw that blood was tricking from her nose towards her mouth. She nodded once.

"I have a few rules," Andrew said evenly. "If they are okay with you, I will take you. The first is that if you have any weapons, you won't be allowed to have them until I escort you away from my home."

She hesitated for only a fraction of a second before nodding.

"The second is that you will be led to where I live blindfolded. When you leave, you will leave blindfolded." When she didn't object, he went on, and Andrew was amazed to find that his mind was settling into a calm logic that helped him to see the steps that needed to be taken. "While in my home you will not be allowed to go outside until it is determined that you are leaving. You can stay until you're well enough to travel. I will give you food and gear, and then escort you back up here. If, at any point, you come back, I will kill you. If you act in any way that is uncivilized while in my home, I will remove you from the property without provisions. If you try to hurt me or my family, I will kill you. Can you live with that?"

She swallowed hard and sat down on the ground shivering. "What... what do I have to do for you?"

The question took him aback for a moment, and he frowned at her, trying to decide what exactly she was asking him. "Nothing, but behave like a good houseguest should."

"Fine," she whispered into the frigid air.

Andrew stood and retrieved the packs. "Do you have any weapons on you?"

She bit her lip. "A knife."

"Is that it?" He asked firmly. "I'm taking you to my wife and daughter. If I find anything else on you, I will be extremely pissed."

Shock covered her face and her eyes went huge as she turned back to him. "You're married?"

"Yes," he lied evenly. "Anything else?"

She let out a long breath and looked up at the sky. She reached under the back on her jacket and pulled out a gun, her finger nowhere near the trigger. She held it out to him, and he took it. He checked the safety and saw it was on before sticking it in the pack. He then took the knife that she was holding out to him, and tucked it in next to the pistol.

He awkwardly shouldered both packs and his weapons and as he walked over to her, pulled his watch cap from his head. "We have a long walk, and this is going over your eyes."

He held it out, and reluctantly she took it and pulled it down all the way over her mouth and nose.

Andrew took her arm and helped her to her feet. He put an arm around her frail waist and started to lead her off down the mountain, not heading anywhere near the shelter. "My name is James, by the way."

"Michelle," she said. Her voice whispered through the fabric of his hat.

They walked around in very wide circles for well over an hour before Andrew gradually began to steer them back towards the shelter. He had to help her stay up a few times, but she was tougher than she looked. It was a sick version of a trust walk, and somehow this woman was so desperate that following him sounded like a good idea to her.

Of course, he had killed the man that she'd been traveling with. He didn't want to even think about what their relationship had been like that they'd stuck together, but she hadn't even flinched at his death.

When they finally reached the rock that hid the shelter, he stopped her. "Stand here for a second." He pulled up the rock and unlocked the shelter, raising the hatch. He took her hand and led her over. "Climb here," he instructed, setting her hand on the ledge, "and step down. Go down five steps then stop. Do not remove the blindfold."

She did as she was bid, and he quickly climbed in behind her. He closed the hatch and locked it again, this time from the inside, pocketing the key. His next priority was Mia and alerting her to the fact that they weren't alone.

"Claire?" Andrew called out loudly.

Michelle jumped a bit, but otherwise didn't comment until he'd guided her to the bottom of the steps and pulled off her makeshift blindfold. He thrust his hat back into his pocket as Mia walked hesitantly into the storage room.

The two women's eyes met. Mia's mouth dropped open, but only for a second before she came forward, hand out. "Hello, welcome. My name is Claire."

Michelle hesitated for a moment before reaching out with her left hand to grasp Mia's, and Andrew knew it was because her right side was too stiff from her beating. "Michelle."

"Come in," Mia said gently, leading her into the living room. "You look hungry, are you?"

"Not so much," Michelle mumbled, looking around her in awe. "Where are we?"

"Our home," Andrew said before Mia could comment. He pointed over to a wide-eyed Jilly. "That's our daughter, Nelly."

Michelle nodded once and shivered. It was only then that Andrew saw just how wet all of her clothes were.

"Would you like a hot shower?" Mia asked her.

Michelle blinked in surprise; her green eyes were startling under the fluorescent lights. "You have a shower?"

The corner of Mia's mouth twitched. "We do. The hot water only lasts about fifteen minutes, but its heaven while it lasts. I can get some clean clothes for you, too. They'll be a bit big, but they'll do until we get yours washed."

"That... would be amazing, thank you," Michelle told her, not looking at Andrew or Jilly.

Mia led her to the bathroom, and told her that she'd drop some clean clothes in for her. "There is plenty of soap and shampoo and clean towels on the rack. Use whatever you want."

The second the door closed, Andrew and Mia sprang into action. As quickly and quietly as they could they stripped the girls' bedroom of all of Mia's stuff, and shoved it into Andrew's room in whatever drawer they could find room. Mia picked out clean clothes for the woman while Andrew stripped the sheets off the twin bed that Mia normally slept on, and threw them in the corner of his room. After Mia put the clean sweats in the bathroom for Michelle, she went to remake the twin bed with clean sheets and blankets while Andrew took down and moved Jilly's crib into his room.

All the while Jilly silently watched them as if it was a tennis match on television.

By the time Michelle came out from the shower, they'd completely rearranged the sleeping area, and Mia was already heating up some beans and rice for her. She smiled over at the painfully thin woman and her bruised face. She was clean now, and it made a world of difference to her appearance to Andrew who was sitting at the table. He'd rescued one of the chairs that had been keeping Jilly away from the stove and put it back at the table. He was going to have to figure out another way of keeping the toddler from burning herself.

She was pretty, or she would have been with another twenty pounds on her, with brown hair that lay in wet tendrils down to just past her shoulder blades. She shuffled slowly over to the table and sat. Mia put a glass of water in front of her, and she sipped slowly.

"Here," Mia said, putting the food down in front of her. "You need to eat something."

As soon as Mia sat next to him, Andrew took her hand. His was so cold, even though he wasn't particularly chilled. He knew he was going to have to tell her about the man, and what he'd done. It was starting to sink in that he'd killed a man, even if it was to stop him from beating this woman to death. He'd taken a man's life.

Michelle took a tentative bite, then another. A slow smile spread across her face as she glanced up at them. "This is really good."

Mia grinned, and Andrew laughed. He picked up the hand that he held in his and kissed the back of it, looking at Mia as he said. "My wife is an amazing cook."

"Mama Dada," Jilly called as she edged around the room, as far from Michelle as she could while still heading towards them.

Andrew pulled her into his lap and cuddled her close. She buried her face into his chest and peeked out at the stranger. "She's a bit shy at first," Andrew told her. "She'll get used to you quickly."

"It's fine," Michelle said through a mouthful. She ate quickly, and then had a smaller second helping. By the time it was done, she was yawning widely.

"You're sleeping in here," Andrew told her as he pointed out the room. Jilly was still firmly attached to him and he had one arm securely around her. "Nelly normally sleeps in here, but we moved her stuff out while you were in the shower so you could have it to yourself."

"Get some rest," Mia encouraged.

Michelle walked in with a murmured word of thanks and closed the door.

"Nap time," Mia told Jilly.

Andrew spooned up a bowl of food for himself and ate quickly. He then went out to the storage room and emptied both of the packs that he'd brought with them. He put all the weapons he found into a small box and stuck them in the storage room along with all of the other guns. He didn't want to be forced to do it, but he knew that if he needed to, he could overpower Michelle without any weapons. He hoped, however, that it wouldn't ever come to that.

Mia walked in just as he relocked the door. She didn't say anything, just took Michelle's bag and, along with the clothes she'd retrieved from the bathroom, started to wash everything that Michelle owned. They worked quickly and silently, getting everything hung on lines. It wasn't much, just a pitiful few items. Andrew took the filthy water out of the shelter to dump it and came back to find Mia cleaning the kitchen.

They moved through their evening as normally as possible. Jilly got up from her nap and they had supper. Michelle didn't wake, and they decided to let her sleep. By the time they went to bed that night Andrew felt like his insides were going to explode.

They curled up together, wrapped so closely in each other's arms that he didn't know where one ended and the other began. "I have to tell you something," he whispered into her hair. He was extremely grateful that he couldn't see her expression. "I killed the man she was with."

"Oh God," Mia breathed out. "What happened? What was he doing?"

"He..." It was difficult to tell her, even more to remember. "He was beating her. She'd said something to him, and he'd gone off. I shot him in the back with the crossbow... it... it killed him almost instantly. By the time I shot him he was kicking her in the gut."

Mia started to cry quietly and Andrew felt a few tears drip slowly down his own cheeks to mingle with hers as his mind relived the horrible moment. "Mia..."

"Shh," she said, kissing him gently. His heart flipped at the contact and his soul lightened just a bit at the unconditional acceptance that he knew she was giving him. "It's okay, you did the right thing. You couldn't let him do that to her."

"I feel..." Andrew let his voice trail in to nothing. He didn't know how he felt, and just then it didn't matter. He was stuck in the position of having ended a man's life, whether he deserved it or not, and he had to deal with that. He could feel remorse, but there was no way to take it back, nor was he sure that he'd want to take it back.

He didn't tell Mia what she'd said to the man. He wanted Mia to form her own impressions of Michelle, and it was possible that hunger and being regularly beaten, because he could tell that not all of the bruises were fresh, had made her snap. It was also possible that she'd seen truly horrible things out on the road. Michelle might not be safe or stable, but by bringing her here, Andrew had given her a chance to get strong enough to live.

"So James," Mia said with resignation. "I need to get used to calling you that again."

He nodded and pulled her in closer, inhaling the scent of her hair and closing his eyes at the comfort it brought him. "I hate calling you Claire. You aren't Claire to me."

"Ah, but you slip so well into husband mode as James," she said teasing. "How long do you think she'll stay?"

"I told her she could stay until she was well and strong enough, and then we'd give her food and send her on her way," Andrew explained as something nagged at him. He couldn't put a finger on what it was exactly.

Mia was quiet for so long that he thought she'd fallen asleep. "I'm glad I'm sleeping with you again. I always sleep better when we're together."

Although he knew what she meant, he was still surprised that she'd said it. "You don't have to move back in with Jilly, you know," he told her haltingly. "I mean… you know you could stay in here if that's what you want after Michelle leaves."

"I think I will," Mia said and yawned. She turned her face more firmly into his shoulder and let out a long sigh.

The first time they'd slept together they'd both woken up stiff and sore. Now that they'd done it so many times, they could be cuddled up together and fall asleep naturally.

Andrew let out a long breath, trying to release some of the tension that was bunching up his shoulders. He couldn't quite let go of the image of the man's blood oozing from the wound in his chest, or the fact that he'd shot a man in the back. It seemed so cowardly to shoot a man in the back.

Then he remembered Michelle's hunched and prone form and anger curled heavily in his gut as he ran a soothing hand up and down Mia's spine. The guy had been kicking the shit out of that woman who couldn't weigh more than ninety pounds, and he'd been a big man, at least as tall as Andrew with a good thirty or forty pounds on him. He clearly hadn't been starving, unlike Michelle.

No one should hit anyone else, but it was inexcusable, in his mind, to take out that much rage on someone so much smaller. It didn't matter what Michelle had said, the man shouldn't have laid a finger on her.

The knot of guilt that was tying him up inside began to loosen. Andrew still hated what he'd done, but he knew deep down that he'd done the right thing. More relaxed, he closed his eyes and drifted off to sleep with Mia's even breaths caressing his neck, and the key to the guns on a chain around his neck.

21

Mid-February

Andrew woke with a start the next morning to find Mia already up and getting dressed. Although he couldn't see her in the dark, he could hear her movements and knew them well enough to know what the rustling meant. Jilly was still asleep, so he crawled carefully from the bed and toed around until he located his jeans. The door cracked open, and she slipped out just as he was pulling them on. Moments later, he joined her in the bright kitchen fully dressed and wincing at the artificial light. They didn't speak as they went through the morning routine of setting the table and preparing breakfast.

When they were finally settled together, Andrew said, "I'm going to wait on trying to find another deer. I just haven't had any luck, and it might be better in another few weeks. We can make do with the rabbit for now."

Mia swallowed the oatmeal she'd just put in her mouth and gave him an appraising look. In her eyes he saw that she got what he was saying, and that he didn't want to leave her alone with Michelle in the shelter. "I can go."

"Really?" he asked, completely bemused. "If you get one how are you going to get it back here?"

She pretended to scowl at him, but gave up quickly. "If I actually get one then we'll figure something out and it will be worth it. I'll go out for a few hours and see what I can find. I'll be back before lunch."

He didn't like it, but didn't have a reason to argue either. He could handle Jilly on his own, and at this point Michelle was unlikely to be much of a threat.

The smaller bedroom's door cracked open and Michelle slowly walked out, blinking at the light. "Hey," she said softly.

After a night's rest Andrew thought her color looked a bit better. If he'd had to guess he would say that she was in her early twenties, but her skin was so blistered from what had to be minor frost bite that it was difficult to tell.

"Good morning," Mia said with a smile. "Are you hungry?"

"Yeah, just... need the bathroom," Michelle said as she shuffled off past them.

Mia got up and fixed a bowl for her. "Go get the weapons ready that you want me to take," she told him quietly. Sighing, knowing he was defeated, he went to get the rifle from the locked storage room. She was gone before Michelle reappeared in the kitchen.

She looked around, but went to sit at the table without comment. Andrew sat with her, not wanting to be rude and also to keep an eye on her. "So..." he faltered, trying to think up something to say. "Where are you from?"

"Vermont," she replied after a small bite of the oatmeal.

"Oh," he said, trying not to feel awkward. Her green eyes flashed to him, then back to her breakfast. "You're a long way from home."

"I'm trying to get home," she told him. When she met his gaze again it was with a smile that didn't completely meet her eyes. "You look too young to be married."

Despite himself, Andrew grinned. "Well, I'd just turned twenty when we got married. I'm twenty two now."

"Wow." Her eyebrow was raised, her head cocked to the side. "I'd never have guessed you were that old. How old is Claire?"

Andrew was ready for this. He'd been rehearsing the details so often that he knew them by heart now. "Twenty."

"Mmhh." Michelle's mummer could have been acceptance or doubt and he couldn't tell which, and that bothered him. Something about her bothered him, but he kept his face passive. Until she proved otherwise, he was going to give her a chance to heal. Her next statement stunned him. "So you had to get married, then."

He felt his mouth drop for a second, unable to believe that she'd been so rude to say it, or that the math of Jilly's age had led her to that conclusion. Unbidden his cheeks started to warm. "No, I mean..." he faltered and took a breath, slowing his heart. He knew what he was going to say, and he needed to stick to his story because clearly this woman wasn't stupid. "Claire and I were going to get married after I was done with school, so it was just moving the wedding up a bit."

She nodded her head once, as if to say, 'yeah, okay whatever'. "So I guess you didn't get to finish school, then."

Andrew wasn't going to tell her this part of the lie, or at least partial lie. He'd decided a while back not to reveal too much, but on reflection he thought it might be a good idea to let her know that she wasn't the only one with brains around here. "I am done, actually. I've got a master's degree in engineering from Johns Hopkins." When her eyes widened slightly, he went on. "I started college at thirteen."

A slow, easy smile flitted over her face, and she was transformed into someone who was decidedly more attractive. "You know," she said, biting her lip and letting it slowly out. "I was going to pin you as the baseball star of your high school, or maybe soccer. You're not the right build for football."

She was definitely flirting with him. Andrew fixed a bland smile on his face, unwilling to acknowledge her attempts. He didn't say anything.

"But," Michelle went on, undeterred by his silence. "I could definitely see you as the class president. You've got the good looks and athleticism down. Clearly you have the brains as well."

"I never went to school," Andrew replied steadily and was even more amused at her attempts to hide her astonishment. "I was homeschooled. That's how I was able to go to college early." He didn't add that a lot of kids would be ready for college early if they were homeschooled. It would ruin the effect he was trying to create.

She leaned forward and laced her hands on the table, never taking her eyes from his. "I wouldn't have guessed that. Aren't all homeschooled kids socially inept?"

"Probably," he said shrugging his shoulders. "I can't imagine a regular kid having political debates with congressmen when they're twelve."

She laughed, but again it didn't meet her eyes. Andrew had met others like her. There was an agenda; he just didn't know what it was, although he had a guess. If he was in any danger, though, he didn't sense it. "I've insulted you," she said bemused.

"No more than anyone else who finds out I was homeschooled," he told her dismissively. "There are a lot of misconceptions"

"Are you one of those radicals that think everyone should be homeschooled?" she asked him, crinkling her nose up in amusement. "I do so love people with a cause."

Andrew shook his head, totally honest now. "No. It isn't practical, although I suppose right now every kid is being homeschooled." He hadn't thought of it, but with the power out and the government gone, most education would have to fall to parents until everything was up and running again.

"So what was it like walking into college that first day?"

He glanced away for a second, trying to collect himself. "It was weird," he sighed. "My mom drove me that morning, and I was not a large kid at that age. I definitely stood out, but I wasn't the only kid on campus, so that helped."

A call from his room made him turn. Jilly was awake. "Excuse me," he said to Michelle, but he didn't look back to see her reaction. He went to his room and flicked the lights. Jilly was standing in her crib, holding on to the rails and smiling at him like he was the best thing she'd ever seen. Her red curls were smashed all around her head from sleep, and her eyes were still heavy but that smile could have melted an iceberg. "Hi, Dada."

"Hey, Jelly Bean," Andrew told her, modifying his nickname for her, as he picked her up and cuddled her to his chest. Love so complete and uncomplicated filled his heart as it always did when he was holding her like this. He kissed her brow and set her on the side of the bed. "Let's get you changed and then we can have breakfast."

He carried her out to the kitchen, and the second Jilly saw Michelle she clung to him like a grasping monkey and wouldn't look at her. It was a dance trying to make breakfast and holding her. She wouldn't go into her high chair, and he ended up holding her on his lap so he could feed her.

"She's not normally like this," Andrew explained as Michelle watched them intently. He half wished that she'd go back to her room so Jilly would relax, but she didn't move. "She hasn't really seen anyone but us in months."

"Makes sense," Michelle agreed. "She doesn't look like you."

"Nope," he said evenly and managed to chuckle. She wasn't related to him, so of course she didn't. He had the story prepared, though. "She looks a lot like Claire, and like Claire's mom, but the red hair was my grandmother."

"I was wondering. It isn't typical to see a red head born to two brown haired parents." Michelle cocked her head to the side and sat back, crossing her arms. She rubbed at her sweatshirt absently. "I can't imagine being that young and becoming a parent."

Frankly Andrew couldn't either. It certainly hadn't been part of his plan, especially because Jilly wasn't technically his. In a way he was more of a substitute or a foster parent in this situation. He wasn't going to comment on that, though. His plan was to stick to the truth when he could, and to the rehearsed story when he couldn't. If he didn't have an answer, he was going to change the subject. "I don't think any of us pictured our lives as they are now. Life can throw us a lot of curve balls. I'm not sorry that mine brought me here with Claire and Nelly."

Michelle nodded in agreement. "Why Nelly? It's such an unusual name."

"Ah," he hedge and was thankfully given time to think as Jilly swiped at the bowl and nearly sent it off the table. Nelly... Nelly... he needed something. Could have been Nelson, but...

"It isn't that singer, is it?" she asked as she watched him straighten up the mess. "That one that was popular a few years ago."

"No," Andrew said before spooning in another bite as the answer came to him. "My hero was Nelson Mandela when I was a kid, and it continued into adulthood. I wrote a paper on him when I was eight." This, at least, was true. He'd been in awe of what the man had gone through for his country. "Claire has always liked him as well. We were going to use Nelson for a boy, and we were stuck for a girl name. When the doctor said girl, Claire said, 'how about we call her Nelly?' and that was it."

It was such a stupid detail. Everyone asks about how they were named, and yet neither he nor Mia had come up with a cover story. This one, however, was brilliant, and Andrew was ready to crown himself the king of bullshit.

Michelle's next question was a kick in the gut that he needed to get his head out of his butt and stop being cocky. She had something she wanted.

"Why is the power still on in here?"

Her eyes were wide, almost innocent. "Well," he began cautiously. "It's because this is a Faraday Cage. Have you heard that term?"

"No," she said sweetly. Her expression was curious and open, but it was too well played and so different from the woman that he'd seen the day before that he knew he wasn't looking at the real her. Andrew had told her to be a pleasant houseguest and she could stay. So far she was acting the part very well.

"Essentially the structure," he was careful not to use the word shelter, "is protected from electrical surges. When the CME hit, the energy was dispersed around everything so that it didn't blow the circuits. There are some places like this around the country, but most of the time when someone builds a Faraday Cage, it's a small one to protect radios and other small electronic devices."

"What's a CME?" she asked.

Andrew tried to set Jilly down, but she wouldn't budge from his lap. "It's a Coronal Mass Ejection, or what most people think of as solar flares although they're not the same thing. It's like a solar flare, but it comes with a bit more power to it."

Michelle opened her mouth to say something, but snapped it shut. She bit her lip again, but this time he could tell it was genuine, and she was contemplating what he'd said.

He stood and went over to the coat hooks to grab the baby back pack. He set Jilly down. Instantly she started crying. "I'm putting you in the back pack, okay?" he said looking down at her pinched little face.

A very pitiful, "Pweas, Dada," popped out of her mouth and she continued to whimper until he'd swung her around onto his back and pulled the straps up so that she could snuggle into him.

"So…" Michelle said slowly, absently watching what he was doing, but not as if she was seeing him. "So it was a solar flare that knocked out the power?"

"You didn't know?" Andrew asked as he clipped the chest clip.

She shook her head. "There isn't much news that's reliable."

"Yeah, it was a CME," he said as he went to wash the dishes, Jilly quiet on his back. "It must have been a really big one, too, for the effects to be so widespread. Where were you when it hit?"

"Atlanta," she sighed.

Andrew turned slowly to look at her. "You walked here from Atlanta?"

"Pretty much," Michelle said through clenched teeth. "We managed to get a ride once for a few hours when we were in Virginia. This guy had a beat up old truck that still worked, and he gave us a lift." Her face darkened and she looked away.

He wasn't sure if it was remembering her dead traveling companion that was making her upset, or something to do with the guy and his truck. A sick wave rushed over him at the thought of how she might have had to 'pay' for that ride. She hadn't brought up the guy she'd been walking with and Andrew didn't want to mention him. He still felt horrible guilt at having shot the man, no matter what he'd been doing to her. He wasn't sure the feeling would ever go away. "That's a long trip," he offered lamely and went back to the dishes.

"What kind of power?"

"Excuse me?" he glanced back at her and saw her staring off thoughtfully.

"The CME, what kind of power?"

"Oh," Andrew shrugged and dried off the bowl. "The rays are full of matter and radiation. It's electromagnetism that actually blew the power grid. It overloads everything and blows it up. It's a bit like when you trip a circuit breaker in your house by putting too much on the same circuit. Do you know what I mean?"

"When you have to flip the breaker back on?"

"Yes," he said putting the bowls away and drying his hands. Jilly was still quiet on his back and not asking to be put down, which was very strange for her. She wasn't even fidgeting much. "It isn't exactly the same thing, but the same concept. If you overloaded something in your house but you didn't have a breaker, it could burn out the circuit and possibly start a fire. That's what happened here. The sun overwhelmed our power grids. The power stations acted like antennas and flooded everything with a lot more power than it could possibly take, which fried all the wires. It would have fried all the cars too, except for the old cars that don't have computers. It would have killed all the satellites, phone lines and all of the cell phone towers."

Michelle let out a low whistle. "So basically we're screwed."

"Basically," he agreed.

"How do you know all of this?" She asked, standing up and stretching in a long, slow arch. "Is it because you're an engineer?"

"Electrical engineer," Andrew added. "That and my father-in-law came to check on us. He was down in Baltimore and they have a bit more information there."

Michelle started to move around the table, and Andrew had to force himself to stand his ground. "Why were you up here? How did you get up here?"

"We came to check on the place for Labor Day," he answered. "Our truck wouldn't start, so we were stuck."

"You didn't leave with your father-in-law?" she asked, coming within a foot of him and looking up at him through her lashes.

Andrew laughed. He couldn't help it, and she stepped back clearly affronted. "He walked here from Baltimore. We couldn't exactly walk back with a baby."

"I guess not," Michelle said reluctantly.

"I need to do a few things around here," he told her, and he stepped around her to go get the vent brush from the storage room. "There are plenty of books on the book shelf in here, and your clothes should be dry soon if you want to change back into your own things. Otherwise I suggest you rest."

With that he walked away, letting her know he was done entertaining her for the moment. Andrew might not have the world's best luck with girls, but he knew when one was hitting on him, and clearly Michelle was, although why she would do that when he'd told her that he was married was beyond him.

He dug out the vent brush as she wandered over to the book shelf and started to peruse. Andrew had been putting off cleaning out the vent because he knew it was going to be nasty work, but they couldn't let the tube build up too much soot from the fires that they'd been burning. He then grabbed a tarp and a bucket before relocking the back storage room and sticking the key back around his neck.

Andrew pulled the filter off of the vent and stuck it on the kitchen table. He moved the couch out of the way, along with the barricade they'd made to keep Jilly away from the potbellied stove, and the stove itself which was just as heavy as the last time when he'd moved it. It was a little more difficult with the baby on his back, but it also meant that she was not going to get hurt while he was doing this. He set the tarp down, along with the bucket and threaded the cleaning brush up the hole. It looked a bit like a bottle brush on steroids. The handle was such that it would extend up almost thirty feet with the handle extensions nestled inside, a bit like an umbrella's handle that would pop up at the push of a button, only with a longer reach. He pushed it all the way up, and as he pulled it down he twisted the handle. Black soot started to fall down into the bucket, although it wasn't as bad as some of the chimney sweeps he'd seen in the movies, probably because it had only been in use for a few weeks.

He saw, out the corner of his eye, Michelle walk back through to her room with a book. It was times like this that he missed Jamal. The kid had been a great help around the shelter once he'd healed up and he'd been eager to learn and contribute. Andrew had thought a lot about him over the past several months. He wasn't sure whether he wanted him to have found his grandmother or not. If he hadn't, he knew Scott would have taken Jamal on with him to the other shelter. But on the other hand, he didn't want Jamal to have lost his entire family.

By the time he'd finished with the vent, Mia was back empty handed. "I didn't see anything."

"I figured," Andrew said as he vacuumed up the last of the ash from the carpet. He'd already put all of the furniture and the stove back, so after this last bit he was totally done with this chore. Jilly had fallen asleep on his back at some point.

"What's up with her?" Mia asked, coming over to help get her down and put her in her bed.

He unclipped the carrier and slowly lowered the shoulder straps so Mia could ease her off of his back. "She's still a bit unsure of Michelle."

Mia's eyes went wide, but she didn't comment. She clearly didn't want Michelle to hear anything. Mia quickly took Jilly into their bedroom to put her down for a nap.

As soon as Mia came back out Andrew took her in his arms and started to kiss her. She didn't resist as he deepened it and pulled her over to the couch. He ran his hands up into her hair and opened his mouth. She nearly retreated, and would have pulled back, but his hands were still in her hair. After a few seconds adjustment, she went with it. Her small body was perched in his lap and he pulled her in closer, willing Michelle to open the door. He wanted her to be a witness.

Then Mia sighed into his mouth and he completely forgot what his original intent had been. Andrew tilted his head and moved to kiss down her jaw, losing himself in the feel of her soft skin under his lips. His body caught fire as she let her head fall back so he could get access to her neck. The words flowed out more naturally than he'd ever said them before, "I love you," a second before they heard Michelle cough. Andrew didn't know how long she'd been there, but his original plan for her to see them together had worked perfectly. Except that everything had changed.

Mia jumped back a bit, and after a second grinned at the other woman. "Sorry," she said and slid off of Andrew's lap. "Are you ready for lunch? I'm starving."

Andrew took a long, deep breath and tried to slow his hammering heart. He didn't know what had just happened, but it was definitely not what he'd expected.

22

Later that Day...

How on earth was he supposed to stop staring at his best friend and imaging pulling her back to the couch to kiss her again? Every feeling he'd ever wanted to feel for Mia was there, right at his fingertips, waiting to be explored. Except it wasn't the explosion that he'd thought it should be, but more a slow burn in his gut.

He didn't touch her, though, as they went about preparing lunch. Andrew knew Mia's body language well enough to know that she didn't want to be touched just then, and he didn't want to make her uncomfortable. He'd achieved his goal of letting Michelle know that he didn't want her, and from the look on her face the message was received loud and clear. It wasn't a friendly look, although she did a good job of hiding it from them. He'd only seen a short flash of it flit across her face before it was gone.

Jilly's nap was short that day, and she was up soon after they'd finished lunch. Andrew went to get her and again she clung to him like a second skin. He changed her diaper then closed the bedroom door so that it was just the two of them in the room. He sat on the floor with her, holding her close and letting her calm down. He didn't know if it was Michelle herself that was freaking the toddler out, or if it was having a stranger in her house.

Andrew could hear Mia and Michelle talking, though it was a bit muffled through the closed door. They were talking about movies, and he tuned them out, focusing completely on Jilly. Her death grip on his shirt began to relax after a few minutes, and eventually she climbed from his lap to patter over to his laundry basket. She picked up one of his socks, looked at him and dropped it daintily to the ground. He grinned, and she giggled, putting her hands up to her mouth.

Michelle's voice cut straight through the door and Jilly froze, staring at it. "The walls are really thin."

"I guess," Mia said cautiously.

"You'd have to be careful not to be heard."

Andrew groaned quietly and let his head fall back against the bed. He got what Michelle was asking, and hoped Mia did, too.

Mia didn't say anything and his heart kicked up. He hated that Michelle was likely making her uncomfortable.

"You're probably worried about getting pregnant again."

"Subtle," Andrew breathed out, barely making a sound as he rolled his eyes.

"I am," Mia finally said. He could hear that her voice was a bit higher than normal. "I suppose everyone is worried about that right now."

"Oh, definitely, although it doesn't stop the men," and even through the door he could hear the bitterness that was dripping from Michelle's words.

"I'm so sorry," Mia told her gently. "I can't imagine what that's been like for you."

"No," Michelle agreed. "You've had it easy here."

"I have," she agreed. Andrew heard a chair scrape and the clank of dishes. "Have you had fruit or vegetables recently?"

Michelle was a moment before answering. "Nope, food has been scarce."

"You're bruising is really bad and it occurred to me that you might be developing scurvy."

Andrew nearly choked as he tried to hold in his laughter. Mia's love of food had range and depth, including nutrition and what different illnesses came from a poor diet. When she'd set out to study food, it had been with the intention of feeding people for wellness as well as taste. She was a fanatic about good foods, and healthy portions.

"You mean like a pirate?" Michelle blurted out.

"Exactly like a pirate," Mia said and he heard her rummaging around. "I've got some canned oranges here. You'll need some vitamin C. I think we've got a bottle of vitamins, but I have to find them."

He heard the can being opened and Jilly walked back over, her task of dumping all the clothes on the floor complete, and he picked her up as he stood. Andrew opened the door with her still in his arms, ready to feed her lunch with Jilly firmly entrenched on his lap.

Even though there were a few other chores that he could do around the shelter, Andrew decided to put them off. He didn't want Michelle asking questions, and he really didn't want her to learn more about the inner workings of the place.

As the day went on Mia got more and more lethargic, so that by the time Jilly was ready for bed, she went along with her. He watched her go with concern, but didn't comment. Andrew got out the manual on how to skin and clean a deer and started flipping through it again. It had been months since they'd cleaned the last one, and if he was going to get one while hunting, he'd need to remember completely how to go about preparing it for freezing.

"What's that?" Michelle asked, coming back to the kitchen from her room. She'd changed into her own clothes again, now that they were dry.

Andrew held up the book to show the picture and she recoiled. He set it back on the table and bit back a grin. "Sorry, didn't think you'd mind."

"I don't like eating meat," she informed him with a sniff. "I've had to, but I hate it."

He'd met several vegetarians and a few vegans over the years. It was something he could respect, even if he didn't agree. "Mention that to Claire. She won't cook meat for you if you don't want it."

He'd read in a novel once that a character was chewing his tongue, and he'd always thought that was the weirdest description ever. Except now he was watching Michelle do just that. Finally she sniffed and nodded. "I will, thanks."

He didn't bother to reply, just went back to reading.

"How did you two meet?"

"We grew up together," Andrew answered, not looking up at her. "We've been best friends since we were young."

"Ah," was her only reply.

He flipped the page, continuing to read up on how to prepare the meat. It was going to be a pain without Scott. Mia was a great help, but hauling in a dead deer that could weigh as much or more than she did was going to be a challenge. It might be worth trying to rig up a pulley system to lower it into the shelter.

He heard a loud sigh, one he'd heard before from his ex-girlfriends when he'd been studying and not paying attention to them. Andrew didn't acknowledge it. To admit it had happened would only bring on something obnoxious and possibly loud. He continued to read as the memories of the procedure solidified back into the front of his brain. Scott had taken the lead the last time, but he'd shown Andrew everything he'd need to know. He was reasonably confident that he could do this again by himself. It would be a lot of hard work, but he remembered well enough to manage alone.

"Well," Michelle stood, her chair legs scraping gently across the floor as she rose. "I'm going to bed."

He glanced up and smiled, "Night." The instructions for smoking were on the next page and he got back into it. They weren't going to be able to smoke it, but it didn't hurt to reread that section.

She waited a moment, but when he didn't give her any sign that he was paying attention, she went into her room and quietly, deliberately noiselessly, closed the door.

Andrew closed his eyes and thanked God she was gone. His nerves were on edge from the earth shattering kiss he'd shared with Mia, and he didn't want to deal with a woman that not only thought he'd cheat on his wife, but couldn't seem to take the hint that he didn't want to play her game. He could imagine that she hadn't met up with a lot of nice people out on the road, but this was unreal. It didn't matter that he wasn't really married to Mia. Certain things were supposed to be sacred, and this was one of them. He could never excuse the man who was beating her up, the one Andrew had killed, but he was starting to wonder just what Michelle had put him through that had made him snap like that. He'd known her for a day and she was already under his skin.

Shaking his head to clear it, he went back to reading. He wanted to finish the section before bed.

By the time he'd shut off all the lights and made his way to his room he was exhausted. He'd gotten caught up in the book, and it was going on midnight. It had happened more than once in his life. He'd been ten when the last Harry Potter book had been released, and he'd talked his mom into going to a midnight release party at a local bookstore. It had been a lot of fun, and the two of them had had a great time arguing over who would get to read the book first. Andrew had won in a rock-paper-scissors contest and he'd stayed up all night and into the next day reading it straight through. He'd ended up with a bad headache and an upset stomach from skipping a few meals, but he'd gone to bed with a grin on his face.

He shuffled carefully over to the bed in the dark and crawled in around Mia. Her shoulders were hunched, and she seemed to be curled in on herself. He wanted to reach out and make her feel better, but he didn't know what was wrong or if he'd only make it worse.

Andrew rolled onto his back and stared up at the darkness above him. Something had shifted for him today. If he'd had to describe it, it would be like saying that something clicked into place that had been off for a long time. Looking sideways, he could almost make out her form in the obsidian that was the world underground. This was probably what miners felt like when they went into the earth.

His stomach clenched as he remembered the kiss. It hadn't only felt right, it had felt so natural that his brain was screaming at him to do it again. It was like breathing. He just needed to. But if Mia didn't feel the same way, then it didn't matter, and they wouldn't be kissing any longer. Andrew closed his eyes and tried to stop thinking about it. If Mia didn't want to be kissing him, then he'd deal with it. She'd still love him, and she'd still be his best friend. It would have to be enough.

But if they did really date each other, which sounded unbelievably ridiculous and childish in their current situation, what if they started to fight? Andrew's luck with women had sucked. It had sucked a lot. He'd always been able to gauge people pretty easily. His dad was the same way, and they'd often discussed motivation and why people acted out. He could remember his dad early on telling him that he needed to think about why he was acting a certain way, and then he'd help him name his feelings. Andrew had understood, later on, that it was a parenting technique, but it had helped him out a lot, especially once he'd gone off to college. Being thirteen in a world full of eighteen-year-olds meant you had to learn fast, or fall hard, and it wasn't all about studies. He'd had to work in groups a lot and while most of the older students had been friendly and helpful, a few hadn't grown out of high school and were more than happy to try to force Andrew into doing all of the work for them.

Or they'd simply ignore his presence. Andrew had worked with people of all ages throughout his life in a lot of situations, but this had been a game changer. He'd had to learn quickly how to read someone and either navigate around them, or stand his ground against them.

Every single encounter gave him either a boost when he did it well or a lesson when he screwed it up. After a few years he'd become really good at understanding people and what made them tick.

Except with girls, of course. As soon as he started to date one, they stopped making any sense at all. Ever. It was unbelievably maddening.

If that happened with Mia he was screwed because the two of them were stuck here for the next few months at least and possibly for the next several years.

His dad's voice floated through his partially manic thoughts. *Step back and think it through.*

He took several deep breaths and calmed his mind. He and Mia had to get through Michelle's rehabilitation. Nothing else mattered until that was done. After that, he could worry about why kissing Mia felt like coming home and catching fire all rolled into one.

Andrew groaned softly and rolled away from her. He decided that counting sheep might be a better way to fall asleep. Except sleep didn't come as his mind filled with the man's face, the one he'd killed. Unbidden images of his eyes losing the light of life smacked him. Had the guy had his mom's eyes? Did he have parents who were missing him? The guilt was so heavy that he wanted to puke from it. Kissing Mia had temporarily driven all of it from his mind, but it came running back to him like a sprinter off the mark. Had the guy been bad before the CME? Had he been keeping Michelle safe all these months, and if so, why was Michelle not sad to be rid of him? He closed his eyes, squeezing them shut tight, and wished it was as simple as that to make the replaying video of the man falling down on the arrow leave his memory.

It begged the question, and Andrew was forced to ask it because he loved difficult questions. Mia once told him that he was just twisted that way. If he, Andrew, had been out on the road, would he have been able to keep his humanity? When faced with starvation and violence, would he have fought back violently? There was a fascinating study done at Stanford that involved dressing students up as either prisoners or guards. The whole thing got quickly out of hand until there was massive abuse and violence. Even the professor had been caught up in it.

The awful, humbling truth that Andrew had taken from that was, given the right circumstances anyone was capable of violence. It was why so many were caught up in Hilter's rampage. Being aware enough of your own faults and failings might lend you enough to be able to walk away, but he doubted that it was a guaranty.

Everyone was capable of good, or bad. It was keeping your head when the shit hit the fan and standing your ground that counted. He hoped he had enough nerve for that, but already he was tainted by one murder. No matter the justification he offered, it was still the taking of a life. He stared at the ceiling for a long time, and wasn't aware of it when sleep finally overtook him.

The next thing he heard was Jilly's soft snuffling as she started to scoot around in her crib. Andrew reached out automatically for Mia, but her side of the bed was empty and cold. He stretched his arms up and yawned widely, trying to rid himself of the late night reading binge's hangover. It didn't help much, but enough that he was able to crawl from the bed and grab Jilly, pulling her sleep warmed body back onto the bed with him so they could cuddle. Amazingly, she settled back down and went back to sleep in his arms, cocooned under the blankets.

Andrew, however, was now wide awake. He could clearly hear Mia and Michelle talking in the kitchen.

"Are you sure you're okay? You look pale." That was from Michelle and it didn't sound flattering.

Mia didn't say anything for well over a minute. "It's cramps. My period is a few days late."

"Oh, wow," Michelle said with a little more edge to it than he thought was necessary. A period wasn't exactly noteworthy since women had them every month. "Do you think you're pregnant?"

Andrew's whole body seemed to drop through the floor, even though he knew it was impossible for her to be pregnant. He wanted to laugh, but he also really wanted to hear what Mia was going to say.

"I think I might be."

It was a close thing, but he managed not to snort out loud. Mia deserved an Oscar for that one. How Jilly was sleeping through his silent laughter he had no idea. Andrew wished he could see Michelle's face.

"I wouldn't have let it happen," was what Michelle said.

"It isn't a good time," Mia told her. "But no time is a good time to have kids. I could be starting my period, though."

"I haven't had one in months."

"I can understand why. You don't have enough body fat. It's called… hmm, let me think. It starts with an 'a'."

They were both quiet for a while until Mia let out a long huff. "It's going to drive me nuts until I remember. Let me get the book."

He heard rummaging around and a large book hitting a flat surface. "It's called amenorrhea."

"What's that book?"

"It's about using your body temperature to predict fertility," Mia explained. "It's actually pretty effective when used correctly."

"But you didn't use it correctly?" Michelle's voice held just a bit too much smugness. Andrew's smile slipped from his face.

"We did," Mia said. "It's just that I'm late, and I shouldn't be. My cycles have been a little weird since I had Nelly. I used to get really bad cramps, but they've been getting better every month. It might be that they're coming back, and that's why I'm late."

"Have you told James that you think you might be pregnant?"

Mia laughed and it warmed Andrew's heart to hear it because he could tell it was genuine. "He won't care. He loves Nelly. He didn't even flinch when we found out I was pregnant before. He just started laughing and spun me around, super excited. Things like that don't faze him."

Andrew tried to picture what would happen if a girlfriend did tell him that she was pregnant, especially right now. Back in his old life he was reasonably certain he'd have freaked. Mia probably knew he would have freaked, but he appreciated her lying to make him sound better than he actually was.

"But have you told him?" Michelle pressed. "I mean, here you don't have a hospital."

"I didn't have Nelly in a hospital," Mia told her.

Andrew knew where this was going, and it was going to be good. This story was a legend among them now. Mia's mom, Diane, had refused to head to the hospital when she went into labor. She'd yelled at everyone who would listen that it had taken her over forty-eight hours to have Mia, and she hated hospitals. She was going to hang out in her own house until the pain really built up.

Diane had been in the bathtub at that point. Andrew and Mia were hanging out downstairs with Andrew's parents and Mia's dad, while the doula was up with Diane. Diane had kicked everyone else out, including Scott. Then the doula had started yelling for help and Andrew's mom had gone tearing up the stairs along with everyone else. Seconds later they heard a loud wail. Jilly had been born in the bathtub a mere two hours after her labor had started.

Andrew's mom had checked the baby out even as the paramedics showed up, but Diane had decided not to bother going to the hospital.

His musings were interrupted by Mia's voice. "So, I accidentally had a homebirth."

"Woah," Michelle said, clearly stunned. "Are you a freaking super woman or something?"

"No," Mia sighed. She sounded exhausted. He heard a chair move and assumed she sat down.

"So have you told him?" Michelle asked, yet again. She was persistent.

"Nope," Mia admitted. "With you getting here I forgot all about it. I didn't get cramps like this before with Nelly, though. I'm pretty sure I'm going to start today or tomorrow."

Jilly began to stir in his arms and before long she'd popped her head up and poked him in the eye. "Dada."

"That's my name," Andrew agreed, and he made them ready for the day.

Mia looked terrible. She was definitely not herself, and as soon as he had Jilly fed and back in the back pack, because she still hadn't accepted Michelle's presence, he sent Mia back to bed with a hot water bottle.

"Isn't she too old to be in one of those?" Michelle asked, pointing to the carrier.

"She still fits, so I'm guessing no," Andrew said, trying not to sound as annoyed as he felt. It was Michelle's fault that Jilly was in it. Most of the time they didn't use the carrier anymore because she was walking so well and could move around without it.

Michelle's nose scrunched up at the tip. He wasn't even sure she was aware that she did it. "I haven't seen one like that before. Most of them are tiny babies on the front."

"Okay," Andrew said deliberately keeping any inflection from the word. He had no idea what she was talking about and didn't want to start a debate over baby carriers. He had hours before it was Jilly's nap time, and she flat out refused to get down, even to sit in his lap. He didn't want to spend it in Michelle's company, but he couldn't do much with the shelter while she watched.

Then he remembered the diapers. Andrew could wash the diapers with Jilly on his back. It smelled and it was gross. There was a good shot that Michelle wouldn't want to hang around for that. He had to hide a chuckle at the look on her face when he told her what he was going to do. She decided to read in her room.

There was peace for several hours. Jilly even got down and played while it was just the two of them.

When lunch came Mia was still asleep, so he reheated some of the leftovers for them, and they all ate in near silence.

Michelle decided to break it with a zinger. "Claire thinks she might be pregnant."

Andrew didn't know whether to laugh or throw his fork across the room. Whatever she was trying to do, it was getting very old, very fast. "I heard you two this morning," he informed her as calmly as he could manage. "If she is, then great, we'll have another baby."

"Aren't you worried at all, James?" She said, narrowing her eyes as she studied him.

"I'm worried about her safety, sure," Andrew said after swallowing a lump of food that felt bigger than it should have. "But I'm always worried about her safety. That's nothing new."

"I can't imagine having a kid right now," she told him flatly. There was something more to it, but whatever it was she didn't elaborate any further.

If he was very, very honest with himself, Andrew couldn't either. He knew he was functioning as Jilly's father, but it didn't seem quite as scary because he wasn't actually her father. He supposed, however, that it was splitting hairs. The split was enough to keep him sane. Michelle turned her head, and he saw that she'd pulled her short, dark hair back in a messy tail at the nape of her neck. It looked oddly out of place, but he couldn't figure out why.

"Dada," Jilly whispered into his chest.

He looked down at her and saw her big blue eyes gazing back up in to his. There was total trust there. Jilly didn't really care that he wasn't her biological father. To her he was 'dada', and every time she said it in that little voice, his heart did an odd tap dance. He wasn't quite sure if it was nerves or joy. Maybe it was a mixture of both.

They were Mia's eyes. They were the exact same shape and color. It was a blue that he'd only seen one other time, at Crater Lake in Oregon. When he'd told her that was her eye color, she's rolled those blue eyes and laughed it off. Mia... it made his head hurt as much as it made his heart ache. She'd kissed him back, but probably because she'd caught on that he was setting Michelle up to see them. Maybe she hadn't been as into it as he was.

The whole situation was complicated, and he couldn't focus on complicated feelings. He had other worries, like a woman who was trying to drive him nuts. Maybe Michelle was just that unpleasant, but he was pretty sure that she was doing it on purpose, and he was starting to really regret bringing her here. Did it make him a terrible person that he was wishing he'd sent a beaten, starving woman on her way alone? Probably.

He went to put Jilly down for a nap, and he knew that whatever happened, he had to let everything go until they were alone again. Mistakes happened when he was distracted, and he couldn't afford any mistakes.

23

After Andrew put Jilly in her crib for her nap, he kicked off his shoes and climbed into bed with Mia. He was exhausted from staying up too late the night before, and from all of the worries that had kept him from falling to sleep. He needed a quick nap, or he'd be a wreck by dinner.

The second his head touched the pillow, Mia rolled over and curled into his side. Instinctively he put his arms around her. "I thought you were asleep," he whispered as quietly as he could.

"I hurt, and I feel awful."

She sounded awful. Her voice was scratchy and there was a hitch to it as she spoke.

"Do you want me to massage your back?" he asked her as he ran her hand down her side.

She gave a short nod and carefully, what seemed like painfully, rolled over.

Andrew slid his hands down her back until he reached her hips and the base of her spine. Slowly, gently he began to knead his fingers into the knots of tension he could feel there.

She inhaled sharply when he hit a particularly large knot, and he eased off the pressure. He worked at her back well past when his fingers had begun to ache. Whatever pain he had in his fingers was nothing compared to something that was keeping her bedridden. He heard her let out a long sigh, and he stopped.

He scooted over to her, spooning up behind her and pulling her back into his arms. It had always been nice holding her, but this was different. Sleepily, she kissed his hand, which was up near her face, and whispered, "I love you."

Andrew closed his eyes and whispered back, "I love you, too," and wondered just what that meant now.

He felt a thousand times better after sleeping for thirty minutes. Andrew quietly made his way from his room and found the shelter silent, with Michelle's door shut. Taking that as his cue, he went to work on a few of the regular maintenance jobs that needed to be done, and did them as silently as he possibly could. After he'd finished, and no one had stirred, he heated up some soup from a can for Mia and carried it in to her. He set the bowl on the night stand and sat down next to her. Careful, so as not to startle her, he whispered her name.

Mia shook her head, and he could tell even in the dim light that she hadn't opened her eyes.

"You need to eat," Andrew told her, and he reached out to gently move her hair from her face and tuck it behind her ear. He couldn't seem to stop himself from cupping her cheek. She was a little flushed, but he thought it was probably from sleep.

"I feel bad," she moaned and licked her dry lips.

"You're going to feel worse if you get too hungry," he reminded her. Mia was always telling him that the body needed fuel to heal.

She inhaled deeply and stretched a bit. "Kay."

Andrew spooned up a small bite and held it to her mouth. Eventually he fed most of the bowl to her before she shook her head and refused any more.

"Michelle..." Mia began, but petered out. He waited to see if she had more to say, and finally she seemed to get to it. "Thinks baby."

If he hadn't heard her conversation that morning he'd have been lost. "I heard you two, it's okay." Andrew didn't want to add more just in case Michelle was eavesdropping. "You know I love kids."

"Mmhmm," she mumbled. It was the last thing she said before sleep claimed her again.

Jilly woke up just as Andrew was walking out of the room. The drudgery of sleep, diaper change, feed, diaper change, sleep should have become old months before, but oddly enough he found comfort in the predictable routine that was Jilly's life. They kept her schedule, adjusting when it needed it, but plowing on with routine had given his life stability and his days a course that they might not have otherwise had. In that way, the predictability was comforting and not tedious.

He found Michelle lounging on the couch reading the Bible. She didn't even look up as she spoke. "How's Claire?"

"I got her to eat something," Andrew said evasively, not really wanting to explain just how sick she was. He tried to put Jilly down, but gave up as her tiny hands clawed at him and sat with her at the table.

"I found your Bible," Michelle intoned conversationally.

It wasn't actually his Bible. After he'd read it at Christmas and realized it had his first name in the front cover, he'd locked it in the wall safe in his room, but there had been another on the bookshelf.

She sighed and set it aside. Sitting up, she crossed her legs and watched him, unblinkingly. "So, you believe in all this?" Michelle nodded her head towards the book.

Andrew wasn't sure what he believed. Right now he'd never felt farther from the God he'd learned about as a child. "I grew up a Christian." He wasn't about to add that his dad was a pastor.

"I met a lot of Christians over the last few months," she drawled softly, and there was definitely a hint of menace in her voice. "I didn't like most of them."

He didn't know what to say to that. Jilly began to whimper softly, and he tightened his arms around her.

Michelle shook her head, lost in thought, and absently started twirling a lock of her hair between her fingers. The dark tresses moved like a snake slithering around her fingers, and Andrew had a hard time drawing his eyes away from it. "How does it feel, as a Christian, to have killed someone?"

She couldn't have affected him more if she'd physically punched him in the gut. "It sucks," he admitted honestly. "But I didn't think about it. I couldn't let him keep beating you."

"You could have though, most out there do. You're the exception out there, not the rule."

It would have been nice, in a different lifetime, to take the compliment and pat himself on the back. Andrew didn't, though. She didn't really mean it as a compliment. It was more of a backhanded slap at everyone else she'd met. "You don't know what I'd do if I were truly stuck out there," he reminded her softly. Maybe he was reminding himself too.

"You?" she laughed, but it was hollow, almost mocking. "I'm pretty sure you'd be fine out in the world. Until you trusted the wrong people. It's the rest of us idiots that are floundering."

Andrew watched her face carefully, looking for anything to tip him off as to what she wanted from him. He still didn't have a clue as to who she really was, but if he had to guess this was closer to her true self. It was almost useless to speculate, though. "Who were you before all of this happened?"

She laughed before replying, "No one. Not really. I read Harry Potter books. I hung out with my friends. I made stupid costumes. I definitely wasn't going to college, or getting married, or having kids anytime soon."

In that statement she'd told him pretty much everything he needed to know. She'd been a decent person, working a job she probably didn't like but paid the bills, and lived a life without much purpose or reason.

It was a snap judgment, but one he'd be willing to bet was reasonably accurate. If she'd had anything to remember with pride, he thought she probably would have said something. "College isn't everything," he told her, watching her closely.

She shrugged and looked away. "And yet you did it with a pregnant wife."

"I had my parents and Claire's parents helping us," Andrew said, and he knew deep down that if it had come to it that would have been what would have happened. Their families would have worked together; after they'd dug Andrew up, of course, because Scott would have killed him for getting his daughter pregnant. "I was nearly done with school anyway. It was just a bit crazy towards the end."

"There aren't a lot of guys like you out there, even before the world went to shit," Michelle grumbled, then glancing briefly at Jilly she muttered, "Sorry. I forgot she was there."

Jilly probably wasn't going to learn to swear right then, but he appreciated the concession. He didn't know what to say to her pronouncement, mostly because her view of him was wrapped around a large handful of lies. He didn't marry his pregnant girlfriend and finish college. He wasn't the man that she thought he was. Andrew was stepping in to fill a role, and trying his damnedest not to screw the whole thing up. "I think there are a lot of guys out there who would do what I did, especially if they have family to help."

"Maybe," she said reluctantly. "You're taking it so calmly."

He was lost. "What calmly?"

"Having another baby," she said, her eyes narrowed. "I would be freaking out."

Andrew shrugged helplessly. He could try to act more panicked but the truth was that Mia wasn't having a baby, and if she was, she'd be getting a Bible story written up about her. "Even if she is pregnant, what am I going to do about it?"

"Pennyroayal tea? I don't know. But I think your view on people is warped, even before the world changed. Most guys freak out. Most would have packed up and set off by now. Granted, some are out there," her focus shifted, and her voice stalled, but then, like snapping out of it, she finished, "But yeah, most guys suck. Especially now."

He didn't know what tea she was talking about, but he had a pretty good idea what it would do. "We wouldn't ever consider an abortion," Andrew whispered. With Jilly on his lap the thought of it left him weak and horrified.

"You'd be surprised at what you'd consider if you were desperate enough," Michelle said through gritted teeth. She crossed her arms and started picking at her sweatshirt, something he'd seen her do before.

"I couldn't," he said and knew he spoke the truth.

Her eyebrow rose. "Is that part of your faith? Being a fanatic about abortion?"

"No," Andrew said as gently as he could because he had an idea that he wasn't just speaking to someone with an opinion on the subject. He'd seen women fighting for abortion rights, and he'd had an in-depth conversation with a girl who had had one. It had changed him so completely that he'd never been able to look back. "I feel bad for anyone who has to do that. I don't think most women want an abortion, and that they grieve even if they feel like it's a relief, too. I just couldn't do that."

Michelle's eyes looked momentarily bright but a second later it was gone. "Yet you killed a man."

"Yes, I did," he agreed. Acid rose in his throat, but he swallowed hard to force it down. Jilly cuddled further into his side, almost like she could sense that he was upset. "I'm going to have to live with that."

"Will your God forgive you?"

Andrew, academically, knew that the answer to that was 'yes'. God would forgive anything if you asked for forgiveness. Where he was stuck now was trying to decide if he was truly remorseful for what he'd done. He'd ended the man's life to save Michelle. Could he go to God with true guilt and ask forgiveness? He didn't know. He didn't even know if he believed he could get into heaven unless he repented. He really wished his dad was there right then to talk to, to get some perspective.

She thumbed the book and said, "You know, sometimes I wish I could believe this." She lifted up the book and added, "Honestly, I think it takes strength to have that kind of faith. The whole world is falling apart, but there's some eternal being out there that loves you no matter what. My dad said I was nothing but wasted potential. I never had the strength to look for some other father who wasn't going to talk to me either."

A light bulb went off in his brain and even more pieces of her puzzle began to fall into place. Andrew had grown up with loving and supportive parents. They weren't perfect, and they'd never be perfect, but they were, at their core, good and had encouraged him in whatever he'd tried to do. His dad, a pastor, hadn't even condemned him when he'd expressed doubts about his faith. It was so much harder to build a life for yourself when you didn't have that. It was possible, of course, but exponentially more difficult. There was nothing he could say to Michelle that would ease the pain of what her father had said to her. There was no magic cure, or fix all to her problems. Even if she did believe in God, she'd have to work at it herself. Miracles happened, but typically it took hard work and help along the way.

What she said, though, was that she couldn't go to a heavenly father when her earthly one was such a joke. Andrew's dad had been anything but a joke, and yet he still struggled to find his place in the church. "I think," he began slowly, because he didn't want to say this the wrong way, "that faith is a journey, and you won't really know where it ends until you get there. The message that Jesus gave us is a good one whether you're a Christian or not. He wanted people to love the poor, sick and outcast and he disliked hypocrisy and the religious who used God as a weapon against others. One of my favorite stories in the Bible was when Jesus saved a woman from an angry mob. Are you familiar with it?" She shook her head once, her eyes riveted on his. "He said to this mob that wanted to stone her that whoever had never sinned should throw the first stone."

"That sounds vaguely familiar," Michelle said with her eyes still fixed on his face.

"If you believe the Bible, Jesus was the only one who had never sinned, so he was the only one who could throw a stone at her, but the crowd left and he told her that he didn't condemn her and to go and sin no more," Andrew finished, and he realized that he'd reached his answer without really meaning to. "To Jesus sin was sin, and there were no levels of sin. I sin every single day, and I can't judge others for their sins because I have enough of my own to deal with. I am sorry that a man died at my hand, but I'm not sorry that I saved your life. I think that maybe Jesus would say to me that he doesn't condemn me eternally, and I should move on in life and not do it again."

Michelle was silent for a long time. "Do you think you'll be able to pull that off? Do you think you'll be able to keep from killing someone else?"

"I'm going to try," he replied.

She nodded slowly and there was a glint in her eyes. "That's a good goal."

Jilly slowly unfurled from him and climbed down. She rested her head on his knee and watched Michelle.

"I'm never going to be perfect," Andrew said honestly. "I think that a lot of the people out there are reacting to a really difficult situation, and they're doing the best they can."

She snorted. "That's sad if that's true."

"Okay," he agreed, "maybe they aren't doing the best they can, but they're doing what they think they need to do to survive. It isn't easy to watch your family suffer and starve. It's going to make some people act badly."

"It's making everyone act badly," she countered. When she stood, Jilly backed further into him until she saw that Michelle was moving to sit with him at the kitchen table. Jilly took off to the back of the couch and peeked out at them.

Andrew watched her go and his concern mounted. He didn't know what was up with the toddler, and he wished like crazy that he could just ask her what was wrong.

Michelle's voice dragged his attention back to him. "Where does your moral compass lie?"

"In what way?" he asked, distracted between her and Jilly.

She didn't get a chance to answer. The door to his bedroom opened and Mia stumbled out, looking like death warmed over. Andrew stood automatically and went to her, catching her before she could fall. "What's up?"

"Bathroom," she groaned, and he picked her up and walked over with her to the bathroom.

He set her down inside the door and eyed her pale face. "Do you need my help?"

"No," she said weakly. "Just... don't go too far."

"Okay," Andrew said and he closed the door.

Jilly came over to him and stood beside him. She pointed at the door and said, "Mama."

"Yep, Jelly Bean, Mama isn't feeling good."

"Why do you call her that?" Michelle called to him.

Andrew grinned over his shoulder at her, "Because she's as sweet as a jelly bean, and she was tiny like one when she was born." That was definitely true. Jilly had been so small when he'd held her that first day. He'd never thought a baby could be that small, even though he supposed she wasn't undersized for a baby. It was just that his hands and arms had felt huge and clumsy when he held her.

Mia came out a few minutes later, and he picked her back up again. He carried her back to bed and set her down, covering her with the blankets. "Do you want anything to eat?"

"Maybe in a bit," she said even as her eyes were drifting shut. "Period started."

"Okay," he said with relief. Her cramps would ease up soon and she'd be back on her feet shortly.

Jilly started to cry from the door of the room. Andrew turned as she toddled quickly over to him, tears running down her cheeks. He scooped her up and held her close. "I'm sorry sweetheart; I didn't mean to leave you."

"Come here, baby," Mia crooned and she held out her arms to Jilly.

Jilly lunged for Mia and she snuggled in to her arms. Mia kissed her brow and whispered loving nonsense words into the baby's curls, stroking her finger gently over Jilly's cheek.

Andrew stared down at them, completely transfixed. His mind was blank even as his heart rate kicked into overdrive. He couldn't have torn his eyes away from them at that moment for anything. They looked so radiant together, almost like a painting. Mia's dark hair fell around her shoulders and commingled with Jilly's red locks, forming a beautiful contrast that was set off by the line of light that poured in from the kitchen. He'd never noticed it before, but they also shared the same small nose that turned up slightly at the end. Mia had been angling for a nose ring for a few years and her dad had been staunchly refusing, but she'd argued she had the perfect nose for it. She probably did, too.

He'd wanted to see what the stud would have looked like, but her dad had told her she had to wait till she was eighteen. Now it didn't matter, except to say that her nose was cute just like the rest of her and Jilly was her spitting image and looking at the two of them together did something very odd to his insides.

He knelt down next to them and leaned in to kiss the crown of Jilly's head. Mia turned her face to his and he cupped her cheek. His eyes met hers and he saw something there that he hadn't seen before. Andrew felt drawn to her and although she didn't move, it felt like she was leaning towards him, willing him to close to distance. He did. He sat up and brushed his lips against hers, lingering just for a second before he pulled back and looked into her stunning blue eyes. Andrew saw only love and acceptance. "You are so beautiful," he whispered reverently, taking in every inch of her face. But it wasn't just her face, because even if she was a lot less attractive, he would still find her beautiful. It was her heart that always drew him back to her, and that had nothing to do with her looks.

How he'd managed not to fall in love with her before now, he had no idea.

Jilly poked him in the chin. He glanced down to see her waving him off. Andrew got the message. This was her 'mama' and she didn't want to share just then. He kissed her noisily on her chubby cheek and rose. "I'll be back with dinner in a bit. Call if you want me to get her."

24

Mia was able to eat some dinner that night and Andrew managed to get Jilly to play with the blocks for a bit after dinner. She wouldn't stay and play unless he was sitting right there, but after a lot of cajoling, he succeeded in getting her off his lap. It wasn't much, but it was progress. Michelle kept to herself, not really seeking him out for conversation while Jilly was still awake.

After Jilly went to bed, though, Michelle wandered back out to the living room. Andrew had known instinctively that she was going to do it, but he couldn't figure out how to divert her attention. Instead of anything intelligent, he asked if she wanted to play a game.

Michelle had stared blankly at him for a full twenty seconds before answering. "What kind of game?"

"We have a bunch of board games or we can play cards," he told her, trying not sound too lame. He knew he was grasping at straws, but he hoped that if she had something to focus on that she would stop trying to needle him.

"Sure," she said slowly, and grinned slyly. "We can play strip poker."

Andrew managed not to roll his eyes, but only just. "We have poker chips."

"Spoil sport," Michelle all but purred. She walked over to stand next to him. "Poker it is. I like Texas Hold'em myself. It reminds me of someone from my old life."

"Fine," he said, and he had to brush past her to get to the cards. He got everything down from a cabinet and set them on the table. He shuffled while she counted out poker chips. He dealt out the two cards that they each held, then laid up the three cards which were called the flop. Andrew checked his whole cards and saw he had a ten of spades and three of clubs. The flop was an ace of hearts, a two of hearts, and a three of spades. He had a pair of threes. Which basically sucked.

"All in," Michelle said with a sweet smile.

Andrew folded, and took her cards back to shuffle again.

"What was your favorite thing to do as a hobby?" Michelle asked him as he dealt again.

"Uhm," his mind went blank as he handed out the new cards. "I liked shooting. My father-in-law is in to guns. I used to play soccer. What about you?"

She shrugged. "I was a bit of a geek."

"Who wasn't?" he chuckled.

"I liked movies, and music," she told him and placed a small bet.

Andrew called, and dealt up more cards. "I really miss Claire's cooking."

Michelle folded and he gathered up his new chips as well as the cards so he could deal again. "What about Claire's cooking?"

"Oh," Andrew shook his head. He needed to focus. "Claire was going to apply to Cordon Bleu this year. She's an amazing cook, but with the limited supply of ingredients she's not really able to do much. Still," he added hastily as he could see the dark cloud brewing over her face at what he'd said, "I'm thankful that we get to eat at all, but another hobby was definitely my wife's cooking. I kept trying to convince her to make me fat."

"So you were going to move to France so she could go to school?"

"We wouldn't have to," he explained and checked his whole cards; king of hearts and a four of diamonds. "There is a campus in Boston. If she'd gotten in, I'd have applied for a job up there."

Michelle sat back, staring at him intently. "You'd have moved so she could go to school?"

"Yeah," he frowned at her expression. "Why?"

She didn't say anything, but frown lines stood out further on her face. "You know," she said slowly. She pushed back from the table and rose. "I'm really tired all of a sudden. I think I'm going to turn in."

"Okay," Andrew said, not at all sorry. "Good night."

Michelle walked back to the door, and looked at him her eyebrow cocked. "You don't have to sleep alone if you don't want to."

"I'm not sleeping alone," he countered as anger started to pump through him. "I'm sleeping with my wife."

"Yeah," she drawled sarcastically. "Okay then."

The door clicked shut behind her.

Andrew stared at the closed door for well over a minute before he could make his muscles move to clean up the game. He was done with this. Whatever it was that she wanted from him, and he had a very hard time believing that she was so desperate for sex that she was truly hitting on him, he just wanted to get it out in the open. So he could tell her no.

The most obvious answer would be that she wanted to stay here in the shelter. If that was the case then there was something very, very wrong in her thought process because he and Mia had done their best to make it plain that they were in love and sleeping together. Could she possibly think that he'd keep her here with Mia and Jilly if he got to sleep with her as well?

Who the hell had she met while traveling? What tricks had she been forced to learn to stay alive? Was she actually really astute when it came to people, or was that a survival technique that had come about when trying to cope with all the people she'd have run into?

Andrew pressed the heels of his hands into his eyes and rubbed. He couldn't believe she'd been so blatant. Did she know, in the fullest sense of the euphemism that they weren't sleeping together?

He broke into a cold sweat. If she suspected this was all a ruse, then they might be in trouble. She'd have to wonder why they were making up this elaborate lie, wonder what they were trying to hide.

Michelle's bruises were starting to fade. Her face was still a wide assortment of colors from deep blue, to purple, to green but she was moving about better and already she was looking healthier. Andrew wasn't an expert, but he was hopeful that he'd be able to walk her out in another week.

A week. He groaned and dropped his head onto his arms. He did not want to put up with her for another week. She'd already pissed him off and she'd only been there... Andrew paused to count, and realized with horror that it was only been two days. It felt like a month already.

Wearily he rose to his feet and trudged towards his room, flipping off the lights as he went. If he was going to have to do battle with her again the next day, he needed a good night's rest.

The following morning Jilly woke up first, and before Andrew really wanted to be up. Mia didn't even stir as he changed the baby and left the room. Michelle's door was still closed and Andrew let out a sigh of relief. He parked Jilly in her high chair and heated up some breakfast for them. He was able to feed her and himself with a lot less juggling.

After she was finished, Andrew set Jilly down and made breakfast for Mia. He took it in to her and woke her up enough to eat some of it, and he left the rest next to her on the nightstand. He'd hoped that she'd be up more that day, which would insulate him from Michelle's flirting, but it clearly wasn't meant to be. He left the door open and went to wash out the pot that he'd not cleaned from dinner the night before. After it was rinsed, he left it on a towel on the counter to dry, which would annoy Mia if she was up, but Jilly had come over to tug at his pants leg.

In her hand was an Elmo book, and on her face was a bit of her breakfast. Andrew swiped at it with his thumb and went over to the couch to read to her.

They played for over an hour before Michelle opened her door and walked out. She didn't say more than a quick, "Morning," as she made her way to the bathroom.

Initially Jilly ran to him, but after she was gone, the toddler relaxed and went back to playing.

Andrew sighed heavily and rose to his feet. Having another person in the shelter was more work when that person didn't offer to pitch in or help. He pulled out a bowl and poured in some oats, added water and stuck it in the microwave.

After the beep, he pulled open the door and removed the steaming oats, cursing silently at the heat. He'd put them in for longer than he typically cooked Jilly's. Andrew quickly dumped the bowl on the table and shook out his hand. He looked down and saw that while his fingers were a little red, they weren't really burned.

Michelle emerged from the bathroom and came over to him. She took his hand and examined it carefully. "It isn't a bad burn."

"No," he agreed and attempted to pull his hand back.

She resisted and he watched, in horrified fascination, as she lifted his hand and kissed the burned spot. "There," she crooned, looking up at him. "All better."

This time he ripped his hand out of hers. "That's enough," he said sharply. "You need to stop that crap."

"Really?" Michelle said, arching her eyebrow as she crossed her arms over her chest.

"What do you hope to gain by this?" Andrew asked her quietly. He realized belatedly that he'd left the door open to his room and Mia was in there sleeping.

Her green eyes darkened. "I can offer you things that your little *wife* can't." She said wife like it was a poisonous word.

Andrew rolled his eyes contemptuously. "I don't need anything you have to offer. I'm doing you a favor, and all I wanted was for you to behave yourself. Is that so effing difficult?"

Jilly let out a small whimper and came over and pulled at his pants leg, but he didn't pick her up. He couldn't focus on the baby when the woman in front of him was making him see red.

"I'm behaving myself," Michelle countered, and this time her voice shook. "I've not done anything to warrant getting kicked out."

"Except hitting on me," Andrew pointed out in exasperation. He slammed his hand against the table frustrated, and glared at her. "I'm married! I love my wife! Why on earth would I want to sleep with you?"

She let out a huff of frustration. "Because you have a dick, and you fiddle with that ring when no one is paying attention. And know what's not on the shelves? Your wedding album. What newly married woman doesn't grab her wedding album when leaving her home?"

Andrew thought fast, but the answer came without much effort. "We didn't know we were staying up here. We didn't pack to be here long term." Then he caught himself doing exactly what she'd said. He'd started to fiddle with the ring that he'd worn for months now, but rarely thought about. He froze and she smirked.

"Quiet nights, and the way you move around her is...stiff. And not in an oh-so-witty that's what she said way. But awkward." Michelle took a deliberate step towards him and if he hadn't been stuck by the table he'd have stumbled. He felt like her gaze held him trapped like a deer in headlights. "You pick her up when she's ill, and your hands are very clearly not touching anything you don't feel like is yours. You're the white knight, not the sex in college type."

"I..." Andrew faltered. "I'm in love with my wife." This, at least, was true. Well, at least that he was in love with Mia as of the last twenty-four hours. Then another bump into his leg made him blurt out, "So how did Nelly get here then?"

Michelle scrunched up her nose considering. "She's definitely Claire's kid. They look too much alike to not be related, but I'd bet anything that the two of you have never had sex. I think you love Nelly, a whole lot, but I don't think she's yours."

"She's mine," he contradicted forcefully. "She's my daughter!"

"This isn't an episode of Montel, so sadly, I can't bring you the DNA results. And sure, she can be yours in that adopted sort of way, which is sweet, but she's not yours." She paused, glaring at him, her eyes widened slightly before she blurted, "You're a virgin, aren't you? Always around kids the wrong age as you. No wonder you're not interested, you don't even know what you're missing."

Andrew was stuck. His limbs wouldn't move and his heart was beating so fast that he was starting to feel light headed and he wanted desperately to reach down for Jilly, but his limbs weren't working properly. A slight movement from his doorway snapped him out of it. He saw Mia, standing in the door looking terrified, and he knew he couldn't just stand there like an idiot. He stared into Michelle's cold eyes. "Even if that was the truth, I wouldn't ever sleep with you." He enjoyed hurting her more than he should have, and a spiteful grin twisted his lips.

"You think I actually *want* you? You wouldn't even know what to do with me if you *had* me. The white knight routine may be good enough for other people who don't know how the real world works. Fucking idiot, this is the real world." Michelle moved so fast that Andrew didn't even register what she was doing until it was too late. She bent down and snatched up Jilly from the floor.

"No!" Andrew hollered and lurched forward even as she stepped back and put her hand up over Jilly's throat.

Jilly let out a strangled squeak and started to thrash and Michelle's knuckles turned white as she closed her fist. "Stop or she dies!"

Andrew stumbled to a stop, staring in horror as panic and fear flooded his senses. "You can't hurt her!"

"I don't want you, and I don't need the friendship of your girlfriend. I want this place, and if you won't play my game and get a little something in return, we're going to play this one instead. Get the hell out of here, or watch *your* Jelly Bean's neck get snapped. Your choice."

He didn't have enough time to do more than open his mouth before Mia had lunged from her spot in their bedroom door. She grabbed the pot he'd left on the counter and swung it hard at Michelle's head just as Michelle turned to see what the movement was.

It connected with her skull with a nauseating *crack*. Andrew leapt forward and snatched Jilly from her just as Michelle crumbled to the floor in an ungainly heap. He pulled the toddler in close, even as she began to flail about.

Jilly started wailing. The sound was absolutely, ear-piercingly, deafening, but he could barely hear her over the thundering of his own heart.

Mia swayed for a moment before kneeling down to check the pulse at Michelle's neck. "Still alive."

His brain kicked back into action and as Mia rose to her feet, her arms out for Jilly, he handed her off and went for the rope from the storage room. He pulled Michelle's hands behind her back and tied them securely. Next he bound her feet. She was either unconscious or dying, but he wasn't going to take a chance.

Andrew moved, almost felt pulled, over to Mia and Jilly. He wrapped them both in his arms. He could feel Mia shaking hard as he guided them back to his room. The door clicked behind them and the sound made Mia jump. He pushed her gently so she sat on the bed, and he knelt at her feet, looking straight into her shattered eyes. "You were awesome, Mia."

Her teeth were chattering hard and she couldn't quite meet his gaze. Jilly was wrapped hard around her, but she'd calmed down and wasn't crying anymore. There was a faint red mark on her neck.

Rage overflowed out of him. He stood and turned, needing to hide the burning anger from her. He didn't want to scare her any more than she'd already been traumatized. He couldn't believe that Michelle had actually been willing to hurt an innocent child just to save herself. What the hell kind of person did that? Who the fuck thought it was okay to screw with a baby? To use her like that?

"Drew." Mia's voice was soft, nearly broken.

He spun back to her and felt his eyes sting at the tears that were pouring down her face. "I'm so sorry!"

"It wasn't your fa-"

Andrew cut her off. "I brought her here. I killed someone for her, and I nearly got my daughter killed because I saved her worthless-" his brain caught up to his mouth and he stared first at Mia and then down to Jilly in disbelief at what he'd said. My daughter. Not Scott's, she's mine; mine and Mia's. He held out his arms and took Jilly back from Mia. He cradled her against his chest and rubbed her back as his tears finally fell freely into her soft curls.

"Dada," Jilly said as she patted his shoulder. It was almost like she was trying to console him.

He was a complete wreck. Andrew stared at Mia, whose hands were over her mouth. It looked to him like she was trying to keep herself from screaming.

"I'm going to take Michelle away from here," Andrew told her firmly, even though he didn't raise his voice. "As soon as she can walk I'm leading her away. She'll never be able to come back."

"She's still not well enough," Mia said dejectedly. "I should care about that, but I just can't. What a flaming psycho."

He sat next to her on the bed and Jilly crawled off him and back towards the middle of the bed where she could jump while they were distracted. Andrew took Mia's hand and squeezed. "She had a chance and she blew it."

Mia shook her head. "How did she figure us out? I can't believe she could tell that we aren't... that we don't... I tried to-"

"Stop," Andrew said mildly. "We did what we could. She still has no idea who we really are and that's all that matters."

Her glance flicked up to his, and it was almost reproachful. "If we can't fool one girl, we're screwed! Dad was adamant about it."

He didn't know what to say. His feelings for Mia had changed so radically over the last few days, and yet he was stuck in this impossible situation with her. Andrew didn't know if Mia felt differently, but from the way she was looking at him he was going to hazard a guess that her feelings hadn't changed. It hurt. A lot.

"Don't look at me like that," Mia whispered, "please don't. I can't take it."

"I don't know what to say," he admitted as he ran his thumb along the back of her hand. He focused on their entwined fingers and wished he had a magic answer.

They both heard a moan and Andrew sprang to his feet. "Stay here," he told Mia. "Keep Jilly in here." He didn't give her a chance to argue as he moved quickly from the room and closed the door behind him.

Michelle's head was shaking slightly, muttering to the kitchen floor. "I - I'm - s--ry. Jus--Just can-n-n-t more. I-I-why-can-n-t s-see. Now. Ho-oh-pe -ha-ha-happy."

Andrew crouched down at her side, and he saw the dejected tears that were spilling from her eyes. "Can you understand me?" He didn't reach out to touch her, much as he'd done the first day he'd saved her.

He'd become a murderer for her, and she'd tried to kill his kid. The whole situation was so far down the road of fucked up that there wasn't any real way to get back with his soul completely intact.

"Can you understand me?" he repeated again, louder this time.

"Yes," she said coldly.

"If this is the real world, you've lost," Andrew told her coldly. "Whatever shred of humanity that might have lived in you? It's gone. No," he cut her off before she could retort, "don't speak. I don't want to hear it. Nothing could have been bad enough to make you hurt a child. Nothing." He grabbed a dish cloth from the counter and forcefully shoved it in her mouth.

Michelle gagged and tried to bite him, but he kept pushing until she was unable to do more than glare wordlessly up at him.

He stood slowly, taking deep breaths to try to calm his fear and rage. If he was pissed, he was going to make a mistake, and he couldn't afford to make any mistakes. Whatever she'd done, she'd be gone soon. He'd tried to help her; she'd screwed herself. Although Jilly was a little hurt, she was still okay, and by that evening they'd all be safe again in isolation.

When he came back, he and Mia would have a long talk about how they were going to cope if they ran into others, but that could wait.

Andrew turned away from Michelle and started to make a mental list as he went to retrieve her backpack.

25

Andrew worked quickly, moving through the shelter to gather what he'd need to get Michelle away, and although he was hard pressed to swallow it, the supplies she'd need to survive for a while. He gathered up her back pack and her weapons. He gave her another round of bullets for her handgun, and grabbed a couple of MRE's for her pack along with some water bottles. When he arrived back in the kitchen, he found Mia on the floor putting Michelle's boots on. Neither looked happy.

"Where's Nelly?" Andrew asked.

"She's in her crib," Mia answered tying one of the laces. "I gave her a few books."

"I'm surprised she let you do that," he mused dryly, nodding at Michelle.

Mia shook her head. "She tried to kick me, but I assured her she could leave without shoes and I wouldn't give a crap, so she stopped. Her clothes are piled over there," she told him and pointed to a stack on the counter.

Andrew took them and shoved until he could get everything in. He zipped it shut and turned to stare down at her. The look in her eyes was pure hatred. He bent and after freeing her feet he pulled her upright. Mia draped Michelle's coat around her and zipped it up, with her arms still bound behind her back. It looked bizarre, but it would work for the hike out of here.

"I'll be back when I can," Andrew promised Mia. "With her tied up it's going to take a couple of hours at least."

"Okay," Mia agreed quietly. She turned to Michelle and bit her lip. "I forgive you."

Michelle stepped back, her eyes widening. The rag was still in her mouth so she couldn't retort, but the surprise quickly faded to something like disdain.

Mia smiled sadly. "I'm sorry your journey has been so terrible. I hope you can make it home."

Andrew didn't wait for her to give Mia another dirty look. He took his watch cap and shoved it down over her head, effectively blinding her. Then he grasped her arm through the thick coat and marched her over to the stairs. "Wait here," he instructed as he climbed up and unlocked the hatch. Mia had come over behind him, and when he came back down she gave him a look that told him she'd lock up behind him.

He guided Michelle up the steps and looked back long enough to watch Mia close the rock. He didn't speak unless he had to. She didn't try to fight him or to communicate in any way. Andrew didn't lead her straight up to the trail. He headed off to the north, parallel to the Appalachian Trail in a long, wending trip that was designed to leave as few foot prints as possible. Certain parts of the ground were rockier than others and he stuck mainly to those. Slowly he started to move in the direction of the trail. He walked up to within ten feet and continued along until he found a way to cross the trail without it being obvious that they were on it. They headed over and continued north for at least another quarter of a mile before he turned her back up to a flat area filled with a lot of evergreens. He wanted a lot of cover to get away from her after he loosened her hands up.

Andrew sat her on a tree root and dropped her pack next to her. "Hold still," he ordered. He pulled a rope out of her pack and tied her upper body to the tree using a simple knot that she'd be able to undo quickly. He reached under her jacket and started to pull the knot free. It would still likely take her ten minutes to get it undone, but she'd be able to wiggle her hands free. More to the point he was going to hide and make sure that she did.

Andrew stood and stared down at her. He blew out a slow breath, calming his pulse much as he'd do before taking a shot with a gun. He put as much steel and resolve as he could into every word. "You will be able to free yourself soon. You're facing northeast which will keep you on the right track to get home. Do not try to find us again. You won't. If I see you again I will kill you. You had your chance, we're done. I wouldn't wait too long to leave. Bears are everywhere around here. Do you understand?"

After a moment she nodded curtly. He still couldn't see her face because of the black watch cap that was pulled down past her chin, but he was sure that if looks could kill he'd be getting one that would lay him out flat. He backed off silently and made his way off the trail on the northern side and found a thick patch that he could blend in to and observe her. The shelter was down from the trail to the south. If she pulled free and went down to the south off the trail he'd know that she knew where the shelter was and would be attempting to find it again.

Michelle sat for a full minute. Her shoulders shook, and Andrew was sure she was crying. After the brief crying jag she started to wiggle her hands back and forth. As he'd suspected it only took her about five minutes to get her hands free. She twisted her shoulders until she'd pushed up the rope and her coat so that she could use her arms.

She ripped off the watch cap and threw it to the ground before pulling the wadded up rag from her mouth. She spit fuzz out onto her fingers and growled in frustration. He watched her right her coat, putting her arms into the sleeves properly. Michelle stood and turned a full circle, scanning the area around her. "You should have just killed me!" she called out angrily. Her voice cracked as she said it.

She stood still looking up the path that was steadily being reclaimed by nature. She stooped and pulled up the bag, slinging it onto her back, and with a huff she took off up the trail, leaving the rope, the rag and the watch cap on the ground where he'd tied her. Andrew watched her go and even followed her for a bit, but she didn't stop or look back. After thirty minutes he back tracked to where she'd left the stuff, collected it, and started to make his way back to the shelter.

He stopped several times to wait and watch. Andrew was reasonably certain that neither she, nor anyone, was following him back, but he wanted to be sure. It was well past lunch by the time he made his way back to the shelter.

Ten feet from the rock opening of the shelter stood a huge buck grazing on some of the vegetation that was starting to peek out through the late winter ground. Andrew froze and stared at it, unable to quite believe what he was seeing. He had a hand gun and the crossbow. Ideally he'd shoot it with the crossbow and save the meat from powder burn, but the likelihood that he'd get it out without startling the deer was slim. Plus there was the cleaning and preparing that was involved in it.

They'd just been through something so traumatic that he didn't want to even be thinking about. Mia was barely on her feet from being sick and getting her period.

Jilly was going to be clingy after what happened.

Getting the buck down into the shelter would be a nightmare and would leave the opening vulnerable for at least thirty minutes while he dragged it in.

He should let it go. Now was not a good time.

But... his mind was racing as a hundred different thoughts threw themselves at him, all vying for supremacy.

Andrew pulled the bow slowly from his back, and as quietly as he could he loaded an arrow in and pulled the string back.

The deer glanced back at him, and he hesitated, even as he was lined up to take the shot.

Life went on and they had to survive. That was real life.

He pulled the trigger. His aim was true and the point of the arrow went straight into the deer's flank, right where its heart was located. It started and jumped a bit before dropping slowly to the forest floor on a bed of leaves. Andrew moved forward and looked into his eyes. He saw the light go out, just as he'd seen in the man.

He didn't know what the man's name had been. He'd never asked.

He felt a lump form in his throat.

He stared down at it for another moment before he went to the fake rock and knocked, calling out for Mia to unlock it for him.

As soon as she had the hatch open, and he'd assured her that he was okay, he went to get the supplies to cut up the deer.

It was miserable work dragging the deer back to the hatch, even though it wasn't a long distance. It was huge, probably weighing a good bit more than he did. He used the deer's hind legs to pull it and he had to stop every few seconds to catch his breath as he dragged it over the rocks and sticks.

"Let me help you," Mia said from beside him. The only silver lining was that Jilly was asleep.

"I don't want you to hurt yourself," he gasped.

She ignored him and went to the head. She lifted it with a grunt and hollered, "Pull!"

It moved a bit more when she did that, but she had to set it down in between each tug. After twenty sweaty minutes they had it to the entrance. Andrew put the tarp down on the stairs and told Mia to hold the end of it. She knelt at the hole and held tight. He could see that her hands were stiff from the cold, but she didn't comment as he pulled, pushed, shoved and swore while getting the deer onto the tarp. When it finally dropped free the end of the tarp was yanked from Mia's grasp, and the deer slid down into the shelter with several loud bangs.

"That went well," Mia said dryly. She turned to him, a look of concern etched on her face. "I'm sorry, I couldn't hold it."

"It's fine," he assured her. He stepped in after her, and they went down to the deer to begin cleaning it and prepping it for freezing.

They worked for hours and the memories of their previous deer came flooding back. Mia nearly threw up twice as she helped him cut the deer up, but after walking away for a bit she held it together enough to continue. He cut up the slices while she used the airtight sealer bags. Mia had to take a quick break to deal with Jilly after she woke up from her nap, and Mia ended up with her on her back as she worked through the rest of the deer. He couldn't believe she'd been able to push herself through her exhaustion. Andrew had said he'd carry Jilly, but on the whole Mia's job was a lot less messy.

Hauling all of the bones, blood and guts up and out of the shelter was the worst part. It was disgusting and heavy hauling the buckets up and away from their clearing. It took him more trips than he cared to count to get the whole thing cleaned up, and by the time it was over he was covered head to foot in grime, blood and other bodily fluids that he didn't want to contemplate. After he had thoroughly cleaned up the shelter, Mia had showered and put Jilly to bed. Then it was his turn. He stripped off in the bathroom and scrubbed until the water went cold.

He came out to find the smell of meat cooking and Mia in sweats and fuzzy socks standing at the kitchen stove pushing something around in the pan. Andrew limped over and sank into a chair. His previously injured knee had started to ache towards the end of it, and now it was positively throbbing.

She dished up the food, and he wolfed it down as soon as she'd set the plate in front of him. He'd missed lunch, and now he couldn't seem to get enough for dinner. Mia normally made enough so that they could get a few meals out of it, but there was nothing left tonight.

Andrew sat back with a groan, and she was staring at him in mild fascination. "I don't think I've ever seen a person eat that much in one go."

"It was excellent," he assured her. He tried to work up the energy to get up and wash the dishes, but his body refused to follow his command.

Besides, there was so much he wanted to talk to her about and right here and now was a perfect opportunity. "Mia..."

"No," she cut in and shook her head resolutely. "I'm not ready to talk about it yet."

He examined every inch of her face, and he saw the emotions that were bubbling just under the surface. "Okay," he agreed. "Later."

They went to bed early that night, and he held her close. By the sound of her breathing, Mia didn't fall asleep any easier than he did. His mind wouldn't stop racing as it played the events of the day over and over again. He could still hear the exact sound that the pot had made as it hit Michelle's head. He could still feel the unbridled terror as he grabbed Jilly.

Andrew could also clearly hear himself saying that Jilly was his daughter. Had it been a Freudian slip? Scott had asked him to watch out for his girls, both of them. He'd asked Andrew to step in as Jilly's father. He'd hinted that it might be forever. Scott hadn't said it outright, but the implication had been crystal clear. Scott hadn't been sure that he'd ever have the opportunity to take over Jilly's care again.

"This is a lot to ask," Scott had said to them when they'd talked a few months back. "I don't think my chances of surviving this are good." He'd met Andrew's gaze, and a lot was said without any words.

It was a lot to ask. It was a lot less when he considered that by allowing him to come to the shelter, Scott had saved his life, but it was still a lot to ask someone to be the father of your kid. Andrew had been telling himself for months that it was temporary, and he was just a stand in. He had no idea when his brain had switched and he'd truly become Jilly's dad. Maybe it had been at that exact moment when Michelle had threatened her, or maybe some other time and he hadn't noticed. It was terrifying, and amazing all at the same time. The thought of handing her back to Scott was unbelievably painful, even though he knew he would if they made it out alive.

Mia sighed gently and rolled over. Her breathing evened out and sleep overcame her. Andrew stared at the darkness and started counting sheep.

It was a week before Mia moved Jilly out of his room. He'd gone up to check the solar panels and come back to find her moving the crib out. Andrew half expected Mia to move back in with her sister as well, despite what they'd discussed before, but she didn't. He'd watched her finish setting up the crib and when she came back out of the other room to see him standing there, she'd burst into tears. He'd held her while she cried, cradling her against him. When she'd managed to compose herself, she didn't want to talk about the tears.

"I need to get started on the garden," she said in a thick voice as she'd wiped her eyes. "It's really time now. I can't put it off any longer."

They spent the next few weeks working most of the day up in the chilly early March sun. Jilly loved it. They showed her how to throw out the weeds, sticks and rocks, and she had a marvelous time taking everything they handed to her and throwing it outside the garden wall. It wasn't the neatest job ever, but it kept her busy and moving.

Jilly had shaken off what had happened to her in a matter of a few hours. She was back to her happy, babbling self so quickly that it was almost like it had never happened. Andrew wished that he could get past it as easily. He kept seeing the man's dead eyes staring up at him. He'd woken a few times from a nightmare where the man lurched back up and grabbed him. The only bright spot was that Mia was right there next to him, ready to comfort him when it happened.

She hadn't escaped the nightmares either. Hers centered on someone finding and killing them, but she could never get a clear image of who was attacking them. This faceless terror had hit her for three nights running before it finally faded.

Andrew's feelings for Mia had been gradually solidifying in to a steady thrum that beat through him whenever he thought about her. She was still avoiding discussing anything, and he wasn't going to push it. They had forever to talk, but not forever to get the spring planting done. He didn't want her distracted when she had a lot of things to keep straight in her mind. They needed to try to plant fruits, vegetables, grains and potatoes in the large garden plot and somehow keep the deer out. That was going to be a feat in and of itself because the deer were everywhere now. They'd had one occasion where a large one had tried to stare Andrew down, but he'd had the pepper spray on him and it had only taken a tiny squirt before the buck had run off.

"We're going to have to make some kind of fence," Mia said one afternoon after they'd put in the broccoli and the snow peas. "We have some wire so conceivably we could make something."

"Do we have enough wire?" Andrew asked as he gathered up the tools.

She shrugged helplessly. "I don't remember. I think there were a couple of miles of wire so I assume so, but I might be wrong."

They did have a couple of miles of wire on several large spools.

"The things your dad thought to stock just amaze me," Andrew told her as they started to lay out a grid in the store room floor later that night.

"I wish he'd thought to just buy fencing," Mia grumbled. "This is going to take us forever."

It didn't take forever, but it did take them almost two full weeks of working every single night to get a fence constructed and put up in the garden. Their hands were raw from handling the wires constantly, and it was definitely flimsy, but it would keep out the deer and the wall would keep out the rabbits. The squirrels were going to be a huge issue, but there wasn't much they could do about them. They could get in practically anything.

Andrew stood back and looked at their handiwork and grinned. He slung his arm over Mia's shoulder and kissed the top of her head. "You did good, kid."

Mia shrugged happily. "It was a team effort."

"Beed!" Jilly cried out happily, holding up a weed for them to inspect.

"Thank you," Mia said with a grin as she took the weed. Then Jilly demanded to have it back. She walked over and threw it through the fence back in to the garden.

"Ah well," Andrew mused, "she'll get it eventually."

They fell silent, watching Jilly walk around, enjoying the clean smell of the forest, and the sounds of the world waking up around them from the winter's sleep.

Andrew let out a sigh. He didn't want to break their peace, but it was time. "We're going to need to talk about what happened."

Mia didn't respond, but he felt her shoulders stiffen.

"Why are you so afraid?" He asked, turning to look down at her.

She looked off, away into the woods. "It hurts."

He didn't know what to say to that.

"I know it's going to keep hurting," she continued. "I know that we have to hash it all out, but I don't want to. I'd rather not face it."

"What's so scary, Mia?" Andrew asked her gently.

Mia turned back to him, and he was startled to see the wet trails that snaked down her cheeks. Her eyes were red, along with the tip of her nose. "I think everything has changed."

"Things always change," he said. "Did you want it to stay the same forever?"

"Yes," she retorted then sighed heavily and rolled her shoulders. "No. No, I didn't want things to stay the same but they aren't what I expected."

"What were you expecting?"

"Fireworks," she whispered and his heart took a flying leap up into his throat as her amazingly blue eyes fixed upon him. "I thought it would be a huge explosion."

Andrew was almost afraid to ask, to hope. "What would?"

She hesitated for only a moment. "Falling in love with you."

26

Andrew felt a grin tug at his mouth as he watched Mia's uncertain face. "Funny, I was thinking the same thing."

"Yeah?" she bit her lip looking uncertain.

"Yeah," he said as he bent to kiss her.

Jilly busted in between them. "Daddy pweas."

Andrew glanced down at her, then back at Mia who was looking faraway and a little anxious. "Okay Jillibean, come on," he sighed as he hoisted her up into his arms.

He didn't normally count down the minutes till Jilly's bed time, but that day it felt like every minute lasted an hour until they finally had peace and quiet in the shelter. It wasn't helped by Jilly needing a shower since she was coated in dirt. It meant extra time and work in the evening for them.

Andrew plopped down on the couch as soon as he'd shut the door to Jilly's room. Mia came out of the bathroom a moment later with a couple of wet towels. She dropped them in a laundry basket and hesitated as she watched him. Her brown hair was getting really long, and it hung in loose curtains around her face. Her eyes looked huge as she watched him. He held out a hand and she walked over to sit with him.

Mia didn't exactly sit next to him, though. She sat close enough to stick her cold feet under his thigh so they'd get warm, but far enough away that she could look at him which meant she wanted to talk. She leaned against the back of the couch and regarded him.

Andrew waited her out. He knew that she had a lot on her mind and that, for her, talking about it was going to be more difficult. He'd wanted to talk weeks ago.

"I thought you were pretending at first," Mia said finally. She blinked and looked away for a second, before meeting his gaze again. "That time you kissed me here on the couch. It felt like it was an act you were putting on for her."

"It started that way," he admitted sheepishly. "Then something just, I dunno, just changed or switched and... and then it wasn't pretend anymore, at least for me."

Mia nodded and tucked her hair back behind her ear. "Then I thought... I thought that maybe it was your way of trying to run away from what you'd done to... that guy."

Andrew closed his eyes and nodded. He hadn't thought of that, but it was a possibility. Or it would have been if his feelings weren't so real, present and solid. "I still feel sick over that," he told her honestly. He looked at her concerned face and shook his head. "I don't know how to deal with it. I did what I thought was right at the time, but the man died because of me." He needed to say the next part, even though it made him feel ill even thinking about it. "I wouldn't blame you if you hated me for it."

"No," she told him frankly. "I couldn't hate you for it. You saved a tiny woman from a larger man. In that situation she looked like the victim."

"You didn't hear what she was saying to him before he started wailing on her," he said softly as the memories flooded back. "It was horrible."

Mia's left eyebrow rose. "Could I say anything at all that would make you beat the crap out of me?"

"No!" he exclaimed, stunned, but her point hit home. "It didn't matter what she said, you mean. He didn't have the right to do that to her. He could have just walked away."

"Yep," she said, and wiggled her feet a bit. Even through the socks and his jeans he could feel how frozen they were.

"I still brought her here," he reminded her. The guilt ate at him constantly. "I brought that crazy woman here where she could hurt you and Jilly."

Mia shook that off, waving her hand like it was nothing. "I'd have done the same thing, and I'd be sitting where you are apologizing for it. It was a mistake, but it's done, and thankfully we made it through. We'll learn from it."

"No more people down here?" Andrew asked, curious as to what she wanted to take away from this.

"Not exactly," she said. "Jamal was great, and I'm glad we saved his life. I think you knew that Michelle was off her rocker. Maybe next time we trust our instincts."

"Okay," he said as he took in her words. He wasn't sure that he was ever going to rely totally on instinct again, but there wasn't much point in arguing about it right now. He *had* known that something was up with Michelle and he'd taken a chance anyway. That wasn't exactly instinct, that was ignoring the obvious. He could have patched her up on the trail, brought her extra food, and sent her on her way. Andrew could easily let himself sit in the guilt and pain, but it wouldn't achieve anything. He had to learn from it and move on. He didn't know what he was going to learn, but he'd work on that. The man he'd killed was likely to always haunt him, and he decided he was okay with that. That wasn't something that should be brushed under the rug.

"I really thought falling in love would feel like I'd been bashed in the head," Mia mused as she traced a finger along the vein on his hand. "I'm not even sure how I know that I am in love with you, just that I am. But I don't feel like I'm tumbling out of control, or like I've been knocked stupid."

"When you put it like that," Andrew frowned contemplatively, "falling in love doesn't sound all that pleasant."

She looked at him expectantly, and he couldn't quite guess what she wanted. That, at least, was typical with girls that he'd been interested in. A sudden horrible thought hit him that maybe Mia would turn into this blank book that he'd no longer be able to read, and they'd end up miserable and stuck together. Then she crinkled up her nose and sighed. She squeezed his hand. "You haven't told me how you feel."

"Oh!" He blurted out while relief flooded his system. Andrew stared at her, completely amazed because all of his fears were gone in the breadth of a finger snap. Mia had told him what she wanted to know. When he'd been confused, she hadn't gotten mad at him. She'd trusted him enough to open up, to be vulnerable while telling him how she felt, and she'd reminded him that he'd yet to reciprocate.

"You think too much," Mia said as her lips twitched.

Andrew chuckled as he tugged her hand, pulling her on to his lap. He ran his hands up her sides and into her hair, burying his fingers into the soft, dark locks. Her long lashes swept down and she looked back at him, a little unsure. "I love you so much, Mia." He ran his thumb along her soft cheek and grinned at a few faint freckles that were starting to peek out along the bridge of her nose, even though it wasn't yet summer. He knew her face so well, from her blue eyes to her slightly upturned nose to her lips, which were right in the middle between thin and full. Yet he'd never felt such tenderness towards her. He'd loved her for longer than he could remember, but when he looked at her now he had such affection mixed in with a healthy dose of awe and longing. "You are incredibly beautiful."

She rolled her eyes, which was a little annoying, but he probably should have expected it. "I think maybe you're a teensy bit biased."

Was he? It didn't really matter. Andrew guided his mouth down to hers and kissed her. This kiss, more than any of the other ones that they'd shared, felt like the beginning of something. They explored each other's mouths, finding new angles and new sensations. Mia gently raked her fingernails through the stubble on his cheek. He wanted to tell her how good it felt but she seemed to know without the words, because she kept doing it. Or maybe she just liked it. It didn't matter why. He splayed his hands on her back and forced himself to keep them there, even though he really wanted to touch her. Andrew clutched at her sweatshirt to keep them still.

Mia pulled back from the kiss, and nearly fell off his lap looking panicked. "Wait!"

"What?" he asked confused. He held her steady so she didn't fall, but let her go when she was able to back safely on to the couch.

She curled into a ball and stared at him. "What the hell were we doing?"

"Kissing?" he said now with total bafflement.

"We can't do this." Mia's whole face was bathed in fear.

Andrew stared at her dumbfounded. If she was in love with him, and he was in love with her then what was wrong with kissing? Then his brain knocked some sense into him and her fear registered. She was truly afraid of something. "Mia, what's wrong?" He held out a hand but she back away, shaking her head violently. Her terror was starting to invade him. Had he done something to frighten her? "I'm sorry, whatever it is, I didn't mean to scare you. I don't want to hurt you," he said, and he couldn't keep his voice steady. He felt terrible that he'd upset her so much. Normally he'd hug her to make her feel better, but she was backing away from his touch.

She started to cry, but they weren't sobs. Mia hesitated for a moment, then came back to his side and curled in to him so he could wrap her in his arms. "I j-just f-freaked out," she hiccupped.

"Why?" He probed gently as he ran his hand soothingly up her back.

"I..." she wavered between speech and tears. After a minute speech won, "I'm not ready to have sex. I freaked."

"Oh!" Andrew breathed out the word in relief. That wasn't a problem; that was just a communication issue. "That's okay. We shouldn't have sex anyway."

"Really?" she asked in a small voice as she looked up at him. "I thought… after everything Michelle said that…"

Andrew had to bite back an angry reply. He needed to stay calm, because he could still feel the tension radiating out of her whole body. "Michelle has nothing to do with this, except that she was right about your safety. We can't risk that. It isn't even about us raising another child at some point, it's about medical care."

"You're nineteen," she said flatly. He knew what she was saying, and that teenage boys were notorious for only wanting sex. They had bigger problems than that. Like fighting to survive.

"You're seventeen," he retorted. "It would be illegal."

Her mouth fell open and after a moment she started to laugh. "There's no law around here."

"It doesn't matter," Andrew told her. He'd been thinking that a lot in the last few minutes. "It's still true. If you got pregnant you or the baby could die, or both of you could die. I know," he added fairly, "that childbirth doesn't have to be really dangerous. I've heard my mom talk about it. But it's a risk we don't need to take. Jilly and I need you. We aren't going to take a chance."

Mia swiped at her eyes with the back of her hand. "I'm sorry I freaked."

"You're allowed to freak," he said with a shrug. "As long as you tell me why you freaked."

"Deal," she sighed. She wrapped her arm around his waist and squeezed. "Things have really changed."

"Yep."

"You're in love with Jilly too."

Andrew blinked. He'd not really thought about it that way, and it wasn't at all how he felt about Mia. "What?"

"You said she was your daughter," she reminded him. Mia climbed back in to his arms, and she stared at him intently. "You looked stunned when you said it, like someone had hit you with a frying pan."

Andrew's cheeks flushed even as a reluctant smile played over his mouth. "Yeah, I guess I am. I didn't really register it until I'd blurted it out. I keep hoping life might get back to some kind of normal. Your dad..." he paused, needing to collect his thoughts. "Your dad didn't say that he'd never be back, but he implied as much when he asked me to take care of you two."

Mia rolled her eyes as she breathed out an exasperated groan. "You'd swear I was the toddler who needed a nanny."

"He didn't mean it like that," he assured her. "It's just that... I don't know how to say this without you getting mad and hitting me."

She gave him an 'oh please' frown. "I don't ever hit you."

"You might," he argued, "if I'd said what I was going to say."

Her blue eyes flashed with temper. "You need to say it. No secrets."

He'd promised her, but he didn't want to say it. Andrew wasn't sure he could explain it well enough. He glanced around the shelter, which had housed them for months now and would be their home for the next several years. If things evened out he might try to make a house over the shelter's entrance just so they could get out from underground, but at the moment that seemed impossible. For one thing he didn't have enough nails.

Andrew glanced back at Mia when he felt her small finger poke his belly. "Sorry," he said awkwardly. "It's... you know how a guy will say something like 'I have to take care of my wife and kids'?"

"Yeah," she said slowly. She reached up and cupped his cheek. "That's what my dad meant? He wanted you to step into that role?"

"He didn't say that in so many words," Andrew told her, "but basically, yeah. It isn't about you, or that you're not my equal partner in this... I guess it's a guy thing."

Mia ran her finger slowly over his cheek to his nose and ran her finger down it. She let her hand fall to his chest. "Okay."

"That's it?" he asked suspiciously.

"Yes indeedy," she laughed. "So am I your girlfriend?" Mia grimaced even as she said it. "That seems so weird."

"Let's just leave it that we're together," he suggested, and she nodded. "It doesn't really matter what we call it between ourselves."

"I can live with that." She leaned in and kissed him.

They lost time as they kissed. It could have been seconds or hours. When they finally pulled apart, a little breathless, Mia's eyes were clouded. "It just hit me... my parents aren't coming back, are they?"

"I don't know." He wished he had a better answer. Andrew wanted something as stupid as a land line telephone so he could call someone. They were completely isolated from friendly faces and the inaccessibility was a constant weight upon him. "If they don't come back we'll be okay. Society will eventually get back to normal, and we can head towards a town when Jilly is old enough to be able to walk."

Mia's expression was far off. "Hunger makes people stupid."

"Come again?" That was a switch of topics.

"People are starving right now. When you're hungry, your brain cells start to cannibalize themselves in order to survive."

He cupped her neck in his hand. It felt so small and delicate under his large hand. He knew he was still getting taller because his new jeans were already fitting perfectly rather than dragging a bit, and he felt awkward right now. They'd used to be closer in size. Mia leaned back against his hand, and he had to stop himself from leaning in to kiss her collar bone. "So..." he grasped for the flow of the conversation. "So you're saying that people won't be thinking straight right now?"

"Yes," she agreed. Mia wrapped her arms around his neck and nestled her face into his neck. "They'll be desperate and not thinking properly. Until the food situation is rectified no one is going to be thinking correctly and society won't be able to get back on track."

She was more than likely right, but with her so close he was having issues thinking clearly himself. "Mia..."

Her lips found the pulse in his neck, although her touch was tentative. "It's probably time for bed."

Not the best thing to say to him at that moment. "We need to keep our clothes on if we keep sleeping together." Then he felt ridiculous. Keeping his clothes on didn't mean he had self-control, and it wasn't a magic answer.

"Okay," she agreed and that one word sounded a bit relieved, even as she kissed him again. Maybe the clothes would help Mia feel better, which would make it worth it.

"Mia, please," he groaned. He wasn't quite sure what he was asking of her.

She pulled back and with one last peck on the lips, rose to her feet. "I'll go get ready, then."

The next few weeks were an interesting mix of bliss, drudgery and tiny spats as they adjusted to being a couple. Mia had pointed out the night before that they'd always griped at each other this much, but it felt different now that they were also kissing. Thus far they'd managed to work through everything by talking it out before bed. Andrew had heard his dad say that was the key to success, not to go to bed angry, so they talked until everything was worked out.

It was more work than he'd ever put in to a relationship, but it was also a lot easier than his previous failures. Mia made him want to work it out.

As March was waning, they spent much of their time in the garden weeding, watering, and tending. They had to keep Jilly out when the plants had started to sprout because she liked to pluck them from the soft ground. On the very last day of March Andrew had Jilly with him in the carrier. He'd been neglecting other projects around the shelter in order to help with the gardening and to learn everything he could from Mia in case he ever had to function on his own.

The thought left him feeling empty. Life was, in a lot of ways, more fragile than it had ever been and he was acutely aware of that fact every time he thought back to what had happened up on the trail with Michelle and the man. He still felt guilty, but it came in waves rather than a constant prodding.

Overall, life was better than he could have reasonably hoped for. He didn't have the job he thought he'd have, and he'd effectively become a father at age nineteen through a weird twist of circumstances. As he walked around a large rock and headed for the solar panels to inspect them, Jilly wiggled back and forth in the baby carrier, knocking him around a bit. He couldn't help but grin. In another time or place it would probably be a pain having her, but life was simple here. It was dangerous and tenuous, but the modern trappings were gone, and there wasn't anything to complicate it.

Except other people. He shook his head and pushed back several branches. One caught on the holster at his hip, but it stayed firmly on his waist. Jilly had kicked it a few times, but Andrew had triple checked the safety and there was no way her foot could arm it.

A small branch had fallen onto the solar panels, and he threw it off and checked for damage. After he was certain that they were functioning, he made his way back to the shelter.

Mia was in the garden by herself, but she had a rifle, and he'd only been gone a few minutes.

"Dadadadaaaahhdadadaddy!" Jilly sang out from behind him.

She was truly an effective bear repellant. There was no possibility that a bear wouldn't know they were coming. Black bears, when warned, would usually walk away from noisy humans.

Andrew came into the clearing and saw Mia kneeling in the garden. The sun glinted off her hair and gave it a coppery hue that made it shine. She didn't hear him come back, so he stood watching her.

He'd wanted to fall in love with Mia for at least a year, maybe longer. Andrew had tried to talk himself into having feelings for her, but she'd stayed firmly in the 'friend' category of his brain. He'd thought about how pretty she was and hoped it would trigger something, but it hadn't. But being here with her and watching her grow and change, and kissing her... if he'd known that making out with her would have triggered the feelings that he'd longed for, he'd have done it a long time ago.

Mia had always been everything he'd wanted. She was funny, smart, and so unbelievably good-hearted. She was beautiful to him, more beautiful than he'd ever realized before.

She was probably it for him. Andrew couldn't say for sure what their future held, but he'd known way back in September that he could be okay with Mia. Now he knew that he could be deliriously happy with her at his side.

A slight movement caught his eye, and before he could blink his gun was out of his holster, and Mia was rising to her feet, the rifle in her arms. Both had their guns trained on two men who had appeared silently from the woods.

They were both built like soldiers, although they were dressed like hikers. Neither looked starved. Even though his heart was racing, Andrew processed that the fact that they'd appeared without either of them noticing. That was a major problem.

"We're not going to kill you," the shorter guy with close-cropped blonde hair said, which was weird because neither he nor the tall, very muscular black man next to him had a weapon drawn. "We're just looking for Scott Harper."

In a voice that sounded so convincingly clueless that even Andrew would have bought it, Mia asked, "Who?"

END

MORE FROM WE ARE THE APEX

After the Flare Book 0: 151 Days

When a geomagnetic storm results from a solar flare and coronal mass ejection the question isn't, "How did this happen?", but, "How do we now survive?"

In a world without electricity, water, constant food sources, or even reliable shelter...how do you live?

This is the question posed to a young man who finds himself stuck 700 miles from home. The best idea is to make his way back...or is it?

Along the journey he will encounter roving gangs of civil war reenactors, a church leading the way to rapture, cannibals, casinos powered by the debts of their customers, and the most dangerous of them all: Boy Scouts.

James P Hassell is back at it with his signature ability to cut through the façade of everyday life and throw our world into chaos while in the process exposing the murky secrets of humanity that no one wants to face. His unflinching style to examine the darkest recesses of humanity's demented nature is as disturbing as it is enlightening.

After the Flare Book 2: Prison

Mia and Andrew's journey into their new world continues September 2015!

Keep an eye on www.wearetheapex.com/aftertheflare and www.wearetheapex.com/denouement for news and updates!

Made in the USA
San Bernardino, CA
11 May 2015